Farewell to Cedar Key

Also by Terri DuLong

Spinning Forward

"A Cedar Key Christmas" *in Holiday Magic*

Casting About

Sunrise on Cedar Key

Postcards from Cedar Key

Secrets on Cedar Key

Published by Kensington Publishing Corporation

Farewell to Cedar Key

Terri DuLong

KENSINGTON BOOKS
www.kensingtonbooks.com

KENSINGTON BOOKS are published by

Kensington Publishing Corp.
119 West 40th Street
New York, NY 10018

All Kensington titles, imprints, and distributed lines are available at special quantity discounts for bulk purchases for sales promotion, premiums, fund-raising, educational, or institutional use.

Special book excerpts or customized printings can also be created to fit specific needs. For details, write or phone the office of the Kensington Special Sales Manager: Kensington Publishing Corp., 119 West 40th Street, New York, NY 10018. Attn. Special Sales Department. Phone: 1-800-221-2647.

Kensington and the K logo Reg. U.S. Pat. & TM Off.

eISBN-13: 978-0-7582-8816-5
eISBN-10: 0-7582-8816-6
First Kensington Electronic Edition: December 2014

ISBN-13: 978-0-7582-8815-8
ISBN-10: 0-7582-8815-8
First Kensington Trade Paperback Printing: December 2014

10 9 8 7 6 5 4 3 2 1

Printed in the United States of America

*With love for Susan DuLong Hanlon
I'm proud of the daughter you are—
and the woman you've become.*

ACKNOWLEDGMENTS

Research is always involved with my stories. When I choose a particular topic to write about, I could easily do a Google search to obtain my information, but I much prefer to seek out people to speak with personally. So I owe a huge debt of gratitude to those of you who were willing to give me your time.

When I did a book signing at A Good Yarn in Sarasota, Florida, I had the pleasure of meeting William Fitzery, who is a member of the shop knitting group. I was in awe of the magnificent knitting projects he had completed, and he was my inspiration to include some male knitters in this story. Thank you for answering all of my questions.

When I attended Stitches in Atlanta, Georgia, I also had the pleasure of meeting master knitter and designer Charles Gandy. He is the author of knitting instruction books, and he was willing to share his lifelong knitting history with me, which in turn sparked my imagination and allowed me to create the character of Gabe Brunell. Thank you so much for planting that seed.

One of my fans, Linda Douglas White, had shared a story with me about her friend, Linda Knight, who happens to be a blind knitter. I was so intrigued on hearing this, I decided to also create a character who was blind and knitted beautifully. Thanks to both of you for allowing my creativity to develop Lily.

In the process of researching knitters who were blind and visiting the American Federation of the Blind Web site, I was fortunate to make a connection with Debra Williamson, who is also a blind knitter. I deeply appreciate all of the information you shared with me about Braille and converting text documents.

I feel uterine cancer in women is a subject not discussed nearly enough. Therefore, I knew my story would have a character with that diagnosis. I was fortunate to meet KG, who was willing to share her positive story with me. Thank you so much for the wealth of information that enabled me to share Shelby's story.

When I was in training to become an RN, I did my psychiatric rotation at Danvers State Hospital in Danvers, Massachusetts. Years later, after the facility closed, I was browsing the Internet to gain more information and connected with Jerry Carroll. Both of us had a profound interest in the history of the structure, and we formed a friendship. Most of the structure is now gone and replaced with luxury condos, and Jerry proves truth is stranger than fiction, because he now resides there. Thank you for all of the updated information.

A huge thank-you to my friend Patricia Smith Zraidi for opening your home and your heart to me when I was in Paris last year. My first experience of sharing a cultural dinner of tajine with you and your family is something I'll always remember and something I tried to capture in my story. *Merci mille fois* for that wonderful evening.

Thank you to Ellen Johnson, owner of Serendipity Needleworks, in Tuscaloosa, Alabama, for offering to design the Healing Cowl for my story.

This year marks my fiftieth high school reunion. Some of us had lost touch over the years, but Facebook reconnected us. Female bonding becomes more precious as the years go by, and one of my classmates, Ellen Tuttle Kennedy, named our group Sisters of '64, which was the inspiration for Sisters of '68 in my story. So to all of my "sisters," thank you for being in my life: Alice Ouelette Jordan, Val Wright Tollo, Linda Kompa Hayes, Alma Pretanik Steele, Deborah Broyer Green, Laura Jackson Ridley, Patricia Bishop Rozumek, and Donna Sherman Reid. I love you all!

Thank you to Kensington for allowing me to share my stories with readers and always making that journey so smooth. And a huge thanks to my editor, Alicia Condon. You're a joy to work with, and I deeply appreciate all of your suggestions and input.

Last, but not least, to all of my wonderful readers, thank you for your loyalty and support! Your interest in my books makes the difficult times so much easier.

1

"You want me to wear *what?*" I gripped the phone to my ear with one hand while I filled my coffee mug with the other. "Mom, come on. This isn't a film shoot for *Gone with the Wind,* and besides, I don't own a fancy *frock.*" Frock? Who even used that term to describe a dress anymore?

I heard an exasperated sigh come across the line. "Josephine Shelby Sullivan, why do you always have to give me such a difficult time? Besides which, I'm not feeling that well."

My mother was really pushing my buttons now. She knew that I had changed my given name to *Josie* the day I began first grade. For three months I had refused to answer to Josephine, causing my mother to finally give in. It was only when she was upset with me that she reverted back to my given name.

"I'm not trying to be difficult, but at thirty-five I think I can be depended on to wear something appropriate for your photo shoot."

My mother was a *New York Times* best-selling author of romance novels. The name Shelby Sullivan was known throughout the world, and while I was proud of her accomplishments over the years, that fact didn't smooth our sometimes rocky relationship. She always meant well, and she was kind and giving, but she was also a control freak and drama queen. I used to wonder if it was because of her writing. If maybe the friction between us was due to the fact that I didn't allow her to manipulate me the way she did her characters.

"Look, Mom, I'll be at your house tomorrow at three. I won't be late. I'll wear that new aqua sundress I bought when you and I went shopping last month. It'll be fine. Now, please, stop worrying and just relax. And why are you not feeling well? What's wrong?"

I heard another sigh come across the line. "Nothing, nothing. Just a little tummy twinge. Okay. Oh, and Orli? Does she have something nice to wear? You know how important this photo shoot is. My publisher is thrilled that such a prominent magazine wants to do a feature article about me with my daughter and granddaughter."

"Yes, I know. And I know you're excited and nervous, but both Orli and I will be there at three . . . appropriately attired. Now go have a glass of sweet tea, relax, and feel better."

"Right. I'll do just that. Oh, but Josie . . . do you think perhaps I should have bought a few parasols that the three of us could hold for the photos? I thought maybe . . ."

"No! Definitely not! No parasols. Bye, Mom," I said, disconnecting our call before she could come up with any other ideas.

Now it was my turn to let out a deep sigh before taking a sip of my coffee. I shook my head and then headed outside to the patio.

I curled up on the lounge and looked at the garden, which was now in full bloom with autumn flowers. Clusters of orange, purple, red, and yellow were arranged along the side of the yard. The rosebushes at the far end were vibrant with color, years after my grandmother had planted them. When she passed away a year after Orli was born, my mother inherited the house. I had been living in a small apartment downtown at the time. My parents lived on the tip of the island, near the airport, in the house where I had been raised. And although I tried to resist, not wanting to feel indebted to my mother, she had insisted that as a single parent raising a baby on her own, I should move into my grandmother's house. Which I did. It had been the smart thing to do. With three bedrooms, two baths, and a good-size family room and kitchen, it was ideal for me and my daughter. Plus, it had a lovely patio and garden, which had been the venue for many of Orli's birthday parties growing up. The location on Second Street also put us within walking distance of school and downtown.

Birthday, I thought. It was hard to believe that in three months my daughter would be turning sixteen. I had only been nineteen when I gave birth to her three days after Christmas. And here she was turning Sweet Sixteen soon, which made me realize I had better start thinking about a celebration for her.

"Are you out back?" I heard my best friend holler as she came around the side of the house.

"Yeah, I am," I said, and looked up to see Mallory walking toward the patio. "What's up?"

She lowered herself into the lounge beside me, reached across, and took a sip from my coffee mug. I was used to Mallory doing things like this. We had shared pretty much everything from the time we were in our mothers' wombs—even a birthday, five hours apart. Our mothers remained best friends to this day, and I guess it was only natural that Mallory and I would do the same. As young children we shared ice cream, candy, and toys. That evolved to sharing clothes, makeup, and ideas when we hit our teen years.

"Did you hear about poor Chloe? I just stopped at Yarning Together, and Dora told me Chloe had a nasty fall down the stairs at her apartment last evening."

I sat up straighter in my lounge. "No. My gosh, is she okay?"

"She broke her arm and is in a cast. Good thing that Berkley was home. She heard noise in the hallway and rushed out of her apartment to see Chloe at the bottom of the stairs. Berkley's the one that drove her to the emergency room at North Florida. They didn't get back till after midnight. Chloe's on something for the pain."

"Geez, that could have been much more serious than a broken arm, so I guess she was lucky."

I watched as Mallory took the last sip of my coffee. "Right. The problem is, Dora has nobody to work the shop with her."

"Hmm, true." Chloe and Dora were partners in the ownership of our local yarn shop downtown. "That does present a problem. With the triplets in day care, I wonder if Monica could help her out."

"Well, that would kind of defeat the purpose of day care. Monica is able to catch up on housework and laundry when the kids are gone those few hours each week."

"I guess you're right. She has her hands full. I know Chloe won't be able to knit.... Oh, God! I can't even imagine not having both of my hands for knitting, but when she feels up to it, maybe she could still go to the shop and assist with sales."

"Possibly, but . . ."

I looked up when I heard Mallory hesitate. I knew that pause had something to do with me. "But what?" I asked, not sure I wanted to hear the answer.

"Well . . . ah . . . since you're out of work at the moment . . . I was thinking maybe you could go in and help Dora out."

"Me?" Yes, I was an addicted knitter. And yes, I had been knitting since I was a child and could probably be considered an expert knitter. But help to run a yarn shop? I didn't think so. When I'd graduated the year before as a registered nurse and took my first position at the Urgent Care Center in Gainesville, I'd hoped the days of part-time jobs were behind me. But unfortunately, due to the economy and being the newest employee, I had lost my job the previous week.

"Sure, you," Mallory said. "You'd be helping Dora out, and hey, you said you'd have to start looking for a new job, right?"

"I meant a new job in *nursing*. You didn't mention this to Dora, did you?" When she remained silent, I said, "Oh, Mallory. You did. You told Dora that maybe I could help her out, didn't you?"

She stood up, and I saw a sheepish grin on her face. "Well, it was only a suggestion. Nothing is carved in stone. I just told her that maybe she should give you a call."

As if on cue, I heard the phone in the kitchen ringing.

"Thanks, Mallory," I said, jumping up to answer it.

"Oh, Josie, it's Dora," I heard after I said hello.

Mallory had followed me inside and was leaning against the counter, chewing on her thumbnail.

"Dora. How are you?" I asked as I shot my friend a menacing look.

"I'm fine, but did you hear about poor Chloe? She had a nasty tumble down the stairs last night at her place, broke her right arm."

"I'm so sorry to hear that," I said, and I did mean it. I braced myself for what I knew was coming.

"She's going to be in a cast for six to eight weeks while it heals. I'm afraid that means she won't be able to help customers with any knitting problems. Poor thing won't even be able to knit the projects she's working on. Now Marin can help out in a pinch, but she's pretty busy with the needlepoint shop and her classes. So . . . I was wondering . . . I heard that you got laid off from the clinic, and I'm sorry about that. But . . . I was wondering if you'd be willing to help me out for a while until Chloe can come back. Of course I would pay you, and we'd work out a schedule that will be good for you."

I let out a deep breath. How could I say no to Miss Dora? I'd known her all my life, and she was one of the sweetest and kindest women I'd ever met. She needed my help, and that's what we did on this island. We helped each other. So of course, I said yes.

Later that evening, I was curled up on the sofa working on a cranberry top I was knitting for myself when Orli walked into the family room.

"Hey, sweetie," I said, glancing up. When did my daughter grow to be so tall? I'd bet anything she was less than an inch away from my five feet seven inches. She had always been a pretty child, but now she had morphed into an extremely attractive young lady. Long, dark wavy hair was pulled back into a ponytail, and just a touch of lip gloss was all she needed to add to her natural beauty. I was quite proud of my daughter. Not just because I had raised her pretty much on my own, but because in addition to being fun and pleasant, she had developed the valuable traits of compassion, insight, and kindness. Yes, I was proud of my daughter and the young adult she was becoming.

"What's going on?" I asked.

"I was going to go over to Laura's house for a while. We're working on a science project together."

"Sure. What time will you be home?"

"By nine," she said, leaning over to kiss my cheek before patting her cat, Clovelly, who was napping beside me.

"Okay, that's fine. Don't forget. We have to be at Grandma's house tomorrow afternoon at three for that magazine photo shoot."

Orli laughed. "I don't think Grandma would let me forget. She's left four messages on my cell."

I smiled and heard the door close behind her. Yup, that was my mother.

✁ 2 ✁

When Orli left for school the next morning, I got busy with laundry and housework. I had to admit that it was kind of nice not to have to zip out of the house by seven-thirty to make the one-hour drive to the clinic in Gainesville. But I also had to admit that I missed my nursing position—a career choice that had never tempted me until three years ago. Having dropped out of college my freshman year when I found out I was pregnant with Orli, I had returned home to Cedar Key. I had managed to get by with waitressing and cleaning jobs, and with the child support that Orli's father paid, we were okay financially. But time was something that I was short on—especially quality time with my daughter. As she grew older our expenses increased, and therefore I found myself working longer hours, giving me even less time with Orli. That was when I made the decision to return to college and become a registered nurse. Despite all the hours of study, it had been worth it. I had been fortunate to get the position at the clinic the month after I graduated—no weekends, a decent salary, and that extra time with Orli. Until last week. The doctor in charge of the clinic felt bad about letting me go, but with patient care down and expenses climbing, I understood he had no other choice.

After punching the button on the washer, I headed into the kitchen and had just placed two slices of bread into the toaster when the phone rang.

"Hey, Josie, how's it going?" I heard Orli's father ask.

I felt a smile cross my face. "Grant. Things are good here. How's it going with you? Enjoying the foliage in Beantown?"

Grant's laughter came across the line. "Not quite yet. But another month and those trees should be gorgeous."

"How's your new place? Do you mind the commute into Boston?"

"Not at all. Danvers is only about a forty-minute drive to my office. And I love my new condo. More spacious and much quieter."

Grant had sold his place in Boston the previous month—an apartment he'd owned since graduating Harvard and beginning his career as an attorney.

"Listen," he said. "The main reason I'm calling is because our girl is turning sixteen in a few months. Have you given any thought as to how you'll celebrate?"

Damn. I hadn't told Grant about the loss of my job, and even though I knew it wasn't my fault, it still made me feel like a failure.

"No, not really. Actually, there have been some things going on here." I paused, and when he remained silent, I continued. "I was informed last month that due to the economy, the clinic would have to let me go. My final day was last Friday. So I'm not really sure what I'm doing."

"Oh, Josie, I'm really sorry to hear that."

I heard the sincerity in his voice. "Yeah, I had been there a little over a year and I really liked it, but . . . I'm in the process of looking for something else." I neglected to mention that I'd be working in the yarn shop for a while.

"Well, I had an idea, and I wanted to discuss it with you before mentioning it to Orli."

I recalled an incident about four years before when Grant had taken it upon himself to ask Orli if she'd like to spend Christmas in Paris with him. Making it even worse was the fact that it was my turn to have our daughter for the holidays that year. I didn't hide my anger with Grant, but after we discussed it, he apologized and promised that would never happen again. And it had not.

"So what's your idea?" I asked.

"Since Orli's birthday is a few days after Christmas, I thought maybe the two of you would like to come up here and spend the holiday with me. I know it's not my turn this year, but turning sixteen is special, and I was hoping the three of us could celebrate it together. Plus, my mother would also love to share Christmas and Orli's birthday. I would pay for your flight, and you know I have a guest room at my new place—so plenty of room for both you and Orli."

I felt a smile crossing my face. I loved the Boston area. I had lived there for a year while attending Emerson College, and when Orli was six I began allowing her to fly up to Boston to spend the summer with her dad and grandmother. During that first trip, though, I had insisted I would accompany Orli on the flight, stay a few days, and return two months later to fly home with her. Grant's mother, Molly Cooper, had extended a gracious invitation, allowing me to stay those days with her at her home in Marblehead. It had allowed us time to get to know each other better, and every year after that I felt secure in letting Orli fly from Tampa to Boston as an unaccompanied minor.

"Oh," I said. "That *would* be nice, and I know Orli would love it. But . . . gee . . . I don't know what to say right now because of my job situation. When I get a new job, it's doubtful that I'll be able to take time off right away, especially around the holidays."

"Not a problem. That's why I wanted to toss the idea out to you now. It gives you some time to think about it. But as soon as you decide, let me know so I can get the flights booked. Well, I'm due in court shortly, so I have to run. Give my love to Orli, and say hello to your parents for me."

"Will do," I said, hanging up the phone.

I tossed out the cold toast and opted for a blueberry muffin instead. Pouring myself another mug of coffee, I sat down at the table to begin scanning the newspaper when the phone rang again. I shoved a piece of muffin into my mouth and picked up the receiver to hear Mallory's voice.

"Are you still speaking to me?" she asked, but I heard the humor in her tone.

"I probably shouldn't be," I kidded her. "But yeah, I am. You are *such* a busybody. I can only imagine what you'll be like when we're old and gray."

I heard her laughter come across the line. "Aw, come on. Working in the yarn shop will be good for you. It'll give you some extra money and you'll be helping Dora. You *are* going to do it, aren't you?"

"You know I am. I called her, and it does sound like she's in a bit of a bind. So I told her I'll be in at ten tomorrow. Friday's are usually pretty busy in there, but hopefully early morning will be a good time for her to teach me the ropes."

"I don't think it'll take much time. You know the shop pretty well as a customer. Plus, I bet it'll be fun working in there. Just be careful not to have too many Y O's."

"Yarn overs?"

"Yarn orgasms," Mallory announced, causing me to laugh. "Being surrounded by all that yarn can be very seductive. Still headed to your mom's for that photo shoot this afternoon?"

I let out a groan. "Oh, yeah. It oughta be great fun."

"Hey, chin up. Besides, you should be proud of her. That's a top-notch magazine. It's quite an honor to be chosen for a feature article."

"I *am* proud of her. You know that. I just wish she was as easy to get along with as your mother."

"Yeah, I did luck out in that department. Anything else going on?"

"Yeah, Grant called a little while ago," I said, and popped another piece of muffin into my mouth before telling her about his idea.

"That sounds great. I bet Orli would love Christmas in Boston. Do you think you'll go?"

"I'm not sure yet. It'll depend on my job situation, but I agree. I know Orli would really enjoy being with both of her parents and grandmother for her special birthday. We'll be celebrating here too, but it's not fair for Grant and Molly to miss out."

"Talk about lucking out—you really hit the jackpot with Orli's father. He's a great dad, and the two of you have the perfect relationship."

She was right. When I found out I was pregnant with Orli, I didn't tell Grant right away, giving myself time to think it through. I was finishing up my freshman year of college, but Grant was two months from graduating from Harvard with his law degree. After much thought, I realized that I wasn't about to deprive him of that—weighing him down with a wife, a child, and a marriage that neither of us was ready for. I loved him and I knew that he loved me. But was it enough to sustain a lifetime together? Especially beginning that lifetime under adverse conditions? I didn't know and I wasn't willing to find out. So after much discussion we had both agreed that I would return home to Cedar Key, Grant would support us financially, and he would be very involved in our daughter's life. And I had to admit that almost sixteen years later, it *had* worked for us—despite, to this day, my mother's vocal and strong misgivings.

"Yeah, Grant is a special guy," I told Mallory.

"Still nobody serious in his life?"

"Not that I'm aware of, and I think he would mention it. He told me about two semiserious relationships over the years, but nothing panned out."

"And where are you at with Ben? You barely mention him anymore."

I let out another groan. "I have *no* clue. You know he was down here this summer for a week to visit his uncle, but . . . I have to say whatever I thought I might have felt for him is gone. We tried, and maybe the problem is the long-distance relationship, his living in Manhattan, but . . . I just don't think we're going anywhere. When he showed up on the island almost four years ago, I think it was simply an attraction for both of us and nothing more. We've just been drifting along—going nowhere."

"Well, my friend, if that's the case, then it's time we get your love life stirred up again."

I let out a chuckle. "Right, Mallory. I'll get right on that." I heard the buzzer go off on my dryer. "Listen, I've got to go. Time for me to fold towels."

"Okay. I'll stop by the yarn shop tomorrow afternoon to see how you're doing. Love you. Bye."

I had no sooner finished folding the towels when the phone rang again, making me wonder if it rang this much when I was at work all day.

I was surprised to answer and hear Dr. Clark's voice.

"Josie, it's Jonathan, at the clinic. How're you doing?"

"Fine. I'm fine. How's everything at the clinic?"

"Well, we're all missing you. And that's the reason I'm calling. I might have a job offer for you."

"Really? Back at the clinic?" I could feel my excitement rising.

"Ah . . . no. I'm afraid not. Nothing has changed there. But . . . I have a colleague, Simon Mancini, and he's also a friend of mine. He's been practicing over on the east coast in St. Augustine, but he's done a fair amount of research and he has plans to relocate over this way and open a practice. He's going to need a good RN to help him run the office. I thought of you immediately, Josie. You're competent and you're great with the patients. Do you think you might be interested?"

Wow! He'd really taken me by surprise—both with his offer and with his praise.

"Ah . . . gee . . . I . . . don't know," I heard myself muttering before his laugh came across the line.

"Sorry to just throw this out at you, but I think you'd be perfect for the position and I wanted you to have the opportunity if you're interested."

"Right," I said, bobbing my head up and down. "So this would be in Gainesville?"

"No. That's the best part. Simon is going to be opening a practice on Cedar Key. Right in your hometown."

Oh. My. God. Our island hadn't had a full-time doctor for over thirty years.

"Seriously? I haven't heard a thing about this."

"Well, there's been a lot of red tape, so the news wasn't made public. Applying for a certificate of need and all the hassles, but yes, he's managed to make it happen. So . . . do you think you might be interested?"

"Oh, yes. Definitely."

"Great. I was hoping you'd say that, because I did take it upon myself to mention you to Simon. So would it be okay to give him your phone number and have him give you a call?"

"Oh, yes. Definitely," I repeated. "And Dr. Clark, thank you so much."

❧ 3 ❧

Orli and I arrived at my parents' home promptly at three o'clock. Leaning out of the golf cart, I pushed the intercom system attached to the brick post and heard Miss Delilah's pleasant voice question how she could help.

"It's Orli and me," I told her just before the tall, decorative iron gate slid open to allow us entrance.

My parents' property hadn't always had such an elaborate security system. The two-story brick house sat by itself on a point overlooking the water. During most of the years that I'd grown up there, the two acres of oak and cedar trees had been unfenced. Once my mother had become well known as an author, a few of her well-meaning fans had simply shown up on our doorstep, hoping to meet their favorite writer. My parents had decided that to safeguard their privacy, it made sense to install both the security system and a wrought-iron fence surrounding the property.

I drove the golf cart along the path bordered by clusters of bright red hibiscus, pink azaleas, and deep green bushes, making my way to the circular driveway in front of the house. Huge ceramic pots of various flowers sat on the wide veranda, and large baskets of marigolds, geraniums and pansies swung from the roof overhang, giving the feeling that this could have been a setting from *Gone with the Wind*.

The front door was pulled open by Miss Delilah. "Hello, girls. It's so good to see you," she said, stepping aside as we walked into the foyer.

"Same here," I told her, and saw my father approaching down the hallway from the back of the house.

"Ah, my girls," he said, scooping both Orli and me into his arms for a hug. "You both look gorgeous."

"Hi, Grandpa."

"Thanks, Dad. Where's Mom?" I asked, and followed him into the family room.

"Putting the finishing touches on herself for the photo shoot. How about some sweet tea or lemonade?"

"Sweet tea, please," I said after Orli chose lemonade.

Delilah headed to the kitchen, and I walked over to the massive window that dominated the entire wall, taking in the view. Beyond the grassy area was the Gulf of Mexico, and I never tired of staring at the beauty that I had grown up with.

"So how's everything going?" I heard my father ask. "I'm really sorry about your job, Josie. I know how much you liked it at the clinic."

"Thanks, Dad," I said, and joined him on the sofa. "Well, I'm sure something will turn up."

I didn't want to risk my mother walking in while I was in the middle of telling him about the phone call from Dr. Clark. What I lacked in a relationship with my mother was more than made up for with my father. We had always shared a close connection. He encouraged me, discussed important decisions with me, and boosted the confidence that always seemed to be absent in my mother's presence. I would never forget the time he came to visit me alone when Orli was about two years old and made a point of telling me how proud he was of the wonderful job I was doing as a single mother; he went on to say that my decision had been the right one.

"You're an excellent nurse, Josie. I have no doubt that you'll find another good position," he said. "And how's everything with you, Orli? Things good at school?"

"Yup." She shot her grandfather a smile. "I'm going to be applying to colleges this year and . . ."

She was interrupted as my mother flew into the room clutching a bracelet to her wrist, saying, "Joe, I just cannot get this clasp. Can you . . . oh, you're here," she said, her eyes shifting to Orli and me. "Oh, Josie, couldn't you have done something nicer with your hair?" She extended her wrist to my father.

My hand automatically reached up to finger my pixie cut—a style that I'd worn for quite a few years, a style that was very becoming with my oval-shaped face and caused many people to comment that I resembled the actress Winona Ryder.

Before I could say a word, my daughter piped in with, "Grandma, her hair looks great. Look at how shiny it is. I wish I could wear my hair that way."

Leave it to Orli. Ever since I could remember, my daughter seemed to run interference between her grandmother and me. Yup, my daughter, the peacemaker.

"Well . . . it just looks a bit windblown. You might want to run a comb through it before the photographer gets here."

"Here we go," Delilah said, placing a tray of glasses on the coffee table. "Help yourself to a nice cool drink." I caught the smile and wink that she sent my way.

My mother twirled around in front of us. "What do you think? Do I look okay?"

At sixty-eight, my mother always looked more than just *okay*. No doubt about it, she was both attractive and elegant, and somehow that gene had skipped me. Her auburn, chin-length hair always looked stylish and perky. She'd managed to keep her trim figure, and the pretty mint green sundress that she wore was perfect with her hair and tanned skin. But something seemed off. I couldn't put my finger on it, but she looked a bit under the weather.

"Feeling okay?" I asked.

"Fine. Fine." She waved her hand in the air to dismiss the subject.

"Beautiful," my father told her. "You look great."

I felt a twinge of stubbornness rise up and couldn't bring myself to vocalize my agreement, but I heard Orli say, "You do, Grandma. Perfect."

"Okay, well then," she said, brushing off the compliments. "You did bring knitted scarves for you and Orli to wear, right?"

Shit. I'd totally forgotten her request. "Ah . . . no . . . I forgot," I was forced to say.

I saw the expression on her face, which I had no doubt meant, *I'm not surprised,* but all she said was, "Okay, then come on. Up to my room so we can find one for each of you to match your dresses."

Fifteen minutes later we descended the staircase—me with an aqua hand-knitted silk scarf perfectly arranged around my neck and Orli wearing a lavender one that matched her dress—just as I heard a voice come across the intercom speaker.

"Oh, he's here," my mother said, nervousness in her voice as she adjusted her own emerald green scarf.

Within a few moments, the doorbell rang and Delilah admitted two men and a woman.

"Hi," the older man said, extending his hand to my mother. "I'm Tom, the photographer. This is Brad, the reporter who will be writing the article, and we brought along our assistant, Kelly. She'll be helping us with the photo shoot."

"It's *so* nice to meet you," Kelly gushed to my mother. "I'm a huge fan, and I've read every single one of your books."

My mother shot her a smile. "Thank you," she told the obvious groupie before introducing my father, Orli, and me.

"Okay," Tom said, clapping his hands together. "Shall we get started? We'll begin with the photos first and get that out of the way and then you can relax while Brad interviews you. You have the perfect setting outside with the Gulf as a backdrop. How about if we get some shots down there by the water?" he suggested, and gestured toward the window.

The three of us followed the crew down to the bench overlooking the water and with Kelly's assistance struck various poses, sitting and standing, for the camera. After about fifteen minutes, Tom said, "Okay. Now maybe we could get a few on the veranda sitting on the swing."

We traipsed up to the house and posed for a few more shots before he said, "Let's do a few in the house, and one with your husband would be nice."

All of it took about an hour, and after a family shot with the four of us, I was happy to hear Tom say, "I think that'll do it." He looked at Orli and me. "Thank you so much for your cooperation. I think the photos will be great, but now we'll get to the interview."

This was my cue that my daughter and I were free to leave.

"My pleasure," I said, going to kiss my father's cheek. "Okay, Mom, I'll call you tomorrow."

I thought I saw a look of disappointment cross her face. She hadn't been expecting me to sit through the interview, had she?

But she walked toward me, gave Orli and me a hug, and said, "Thank you so much for being part of this. I love you both."

"That was fun," Orli said as we got into the golf cart and headed home.

Fun? I'm not sure that's the word I'd use to describe the past hour. More like *duty* was what I was thinking, but all I said was, "Good. I'm glad you enjoyed it. So what are you up to this evening?"

"I told Grace that I could babysit Solange. She and Lucas are going to dinner at the Island Room, and I have to be at their house by six."

"Okay, then let's get you home so you can change. Your dad called this morning and there's something I wanted to discuss with you." I glanced at Orli and saw that she was staring at me, a concerned expression on her face. Reaching over, I patted her knee. "Don't look so worried. He suggested that maybe you and I could fly up to Boston to spend Christmas and celebrate your special birthday."

"Oh, wow! Really? Could we, Mom? Could we?"

The excitement in her voice told me how she felt. "I told him I'd have to think about it, because it will depend on whether I'm working at a new job by then. So we'll see." My daughter remained silent, causing me to add, "But I think it's definitely a possibility."

Orli leaned over and kissed my cheek. "You're the best, Mom," she said, to which I replied, "No, *you're* the best. The very best thing that ever happened to me."

4

I walked into Yarning Together the following morning to find Dora behind the counter and the shop empty of customers.

She looked up with a bright smile on her face. "Good morning, Josie. Thank you again for helping me out."

"Not a problem. How's Chloe doing?"

Dora walked toward the coffeemaker and began preparing the pot. "I haven't heard from her yet this morning, so I'm hoping she had a comfortable night."

I looked around the shop and noticed two large boxes on the floor. "Is that a UPS delivery? Do you want to start unpacking those?"

"Yes, we'll get to those shortly. But first, we'll have coffee while I explain the stock—which you probably know as well as I do."

I chuckled and followed her through the back room and outside to the narrow, screened area used for customers to relax and knit. She opened the door of the carriage house, which was attached to the screened enclosure.

"Chloe mostly handles all of the stock in here," she said, gesturing with her hand. "We've put all of the cashmere, Qiviuk, and mink yarns out here in addition to many of the yarns used for knitting lace—the luxury fibers."

"In other words, the very pricey yarns," I said, walking toward the mahogany antique armoire that held shelves of displayed yarn. Reaching out, I stroked a skein of pale pink cashmere.

Dora laughed. "Exactly. When Sydney owned the yarn shop, there wasn't much of a demand for these fibers, and even when Monica took over the shop it didn't make business sense to stock them. But in the past year or so, Chloe and I have found there are a lot of women who will give up other things in order to spend their disposable income on these yarns."

I nodded. My mother was one of those women.

"So," Dora said, "if somebody is looking for one of those, you can direct them out here. And this is where Chloe does her knitting classes." She indicated an area to the side, complete with long table, chairs, and a galley kitchen built along the wall. "As a matter of fact, we were trying to come up with an idea for another class. We already have a mother and daughter group that comes to knit on Saturday mornings, but we were hoping to develop something new. If you have any ideas, please jump in with your suggestions."

"How about men?" I blurted out.

"Men?" she questioned, a bewildered expression on her face.

"Yeah, a men's knitting class. I belong to a few knitting groups online, and from everything I'm reading, men are becoming more and more involved in knitting. They're also wonderful designers of patterns."

"Oh, yes," Dora responded. "I'm well aware of that. We carry a few books in the shop written by male designers. But . . . I'm just not sure there would be much of a call for men to join a knitting class here on the island."

"You mean the macho thing?"

"Well . . . possibly."

"That's just it," I said, not even sure where I was going with this. "Maybe they just don't realize yet how enjoyable it could be if they didn't allow gender to get in the way."

"Hmm, you could be right," Dora said as I followed her back to the shop, but I heard the doubt in her tone. "Let's have that coffee while I mull this over."

She had just passed me a mug when we turned to see Chloe walk in.

Dora rushed over to give her a gentle hug. "How're you feeling? Join us for some coffee?"

"That would be great. Thanks. Josie, I heard you're going to help Dora while I'm . . . incapacitated. I really appreciate it."

She held up her right arm encased in a cast from elbow to fingertips.

"My pleasure. Are you doing okay?"

Chloe reached for the mug of coffee with her left hand and laughed. "Yeah. Actually, not too much pain. More a discomfort and a pain in the neck. And I am definitely a right-handed person. I could barely get the toothpaste cap off this morning. It's amazing how much we take our hand dominance for granted."

"I can imagine," I told her.

"So what's going on here? I know I can't do anything as far as work, but I thought maybe I could help get Josie settled in."

"Yes, that would be great," Dora said. "Especially if we get busy. Well, Josie and I were just having an interesting discussion. I told her that we'd like to come up with an idea for more classes and she suggested a men's knitting group."

"Oh, that's a brilliant idea. Now why didn't I think of that?"

"Really?" Dora questioned. "You think it might work? That we'd even have enough men on the island who would take an interest?"

Chloe headed to the sofa and sat down. "Well, I'm not sure. But we'll never know unless we put the word out there, will we?"

I leaned against the counter and took a sip of coffee. "Dora seems to think that the men might reject the idea because knitting is normally associated with females."

"But that's not really true. When I was a student and working toward my textile degree in college, we studied the history of knitting. Look at James Norbury."

"Who?" Dora and I said at the same time.

Chloe laughed. "He was British and he was a pioneer in the world of knitting following World War Two. Quite accomplished in his field. Do a Google search and you'll find out more about him."

"I had no idea," Dora said. "But that doesn't mean we'd be able to lure any men in this area to knitting classes."

"I like the idea," Chloe said, looking over at me. "And I hate to put this in your lap, but . . ." She raised her casted arm. "I think you'd be great doing a male knitting class, Josie. Obviously, it would have to be a beginner's class, teaching the basics of knit and purl, but it shouldn't be too difficult. After all, we teach knitting to children and they do well."

"Me?" I said with surprise.

"I agree." Dora patted me on the shoulder. "I think you'd be perfect. And hopefully you'll be back to work nursing soon, so we could arrange for the classes to be in the evening. I don't want to pressure you, but I'd like you to give it some thought. I think it could be a lot of fun."

Fun? That wasn't the word that came to mind. "Okay," I mumbled.

Dora took the last sip of her coffee. "Now if you'd like to start unpacking one of those boxes, Chloe can explain where the various yarns should be placed. I'm going to get on the computer and check for any online orders."

The next few hours passed pleasantly, with Chloe as my guide, and when lunchtime arrived, I realized that I had actually enjoyed learning my new tasks.

"Josie, why don't you go to lunch now? I'll eat here and, Chloe, you really should go home and get some rest."

"Yeah, I'm a little tired. Since I won't be knitting for a while, and believe me, I'm already going through withdrawal, I think I'll stop by the book shop and stock up on some reading material."

I was getting ready to head home for lunch when the phone rang, and Dora informed me it was my mother. When she'd called me the night before, I had explained to her that I'd be working in the shop for a while to help Dora out. To my surprise, she thought it was a good idea. So I figured she was calling to see how I was doing.

"Hey, Mom," I said into the phone.

"Josie, can you come over to the house? When do you get a break for lunch?"

"Actually, I'm leaving now to go home. Why? What's up?"

"No, no. You can't go home. Come here to eat. I'll have Delilah fix you something nice. I need to talk to you."

"What's going on?"

"It'll keep till you get here. See you soon." And with that, she disconnected the call.

I let out a sigh.

"Everything okay?" Dora questioned.

"Oh, yeah, I'm sure it is. Just my mother in her drama queen role. I'll be back in about an hour."

My mother had the front door open before I barely got out of the golf cart. Now I was worried.

"Are you okay?" I asked, running up the steps. "Is it Dad?"

She shook her head from side to side. "No, no. We're fine. Come on into the kitchen. Delilah prepared you a nice crabmeat croissant."

I followed my mother to the back of the house and sat down at the table while she began to pace the floor.

"It's CC," she said. "She called me this morning."

Now I detected agitation in her tone. CC—whose given name was Catherine Carol—was one of my mother's close college friends. Five of them belonged to a group that they had dubbed Sisters of '68, the year they graduated college. Elly Bishop, Maggie Seymour, and Jane Carlisle, who was Mallory's mother, composed the rest of the group. Although they had been scattered along the East Coast since graduation, they had managed to stay connected and had forged a strong female bond. As an only child, I had adopted all four as my surrogate aunts and always looked forward to their visits.

"Is CC okay?" I asked with concern.

"Okay?" My mother threw her hands up into the air. "I think she's gone mad. She's making no sense at all."

I felt a sense of dread, wondering if perhaps she was showing signs of Alzheimer's. "What do you mean?"

"It seems," my mother said, pausing only long enough to take a quick sip of her sweet tea, "that CC has taken up with a younger man. *Much* younger."

So far I was failing to see any crisis; I waited for her to go on.

"Somebody that she met at that fancy advertising firm in New York where she works. They've been together for about a month now, and since the relationship is still going on, she wanted me to know and asked if it would be all right if she brought him here during her Christmas visit."

CC was divorced, had no children, was sixty-eight years old, and I was still failing to see the problem.

"Mom, I guess I'm missing the point here. So maybe she's happy." I took a bite of my sandwich as my mother continued to pace.

"Happy? How can she be happy with somebody young enough to be her son?"

"How much of an age difference are we talking about?" I asked between bites.

"Oh, I don't know." She waved her hand in the air. "About twenty years, I guess. And what does that matter anyway?"

Excuse me? I thought the age difference *was* the problem. But I had to admit that I was a bit surprised at this revelation. CC had always struck me as an elegant, well-put-together career woman, so I did think it was a bit out of character for her.

"Oh," was all I said as I continued to wolf down my sandwich.

"This is just insane," my mother continued. "Don't get me wrong, I do think CC should finally be out there dating. After all, she's been divorced for five years. But dating a kid? I can only imagine what the others will think."

I took the last bite of my sandwich and smiled. I had a feeling that it wouldn't bother the rest of the group nearly as much as it seemed to be bothering my mother.

"Well," I said, standing up and wiping my mouth with a napkin.

"I don't think you need to be so upset about this. CC is a grown woman. She's always been responsible. So let her be."

I headed toward the front door. "I need to get back to the yarn shop. Thanks for lunch. I'll call you later, but cut CC some slack. It might be just a fling."

"I should have known better than to think you'd agree with me," were my mother's parting words.

I couldn't argue with her on that.

5

By the end of the following week, I'd given up on Simon Mancini calling me for a job interview. I figured if he was interested, I would have heard from him by now. But gossip *was* circulating the island about a new doctor coming to town.

I was in the yarn shop with Dora when Raylene Samuels— known as the island busybody—walked in.

"Have you heard?" she asked, while swiping a tissue across her brow. "Have you heard we're getting a doctor here on the island?"

I wasn't about to divulge what I already knew, and Dora remained silent, both of us certain that Raylene would continue.

"Yup," she went on. "It was just confirmed to me. He bought the house on the corner of Twenty-Fourth and D Streets. There's a contractor in there now doing all kinds of renovations. He told me. Seems the new doc is going to live upstairs and his office will be on the first floor. After all these years . . . now why would a doctor want to come here to Cedar Key?"

"To heal the sick?" Dora asked, and I caught the smile on her face.

I had to admit that Raylene did have more information than I did, since I hadn't known where Dr. Mancini would live or set up his practice.

"Oh, I don't know," she said. "Just seems mighty strange to me. And I wonder how his wife will take to living in such a small town."

How on earth did she know he had a wife?

"Raylene." Dora shook her head. "Why must you always lean toward the negative? Are you saying he has a sinister reason for coming here to set up a practice? Don't you think it could simply be that he likes the location, realizes we have no doctor on the island, and might want to help the community?"

Raylene remained silent for a moment, giving an indication that no, she hadn't considered that option at all.

"Well," she sniffed. "It just seems mighty odd to me, that's all I'm saying. I wonder where he's coming from. You think he's a big fancy doc from the north? A lot of them like coming down here for the golf. Not that we have a golf course on the island, but there is one in Chiefland."

"He's coming from St. Augustine," I blurted. When I get annoyed, I have a tendency to just blurt things out.

Dora and Raylene both stared at me.

"And how do you know that, Miss Josie?" Raylene questioned.

Damn. I hadn't intended to share my possible news with anyone just yet. Especially since it looked like it wasn't going to work out for me anyway.

"The coconut pipeline," was all I said. Everybody on the island referred to the vehicle for gossip as the coconut pipeline.

"Hmm." Raylene pointed a finger at each of us in turn. "See, why would he leave St. Augustine to come here?"

Dora shook her head and laughed. "Why wouldn't he? Raylene, I think you're reading too much into this. Remember the movie company from last year? You let your imagination run away with you."

I felt a smile cross my face. Raylene and her husband, Carl, had been convinced that a film company was coming to Cedar Key to use the town as the setting for a movie. She was determined to get a walk-on part. Raylene had been correct about a crew coming to the island to do some filming. Unfortunately, it wasn't a Hollywood film producer. It was a few fellows from the university who came to do a short documentary on Cedar Key as a fishing village.

Raylene tossed her chin and headed for the door. "Well, mark my words. He just might be up to no good," she said without even a good-bye.

Dora and I burst out laughing.

"Good Lord," Dora said, still chuckling. "I wonder if every small town has a Raylene Samuels."

"Probably," I replied, and returned to emptying a box of scrumptious baby alpaca when my cell phone rang.

I fished the phone out of my handbag to hear Mallory's voice.

"Hey, working girl. How about meeting me for lunch at the Pickled Pelican?"

I glanced up at the clock on the wall and saw it was just before noon.

"Sure," I said. "How about in an hour?"

"That'll work for me," she said. "See you at the Pelican."

Mallory had already secured an outside table on the deck and was sipping sweet tea when I arrived. She got up to give me a hug.

"I like you working right here on the island," she said. "This beats Gainesville, doesn't it?"

Being able to have lunch with my BFF on a weekday was definitely a plus. "It does," I said, sitting down across from her.

"So what's up?" she asked. "Any word yet from Mystery Doc?"

I had confided in my best friend a few nights before I realized that my possible job offer was unlikely to materialize.

I waited for the waitress to take our order before I replied.

"Nope. Nothing. Not a word. He probably changed his mind."

"Now, now," she said, reaching over to pat my hand. "Think positive. He's probably pretty busy trying to get everything organized. Oh, did you hear he bought the house on the corner of Twenty-fourth and D Streets?"

Sometimes that coconut pipeline got a glitch, leaving me on the slower end of receiving news.

"Yeah. Raylene just came into the yarn shop to tell us. That's a good spot for a doctor's office. Right downtown and convenient for people to get to. By the way," I said, wanting to change the subject. "Did your mother mention anything to you about CC dating a younger man?"

Mallory laughed. "She told me last night. CC called her to share her news. Hey, good for her is what I say."

"Me too, but my mother doesn't feel that way. What was your mother's reaction?"

"Oh, she's happy for CC, but a little concerned. Apparently, CC has planned a trip to Tuscany with him next month."

"Really?" I doubted that my mother had that piece of information.

Mallory nodded. "Yeah. I mean it's great, but my mom's a bit concerned that he might be taking CC for a ride financially. Guess it sounded like she was footing the entire bill. Airfare, renting a place over there, all of it."

"Hmm," was all I said, but I wondered now if perhaps my mother had been right to worry. "What's your take on it?"

Mallory waited while the waitress placed grouper sandwiches in front of us.

"Well, I'd hate to see her taken advantage of. But . . . CC's a grown woman. She's entitled to make her own choices. Good or bad. And hey, if this fellow and the trip make her happy . . . why not?"

I took a bite of the delicious fish and nodded. I, of all people, should know how important it is for a woman to make her own decisions. Not what somebody else wants. Or what they think you should do. But a decision based on your own wants and needs.

"Yup, I agree with you," I said. "But convincing my mother isn't going to be easy."

"She's that upset?"

"That's probably putting it mildly. She calls me constantly to discuss the *situation,* as she calls it. You know my mother."

Mallory laughed. "Oh, yeah. Speaking of decisions, have you decided yet if you and Orli are going to Boston for Christmas?"

"Not yet. I'm holding off, waiting to see if I get a full-time job. Which, at the moment, isn't looking hopeful. At this rate, I could be fully unemployed come Christmas. Chloe will be back to work by then, so Dora won't need me at the yarn shop."

We both looked up as the waitress came rushing out to the deck, waving her hands at the few locals seated outside.

"Hey, did y'all hear? Mr. Al passed away. His housekeeper found him this morning in his bed," she said before running back inside.

Mallory and I looked at each other, and I felt my heart drop. Mr. Al had died? The entire town loved Mr. Al—especially my daughter.

"Oh no," Mallory said. "How sad. He was such a sweet old guy. But when his beloved Pal passed away last month, everybody said Mr. Al took it pretty bad."

"True." I nodded my head and recalled how Orli and I had stopped by his house to offer our sympathy on the loss of his dog. "He had developed a heart problem this past year, and I think the loss of his best friend made it worse."

I was concerned about how Orli would take this news when Mallory said something that added to my concern.

"Oh, gee. I guess this means that Ben will be returning to the island to make funeral arrangements."

"I'm sure you're right," was all I said.

"Poor Mr. Al," Orli said as she helped me clear the supper table. "Maybe he just didn't want to go on without Pal. He sure did miss that dog."

I began filling the dishwasher and nodded. "You could be right. Sometimes people hit a certain age and they feel they've lost enough in life. But it was a cardiac problem and I'm glad that he went peacefully in his sleep."

"Oh, me too. He was such a sweet man."

It was obvious that Orli was bothered by his loss. "But he never forgot the kindness that you showed him, helping clean up his yard and preventing him from going to a nursing home."

Four years before, it was my eleven-year-old daughter who was instrumental in bringing the community together to organize a weekend cleanup at Mr. Al's house. Everybody had pitched in to replace shutters, paint the house, clean up the yard, and tend to the gardening. Even his nephew, Ben, had a change of heart regarding his uncle, and it brought the two of them together, which was also the beginning of our uncertain relationship.

This brought a smile to Orli's face. "Yeah, I know. I'm glad I did that. It was a fun weekend, and Mr. Al was able to stay in his own home with Pal. Have you called Ben? Do you know when the funeral is?"

I was ashamed to admit that I had not. "No, not yet. I heard that the housekeeper notified him. So I thought I'd wait till after supper and give him a call."

"Do you mind if I go to Laura's house when we're finished cleaning up? We were going to do homework together."

"Sure. That's fine."

When Orli left, I stared at the phone for a few minutes working up my courage to dial Ben's number. It was always awkward when somebody died. No words ever seemed adequate, but what made it worse was the fact that Ben and I had not been in touch since his visit to the island two months before. We had shared a few dinners together, but it became obvious that our relationship had stalled. The original zing that I had felt with him had slowly diminished over the past few years, and during his most recent visit, I sensed that he was less excited too.

But it wouldn't be right not to call him and at least offer my condolences, so I dialed his number and after two rings heard his voice on the other end.

I cleared my throat and began fiddling with the ballpoint pen on the counter. "Ben? It's Josie. I'm so sorry about Mr. Al. I heard the news this afternoon and wanted to make sure you were okay."

There was a pause before he said, "Oh . . . Josie. Yes, I'm fine. I knew his heart was getting worse, and I think the loss of his dog just put him over the edge. I'm grateful, though, that we were able to have these past years together."

I had to give Ben credit. As he had promised four years before, he had managed to stay in touch with phone calls and infrequent visits, which I knew had made Mr. Al happy.

"I know it meant a lot to him," I told him. "Have you made any plans for a funeral yet?"

"Oh . . . well . . . ah. According to his will, he wanted to be cremated and he had very specific instructions. If Pal predeceased him, he wanted me take their ashes and distribute them from a boat near North Key."

This brought a smile to my face. "That sounds like Mr. Al. Have you made the arrangements yet? Will there be a memorial service?"

"That's what I'm working on right now. He did arrange for a memorial service at the church, followed by a lunch in the church hall. I'm just so busy at the moment with work. The autumn months are pretty filled at a publishing company. You know how it is."

Hmm, no. I didn't know how it was. Work took precedence over tending to your uncle's funeral?

"Oh," was all I said.

"So I was thinking . . . I'll fly down there in about a month. Before the holidays. I'll stay a day or two and then get back here so I don't fall behind with the publishing production. As soon as I have a definite date, I'll give you a call, okay?"

"Sure. Thanks," I said, before hanging up and realizing that he had not mentioned one word about the two of us getting together.

6

The following week I was stocking a new shipment of Euroflax linen yarn on the shelf when I remembered a pattern I'd recently seen calling for this exact yarn to make lace facecloths. I fingered the texture and checked the label to make sure it was machine washable, which it was. With a nice bar of scented soap and tied up with a ribbon, these would make ideal Christmas gifts for Orli's teachers. I put aside two skeins of dusty rose to ring up for myself later. Mallory had been right. Working in a yarn shop made it difficult to resist purchases.

I turned around as I heard the chimes on the door tinkle and saw a middle-aged man enter. Probably had a shopping list from his wife.

"Hi," I said. "Can I help you?"

A sheepish grin crossed his face as he pointed to my handmade sign in the window. "Ah, yeah. I'm curious about that men's knitting class."

"Oh, great. Well, it's scheduled to begin on October first, and I'll be teaching the class. You're certainly welcome to sign up, but I'm afraid so far we have only one other man interested. My father."

He chuckled and smiled. "Hmm, did you browbeat the poor man into signing up?"

I shook my head and laughed. "Actually, no. My mother and I are both huge knitters, and my dad said he'd often thought about learning himself. But I do think part of it is because I'm the one teaching the class and he doesn't want it to fall apart before it even begins."

"Well, then. I agree with your father. We can't have that. Where do I sign up?"

I walked to the counter to get my notebook. "I can do that for you right now." I knew he wasn't a local and he didn't look familiar to me. "Do you live on the island?"

He extended his hand in greeting. "I'm Gabe. Gabe Brunell. I do live here for now. I'm renting a house over on Third Street. Just for the winter. Do you think that'll give me enough time to perfect my knitting skills?"

I smiled as I wrote his name down. "It should. It's forty dollars for the four-week class. And then based on interest, we can begin another more in-depth class after the holidays."

"Great," he said, reaching for a checkbook and pen inside his shirt pocket. "Make it out to Yarning Together?"

"Yes, please."

He handed me the check and said, "Now, what exactly will I need for the class?"

"After I teach you the basics of knit and purl, we'll be making a scarf. You'll only need to choose yarn for the scarf and needles, because we'll supply the scrap yarn for you to practice on."

I led the way to the shelves holding yarn that would be good for a scarf. "Any of these would be fine. So this is the fun part, choosing what you'd like. Take your time and browse," I said as I heard my cell phone ring.

"Is this Josie Sullivan?" a male voice said.

"Yes, it is."

"Hi, this is Simon Mancini. I believe Dr. Clark mentioned I'd be calling you?"

My first thought was, *Yes, he did. But that was two weeks ago.*

"Yes, he said you might get in touch with me," was what I replied.

"Great. I'm sorry it took me a while. I'm afraid I've been a bit overwhelmed trying to get my new practice up and running. He tells me you're an excellent RN, and I'm certainly in need of one. Would you be interested in meeting me for an interview?"

I could feel my excitement starting to build, but I didn't want to seem desperate. "Ah, yes. That would be fine."

"Great," I heard him say, and I thought I detected a sigh come across the line. "Hmm, let's see . . ."

He paused, and I was certain he was checking a calendar. One point for him. He appeared to be organized.

"Okay. Yes. How would this Friday work for you? Let's say twelve noon at the Pickled Pelican for lunch?"

A lunch interview? "Sure. That would be fine. I'll see you there on Friday, and thank you."

I disconnected the call, felt a smile cross my face, and looked up to see Gabe Brunell holding out two skeins of yarn in front of me.

"Would these work for the scarf?" he asked.

He had chosen a tweed DK weight in shades of tan and brown.

"Perfect," I said. "Now, let's get you those needles." I walked to the rack and removed a packet. "Size 10, and I think you'll like working with the bamboo to start with."

"Great. Then I'm all set?"

"I believe you are. I'll ring you up."

We both glanced toward the door when the chimes rang, and I saw Chloe walk in.

"Hey, how're you doing?" I asked.

Before she had a chance to reply, Gabe said, "Oh, it sure looks like you had a tumble."

Chloe laughed and held out her casted arm. "Yeah, I sure did. Right down my stairs."

"This is Gabe Brunell," I said, introducing them. "My second pupil to sign up for the men's knitting class."

I saw him extend his hand to Chloe. Was it only my imagination, or did he seem to hold on to it a bit longer than necessary?

"Hi," she said, returning his smile. "How nice you're going to learn to knit. Is your wife also a knitter?"

Oh, clever, Chloe. Very clever. I smiled as I placed his purchase into the bag and watched the interaction.

"Oh, no, I don't have a wife. I'm afraid I've been divorced for many years."

"Same here," Chloe said, without hesitating. "Do you live on the island?"

Gabe nodded. "I do for the winter. I'm renting a place over on Third Street. I retired last year from teaching, and a few of my friends from Philly have visited here. After a little research, I decided it might be a great place to get out of the cold for the winter months."

Chloe's smile increased. "Well, great. Welcome to the island. Actually, I'm part owner of the shop, with Dora Foster. But as you can see, I'm out of commission at the moment, and we're very fortunate to have Josie to help out."

"Wonderful," he said, taking his bag of supplies. "Then I certainly know where to go when I have a problem with my knitting. Thanks again, Josie, and I'll see you on the first."

I leaned on the counter, chin in my hands, and stared at Chloe, who was watching Gabe leave and walk down Second Street.

She turned around to face me. "What?" she said, and I swear that was a blush moving up her neck.

I smiled. "Hmm, interested?"

She waved her left hand in the air. "Don't be silly. But he *is* good-looking."

I nodded. "He is."

"And he looks to be around midsixties."

I nodded again. "He does."

"Oh, stop it," she said, reaching across the counter to jab my arm. "What else is going on here?"

"Well," I said, figuring I'd teased her enough. "It just so happens I might be on my way to a job. An RN position."

"Really? Oh, Josie, that's great. The new doctor called?"

"He did. Just a few minutes ago. He wants me to meet him for an interview at noon on Friday and lunch at the Pelican."

"Aha," I heard her say.

"What does that mean?"

Chloe laughed. "Well, hey, a lunch interview? Whatever happened to a formal interview in his office? He could be like that TV character, Doctor McDreamy. You never know."

Now I was positive I was the one who had a blush creeping up her neck. "Yeah, right. Well, first of all, the man does not yet have an office where we can meet. And second, he most likely has a wife."

Chloe nodded and a smile crossed her face. "Right," was all she said.

I returned home from work late that afternoon to find a message from Ben on the answering machine informing me that a memorial service would take place on Friday, October tenth, at the Methodist church. That was it. No *See you there*. No *Will we get together?* Nothing. As I stood there staring at the machine it also hit me how he'd chosen to contact me—not on my cell phone, which I was likely to answer, but rather by leaving a brief message. Was he trying to avoid me?

I turned around as Orli came in the back door loaded down with her backpack, posters, and a small bouquet of freshly picked wildflowers.

Extending her hand, she said, "For you," and placed a kiss on my cheek.

She had been doing random kindnesses like this as long as I could remember. I knew all children were special, but I always thought my daughter was one in a million.

"Thank you so much." I placed a kiss on her cheek before reaching into the cabinet for a vase. "Very pretty," I said as I began arranging the various blossoms of purple, blue, and yellow.

"Nana and Grandpa's for dinner at six, right?"

Oh, geez. I had completely forgotten and had planned to whip up Orli's favorite—baked macaroni and cheese.

"Right," I said. "Oh, hey, I think I have some good news."

"Great. Are we going to Dad's for Christmas?" she asked while removing the pitcher of lemonade from the fridge.

"Ah, that's not my good news, but . . . we might be one step closer to figuring out whether I can go."

I joined her on a stool at the counter while she munched on a freshly baked oatmeal cookie, courtesy of my mother, and told her about my job interview.

"That *is* great news. I'm happy for you, Mom. Really. I just hope if he offers you the job, you'll be able to get away so we can go to Boston."

That was my wish, too, although it seemed pretty doubtful that as a new employee it would be possible, but I planned to stay positive.

"Well, we'll know more on Friday. Going to get your homework done before we leave for Nana's?"

"Yup," she said, grabbing another cookie and heading to her bedroom.

I was putting the kettle on to make a cup of herbal tea when the phone rang. It was Mallory.

"Holding out news from your best friend, huh?" she said.

"I only found Ben's message on the recorder when I got home," I told her.

"Ben's message? I'm talking about your job interview on Friday. Actually, your *lunch* with the new doc in town."

I heard the humor in her tone. "Oh, right. I was going to call you about that, and then I got busy at work and only came in a little while ago. But yeah, I do have an *interview*. How'd you find out so fast?"

"I bumped into Chloe at the chocolate shop. You don't sound very excited about it. What's wrong?"

"No, I am excited. But it's not definite that he'll hire me, so I don't want to get my hopes too high. And if I do get hired, it'll most likely interfere with the trip to Boston that Orli has her heart set on."

"Hmm, I see what you're saying. Well, my fingers are crossed that it'll all work out perfectly for you. Are you busy this evening?"

I let out a groan. "Dinner at my mom's. Why?"

"Oh, okay. I had a question about that new sock pattern I'm working on. Not a big deal. I'll be at the knitting group tomorrow evening and you can help me then. It's not as if I don't have another dozen or so projects in the works that I can do this evening."

I let out a chuckle. She was right. Was there any serious knitter who didn't have way more than one project going at the same time?

"Okay," I said. "If I don't see you before, I'll see you at the shop tomorrow evening."

7

"That was delicious, Mom," I said as I helped her to clear the table. Although Delilah did cook most of the meals for my parents, on her evenings off my mother proved herself to be a very adequate cook.

"Oh, thank you. I was lying down for most of the afternoon, so I wanted something that would be easy to put together. The chicken dish was a recipe from an old *Good Housekeeping* magazine. I'm glad you liked it. I can copy the recipe for you."

"Great," I said, knowing I'd probably never use it. While I wasn't a bad cook, I tended to lean toward the simple, and I knew that despite what she said, the chicken had involved at least an hour of prep time. "You're not feeling well again?"

She waved a perfectly manicured hand in the air. "No, it was nothing. Just a tummy twinge and could have been something I ate."

Orli began to help my mother fill the dishwasher.

"Want me to get the coffee ready?"

"Yes, that would be good, Josie. We'll have it outside on the patio."

After I filled the paper coffee filter and poured the carafe of water into the machine, I reached into the cabinet for the tray and arranged three mugs along with the sugar bowl and creamer. So far, so good with mealtime conversation. We had kept it light, mostly about the current novel my mother was working on, some local gossip, and Orli's school activities.

"So," my mother said as the four of us sat at the patio table. "Hasn't Ben even contacted you about the memorial service for his uncle?"

I took a sip of coffee and nodded. "Actually, he did this afternoon. It's being held in a few weeks."

"Yes, I knew that. October tenth at the Methodist church, with a lunch after. Sydney called and told me all that. But what else did Ben have to say? Will he be keeping Al's house and stay there when he visits? Is he going to move here permanently now?"

"I have no idea."

"No idea? What on earth *did* he tell you?"

"He didn't actually tell me anything. He left a message on my home machine with only the details about the service. That was it."

My mother shook her head. "I swear, Josephine, you have the strangest relationships with men. I'll just never understand. You two barely see each other, it doesn't seem you're in contact very much, his uncle passes away, and you don't seem to know anything. You call this a romance?"

I knew I was gnawing on my lower lip and didn't care. "I've never called *this* a romance—whatever it is. It's not one of your novels. Ben and I have been trying to figure out exactly what it is we have. Which at this point doesn't seem like very much. So let it go, Mom. Please."

My mother was about to say something more, but my father interrupted her. "So, Josie, am I still the lone pupil for those knitting classes?"

Bless my dad. "No, actually, you're not. I had a man sign up today. He's new in town and renting a place on Third Street for the winter. He's in your age group and seems very nice."

"Terrific. I look forward to meeting him. I think it'll be a fun class."

"Oh," my mother said, "and I forgot to tell you, I bumped into Doyle Summers at the book shop earlier today and he plans to drop by and sign up too. So you'll have at least three."

"Very good. And maybe there will be a couple more," I told her, grateful that she'd gotten off the subject of Ben. "And . . . I think I have some good news to share. You know the new doctor who's opening a practice here? Dr. Clark had recommended me, and Dr. Mancini called me today to set up an interview for Friday."

My father reached over to squeeze my arm. "That *is* good news, Josie. It would be great if you could work right here in town instead of having to do the commute to Gainesville."

When my mother didn't comment, I looked over at her, waiting for a reaction.

"Well . . . yes. That does sound promising. Of course, there's a huge difference between working for a small-town doctor and a large city hospital. But . . . of course that's your choice."

Yes, Mom, I thought, *it is.*

"So," she said, "I don't think I've told you. The foolishness with CC? It's only getting worse. Now she tells me she's planning a trip to Tuscany with this young guy. Not only that, it seems she's picking up the tab. Can you imagine! I have no idea what on earth has gotten into her."

I caught the wink that Orli sent me across the table and smiled.

"Mom, maybe he makes her happy. Did you ever stop to think about that? Just because she's paying, it doesn't mean he's taking advantage of her. Maybe she enjoys his company, he couldn't afford his share of the trip . . . and rather than not go at all, CC is paying."

My mother waved her hand in the air. "Crazy. That's what it is. Just downright crazy. And Jane? I spoke to her again today and she doesn't seem to have a problem with it either." My mother shook her head before taking a sip of her coffee.

I let out a deep sigh. "Maybe Jane's right. Maybe CC's reached an age when she's entitled to do stuff like this. Act silly. Be spontaneous. Enjoy the moment." Saying this, I realized that my mother had probably never once experienced any of those things.

After we got home, Orli curled up at the other end of the sofa to watch a rerun of *Downton Abbey,* the British TV series that we were both hooked on.

With Clovelly stretched out between us, I began casting on stitches for the first facecloth I planned to make.

During a commercial, Orli glanced over and said, "Oh, pretty. I love the color. What's it going to be?"

"A lacy facecloth. I thought they would be nice Christmas gifts for your teachers, with a bar of scented soap wrapped inside."

"Perfect. Sometimes I think my teachers are thrilled to have me at the beginning of the year because they can count on a nice hand-knit Christmas gift from you."

I looked over and saw the smile on her face. "Oh, I doubt that. They know what a superb student they're getting. Speaking of which, any more thought about where you'll be applying for college? Is the university in Gainesville still in the running?"

"Oh, definitely. I'm just not sure if I want to go to a town I'm so familiar with. Maybe it would be better to go to school in the northeast."

I could feel a lump forming in my throat at just the thought of Orli leaving home for college, but I nodded. "Yeah, time to spread your wings, huh? Like where? Boston area?"

"Hmm, maybe. Or New York. There's lots of great colleges there too."

The show resumed and I stayed quiet, lost in my own thoughts while I knitted. Who was I to say anything? I had done exactly the same thing when I graduated high school. Left my small-town life and headed to Emerson College in Boston. And of course, I'd never regretted it for one minute. It was where I had met Grant. It was where I had conceived my daughter. But still . . . the thought of Orli so far away made me feel sad.

I recalled the conversation earlier with my mother about CC. Here I was thinking that my mother had never done anything silly or spontaneous. But had I? Sure, I'd left home for college, but that wasn't so remarkable. Sure, during my first few months in the dorm, I drank beer under age, took a few hits of pot, but beyond that, when was the last time I'd done anything that wasn't responsible or practical? After having a daughter at nineteen, I'd chosen to skip those silly moments, trading them in for motherhood instead. And I wasn't sorry. Not in the least. But now at age thirty-five, I could understand even more why CC wanted to make her moments count—no matter who didn't agree with her.

Orli had gone to bed and I was still sitting on the sofa knitting when the phone rang. I glanced at the clock on the mantel as I headed to the kitchen. Who would be calling at close to ten-thirty?

I answered and was surprised to hear Ben's voice.

"Josie?" He hesitated before saying, "I'm sorry to be calling a little late, but I wanted to discuss something with you."

His voice sounded odd. Had he been drinking?

"No, it's okay. I'm still up. What's going on?"

"Well—" He hesitated again before saying, "Well . . . um . . . you see. It seems that I've met somebody. . . ."

Now I realized that what I heard in his voice was nerves and uncertainty.

"It *seems?*" I asked.

I heard a forced chuckle before he said, "Right. Well, I *have* met somebody. Her name is Dawn. She works with me, you see. A fairly new editor at the company. It started off with just a drink after work. You know."

Why did he always assume that I *knew* things? When I remained silent, he went on in a rush.

"One thing led to another, drinks and then dinners and then, well, ah . . . Dawn informed me this evening that she's pregnant. She just found out. She's about ten weeks along. I thought you should know."

On wobbly legs, I found my way to the stool at the counter and managed to plunk down while trying to absorb what he'd just told me. He'd met a woman. She worked with him. They had drinks. Dinners. And now she was pregnant? There was no assumption involved on my part to *know* that he'd slept with her.

"Oh, I see," was all I could say. Yes, this time I did actually see what he was saying, and doing a quick calculation in my head, I realized he had slept with her in July, either before coming to Cedar Key or shortly after returning to New York.

"Good. Good," I heard him say.

Good? For who? For him? For me?

"And so . . . where does this leave us?" I asked, and then let out an exaggerated chuckle. "Oh, wait. There is no *us,* right?"

"Well, no . . . not anymore. I wanted you to know before I came there for my uncle's memorial. And I thought it might be easier to tell you on the phone. Dawn and I are planning to get married, but we're not sure when. I just wanted you to know."

"Gee, that was really generous of you," I said, and didn't try to disguise the snarkiness in my tone. "Well . . . thank you so much for telling me, Ben. I do appreciate that, rather than finding out from somebody else."

"Oh, good," I heard him reply, followed by a deep sigh across the line. "And just so you know, Dawn won't be coming with me to Cedar Key next month. I'm going to get my uncle's house listed with a realtor and put it up for sale. I'm really sorry it didn't work out for us, Josie. You know how it is."

"I certainly do," I said before hanging up the phone.

I stood at the counter for a few minutes, not exactly sure what I was feeling. Sorrow? Rejection? Happiness? Relief?

I walked to the fridge, removed an open bottle of Pinot Grigio, took a wineglass from the cabinet, filled the glass halfway, and then took a long sip. I sat back down on the stool and shook my head as laughter bubbled out of me.

"What the hell just happened?" I said out loud to the empty kitchen.

I took another sip of wine and shook my head again. One thing I knew for certain—sorrow was not among the emotions I was experiencing.

8

I wasn't due into the yarn shop until noon, so I had called Mallory at seven in the morning and asked if she could join me for breakfast downtown at Ken's Diner in an hour.

When I walked upstairs, she was already seated at a booth near the window.

"Hey," I said, sliding in across from her. I waved my hand in the air at the waitress passing with the coffeepot. "Thanks," I told her as she filled my mug. We gave our order and then I launched into an account of Ben's call the night before.

Mallory rested her elbows on the table and leaned toward me. "What. A. Shit. I can hardly believe this! So he goes back to New York, meets this woman, gets her pregnant . . . and all without formally telling you whatever you had together is finished?"

I nodded. "Yup, that pretty much covers it."

"Thank God you never slept with him," Mallory said, and when I remained silent, she asked, "You didn't, *did* you?"

I shook my head. "No, I did not. There was just never that attraction there for me. Not to mention the difficulties of maintaining a long-distance relationship."

"You seem a little down though. Are you sad it's officially ended?"

"No. Not really. But it does sting a little to be rejected."

Mallory let out a snort, causing me to smile. "Rejected? In my opinion, he did you a favor." She took a sip of coffee. "Will you still go to Mr. Al's memorial with him there?"

"Of course I will. I'm sure as hell not going for Ben. I'll be going for Mr. Al."

She reached across the table and patted my hand. "Good girl."

"You're right," I said. "He is a shit. Didn't even have the nerve to tell me in person. Which is actually probably for the better. I have to admit, though, I sure didn't see that coming. I guess I thought . . . oh, hell, I have no idea what I thought. Maybe you're right. We were definitely going nowhere. I'd rather be alone than hooked up in such an iffy relationship."

"Exactly, and from what I hear, you just might be working for a mighty good-looking doctor."

My head snapped up to stare at her. "What do you mean? How do you even know what he looks like?"

"Well," she said, dragging out the word and waiting till the waitress put our breakfast plates in front of us. "Seems that Marin saw him yesterday afternoon sitting on the steps of the building that's being remodeled. She had just come out of the chocolate shop, so she went over and introduced herself. She said he was very nice and *very* good-looking."

I shook my head and let out a chuckle. "And as we know, Marin has very good taste in men."

Mallory laughed. "Right. She said that Worth is a keeper but that a lot of the younger women in town will enjoy the eye candy with the new doc." She paused for a moment. "Just sayin'."

I saw the grin on her face and took a bite of my eggs before saying, "Yeah, well, I don't think I'm in the market for a new relationship right about now."

I walked into the yarn shop at noon and heard baby sounds coming from the needlepoint shop. After putting down my handbag, I went through the archway and found Marin sitting beside the portacrib working on a piece of canvas that was coming alive with various colored threads to form a teddy bear.

Peeking into the crib, I smiled at Marin's granddaughter, Andrea. "I swear she gets bigger every time I see her. Hi there, sweetie," I said, reaching out my hand to touch her foot and receiving a beautiful smile.

"I know. Hard to believe she turns five months old in a couple weeks. I love having her here with me at the shop on Thursdays. Gives us more time to bond, and she's such a good baby."

"She's certainly beautiful, and it's obvious she loves her Nana. How's the day care going on the other days?"

"Wonderful. Leigh is just great with all the kids there, but it's nice to have Andrea to myself one day a week."

I nodded. "And Fiona's classes? Everything going okay?"

"Great. She loves the university, and she's anxious to graduate as a registered nurse in three more years."

During the past year Marin had experienced a life-changing event. After her husband passed away, she'd discovered that he had a grown daughter in the Boston area whom she knew nothing about. It had been a devastating ordeal for Marin to go through, but one that had changed her life in ways she'd never thought possible. After much soul searching, she met Fiona, her husband's pregnant, nineteen-year-old daughter, introduced her sons to their half sister, and discovered that not only did her two boys accept Fiona but that she had also developed a connection with her. Marin had encouraged Fiona to contact Greg, the father of the child. It was easy to see the love that the couple shared, both for each other and their newborn daughter.

"Oh," Marin said, getting up to put the needlepoint on the counter. "Fiona is so excited. It seems that Greg got the word yesterday that a position is being offered to him at the university in January."

"That's wonderful news! I can only imagine how happy they both are."

The couple had decided that Fiona would finish her nursing education in Gainesville while she continued to live with the baby at Marin's house. Greg would continue to teach in the Boston area while they both hoped that his connections in Gainesville would pay off, enabling him to relocate.

"Does that mean that Fiona will be moving?" I asked, knowing how attached Marin had become to both her stepdaughter and her new granddaughter.

She nodded and looked down at Andrea, happily kicking her legs while watching the mobile that turned above her head. "Yeah, I think it will. But . . . I'm okay with it. They're going to wait until Fiona graduates to get married, but they should be together—raising their daughter as a couple. I knew that day would eventually come, and it's fine. Besides, Fiona has already said not too much will change. It's only a one-hour drive to Gainesville, and she said that I can keep Andrea every Wednesday evening overnight, so I'll still have the baby one day a week."

"Oh, that *is* good news. I'm very happy for you, Marin, and I'm sure it'll be nice to have more private time with Worth. Gosh, Fiona and the baby have been with you ever since Worth moved in."

"I know, and you're right. We're both thrilled to have them with us, but . . . yes, it's time for us to be alone. Oh, hey, I met the new doctor who's coming to town. He is very nice, not to mention quite good-looking. Is your interview tomorrow?"

"Yeah, it is. Fingers crossed that it goes well. I really need this job. As much as I love working in the yarn shop, it would be nice to get back to nursing." I heard the chimes on the yarn shop door and turned to leave.

"Well, good luck tomorrow. See you at the knitting group this evening."

I had closed the shop at five, raced home to have dinner with Orli, and was back just before seven. Dora had already arrived and was preparing the coffeemaker.

"How'd it go today? Were you very busy?"

"Yeah, it was a good afternoon, and oh, Doyle Summers stopped by to sign up for the knitting class. So that's three confirmed."

"Wonderful. I'm sure it'll be a fun class for the men."

We both turned toward the door as knitters began arriving, and I was quite surprised to see Mallory's mom walk in with my mother.

"Jane," I said, going to give her a hug. "I didn't know you were coming to the island."

"Yeah, your mom invited me for a few days and I had some vacation time, so I thought I'd come for a long weekend."

I couldn't help but wonder if part of the reason was to calm my mother down about CC.

"Well, that's great," I said, giving my mother a hug. "Glad you could join us tonight. Is Mallory coming?"

"Just spoke to her on the phone, and yes, she's on her way."

Within a half hour, the aroma of coffee filled the air while ten of us sat around gabbing with needles clicking.

"Oh, meant to tell you, Josie," Berkley said. "Saxton is going to stop by to sign up for your knitting class."

"That's great. Then we'll have four."

I looked up from the vest that I was working on for Orli as I heard Raylene sniff. "Something wrong?" I asked.

"I just can't get over men wanting to learn to knit. Silliest thing I've ever heard of. You'd never see my Carl getting into knitting."

"It's not silly at all," Dora said. "Chloe was telling us about this British fellow who was quite prominent in the area of knitting. He had a strong influence on knitting after the war as a teacher and designer. So I don't think it's as uncommon as you might think."

"Well . . . I just hope they don't decide to join our knitting group," Raylene said.

"I'm sorry you feel that way." I heard the edge in Dora's tone. "But this group is open to anybody who would like to join us."

So there, I thought, and bent my head to continue knitting so Raylene wouldn't see the smile on my face.

"Speaking of silly things," my mother said. I knew where she was headed, and my smile vanished. "You know my friend, CC? You've all met her when she's visited here. Well . . . it seems she's taken up with a fellow young enough to be her son."

"No," I heard Raylene say, clearly relishing the fodder this provided for gossip. "You can't be serious. Why on earth would she do such a thing?"

My mother shrugged. "I have no idea. I think she's going through a postmenopause or something. She's planning a trip to Tuscany with him . . . and . . . she's footing the bill."

"Oh, my goodness." Raylene leaned forward, caught up in the

drama. "That sounds like he could be one of those...what are they called? Jigglers?"

This did bring forth a round of laughter, but I'd heard enough.

"I think you mean *gigolo,* Raylene. And Mom, give CC a break. You should be glad that she's happy."

"Well, I just don't understand how she could be happy being taken advantage of."

"Bottom line, it's not up to *you* to decide."

"Josie's right," Jane said. "We need to let go of it. CC's a big girl and she's not stupid. She's always been very responsible. The person she chooses to travel with is her choice."

"Well, she'd better be careful," Raylene said. "Or she'll get herself labeled as one of those panthers."

Flora choked on her coffee and shook her head while trying to control her laughter. "Good Lord, Raylene. I think you mean a *cougar.*"

"Right. Whatever."

I looked over at Mallory and was certain the grin on her face matched mine.

9

I glanced over at my bed and realized that it looked the way it had when I was dating in high school. Slacks, dresses, and blouses were flung every which way across the bedspread. Shoes were scattered over the floor. I let out a deep sigh.

"Cripe, get a grip, Josie," I said to myself in the full-length mirror. "It's an interview, not a *date*."

I decided the white cropped pants, aqua hand-knit cotton sweater, and gold sandals would have to do. Casual, dressy, and appropriate.

I glanced at the bedside clock and saw that it was 11:45. Time to head downtown and meet Dr. Simon Mancini.

When I arrived on the outside deck of the Pickled Pelican, I saw a man who appeared to be in his early to midforties sitting alone at a table in the back. That had to be him. I let out a deep breath, hoping to control my nerves. *Geez,* I thought, *Chloe was right. He does look like Dr. McDreamy.*

I let out a sigh and walked toward his table. "Dr. . . ." I had to catch myself from saying *McDreamy.* "Mancini? I'm Josie Sullivan."

"Josie," he said, a huge smile covering his face as he stood and extended his hand. "Yes, but please, call me Simon. Have a seat. It's very nice to meet you."

It only took a nanosecond to take in his height, which was a good five inches above my five seven; his dark hair, which was on the longish side, shot through with flecks of gray; and his incredible good looks. Oh, yes, this doc was going to create quite a stir on the island.

"Thanks," I said, sitting opposite him.

"I feel fortunate that Jonathan contacted me about you. It's not always easy finding competent RNs, especially in such a small town."

"And I feel fortunate to be considered. I loved working with Dr. Clark in the clinic and hated losing my position there."

"Hey, Josie, you guys ready to order?"

I looked up to see our waitress. "Hey, Brandy. Yes, I'll have a burger, fries, and sweet tea, please," I said, realizing it probably wasn't the healthiest meal to have with a doctor.

But I smiled when I heard Simon say, "Sounds great. I'll have the same."

Shifting his focus back to me, he said, "Well, I'm sorry about the loss of your job, but hopefully Jonathan's loss will be my gain. So let's discuss hours and salary."

By the time our food arrived, I knew the pay was more than generous and the schedule of eight till five, with an hour for lunch, was fair. I prayed that I'd get the position.

"Now, there is one other thing," he said. "I plan to be open every other Saturday morning, to accommodate patients who work during the week. However, on the Saturday that I'll need you to work, you can have the previous Wednesday off. Would that work for you?"

"Oh, definitely. That would be great."

He nodded and took a sip of his tea. "Good. Now on to when I would need you to begin work. I hope that won't be a problem."

He took a bite of his burger, chewed, swallowed, and wiped his mouth with a napkin. I suppressed a smile as I realized that despite being a doctor, he had a healthy appetite for burgers.

"As you might know, I'm having the entire building restored. I bought the house over on D Street."

I nodded and continued to eat.

"I plan to live upstairs and my office will be downstairs, so it'll be ideal. I have contractors working in there now, but they tell me it will be early to mid-January before it's entirely finished."

"Okay," I said.

"Would that be a problem for you? It's only mid-September. Would you be able to wait until January to begin work?"

"Gosh, that would be perfect for me. At the moment, I'm working at the yarn shop in town. Helping out Miss Dora, because Chloe fell and broke her arm. She won't be able to return to work till December, and I'd like to be able to stay and help them out until that happens."

"Wonderful."

"Plus . . . my daughter's father lives in the Boston area. Orli is turning sixteen a few days after Christmas, so he's invited us up there to spend the holidays and celebrate her special birthday. I've kind of put that on hold waiting to see about this job."

He nodded his head slowly, as if thinking. "I see," he said, after a few moments. "So if I had asked you to begin work before the holidays, then you wouldn't have gone on the trip?"

I wasn't quite sure what I was supposed to say. "Well, no. Orli knows that as a single mom, my work is important. She would have been disappointed and so would I, but . . . I've always worked to support us."

"Well, then, Josie Sullivan . . . if you would like this position, I'd be very happy to hire you as my RN."

I felt a giggle escape me and blurted, "Just like that? Don't you want to interview anybody else?"

He threw his head back, laughing. "Yup. Just like that. Jonathan gave you an excellent recommendation as a nurse, but I can see for myself that you're also a conscientious and motivated employee. So, yes, if you would like it, the position is yours."

"Oh, gosh. Yes. Definitely. Yes, I'd love the position, and thank you. Thank you so much." I knew I was babbling, but I couldn't help it.

He laughed again and reached his hand across the table to shake mine. "Well, welcome aboard, Josie. I think I'm going to enjoy working with you."

Brandy cleared away our lunch plates and asked if there would be anything else.

"Coffee?" Simon asked.

"Sure," I said, not knowing his schedule. "Sounds great."

"So," he said. "Tell me about yourself. You're originally from Cedar Key? Do you have siblings? Do they live here too?"

I nodded. "Yes, I'm originally from here. I'm an only child, but my parents live on the island. My mom's an author, and they live out near the airport."

"No shit," he said, causing me to smile. I liked this guy. He was a doctor, but he was down to earth and easy to talk to. I had a feeling he'd be a hit with the locals. "Your mom's an author? What does she write?"

"Romance novels," I said, and heard him say *No shit* again, followed by laughter.

"Wow. I don't think I've ever met a romance writer before. Do you also write?"

I shook my head, and it was my turn to laugh. "Ah, no. Much to my mom's disappointment, I am not a writer. She had a degree in journalism and was working as a journalist when she met my dad. She was hoping I'd follow in her footsteps."

"But you chose the noble profession of nursing. Good for you. Sounds like you're quite an independent woman. Raising a child alone, living on your own, doing what you enjoy for work rather than something you felt obligated to do."

"Thanks," I said to Brandy as she placed the coffee in front of us. "Hmm, I guess you could say that," I told Simon. "Actually, my mom would probably say I'm much *too* independent. How about you? Are you originally from St. Augustine? Dr. Clark said that's where your practice was located."

Simon took a sip of coffee and shook his head. "No, I'm originally from Gainesville. Born and raised there, went to the university, and that's why I wanted to set up a practice here. I come from a pretty large Italian family—two brothers and two sisters. My dad's Italian, but my mom is British. They met when she did a transfer year at UF, where he was also a student. We used to come to Cedar Key for long weekends when I was a kid. Boating, fishing, that kind of thing. I always loved it here, and it brings back happy family memories, so when the opportunity arose, I thought, why not? Just do it, Simon. Live on the island and open up a practice there."

I nodded. "Well, good for you. Sounds like you also do what will make you happy. Gosh, I can't even imagine having four siblings. Are you close? Do you still see each other?"

Simon laughed again. "Oh, yes. My parents insist on it. They're very big on family. So at least once a month we gather at their house in Gainesville for dinner and to catch up on things. My brothers live in the Tampa area, and both sisters live near Jacksonville. So getting to the folks' house for dinner is easy logistically."

The more Simon talked, the more I liked him. "And so," I said, remembering Chloe's words to Gabe, "how do you think Mrs. Mancini will like living here on the island?"

Without hesitating, he said, "Oh, there isn't a Mrs. Mancini. Not anymore. I've been divorced for over ten years. She remarried—a lawyer this time. So she's Stephanie Pope and lives on Amelia Island."

I knew Amelia Island was on the east coast and close to St. Augustine, where Simon's previous practice had been located. I thought it odd that he would stay in the same area for ten years after divorcing his wife.

As if reading my thoughts, he said, "We have a daughter. Lily. I needed . . . wanted . . . to be close to her, so that I could see her often."

"That's understandable. I've always felt bad that Grant is in the Boston area, but it's worked okay all the way around for both Grant and Orli. He visits here occasionally, and Orli spends some holidays and summers up there with him and his mother. So I think he's always felt very included in her life. That's why this birthday celebration is so important to both of them, and they feel that I should also be there."

"Oh, I agree," Simon said. "Yes, family is very important no matter the miles that separate you or the circumstances that make you a family."

"How old is your daughter?" I asked.

"Lily just turned 18."

Before I could ask any more questions, he called Brandy over for the check, passed her his credit card, and said, "Well, I'm very glad we had this lunch, Josie, and that you've accepted the position. Would it be all right if I called you should I have any questions concerning the office or if I'm looking for ideas and suggestions? I'm traveling back and forth to St. Augustine until the apartment here is finished, so maybe we could get together again when I'm on the island."

I got the feeling that the subject of his daughter was closed, but I also felt that there might be more to his story.

"Sure," I said, standing up to leave. "And again, thank you so much for offering me the position. You have both my home and cell numbers, so just give me a call anytime."

He bent his head to sign the receipt and said, "Great. I'll be in touch."

As I walked toward the stairs, I could feel his eyes on my back following me as I left.

10

"Oh, Mom! I love you so much," Orli squealed as she enveloped me in a tight bear hug. "You're the best. You really are! We can go to Boston for the holidays?"

"We can," I said, sharing her excitement. "Not only do I have a new nursing position, but I don't have to start till January, so that will free us up to go. I'm going to call your father now to let him know."

"Great," she said, heading to her room. "I'm calling Laura to tell her. Tell Dad I love him when you talk to him."

I dialed Grant's cell phone, and he picked up right away.

"Hey, Josie. How's everything going?"

"Very well," I said, and proceeded to tell him about my new job and that we could accept his offer to spend the holidays with him.

"That's wonderful news. I'm so happy for you that you got the job, and I'm happy for me that you guys will be up here for Christmas and Orli's birthday. I know my mom will be excited too."

"Do you have a date in mind for us to fly up there?"

"Hold on, I'm looking at my calendar." There was a pause, and then he said, "Okay, Christmas is on Thursday and Orli's birthday the following Sunday. Why don't I book you on a flight for Monday, December twenty-second, and you can fly back home on Tuesday, the thirtieth. Would that work for you?"

"It would. Sounds great."

"Okay, I'll get everything booked and I'll be in touch soon."

"Orli sends her love, and, Grant, thank you."

"Love back to her and it's my pleasure."

I hung up the phone and felt a smile cross my face. He really was a very special man. Sometimes I wondered if maybe I had been wrong not to marry Grant almost sixteen years ago when I realized I was pregnant with Orli. But no, I think our relationship had evolved over the years the way it was supposed to, minus a marriage contract. It would have been very difficult for Grant to support a family as a new grad trying to get established with a law firm. I most likely never would have become a nurse, and I had to admit, I did value my freedom and the independence of not having to answer to anybody.

I was just about to make myself a cup of tea and settle down with some knitting when the phone rang. I thought maybe it was Grant calling back with details, so I was surprised to hear Simon's voice.

"Hi, how are you?" I said.

"Fine, and I'm sorry to bother you so soon, but on the drive back to St. Augustine I had a million things floating around in my head. I'm thinking I should hire a girl to cover the desk. You know, like a receptionist. I don't expect you to make and confirm the appointments and be in charge of the general office work. You'll be busy enough doing nurse-related tasks. So I was wondering if maybe you knew of somebody who might have adequate office skills and would like a job."

"Hmm," I said, trying to think of somebody. I hadn't even thought to ask him about that, because many times in a small office the nurse also handles the front desk. "Well . . . not off hand. But let me think about it. I'm sure there's somebody on the island who would love that position. Call me back next week and hopefully I'll have found somebody for you."

"Great. Thank you. Oh, and Josie . . . I really enjoyed having lunch with you today and getting to know you."

"Same here," I said before hanging up.

I poured water into my mug and added an herbal tea bag. I got the feeling that our meeting might have meant a little more to him than simply an interview for a job. Based on his good looks and personality, I realized that might not be a bad thing. *Forget it, Josie,* I thought. *You're barely out of whatever it was that you had with Ben.*

Saturdays were usually busy at the yarn shop, so I wasn't surprised to glance at my watch and see it was going on four. Dora had left at two and I wouldn't be closing for another hour, so I decided to unpack a new shipment of yarn that had arrived earlier.

I opened the box and discovered some yummy Manos del Uruguay Fino, an extrafine merino and silk. The colors were gorgeous, and I loved the names that went with them—Watered Silk, Silhouette, and Antique Lace. One was called Crystal Goblet and was a beautiful greenish beige. I recalled that I had recently seen a pattern for a shawl called Pluma Shawlette and knew I was going to have to search for the pattern and purchase the yarn. I also knew that once I returned to my nursing position, I'd probably be saving myself some money.

I turned around when I heard the door chimes, and I saw Saxton Tate walk in.

"Hey, Josie," he said, looking around. He appeared to be hesitant about walking farther into the shop.

"Saxton, good to see you. Berkley mentioned you'd be stopping by to sign up for the class."

"She did? Am I the first one?"

"No, not at all," I said, attempting to put him at ease. "You'll be number four."

"Really?"

I laughed. "Yes, really. My dad has signed up and so has Doyle, and we have a winter resident on the island who is also confirmed."

"Oh, good. Good," he said, and I saw the expression on his face relax. "So just tell me what I need to do."

"The class is forty dollars for the four weeks. You'll be using our stash yarn to begin with, but then you'll be making a simple scarf." I walked to the wall and gestured. "So choose a skein of anything in here that you think you might like as a scarf, and I'll get your needles for you."

He returned to the counter a few minutes later with a skein of Berroco worsted in shades of blue.

"Very nice," I said. "And it's machine washable, which is great. Okay. I'll total you up."

"I'm not sure I'll get the hang of this knitting, but I thought I'd give it a shot. I thought it might be fun for Berkley and me to knit together."

I laughed. "Hey, the couple that knits together stays together. Are you working on another mystery?"

Saxton was originally from England and a best-selling mystery author. He was now with a publisher in the States, and everybody on the island enjoyed his books.

"I'm on a break at the moment, till after the holidays. That's why I thought it might be good to do the knitting class now."

I passed him his bag. "Well, I think you'll enjoy it, and I'll see you on October first."

I watched him leave and thought that Berkley was pretty fortunate to have found such a nice man to spend her time with, which caused me to question if perhaps I wanted a man in my life. I knew for certain that Ben wasn't that person. I thought back to when I'd first met Grant, the fun we'd had together, the mind-blowing sex and the love that we shared. Even though it probably wasn't meant to be a permanent kind of love, he had taught me that being with one special person could make life a lot more fulfilling.

I pushed those thoughts out of my head and prepared to close the shop for the day. That was when I remembered that Orli and I were expected for dinner at my parents' after I left work. *Oh, great,* I thought, *now I have to go deal with my mother's attitude about Orli and me not being here for Christmas.*

"Delicious, Dad," I said, wiping my lips with the linen napkin. Even dining on the patio for a barbeque, my mother used her good china, glassware, and linen napkins.

My father laughed. "Only hamburgers and hot dogs, but glad you enjoyed it."

"More wine?" my mother asked, holding up the bottle of Bella Sera Pinot.

"Yes, please. That's a good one." I was like my mother in that respect. Very fussy about my wine selections and usually leaning toward reds or a dry white. "It's a shame Jane couldn't have stayed till tomorrow. I was looking forward to visiting with her."

"Yes, I know, but she got that call about the plumbing problem at the library, and as the director she felt she should head back and make sure everything was taken care of, so she left this morning."

"Yeah, I wanted to see her, too, and she missed a good dinner. That was great potato salad, Nana," Orli said.

"Thanks, honey. I got the recipe out of some magazine. So how's school going? What's new with you?"

"Fine," Orli told her as she shot a glance to me across the table. We had agreed that I would bring up the subject of my new job and our trip following dinner. "Yup, everything is good."

I took a sip of wine, attempting to boost my courage. I dreaded confrontations with my mother, and I knew not spending Christmas with her would create one.

"Well," I said, and began fingering my napkin. "I have some good news for you."

"Great," my father said. "Let's hear it."

"First of all . . . I have a new nursing position. I was hired yesterday by Dr. Mancini to work in his office."

"That's terrific," my father said, reaching over to give my hand a squeeze. "Good for you. I'm very happy for you, Josie."

"Thanks, Dad." I glanced over at my mother and saw her pursed lips.

"So," she said. "I guess you've given up on trying for a hospital position?"

No *That's great, Josie.* No words of support.

"Well . . . right now hospital positions are at a minimum, and besides, I much prefer to work right here on the island rather than spend time and money traveling back and forth to Gainesville."

My mother nodded. "Hmm, that's true. Well . . . yes. Of course I'm happy for you, too, Josie. When do you start?"

I took another sip of wine. "That's the great part. Simon said . . ."

"Simon?" my mother questioned. "You're calling your employer by his first name? That was unheard of in my day."

"Mom, you're only sixty-eight, and yes, he told me to call him that. Of course in the office I'll refer to him as Dr. Mancini. But anyway, he said, due to the remodeling of the office, he's not planning to open until January. So I'll be able to finish up at the yarn shop till Chloe comes back and it'll work out great."

"Yes, I'm sure Dora will appreciate that. Well, good. If you're happy with this position, then so am I."

I saw Orli stare at me with raised eyebrows as if to say *Keep going.*

"Also," I said, "there's another reason why the starting date works out so well." I paused and saw the expectant look on my mother's face. "Grant called a few weeks ago. As you know, Orli has a special birthday this year. So . . . he's invited both of us up there to spend Christmas and celebrate her birthday. He's purchasing the plane tickets for us, and we can stay with him at his new condo."

I took a deep breath after I got it all out and waited for my mother's reaction, but she remained silent, leaving it once again to my father to pick up the slack.

"Oh, that's a great idea," he said. "That's very generous of Grant, and I know he'll love having you both there for the holiday and the birthday."

Still my mother said nothing.

"Mom?" I questioned. "Are you okay with this?"

She took a sip of wine before saying, "Well . . . I suppose I have to be. It seems the plans are all in place. So . . . you won't be here for Christmas? I mean, even when Orli spends the holiday up there, you're here with us."

"But Nan," Orli said, "we'll both be here for Thanksgiving. We'll be spending that holiday with you. You know how we always enjoy that day together."

My mother nodded. "Yes . . . you're right. I'll just have to get used to the idea of not having either one of you here for Christmas."

Yes, you will, I thought. But I wasn't convinced that I'd heard the last about this subject.

11

"I am *so* happy for you, Josie," Mallory said as she leaned across the table at the Pickled Pelican. "Both because of the new job and your trip to Boston. It seems things are heading in a good direction for you."

"Yeah, all except for my mom. I don't think she's too thrilled about me working in a doctor's office, and I know she's not happy about Orli and me not being here for Christmas."

"Ah, well, she'll have to adjust."

"Anything else?" Brandy asked as she waved our check in her hand.

"Coffee for me," I said. "I'm off work this afternoon so no rush."

"Same for me," Mallory told her.

I watched Brandy go back inside to get our coffee and wondered if she was happy with her waitressing job. She always struck me as bored, as if she'd much rather be doing something else.

When she returned and placed the coffee in front of us, I said, "Brandy, can you type?"

The wide streak of red in her dark hair seemed to glow in the sun, and her nose and eyebrow rings always made me feel this was some sort of statement she hoped others would notice.

"Can I *type?*" she asked, clearly surprised by my question. "Yeah, I can type. I learned in high school. Why?"

"Well, I don't want to overstep my bounds, but . . . we have a new doctor coming to town to open a practice. I'll be working there as his RN, and he's looking for an office girl."

"Oh, you mean that dude you had lunch with here last week? Was that him?"

"Right."

"Whew, he sure is hot, isn't he? My friends are calling him Doctor McDreamy."

I laughed. Leave it to the kids to notice a good-looking guy on the island.

"Well . . . gee . . . I don't know. I mean, yeah, I'd love to quit waitressing. But what would I have to do in a doctor's office? I'm not into giving shots and that kinda stuff."

I laughed again. "Ah, no. That would be my job. You'd be expected to answer the phone, make appointments, greet the patients when they arrive, that sort of thing, and we'd teach you anything else you might need to do."

She plunked down on the empty chair at our table. "Really? Well, heck, I could do that. I know I could. Geez, yeah. I'd love to work in a doctor's office. I mean . . . wow, that's like a professional job, isn't it?"

I felt a smile cross my face and said, "Yes, it could be. So you think you might be interested? It wouldn't start until January. The office is being redone, so would January work for you?"

"Sure. That would be great. I could give my notice here and even take the holidays off. I still live at home, so I don't think my parents would mind if I don't pay rent for a couple weeks."

"Well, give me your phone number, and I'll have Dr. Mancini give you a call. He'll want to meet you for an interview."

"Oh," she said, and paused. "Well . . . gee . . . I kinda met him the other day. Doesn't that count?"

"Ah . . . no. 'Fraid not. You'd have to do a formal interview with him. You'd discuss hours, salary, that sort of thing. It's a *professional* job, remember?"

"Oh, right," she said, but her expression showed concern.

"Don't worry. I'll get together with you before you go and kind of walk you through a practice interview."

"Really? Oh, Miss Josie, that would be super. Thanks. Thanks so much. I'll get my number to you in a minute." She jumped up and ran inside.

Mallory laughed. "Hmm, I'd say you made that girl's day. Actually, you may have made her month."

I nodded and smiled. "You think?"

Brandy returned and handed me a piece of paper with her phone number scribbled on it.

I tucked it into my handbag. "Okay. I'll give Dr. Mancini your number, so you can expect a call from him. When is a good time to get together for our mock interview?"

"I'm off work tomorrow morning."

"Good. I don't have to be at the yarn shop till two. Why don't you come by my house in the morning? Like around ten?"

"Sounds great," she said before rushing back inside the restaurant. Then she paused and turned around. "Oh, and thanks, Miss Josie."

I had called Simon the night before to tell him about Brandy. He was quite interested in doing an interview with her and planned to call her when we hung up.

I began slicing the banana bread that had been cooling on the counter when I heard the doorbell. Glancing at the clock, I saw it was just before ten. A good trait for an employee to have—arriving on time.

"Hey," I said, opening the door wider for Brandy to enter. "Come on in the kitchen. I have coffee and banana bread."

"This is so nice of you to coach me. I've never done a formal interview before. And the doctor called me last night. I have an interview with him this Friday at eleven."

Brandy took a seat at the table while I filled two mugs. "Really? How'd you get the job at the Pelican?" I asked, as I made a mental note that Simon would be back on the island in a couple days.

"Oh, well, my sister worked there, but she quit when she got married, so she just told the owner that I'd take her place. I mean, we met for a few minutes so he could explain the job and hours, but . . . that was it. What will this interview be like?"

I placed two plates of banana bread on the table and joined her. "Not really that different. Dr. Mancini will explain the hours and your salary." I glanced at her very short cutoffs and stained T-shirt. "But you'll want to dress appropriately for the interview."

I saw by the expression on her face that she wasn't following me, and she remained silent.

"You know," I said, pausing to take a sip of coffee. "Like a nice pair of slacks or skirt and a top."

She nodded. "Oh. Right. I have the ones I wear to church."

"Exactly. Something like that." I watched her break off a piece of banana bread and pop it into her mouth. "Make sure your hair looks good, too, and not too much makeup." I wasn't sure there was much hope for the red-streaked spiky hair, but I hoped that maybe she'd tone down the heavy makeup. She was such a pretty girl, but the black lining her eyes made her look a bit fierce.

She ran a hand through her hair and nodded. "Oh . . . Like the way I look when I go to church?"

"Exactly," I said again. "You want to present a professional appearance. So, yes, copy the way you look when you go to church." I took another sip of coffee, feeling that our practice session was going well.

"Right . . . but . . . I don't have to look like that when I'm actually working, do I?"

Maybe this wasn't going as well as I'd thought. I cleared my throat and said, "Well, that's one of the questions that you'll need to ask Dr. Mancini. Jot down some questions that you have before the interview and bring them with you. Ask him about a dress code—what he expects you to wear in the office."

"Oh, like a uniform?"

I laughed. "You won't be expected to wear a uniform, but he might tell you that he doesn't want you working in the office in shorts or tank tops, or . . . I really don't know what his dress code will be, but just bear in mind that a skirt, or cropped pants or slacks, and a nice blouse or top is always appropriate. But that's something that you need to discuss with him."

Brandy nodded her head emphatically. "Okay. Got it."

I smiled. "I'm sure he'll ask how your typing is, if you understand a filing system and that sort of thing. But you certainly can't be expected to understand the duties of a receptionist right away. He knows this will be your first job doing this type of work, so I'm sure he'll explain how he'd like things to be done. Now let's just role play here a little bit," I said, and saw the bewildered expression on her face. "You know—let's pretend. I'll be a patient coming into the office. You're sitting here at your desk. What's the first thing you'd say to the patient?"

I saw Brandy's shoulders go back, and she sat up straighter in the chair. "Hello?"

I laughed and nodded. "Yes, hello is good. But people like to be referred to by their name. So even better would be something like, 'Hello, Miss Chloe.'"

"Oh, is Miss Chloe going to be seen there for her broken arm?"

Maybe this wasn't going to be as easy as I thought. "I'm just using Chloe's name as an example."

"Oh . . . gotcha."

"Okay, so you've said hello. Now what?" I asked, and saw another confused expression on her face. "You might make a little small talk, like about the weather or something. People are normally a bit nervous when they're seeing the doctor. They're there because they don't feel well, so it's nice to put them at ease."

"Okay. Right. Do you have . . . ah . . . like a piece of paper and pencil? Maybe I should write all of this down."

Not a bad idea. I got up and rummaged in my counter drawer and gave her a small notebook and ink pen, and then waited while she made some notes.

She then glanced up at me, an expectant look on her face. "Got it. Then what?"

"Well, now this is when you'll check your appointment book against the actual time. Sometimes patients arrive early or late. You'll also have to determine if the doctor is running behind, and if so, you should let the patient know this. For instance, you might tell her that Dr. Mancini is running about ten minutes behind. This is a courtesy to the patient. If it's longer than ten minutes, the patient might want to run to the post office or something, rather than have to wait in the office."

Brandy scribbled away and then looked up. "Right. That makes sense."

"And if the doctor is on schedule, you can just say, 'Please have a seat.' "

Again, she wrote down what I'd said.

"Anything else?" she asked.

"Well, you'll be answering the phone, and phone etiquette is important too. How do you answer the phone at the restaurant?"

I saw that bewildered expression again.

"I . . . um . . . just say 'Pickled Pelican.' "

I nodded. "Which is fine for a restaurant, but you want to be a little more professional at a doctor's office. So you should say, 'Good morning, Dr. Mancini's office, this is Brandy speaking. How may I help you?' "

She blew out a breath and giggled. "Wow! That's a mouthful, isn't it?"

I smiled and nodded but saw her once again writing everything down.

After a few moments, she said, "Okay. Got it."

"Well, I think the rest of your job duties will be explained to you once you actually begin working. I'm sure Dr. Mancini will have a certain way he wants you to deal with the patient records, how close to book appointments, what to do if somebody calls in with an emergency, that sort of thing."

I saw a huge smile cross her face. "I sure hope I get this job. It all sounds so . . . *grown-up*. I think I'd like having a job like this."

"And I think you'd be very good at it. You have a friendly personality and that's important when working with sick people. Plus, you're used to working with the public, and that isn't always easy."

Brandy laughed. "Boy! Don't I just know that."

By the time Brandy left, I felt she'd absorbed everything that I'd tried to help her with. I was hopeful that she'd be hired, and I was happy for her. I was happy for myself as well because I thought she'd be a very pleasant employee to work with.

As I headed to do some laundry I remembered that Simon would be back in Cedar Key in two days, and I felt a smile cross my face.

❧ 12 ❧

By the following week, I still hadn't heard from Simon even though I knew the interview with Brandy had gone well and she had been hired. It was Brandy who excitedly shared the news with me and not him.

Who cares anyway, I thought. I was simply going to be his nurse in a working relationship, so he certainly had no obligation to be in touch.

I was applying my makeup before heading to the yarn shop for my first men's knitting class when the phone rang.

I answered to hear Simon's voice, and all thoughts of *Who cares?* vanished.

"Josie, I've been meaning to call you and I'm sorry it's taken a while. Something came up with my daughter and I've been busy since I left Cedar Key last Friday."

"Oh. Not a problem," I said.

"I'm sure Brandy told you that I hired her as our receptionist?"

I smiled. "Yes, she did. She's pretty excited about her upcoming job."

Simon's laughter came across the line. "She's quite a character, but I think she's exactly what a doctor's office needs. Somebody who doesn't get too stressed. She knows the locals, and I think she'll be both competent and easy to work with. So I want to thank you for recommending her."

"I totally agree, and it was my pleasure."

"I also know I mentioned getting together last Friday when I was here, but I had to leave as soon as I did the interview with Brandy."

"Oh . . . no . . . that's fine. I understand."

"Thanks, but I'd like to take you to dinner. Are you free this evening? I know it's short notice, but figured I'd ask."

I felt my heart drop. Damn. "Oh, geez, no. I'm sorry. I have my first knitting class in about an hour."

"Well, I'm here till Friday morning. Would you be free tomorrow evening?"

I normally went to the knitting group on Thursday evenings, but let's see—Doctor McDreamy or knitting group? "Actually, yes, I am."

"Great. How about if I make a reservation for seven at the Island Room? Would that work for you?"

"It would," I said, knowing I was feeling more excited than I should be.

"Great," he said again. "So we'll meet there at seven?"

"Sounds good," I told him before hanging up.

You silly goose, I thought. I'm meeting him at the restaurant. That doesn't really constitute a date. Does it?

I looked across the table at four men with anxious expressions on their faces.

"Okay," I said, leaning forward. "First rule of knitting. Relax. Have fun. No need to be stressed."

I heard four collective sighs, and my dad threw me a smile and a wink.

"First I'm going to teach you to cast on. There's lots of ways to do this, and over time you'll learn different ones, but I think the easiest for a beginning knitter is the long tail cast on." I proceeded to demonstrate how to hold the yarn and the needles and slowly began casting on as I explained to them. "So take your time, there's no rush, and if that's all you learn tonight, that's fine."

I watched as Doyle, Saxton, Gabe, and my dad fumbled with their yarn and needle.

"Like this?" Doyle questioned. "Am I doing it right?"

I got up to stand behind him and check his work. "You are," I told him. "Yay for you." I peeked over the shoulders of the others and saw the only one who seemed to be a bit clumsy was my dad. I leaned over to position his fingers a bit better. "Try holding it like this."

After a few moments he nodded. "Much better. Thanks, Josie."

Within a few more minutes it was easy to see that all four men had gotten the hang of it.

"Okay," I said. "Now I want you to take that apart and start over. This time cast on thirty stitches, not too tight, not too loose."

I did the same with my sample as I kept one eye on them.

When they had finished, I inspected their work. "Perfect," I said. "You guys are born knitters. Now I'll teach you how to do a knit stitch."

Again, I demonstrated while sitting with my back to them and holding my knitting to the side so that they could see it from the correct position. Slowly I inserted my right needle while explaining what to do. I finished my row and turned around.

"Any questions?" When all four men said no, I said, "Okay. Now you try. I'll walk behind to make sure you're getting it."

They were slow, they were a bit clumsy, but by golly, they were knitting stitches.

At one point, Saxton got a little tangled with the yarn and Doyle realized he'd dropped a stitch, but I helped them out and they kept going.

"So if I kept doing this, I could make a scarf?" my father questioned.

"You could, and that would be the garter stitch. You just knit every row. So let's do a few more rows and then I'll teach you how to purl. When you alternate with a row of knitting and a row of purling, that's the stockinette stitch. In many basic patterns, those two stitches will be all you'll need to know."

The room became very quiet as each of them plodded along. After a few minutes, I said, "We can talk, you know. Knitting doesn't have to be a silent pastime when you're in a group." They all laughed and I saw them relax a bit more. "When you're working on a lace pattern or cables you'll probably have to focus, but straight knitting and purling allows you to socialize."

My father began chatting with Gabe, asking him questions about spending the winter on Cedar Key. "How do you like the island so far?"

"I like it a lot," Gabe said. "Quiet and beautiful scenery. I'm very much enjoying the wildlife."

"Do you fish?" Doyle asked.

"I do, although I haven't had the chance in a few years."

"Well, you'll have to go out with us," Doyle told him. "I have a boat, and the three of us try to get out there at least once a week. You're welcome to join us."

"That sounds great. Thanks."

The conversation went back and forth as they discussed current events, sports, books, boating, and fishing. I smiled as I listened to the male chatter. It wasn't any different from females getting together over knitting. The topics might not be the same, but the result was the same. Bonding. Making a connection with other people. Socializing.

I saw that all four of them now had a few rows finished. "Okay," I said. "Ready to learn how to purl?"

I heard a resounding yes and proceeded to teach them the purl stitch. This proved a little more difficult as they had to learn the exact opposite of knitting by inserting the right needle in front of the left one. I helped each one individually and, except for Gabe, I could see this stitch slowed them down a bit and created a bit more clumsiness.

"It's just going to take practice," I explained. "Once you've done purling for a while, it will feel almost as comfortable as knitting. But the main thing tonight is that you're learning the difference between knit and purl stitches."

"I don't think I like this as well as straight knitting," I heard Doyle say, and I laughed.

"Don't feel bad," I told him. "Many knitters would much rather knit than purl, so you're not alone. But it's a needed stitch, as you'll see when we begin working on your scarf."

I checked my watch and was surprised to see we had been working for an hour and had only thirty minutes left to the class.

I got up and walked to the counter area. "You guys keep going. The coffee is ready, and I brought some cranberry bread that I made this morning. During knitting night we always end with a snack, so I thought you guys would enjoy this too."

I proceeded to slice the bread and heard Gabe say, "I'd be more than happy to bring something to go with the coffee next week. I make a pretty good pound cake."

"Ah, so you're a chef too?" I heard my father kid him.

"Well, I've been divorced for years, so it was either starve or learn how to cook properly," he said, causing the others to laugh.

"That would be great, Gabe," I told him as I placed the platter of bread on the table. "Thanks. You guys can stop anytime you want. I'd say you did exceptionally well for your first class. So keep practicing all week on that piece, and next week I'll teach you how to increase. Many patterns call for adding an extra stitch. Help yourself to the coffee and bread," I said, and looked up as the door opened and Chloe walked in.

"Oh, sorry," she said. "Is the class still going on? I just wanted to drop by and say hi."

I saw her eyes dart directly to Gabe, and I smiled. "No, we're finishing up, and you're just in time for coffee and cranberry bread. Come and join us."

"Thanks," she said, grabbing the empty chair next to Gabe.

The men said hi, and I heard Gabe say, "Nice to see you again. How's that arm doing?"

"It's putting a real damper on my knitting, but no discomfort."

"More of an annoyance, huh?" he asked, standing up. "Can I get you some coffee?"

"That would be great. Thanks."

I sat there and observed the interaction. Call me silly, but I was pretty sure I saw some interest between them.

"So the class went well?" Chloe asked.

"It did," I told her. "I think we have some natural knitters here. They've done very well learning to cast on and knitting and purling."

"Wonderful. Who knows, we might just have a potential master knitter in our group."

Gabe placed the coffee in front of Chloe and sat back down. "Yes, on my flight down here from Philly I noticed a man in first class knitting away. I struck up a conversation with him, and he was working on a gorgeous lace shawl for his daughter. Told me he's been knitting for about ten years now and has even written some books with unusual designs for socks."

Chloe nodded. "Oh, right. Not only are more and more men learning to knit, many are so creative. Hey, knitting is an art just like writing or music. Some do it only as a hobby or pastime, but we have some great male designers around now. It's a terrible stereotype to say knitting is only for women."

"Hear, hear," said my father, holding up the piece he'd been working on. "Remember that saying years ago, 'Real men don't eat quiche'? That was downright false. Like masculine men choose steak and gravy and hearty meals over something like quiche? It isn't always true, and people shouldn't lean on stereotypes."

"Is that why you took up knitting, Dad? To dispel this idea?"

My father laughed. "Not really, but now that you mention the idea, it never hurts to be a bit of a rebel."

"While I certainly agree with you, Joe, let's bring a little testosterone into the conversation," Doyle said. "Who's free to go fishing on Friday?"

By the time the men left the carriage house of the yarn shop, plans had been made for a day of boating and fishing.

"That really seemed to go well," Chloe said as she helped me clear off the table and I began washing the cups and plates.

"I think it did. I'm glad I mentioned the idea of this class and agreed to teach it. I think it'll be fun. And so . . . what's up with you and Gabe?"

She turned her back to remove the last of the cups from the table. "Me and Gabe? Nothing. I don't even know him."

"Right," I said, and felt a smile cross my face. "But I'm betting anything you'd sure like to have that chance."

13

Orli had just left for school and I was savoring my first cup of coffee when I answered the phone to hear my mother say, "Is it true? Did Ben really get some woman up in New York pregnant?"

A groan escaped me. Hearing my mother's drama queen tone of voice was not my idea of waking up slowly.

"How the heck did you hear about that?" I questioned.

"What does it matter where I heard it? Is it true?"

"Yes. It's true."

"And it never occurred to you to tell me this?" I heard the annoyance in her voice.

"Why? It's not like you could change anything, and besides, I honestly don't care."

I heard her sigh of aggravation come across the line.

"You don't care? You've been dating him for a couple years now and you don't care?"

"Mom, look. I'm still not quite sure what Ben and I had together. At best, it was a long-distance relationship that was simply going nowhere. I liked him well enough in the beginning, but . . . there just was never any . . . sexual chemistry with him. And it's pretty tough to even attempt a relationship with over a thousand miles between you."

"Hmm. He certainly seemed to find some sexual chemistry with whomever he got pregnant. So . . . you're okay with all of this?"

"Yes, I'm perfectly fine with it." The initial stab of rejection I'd felt had disappeared within a day or so of hearing his news. "And I'm still planning to attend Mr. Al's memorial next week."

"Won't that be awkward?"

"Not at all. I don't plan to go out of my way to speak to Ben. I'll go to the church and skip the gathering after. Not a big deal."

"Okay," my mother said, and I heard the hesitancy in the word. "Well, personally, I never thought you two were suited for each other, so it's probably all for the best."

I had a feeling that, in my mother's opinion, Grant would probably always be the only man she thought was suited for me.

"Your father said the knitting class went very well. He seemed to really enjoy it."

"I think it did too. They're a nice group of men, and it was fun. I think all four of them caught on pretty fast with the basic stitches."

"I'm about to make some meatballs and sauce to go with pasta tonight for supper. Are you and Orli able to come?"

Damn. I really didn't want to tell my mother about dinner with Simon. "Well . . . I'm sure Orli can make it, but . . . I've already made other plans."

"Oh, really? For dinner? Who are you having dinner with?"

"Simon. Dr. Mancini." It was times like this that I thought living anywhere but in the same town as my mother might be a good thing.

"Oh!" There was a pause. "So you have a date with him?"

"It's not a *date,* Mom." I heard the aggravation creeping into my tone. "I had suggested Brandy as his new receptionist. He interviewed and hired her. So he just wanted to thank me, and I'm meeting him at seven at the Island Room."

"Oh, I see," was all she said.

"I have to go, but I'll tell Orli to give you a call about dinner."

I hung up before she could ask any more questions and took my mug of coffee out to the patio.

Sitting on the lounge I relished the great autumn weather that had arrived on the island over the past week. A definite drop in humidity, cooler mornings and evenings. I loved this time of year in Florida. I let my mind wander and found myself wondering what I should wear for dinner. I wanted to look nice, of course, but I didn't want to appear too dressy. Thinking of the advice I'd given Brandy, I thought perhaps a sundress, sweater, and flats might work well. I'd be home from work by two, so I had plenty of time to think about that.

The phone rang again, interrupting my thoughts.

"I didn't wake you, did I?" Grant asked.

"Not at all. I'm just enjoying my coffee. What's up?"

"I wanted to let you know that the flights are all booked for you and Orli. First class on Delta, Gainesville to Atlanta, and then on to Boston. You'll leave on Monday, the twenty-second, and are back on the thirtieth, as we discussed. I'll e-mail you all the info, and you can print out the boarding passes the day before, okay?"

"It's great, but Grant, you didn't have to book us in first class. Really."

I heard his laugh across the line. "I know I didn't *have* to. I wanted to. Hey, my two girls deserve the best, right?"

Even after sixteen years, even with no certificate of marriage—he still considered me his *girl,* causing me to smile.

"Well, that was very nice of you, and Orli will be thrilled. I'm really looking forward to the trip. So how's your condo? I take it you like it there? Seen any ghosts yet?"

I heard Grant laugh again. "Not yet. I like it here a lot, and I have very nice neighbors in my building. You'll meet them all when you come up. I think you'll really get a kick out of one in particular."

"Why's that?"

"Well, Estelle Fletcher is a hoot. Elderly woman who lives in the condo across from mine. Her husband passed away last year, but she's pretty independent, not to mention feisty. In addition to being a psychic."

Now it was my turn to laugh. "No! Seriously? She thinks she's a psychic?"

"Oh, trust me. She doesn't *think* it. She says she has the gift, and she's dead serious."

The building where Grant now lived had been part of the ancient and historic Danvers State Hospital. Perched high on a hill overlooking the town, it had closed its doors in the 1990s and then over the years fell into a state of disrepair with numerous rumors about ghosts and spirits. A developer had bought the land and turned the buildings into a luxury condo complex.

"Hmm," I said. "Interesting. I remember your mother driving me past there once when I was visiting, and she told me quite a few stories about the structure and patients. It sounded like a horrible place; just the sight of that gothic structure gave me the creeps. I couldn't believe it was the same place when you sent me the photos. Maybe this Estelle just got caught up in the drama of the history behind the building."

I heard Grant chuckle. "Yeah, maybe. Listen, I have to run. I'm due in court. So I'll e-mail you the flight info. Will you tell Orli to give me a call this evening?"

"Will do," I said, hanging up the phone. I smiled as I thought about Estelle and Danvers State. I felt it was all hooey, but I knew that somebody like Berkley Whitmore would gobble up something like this. She was originally from Salem, the next town to Danvers, so no doubt she had a lot of background on the place.

I scarfed down a quick sandwich for lunch at the yarn shop, locked the door behind me, and headed to the chocolate shop down the street.

"Hey," Berkley said as I walked in. "Here to replenish your chocolate supply?"

"I am. Orli reminded me last night that we need more Cedar Key clams and some truffles. So I'll take a pound of each. Can't have us running out of our chocolate. How's things with you?"

"Great," Berkley said, putting on a pair of plastic gloves before bending down to reach into the glass display case. "Oh, Saxton seemed to really enjoy his first knitting class last night. Gosh, he was up till after midnight knitting away on that practice swatch."

I laughed. "That's great. Yeah, I think it went very well, and I was surprised at how quickly they all seemed to catch on."

"What's with this new man in town? Gabe Brunell."

"He's here for the winter, and he's in the class too. Why?"

Berkley continued to fill the box with chocolates and looked up to shoot me a smile. "Well, Saxton said that Chloe arrived just as you were finishing and about to have coffee and that she settled herself next to Gabe. He said they were still chatting away when he left."

"Yeah, although she won't admit it, I think she's attracted to him. He seems like a really nice guy too. From Philly, retired teacher, divorced. They did seem to hit it off, so who knows."

"I think it would be nice for her to have a male companion again. She had Cameron for a while, but that really didn't go anywhere."

I nodded. "Oh, hey. I wanted to ask you about Danvers State Hospital. Do you remember it from when you lived in Salem?"

Berkley stopped putting chocolate in the box and stood up. "Oh, yeah. Why would you want to know about that gruesome place?"

"That's where Grant purchased his new condo."

"Oh. Really?" She bent back down and continued reaching for chocolates.

"A developer has turned what was left of the buildings into a luxury condo unit."

She nodded and closed both boxes with her signature gold seal. "Yeah, I'd heard that. In all honesty, I couldn't imagine anybody wanting to *live* there."

"Why not?"

She shook her shoulders and made a distasteful sound. "That place is so creepy. All the horrors that took place there over so many years with those mental patients. God, some of the stories I heard made it sound like a snake pit. I just don't think that, after so much sorrow, that place would have very good energy. You know . . . all that bad karma hanging around."

I laughed. "Oh, Berkley, you don't really believe that, do you?"

She totaled up my sales on the register and shrugged. "I do believe in energy and karma . . . but I don't mean to offend Grant or his choice of residence. I just know that I couldn't live there."

I reached for the bag. "Thanks. He told me his neighbor is a real character. She sounds like a few people here on the island. Elderly woman, and she claims she's a psychic."

"Really? Well, don't be so quick to dispute that. People with gifts are drawn to certain places for various reasons. I'll be interested to hear what you think of the place after you visit there over Christmas."

On the ride home I replayed the conversation with Berkley in my mind. I knew she was into all the New Age stuff with crystals and horoscopes and anything to do with the occult. But I wondered if what she'd said could have any truth to it. I knew there were many claims about old houses harboring ghosts. We even had our fair share of those on the island, and I recalled how Saren Ghetti, Sydney's father, had insisted a lovely ghost named Miss Elly used to visit him every evening for cognac, but most of us just chalked that up to a vivid imagination on his part. By the time I pulled into my driveway I realized that in addition to visiting with Grant and his mother, I was also very much looking forward to meeting Estelle Fletcher.

14

I had driven myself to the Island Room, but walking from the car to the restaurant I still had a silly assumption that this evening with Simon was a date and not just a dinner. And from the look on his face when I walked in, I couldn't help but think that perhaps he felt the same.

He was already seated at a table by the window but stood up as soon as I walked toward him. I couldn't miss the head-to-toe glance he gave me or the huge smile covering his face. He looked great in a pair of tan dress slacks and a chocolate-brown, open-collar shirt. I was glad I'd chosen my black and white sundress and the pretty black shrug that I had recently finished knitting.

"Good to see you again, Josie," he said, sitting back down. "I'm glad you could join me for dinner. Would you like a drink or some wine?"

I sat across from him and realized again what a great-looking guy he was, in addition to having a pleasant personality. "Yes. White wine would be nice."

After the waiter took our drink order, Simon said, "So you're doing a knitting class at the yarn shop? How'd that go for you last night?"

"Oh, very well. The guys caught on even better than I'd expected."

"Guys?"

I saw the look of surprise on his face and smiled. "Yeah. It's a men's knitting class and I have four students learning how to knit. One of them is my father."

"Well, that's wonderful. Knitting, along with many other things, has been seen as the domain of women for too long. I've never understood the reasoning. Look at all the great male chefs and clothes designers."

I liked how this guy thought. "Exactly. I'm afraid up until recently there's been a stereotype attached to men who knit, but . . . more and more are now coming out of the closet, so to speak. Which I think is great."

"I agree. My daughter is quite an accomplished knitter, so I know how enjoyable knitting can be just from watching Lily."

Now it was my turn to be surprised. "Oh, I love to hear about young people knitting. We also have a children's class that we hold at the yarn shop. Has she been knitting since she was a child?"

"Thanks," we both said as the waiter placed our wine in front of us.

"Give us a little while before we order," Simon told him. "Yes, she began knitting around age ten, I think it was." He lifted his glass and touched mine. "Here's to a great working relationship."

I nodded. "Yes, a great working relationship." I took a sip and then asked, "Does your wife also knit?"

Simon shook his head. "No, my ex-wife was never into that sort of thing. I'm afraid Stephanie was more caught up in spas, shopping, and socializing."

I noticed how he used the word *ex* in relation to his wife, and I also noticed that just from his brief description of her, she sounded vain and superficial. "Right. Knitting and needle crafts aren't for everybody. You mentioned that something came up with your daughter last week. I hope everything is okay."

He took a sip of wine and nodded. "Oh, yes. Fine. Lily will be going off to college next year, and she's been accepted at a few, so we're still doing the parent/student visits to check them out. We drove to the University of Tampa, and it was kind of a last-minute thing. Her mother had been scheduled to take Lily but . . . realized she wasn't able to."

I thought it was odd that the mother had had a change of plans last minute, but I didn't say anything. "Oh, I thought Lily graduated this past June from high school."

"Yes, she did," Simon said before pausing for a moment. "She wanted to take a year off before beginning college . . . which I thought was a good idea. So she's all set to begin next summer."

"That's great. Such an adventure ahead of her. Does she live with her mother?" I asked.

"Right now, Lily is splitting her time between my parents' home in Gainesville and a few days a month at Stephanie's on Amelia Island. She was spending a lot of time with me, but I've been so busy trying to set up the new office and I really don't have a proper home at the moment, so staying with my parents is good. I can see Lily when I'm there."

It was obvious that he had a close relationship with his daughter. "Oh, that's great. I know Orli loves going to the Boston area to spend time with Grant and his mother."

Simon nodded and picked up the menu. "I guess we should decide on what we're having."

By the time the waiter approached our table I'd decided on a pasta dish, and Simon requested chicken.

"Did everything work out for your trip to Boston?" he asked.

"It did. Grant called and has e-mailed me all the info for the flights. Orli and I will fly up there on December twenty-second and fly home on the thirtieth."

"That's great. I'm sure you're looking forward to it."

I nodded. "Yeah, I am. I love it up there, and I know that Orli and I will have a good time, so it'll be fun."

He shifted in his chair, and I saw a grimace cross his face.

"Are you okay?" I asked.

"Yeah, fine. Just an old back injury that nags me sometimes. So, does your daughter also knit?"

I got the feeling he wanted to change the subject. "Strangely enough, no," I said, then laughed. "I think she figures I do enough knitting for both of us. But I wouldn't be surprised if in a few years she'll be itching to learn. So if your ex-wife doesn't knit, how did Lily learn?"

He paused a moment before saying, "In school. One of her teachers taught her, and my sister is a huge knitter, so she helped Lily in the beginning."

"Oh, that's great. How nice to have a teacher to do that after school hours."

"Right," was all he said. "I know Gloria normally frequents the yarn shop in Gainesville because it's close, but I'll have to mention the one here to her."

"Yes, I also love the Yarnworks in Gainesville. We knitters usually have one local shop we're loyal to, but if she's like the rest of us, I'm sure she's probably already visited here. Somehow we can track down a yarn shop within a hundred mile radius."

He laughed. "You're probably right. So, besides knitting, what else do you do for enjoyment? Do you fish?"

"Not really. Having been brought up on the island I've done my fair share of fishing, but I can't say I've really ever enjoyed it. How about you? Do you like to fish?"

He nodded. "I do. I just don't seem to find as much time to do it as I'd like."

"Well, maybe actually living here will help that situation. Plus, I'll introduce you to Doyle Summers and my dad. They and a small group of guys go out on Doyle's boat at least once a week."

"That sounds great. Thanks."

The waiter approached with our dishes.

"Looks good," I said.

"Yes. *Bon appétit.*"

I began eating my pasta and realized I was having a really nice time being in Simon's company. He was so easy to converse with, and I recalled the dead silences that Ben and I had encountered during dinners out. It even *felt* different being with Simon. Ben could be a bit strong-willed about certain things, and many an evening had ended in a heated debate. I often wondered if he had a bit of that control streak that my mother possessed. Perhaps that's why we clashed. My independent personality never went well with a control freak.

As if reading my mind, Simon asked, "So, you're not dating or involved with anybody right now?"

I wiped my mouth with the napkin and shook my head. "No. I'm a free agent again. I had been in a long-distance relationship with somebody—his uncle lived on the island. Mr. Al recently passed away. But we both came to realize that whatever we had, if anything, was going nowhere." I neglected to mention that in all truth, Ben had dumped me.

"Yeah, I would think that could be pretty difficult. Trying to keep a relationship going with miles separating you." He took a bite of chicken and was silent for a few moments. "So . . . your mother is a romance author. My sister is an avid reader, too, so I'll have to ask if she's read your mom's books. Does she write under her real name?"

"Yes. Shelby Sullivan. She and I have our moments . . . but I have to admit that she's done very well over the years with her writing."

"Sounds like you're proud of her."

I'd never given this too much thought. "I guess I am. Maybe I take her career for granted sometimes, but I know it's become more difficult to even get published, so yeah, I am proud of her for turning out a best seller every year. She can just be a bit difficult at times to get along with."

Simon laughed. "Ah, that old mother-daughter thing, huh?"

I let out a chuckle. "Yup, I'm afraid so. I've always envied mothers and daughters who get along like best friends. I've never had that with my mother. It's been a constant battle filled with tension. My best friend Mallory . . . she and her mother get along so well. Once I got older, I realized that my mother is a control freak and that's the root of our problem."

Simon nodded. "Yeah, I can understand that. My sisters have had their moments with my mother, but overall I'd have to say they all get along pretty well. And just from what you've told me about being a single mom, I can certainly understand how your mother's personality might rub you the wrong way."

He understood? This was the first time I could recall a man saying that and agreeing with me. Even thought I felt that Grant probably did, he'd never come out and said it in so many words.

"Thanks," I said. "I have to admit that I also envy you your large family. Being an only child isn't all that it's cracked up to be. That's why I've always felt bad that my own daughter has ended up as an only child."

"I probably don't tell them nearly enough, but yeah, I do feel fortunate having my siblings and now their families added to the group. But hey, never say never on that sibling for Orli. Gosh, what are you, barely thirty? Women are having children much later in life now."

Hearing his assumption about my age caused me to laugh. "Thank you for the compliment, but no, I'm not barely thirty. I'm thirty-five."

I heard Simon chuckle. "You're a mere babe," he said. "I just turned forty-seven."

"Really?" I heard myself say. Whew, he looked pretty damn good for a guy pushing fifty. "You sure don't look it," I said, and realized that was an awkward thing to say.

But he laughed again. "And thank *you* for your compliment."

By the time coffee arrived I could hardly believe that two hours had passed. I glanced at my watch and saw that it was almost nine. I couldn't recall the last time I had enjoyed an evening out as much as this one.

Simon walked me to my car in the parking lot. "I'll follow you home," he said.

"Oh, no, really. You don't have to do that. Cedar Key is quite a safe town."

"I know that, but I want to. I'm leaving in the morning for Gainesville. Lily is at my parents' house and I'll be staying there for a few days. Then I have to head to St. Augustine for a couple weeks, but I'll give you a call when I'm coming back to Cedar Key."

"Great," I said, getting into my car and starting the ignition. "Thank you so much for a lovely dinner."

"It was *my* pleasure, Josie. Really," he said, and headed to his car.

When I pulled into my driveway, Simon gave a short toot of his horn and I saw him lift his hand in a wave as he headed down Second Street.

❧ 15 ❧

I walked into the coffee café at the bookshop and saw it was filled with the usual early morning patrons. After chatting with Suellen for a few minutes, I took my latte and found an empty table. Mr. Al's memorial was later that day, and I found myself thinking about the differences between Ben and Simon.

Although I didn't know Simon well, I knew I enjoyed being with him. Not to say that Ben and I hadn't shared some fun moments during our brief time together, but Ben could be a bit difficult when it came to having ordinary discussions. He was extremely opinionated, which was fine, but I always got the feeling he expected me to agree with him on all subjects, and that had caused a bit of tension between us. Whereas chatting with Simon just seemed so easy. Relaxed. Comfortable. I felt that we were going to form a pleasant friendship.

I took a sip of coffee and questioned if friendship was all I really wanted. Of course it was. I wasn't so sure I wanted to get into the dynamics of anything more. Friendships were so much easier than involved relationships. And being friends with a handsome doctor was an extra plus.

"Hey, Josie."

I looked up to see Fiona standing beside my table with Andrea in her stroller.

"Good morning," I told her. "And you, you get prettier every day." I reached over to touch the baby's hand. "Can you join me for coffee?"

"Yeah, thanks. I just gave Suellen my order," Fiona said, sitting down.

"No classes today?"

"Not till later this afternoon. So I thought I'd spend some mommy time with Andrea. Sometimes I feel guilty for all the time my classes and study take away from her."

I nodded. I recalled the feeling from my days of raising Orli. "Yeah, that's understandable, but it'll all be worth it in the long run."

"I think so, and guess what? Greg called last evening. He got the position teaching at the university. I'm so excited. He'll be starting the new semester in January."

"Oh, that's great, Fiona. Marin had mentioned that you were hoping it would happen. So how soon do you think you'll be moving to Gainesville?"

"Thanks, Suellen," she said as her coffee was brought to the table. "Well, this will be Andrea's first Christmas, and that's a special one. I don't want Marin to miss out on that. So Greg and I will stay with Marin and Worth through the holidays. We have it all arranged to move right after the first of the year."

"That's really thoughtful of you. I know Marin will enjoy having all of you with her for Christmas."

"Can I join your table?"

I looked up to see that Grace had arrived with her daughter, Solange, in a stroller.

"Of course you can," I said, scooting my chair over to make room. "Good morning. I can't get over how fast Solange is growing."

Grace laughed and bent over to touch Andrea's hand as she positioned her stroller so the two babies could see each other. "I know. Eighteen months old already. And what's Andrea? Four months now?"

"Actually, she just turned five months. Time seems to be flying by."

It seemed like yesterday that Orli had been those ages. "Don't blink," I said. "Because before you know it they'll be celebrating their sweet sixteen like my daughter."

"I can hardly believe Orli is turning sixteen. So you're right. We have to savor these moments now, right along with all the sleepless nights. Is she teething yet?"

"I think she might be starting," Fiona said. "Lots of drooling going on as you can see." She reached over to wipe her daughter's chin with a napkin.

"How's your aunt doing?" I asked Grace. "I heard she was under the weather."

"Yeah, I'm not sure what's going on. She has the heart condition of course, so I hope that's not acting up again. But she told me last night that she won't be doing the knitting retreats anymore. She said it's just become too much for her, and with me tied up with Solange and Chloe being a partner at the yarn shop, I think she's finding it difficult to manage on her own."

I nodded. "I can understand that, but it's a shame. She really enjoyed doing that at her carriage house, and I'm sure her knitters will be disappointed. But everyone does reach a point when they simply have to slow down a little. That's one of the biggest downfalls that I've seen with my patients—the reluctance to give things up that they're no longer able to do. It's a difficult decision to make when the time comes."

"I know, so I'm hoping that she's really going to be okay about not doing the retreats anymore."

"Good morning. Got room for one more?"

We looked up to see that Chloe had joined us.

"Of course," Grace said, getting up to give her sister a hug. "How's your arm today?"

"Itchy," she said, sitting down. "But I think that means its healing?" She looked at both Fiona and me.

"It does," I told her. "So that's a good thing. When do you see the doctor again?"

"Next week, and I'm hoping this silly cast can come off sooner than he said. I've been a model patient, but I'm having terrible knitting withdrawal."

All of us nodded and laughed because we understood her feelings.

"So," Chloe said. "When does Doctor McDreamy open that practice of his?"

"After the first of the year," I told her. "It couldn't have worked out better for me. Now Orli and I will be able to fly to Boston for Christmas and her birthday."

"That really did work out well. And it seems that you were spotted at the Island Room having dinner with him last week. What's that all about?"

I felt a flush creeping up my neck. "Geez, it was only a dinner. A thank-you dinner. For recommending Brandy as his new receptionist."

Chloe laughed. "Right."

"While we're on that subject, how're things going for you and Gabe?"

"Who?" Grace asked, leaning toward her sister.

Chloe waved her hand in the air. "Oh, come on. He's just a nice guy taking Josie's knitting class. That's all."

"That's all? Gosh, I thought I'd never get the two of you out of the carriage house after the class so that I could lock up and go home," I kidded her.

Grace held up a hand. "Wait a sec. Back up. I seem to be missing a lot of details here. Start at the beginning, Chloe."

Chloe laughed and shook her head. "There isn't much to tell. Gabe Brunell is here for the winter. He signed up with Josie to learn how to knit. I happened to drop by toward the end of the first class and . . . well . . . we just got to talking. That's it."

"Hmm, that's it, huh?" Grace shot me a wink. "Well, if *it* turns into anything else you'd just better share it with me."

"Ah, female gossip," I said, then took my last sip of coffee. "Nothing beats it. I have to get going. Will I see you guys at Mr. Al's memorial today?"

"I'll be there," both Grace and Chloe said.

"Good, I'll see you there," I told them, and got up to leave before they could start hitting me with questions about Ben.

* * *

I had purposely arrived at the memorial only a few minutes before it was due to begin and slipped into the last pew next to Sydney Webster.

She touched my hand, gave me a smile, and whispered, "How're you doing?"

"Fine," I whispered back, and shot a smile and nod to Noah Hale sitting beside her.

Mr. Al had a good turnout for his final good-bye. I saw my parents sitting up front, along with many of the women from the yarn shop, fishermen, locals, and merchants. Then I spotted Ben sitting at the end of the first row. I craned my neck to see who was next to him, half expecting to see his pregnant girlfriend even though he'd said she wasn't coming. But it was a neighbor of Mr. Al's.

The pastor began the ceremony with lots of nice words about Mr. Al, followed by music, some heartfelt eulogies, and before I knew it, Ben was heading to the podium.

"I want to thank everybody for coming today," he said without a trace of emotion in his voice. "My uncle would have been very happy to see so many friendly faces. Uncle Al loved Cedar Key and all of the people here." He then paused as if uncertain how to continue. "Although I spent childhood summers here, I'm afraid I just never felt the same attachment, so I've decided to put his house up for sale rather than keep it myself." He cleared his throat and coughed.

There was a pause before he said, "So . . . thank you again for coming. We're having coffee and pastry in the church hall, and I hope you'll join us there."

That was it. No *I'm going to miss my uncle* or *My uncle was a great person*. No mention of his love of fishing. Nothing.

I was struck by the lack of emotion and intimacy that he had conveyed. And just before I stood and slipped out of the church, I was convinced that Ben Sudbury was definitely not someone I wanted to be around—and it had nothing to do with the fact that he had dumped me.

≈ 16 ≈

I looked across the table at the four men diligently knitting away. I was surprised at how quickly the month had flown by. During that time they had learned all the basic knitting stitches and techniques and were coming to the end of working on their scarves.

We had also learned that Gabe Brunell would be on the island until late April. He hadn't decided yet if he'd be returning to Cedar Key the following winter, because he had one married daughter and a granddaughter living in the Atlanta area. It also seemed that nothing was stirring between him and Chloe.

"So," I said, standing up and heading to the counter. "I'll get the coffee going. Dad, thanks for bringing the monkey bread tonight."

I heard my father laugh. "Oh, I'm afraid I can't take credit for that. I coerced your mother into making it for us."

I smiled as I spooned coffee into the filter and heard the guys discussing their fishing trip for the next day. Gabe had fit right into the group and had joined them each week for boating and fishing.

"Well, tonight marks the end of our four-week beginner class," I said. "I'm not sure if you guys would like to continue with another class or if you've had enough of knitting."

"Oh," Gabe said. "I guess I just assumed we'd go on to the next level for another class."

"Right," Doyle agreed. "Now that I've mastered the basics, I'm not about to give up."

"Same here," my dad and Saxton said.

"Well, that's great," I told them. "Okay. Then we have to decide what you'd like to learn to do. And we can set up some more classes."

"How about a sweater?" Gabe offered.

"Yeah, maybe with some cables in it, so we can learn how to do those," Doyle said.

"Sure." I felt a smile cross my face. This class had definitely been a success. "Actually, a sweater is pretty much straight knitting and purling, except for the cables, and on a larger scale than your scarf. If you all agree, that's fine with me. I'll teach you how to do the neck and the sleeves and then put it all together."

"Great," my dad said. "Bring on the sweater."

"Okay. While you have your coffee, I'll go into the shop and bring back some patterns for sweaters and you can decide which one you'd like to make."

When I returned with five different patterns, the men were enjoying their coffee and snack while chatting away.

I placed the patterns on the table and went to fill my mug. "Here's a few to look at. Unfortunately, there just aren't as many patterns around for men's designs as there are for women."

"Yeah," Gabe said, picking up one to look at. "I've noticed that, and it's a shame."

"Maybe we need somebody like you to start designing some," my dad kidded him, but I noticed that Gabe didn't make any comment.

"So once you decide which one you'd like to make, come into the shop to purchase your yarn and needles and you'll be all set." I reached for the calendar in my handbag. "Why don't we take next week off and start the new class the first Wednesday in November? Will that work for you?"

Without hesitation four heads nodded.

"And since we'll be working on a sweater, it will take longer. How about if the next class goes for seven weeks to begin with and we can extend it if we have to."

"Sounds good," they all agreed.

"So that'll take us till the week before Christmas, which will work well for me because I leave that following Monday for Boston. And as I said, if you feel we need more time, we can resume after the holidays."

"Great," Gabe said, and I saw him turn his head toward the door with a huge grin covering his face.

I looked over to see Chloe walk in. She hadn't been back since our first class.

"Hey," she said. "I just wanted to congratulate you guys for finishing up the knitting class. Did you enjoy it?"

Gabe laughed as Chloe again took the seat beside him. "We enjoyed it so much, Josie has agreed to do another class for us. We'll be starting in a couple weeks and making a sweater."

"That's great. Well done, Josie. You're an ace teacher."

I smiled. "Oh, I don't know about that. I have some prize pupils here."

After a few minutes the other three men drifted into generic conversation, but Gabe had his attention focused on Chloe. I picked up the vest that I was finishing for Orli, began knitting, and tried not to eavesdrop on what they were saying, but since I was just across the table, that was pretty much impossible.

"So how much longer until that cast comes off and you can resume knitting?" he asked.

"Actually, only one more week. I saw the doctor yesterday and he assures me that he can remove it next week. Believe me, I can't wait. It'll be nice to be a free woman again."

Gabe laughed. "Yes, I'm sure. The cast is such an inconvenience, but I'm sure you were a great patient and allowed that arm to heal properly."

"I was. The doctor said I can go back to knitting, but I'll be limited at first—only a couple hours each day—but he also said that knitting was great therapy. Many people with arthritis find that it eases their discomfort and keeps their fingers and hands limber."

"Very true," Gabe said. "Knitting can be good for *all* kinds of reasons."

I glanced up and saw the smile he gave Chloe and wondered if that statement had a double meaning to it.

I looked over and saw Chloe's face had taken on a crimson hue.

"Oh . . . by the way, Josie . . . I wanted to tell you," she stammered, and I realized that she was flustered by the flirty way Gabe was looking at her. "Just because the cast is coming off, you're not going to be out of a job next week. The doctor said that I can do light work at the yarn shop, but Dora and I agreed that if you can, we'd like you to stay on till the first week in December."

"Terrific," I told her, then smiled because I had an idea that Chloe wasn't thinking about my position at the yarn shop at all.

"So which day next week is it coming off?" I heard Gabe ask her as I looked back down at my knitting.

"Ah . . . Tuesday. I have an appointment with the doctor in Gainesville next Tuesday."

"Great. How about if I drive you to the doctor and then take you out for lunch or dinner after, so we can celebrate. You know . . . the removal of the cast and . . . being a free woman again."

I kept knitting away, but from the corner of my eye I saw a huge smile cross Chloe's face and heard her say, "Oh. Oh, well, yeah. That sounds like fun. Thank you."

"What time is your appointment?"

"Eleven."

"Okay, why don't I pick you up about nine-thirty, we'll go to your appointment, and then we'll have lunch in Gainesville."

"That's great. I live just up the street, upstairs from the chocolate shop. I can meet you outside at nine-thirty."

"Sounds like a plan to me," he said. I could have been wrong, but I thought I saw an expression of complete happiness cross his face.

So, I thought, *we just might have a little romance brewing here, after all.*

"Well, this was a great evening, Josie," my father said as he stood up and brought his cup and plate to the sink.

"It certainly was," Saxton agreed as he did the same.

"Yeah, I'm looking forward to the new class starting in two weeks." Doyle put his cup and plate on the counter. "Thanks for your great instructions, and I'll drop by the shop to get my yarn and needles for the sweater."

I stood up and began filling the sink with water and detergent to wash up the few items. As the three men left, I turned around and saw that Gabe and Chloe were still quietly chatting.

"Well," I heard him say, "I need to get home and let my dog out. Thanks for a great evening, Josie," he said, but I noticed that his eyes were on Chloe. "And if I don't see you before, I'll see you next Tuesday," he told her.

"Take care," I hollered as he left the shop.

Chloe joined me and picked up a dish towel to begin drying mugs.

"So," I said. "Looks like you snagged yourself a bona fide date."

She laughed. "Oh, I think he felt sorry for me and he was just trying to be nice."

"Why would he feel sorry for you?"

"Well . . . you know . . . because I broke my arm and I haven't been able to knit."

"I seriously doubt that. That man is smitten."

Now Chloe let out a belly laugh. "He's what?"

I joined her laugher. "*Smitten.* You know . . . besotted. Infatuated."

She whipped my arm with the dish towel. "Don't be silly."

"Yeah, well, you didn't see the way he looks at you when you're looking the other way."

"Oh, Josie, you're too funny. Guys in *my* age group are not smitten."

I finished washing the final plate, dried my hands, and put them on my hips. "Really? And you would know this how? And besides, your age group is the fifties and sixties—far from ancient in today's world."

I saw a serious expression cross her face. "Hmm. You mean you think he could be . . . interested in me?"

I smiled. "Gee, Chloe, yes. I think that could be a distinct possibility."

"Oh, I don't know. I thought he was just being nice. Although . . . I do have to say, he's pretty damn attractive."

"I gathered you thought that from the first day you met him in the yarn shop."

"No . . . was I that obvious?"

I laughed. "Hey, I thought it was cute."

"Cute? We're not teenagers."

"True, but there's no expiration date on being attracted to somebody. Having a relationship. Enjoying each other's company."

"I know that. I mean, I did date Cameron after Parker and I got divorced, but . . . we just didn't seem to . . . click. You know?"

I nodded. "Oh, yeah, I certainly do."

"Ah, Ben?" she asked.

"Yup. We hated each other at first, then we seemed to work through that and then . . . we seemed to just settle into this . . . static relationship, so yeah, I hear what you're saying. But I also have to say, from what I've witnessed between you and Gabe . . . I don't detect one ounce of static there."

Chloe laughed and squeezed my arm. "Come on," she said. "Time to lock up and go home."

∽ 17 ∽

Two days later I had unlocked the yarn shop at ten and was just taking my first sip of coffee when the door opened and two women walked in.

"Good morning," I said. "Can I help you with anything in particular?"

"Hi," the taller one said. "Are you Josie?"

I nodded. "Yes, but I'm not the owner. Eudora and Chloe are the owners, and Dora will be here around noon."

She waved a hand in the air while the other woman began fingering the yarns on the front display table.

"Oh, well . . . we wanted to meet *you*. I'm Eva. Eva Franklin, and this is my sister, Gloria Tucci. We're Simon's sisters."

"Oh," I said, and felt my hand go to my hair as I wished I'd taken a bit more time with my makeup that morning. I walked toward them, extending my hand. "How nice to meet you. Simon said that you were a knitter."

"Oh, I dabble a bit, but Gloria here is the advanced and addicted knitter."

"Hi," the other woman said and shook my hand after she replaced two skeins on the table. "As you can see, I get a little carried away in a yarn shop."

I laughed. "Is there any other way to be?"

Gloria glanced around and nodded. "This is a lovely shop. I can't believe I've never taken the time to come here."

"Thanks. We have the carriage house out back too. We keep the luxury yarns in there, so feel free to browse around."

"Great," Gloria said. "I love working with cashmere. Simon told us you're going to be his new nurse but that you're helping out in here for a while. We wanted to come and see his new office and thought we'd check out the yarn shop while we're here."

"Well, that's great," I said. "How's Simon doing?"

"Busy," Eva said. "He's really got his hands full at the moment, as you know. Between getting the new practice up and taking Lily around for her college tours. But he's great. He'll be back on the island on Monday."

"Terrific," I said, and hoped I didn't sound too excited by that thought.

Both women wandered toward the cubbyholes containing yarn, and I realized that while Eva was tall and slim and Gloria shorter and a bit pudgy, they both resembled Simon, especially around the eyes. Once again I wondered what it would be like to have a sister. I would see Grace and Chloe together and even Sydney and Marin, although they were cousins and not sisters, and a sense of emptiness would come over me. Glancing at Gloria and Eva, I once again felt that childhood ache that I had no family member close to my age. Somehow with just my parents and me forming a threesome, I never seemed to have that sense of *family* that so many other women had. And unfortunately, my daughter was also destined to be an only child.

"Oh, this is gorgeous," I heard Gloria say. "You have a wonderful selection of baby alpaca."

"Thank you," I said, even though I had nothing to do with the stock or the ordering.

"Lily would love this. I think I'll get it for her." She placed the skeins into the basket she was now carrying. "It's okay if I browse in back?" she asked.

"Certainly. Go right through the screened area out back to the carriage house. It's open, so just walk on in."

Both women headed out back, and I began opening a new shipment of yarn. I looked up to see Mallory walk in.

"Well, good morning, girlfriend. You're early for a yarn stop."

"Oh, I know. I found a pattern last night when I was going through a new issue of one of my knitting magazines. Those magazines' *sole* intent is to get you to buy more yarn."

I laughed. "No! You think?"

"Right. Silly me, huh?"

"So let me see what you've got there. Oh," I said, and dropped my voice to a whisper. "Simon's sisters are out back in the carriage house."

"Simon's *sisters?* What're they doing here?"

"One is an avid knitter and he told her I worked here and am going to be his new nurse, so when they drove over to see his office, they stopped in."

"Aha," she said.

"What's that supposed to mean?"

Mallory laughed. "Checking out their bro's future romantic interest, I'd say."

"Don't be silly," I said, and recalled Chloe saying the same thing to me a few nights before. "Let me see the pattern."

"It's this," she said, pointing to a loose, boxy sweater in a luscious shade of coral.

"Gorgeous." I began reading the instructions. "So you need some Ella Rae yarn, and I think we just happen to have that particular color."

"Great," she said, and followed me to the cubbyholes.

"Here ya go." I pointed to the yarn. "You'll need eight skeins."

"Thanks. So when are you seeing Simon again?"

"Shh! Geez, we don't need his sisters hearing you, and I have no clue. He said he'd call when he got back here on the island."

"And when's that?" she asked, filling her arms with the yarn.

"Monday, according to his sister. Here." I passed her one of the shop baskets.

"Well, as you can see, I couldn't resist your cashmere."

I turned around to see Gloria with her basket nearly full, and laughed. "Yeah, there's something about cashmere, isn't there?

Mallory, this is Gloria and Eva, Si . . . Dr. Mancini's sisters. This is my best friend, Mallory Wilson."

"Nice to meet you," they both said.

Mallory nodded toward Gloria's basket. "Same here. I see you're another addicted knitter."

Gloria laughed. "Ever meet a serious knitter who wasn't?"

"I hear ya," Mallory said.

"Oh, what have you got there?" Gloria walked over and touched the yarn in Mallory's basket.

I held up the photo in the magazine. "Mallory found this last night and of course had to rush over this morning to purchase the yarn."

"Oh, that's beautiful," Eva said. "I love it. Making it for yourself?"

"Yeah. I couldn't resist."

Gloria passed me her basket. "Well, before I do any more damage here, you can ring me up."

I went over to the desk and began totaling her purchase. "This is a gorgeous shade of blue in the baby alpaca. You said it was for your niece? Isn't it great that she also knits, and she learned at such a young age?"

Gloria nodded and passed me her credit card. "I know. I have two boys, and they're into sports, not knitting, so yeah, it's nice to have a knitting partner in the family. But what really impresses me is the fact that she's blind. You'd certainly never know it though if you could see some of her finished knitting projects. Lily is quite the inspiration."

Blind? Simon's daughter is blind? I fumbled with the credit card twice before I finally managed to swipe it correctly. "Oh, I know," was all I could say and was grateful when I heard Eva holler to her sister.

"Now, look at this sweater," she said, pointing to a finished piece hanging on the door of the armoire. "Christmas is coming, sis, so keep that in mind."

Gloria laughed. "Sure. Well, Josie, it was so nice to meet you after hearing all about you from Simon. I just love your shop, so I'll definitely be back, and who knows; maybe we'll get to see you again over one of the family's big Italian dinners."

"Thanks," I said, and watched them both walk out of the shop.

"*What* the hell? Did I hear her right? Simon's daughter is blind? Did you know this? Did he tell you?" Mallory's bewildered expression mirrored exactly what I felt.

I shook my head. "No. He never once mentioned that fact. I had no idea. But you know . . . I can't put my finger on it, but whenever he mentioned her . . . I just had a feeling that something wasn't quite right. But I sure had no idea that she was blind."

"Gosh, I wonder if she's been blind since birth. But can you imagine? She knits, and knits pretty damn good according to her aunt. That's amazing."

It *was* amazing. "Geez, I'm beginning to think my mother is so right. She's always said that everybody has a story. We never know what some people have endured. They go along, day to day, living their life, and we just never know what sadness they might have encountered."

Mallory nodded. "That's for sure. I wonder if it was Gloria who taught her how to knit."

I recalled what Simon had told me. "No, he said she learned from a teacher at school. I thought that was a bit odd because they don't offer sewing or knitting classes anymore, so I figured the teacher probably taught her after school. But now I'm wondering if maybe she attended a special school for the blind and that's where she learned."

"Oh, wait a minute." Mallory held a finger in the air. "There *is* a school for the blind over on the east coast. Near St. Augustine, actually. I just recently read an article about it in some magazine."

"Hmm. So that could be the reason why he chose to live there even though his ex-wife lives nearby. Maybe he wanted to be close to his daughter and now . . . she's graduated high school, so he doesn't have to stay in that area anymore."

"Exactly," Mallory said. "I'd bet anything that's why he's relocating to Cedar Key. You said his daughter will be off to college next year."

I nodded. "Right," I said, and realized that much like Ben, I truly didn't know Dr. Simon Mancini at all.

❧ 18 ❧

Sunday evening Orli was helping me wind some skeins of yarn when the phone rang. She draped the yarn across my knee and ran to answer.

"Yes, she is. Could you hold, please?" I heard her say before she walked toward me and passed me the phone.

I raised my eyebrows, asking a silent *Who is it,* but she just smiled.

I said hello and heard Simon say, "I hope I'm not interrupting anything."

"No. Not at all. My daughter is just helping me wind some yarn."

"Well, I wanted to let you know I'm coming to Cedar Key in the morning. So I was wondering if maybe you'd like to get a pizza at the Blue Desert tomorrow evening."

"Sure. That sounds great. What time?"

"Can you meet me there at six?"

"Perfect."

"Great. Oh, my sisters told me they dropped by the yarn shop and met you the other day. They seemed to like you a lot, and I hear Gloria went overboard purchasing yarn as usual."

I laughed. "Yeah, she did. They were both very nice, and I enjoyed meeting them. Did they get to see your office?"

"They did. I told the contractor they'd be stopping by. Okay, so I'll see you tomorrow evening. I'm looking forward to it."

"Same here," I said before hanging up.

I looked up to see Orli staring at me. "Well?" she questioned, with a grin on her face. "Mom, don't keep me in suspense. Who was that?"

Sometimes I found it difficult to comprehend that this young lady joking with me was my grown-up daughter. Where had that little girl with braids and skinned knees gone to?

"It was Dr. Mancini. His sisters stopped by the yarn shop the other day before going to see his office."

"Hmm," was what my daughter said.

I began winding more yarn. "What does that mean?"

"They drove all the way over here to meet you?"

"Of course not. They were coming to see his office and . . . well, one of them, Gloria, is a knitter so she wanted to purchase some yarn."

"So that was why he just called you?"

"Not exactly. He's coming back to the island tomorrow. So he called to see if I'd like to meet him for a pizza tomorrow evening. And I said yes."

"Well, good for you. I've been telling you for a while that you need to find somebody in your life, so yeah, *good* for you."

How is it that sometimes one's own child can sound more like the parent?

I laughed. "Well, thank you, Orli. I'm glad you approve."

"Oh, I do, but next time you should invite him here for dinner. I'd like to meet him. Uh-oh."

My head shot up. "What?"

"We're due at Nana's for dinner tomorrow evening. This will be another one you have to cancel."

Shit. She was right.

"Yeah, I'd forgotten. Well, not to worry. I'll handle Nana."

* * *

I dreaded dealing with my mother, but the next morning I knew I had to bite the bullet and give her a call about skipping out on another dinner.

"Josie, I was just going to call you. What's up?"

"Well, I wanted to apologize, but . . . well . . . I'm not going to be able to make dinner this evening. But Orli will be there," I hastened to add.

There was a slight pause before she said, "Again? What's going on this time?"

Same thing, I thought, *dinner with Doctor McDreamy,* but said, "Well . . . Dr. Mancini called last night and wanted to discuss some office stuff with me, so he asked if I could meet him for pizza at six."

Why on earth did I feel that I had to lie to my mother about this? I was a thirty-five-year-old *woman,* for heaven's sake. Not some silly teenager. But somehow she always managed to make me feel like one.

"Oh, I see," she said, and I heard that frosty tone.

"I'm really sorry, but this new job is important to me and it's part of my job to help him get settled in."

"So nothing seems to have changed over the years. Nurses are still the doctor's handmaidens."

"Mom, for God's sake. It isn't like that at all. I said I'm sorry, and I promise I'll make the next dinner."

I heard my mother give a nasty chuckle. "Hmm, so you say now."

I took a sip of coffee and wished it were wine. "So why were you going to call me?" I asked.

"Oh . . . that. It's about CC."

Here we go again, I thought. I wondered if CC knew that she was my mother's new obsession. Poor CC.

"Well, I spoke to her on the phone last night. She got back from Tuscany on Friday."

"So she did go?"

"Yes, of course she went. With that boy toy. You know CC. Once she gets a thought in her head, there's no turning back for her."

Strange that my mother couldn't see that she had the same trait.

"So did she have a good time, or did her companion abscond with all of her money as you predicted?"

"Not funny, Josie. And yes, of course she *says* she had a good time. But who really knows."

I couldn't suppress a chuckle. "Mom, why the heck would she lie to you?"

"Well, I'm sure she'd never admit that I was right."

"So she went. She says she had a good time, so now what?"

"Well, she's coming for Christmas like she always does, but this time she's bringing him. And I guess she must think I'm not real fond of this arrangement."

Gee, I wonder where she ever got that idea.

"So instead of staying here," my mother continued, "they're booking a room at the Island Hotel. I told her that was downright silly with two perfectly good guest rooms here, but she won't listen."

I rolled my eyes and smiled. *Two* guest rooms? Two grown adults who were obviously sleeping together and she expected to separate them? No wonder they were booking their own accommodations.

"Well, Mom, just be happy she's still coming. You know damn well you'd be pretty upset if she broke the tradition of coming for Christmas."

"Yes, yes, I know. Oh, and guess what? It's not definite yet, but Mags thinks she might fly down this year for Christmas also."

Good old Maggie. She was such an eccentric, but I adored her. She was the aging hippie in their group and lived up to her title with honor. It was impossible to be in Maggie's company and not just plain feel good.

"Oh, that's great! So, see, your Christmas will be just fine. Maggie will really perk things up, and hey, look on the bright side—at least one of your guest rooms will get put to use."

"Yes, I suppose," I heard my mother say grudgingly.

A few hours later my mother called back. "Listen, Josie," she said. "I'm not feeling all that great, and I think I'll have to cancel dinner with Orli this evening. I'm really sorry, but I think she'll understand."

"Of course she will, but what's going on? You're never sick."

"And I'm not *sick* now. Just a little tummy twinge. I'll be right as rain by tomorrow."

"Mom, this *tummy twinge* seems to be hanging on. Don't you think you should get in to see the doctor?"

"Don't be silly. I'm sure it's nothing."

It was times like this that I became more exasperated than usual with my mother. "I know you like controlling all situations, but Mom . . . when it comes to your health and not feeling well, you simply have *no* control over it. At least go get checked out."

"Right. If it doesn't go away soon, I will. Have Orli call me later and tell her I'm sorry."

I hung up the phone and shook my head. If I lived to be a hundred, I'd never understand why my mother was such a control freak.

Pizza at the Blue Desert called for jeans and a lightweight pullover sweater. I chose the cotton one that I'd finished a few months ago—the yarn was from Kollage and the fiber was 100 percent recycled from blue jeans. I had made it in a shade of terra cotta, and it did go perfectly with denim.

When Orli found out that dinner at my mother's had been canceled, she asked if she could join Laura at the Pickled Pelican for a burger; she had just left. I grabbed my car keys and headed out the door to meet Simon.

On the drive over I'd made up my mind not to mention what I'd learned about his daughter. It was none of my business, and I felt that if he wanted me to know, he'd tell me.

I drove slowly past the restaurant on SR 24, saw that he was already seated at a table outside, and gave a short toot of my horn as I waved my arm out the window. I had to drive farther down the road and found a spot to park across the street.

As I approached the restaurant, Simon stood up with a huge smile on his face. Damn, but he looked good. I'm not sure why it is, but I get a bit fluttery inside when I see a good-looking guy wearing an open collar, long-sleeved white shirt, untucked, with jeans. It suddenly occurred to me that Simon reminded me of an actor that

I'd seen in some British series about a Scottish laird. And just like that actor, Simon Mancini exuded a fair amount of sex appeal.

"Josie," he said, reaching out his hand. "Good to see you again. It's so nice out this evening, I thought we'd sit outside."

I felt my hand in his and had to admit that his touch had a certain electricity to it. No wonder he had a gift for healing people. "Great idea," I said, letting go of his hand and sitting down across from him. "I do think autumn is definitely in the air."

"You probably enjoy wearing all of your knitted items this time of year. That's a nice sweater. Did you make it?"

"I did. Thanks," I said just as the waitress came out to take our drink order. "I'll have a glass of cabernet. I prefer the red wines in the cooler weather."

"Same here," Simon told her.

"So how's the remodeling going?" I asked.

"Right on schedule. Actually, I think my apartment will be ready right after Thanksgiving and I'll be able to move in."

"Oh, I'm sure you'll enjoy that."

"I will. I'm getting a bit tired of living here and there out of a suitcase. It'll be nice not to have to leave the island as frequently and to have my own place."

"And the office is also coming along okay?"

Simon laughed as the wine was placed in front of us. "Yeah, with the help of my sister. Is it okay if we wait a bit before ordering the pizza?" he asked me.

I nodded. "Sure. Fine."

"I'll be back," the waitress said.

"Your sister is helping on the renovation?"

"Cheers," he said, touching my wineglass. "Well, she's helping with the decorating. I'm hopeless when it comes to things like that. So Gloria has given me her input on colors, furniture, that sort of thing. She's pretty good at it, so I always welcome her suggestions."

I smiled. "Yeah, always good to get a second opinion."

He caught my meaning and chuckled. "Right. Even with a doctor. So as I'd mentioned, both of my sisters really enjoyed meeting you, and I know Gloria loved the yarn shop. She came back to my mom's house with a bag full. She even got some for Lily, which made her happy. It always amazes me how much yarn can delight a woman."

I laughed. "Well, if she's a knitter, yes."

"It's hard to believe that it'll be November already next week. Before we know it, I'll be opening my practice here. Oh, by the way, my daughter is going to move in with me for a few months. We want to spend some quality time together before she heads off to college next summer."

"How nice for both of you," I said. "Has she made a choice on a college yet?"

"Not yet, but I think she'll choose somewhere in the southeast so she won't be too far away to visit me and the family."

"That's really nice. You seem to have a very close relationship with her."

I noticed that a sad expression briefly crossed his face before he said, "Yeah, we're very close. Lily is everything to me. She's never been all that close to her mother. When she was a kid, I often thought that she looked to my sisters as more of a mother figure than her own mother."

I couldn't think of anything to say.

Simon took another sip of wine and then said, "We divorced when Lily was around eight, but even before the divorce there was never a special bond between them. Soon after Lily was born, I discovered that Stephanie just wasn't one of those mothers who considered motherhood the focus of her life." He tapped the table with his palm. "So . . . enough about me. Let's get that pizza ordered."

Driving home later, I realized that I very much enjoyed being in the company of Dr. Simon Mancini. Once again an entire evening seemed to have flown by, allowing us to learn a little more about each other. But I also realized that although he had discussed his daughter, he had never once made mention of the fact that she was blind.

19

I was just sliding pumpkin bread into the oven when the phone rang.

I answered to hear Mallory say, "Can you believe it's the morning before Thanksgiving already? Are you busy?"

I reached for my coffee mug. "I know. This year has really flown by. And no, I just got a pumpkin bread into the oven for the knitting class this evening."

"That class is going so well, isn't it? The guys seem to really enjoy it."

"They do, and I enjoy it as well. So what's up with you today?"

"I have to make a run to Publix in Gainesville. Do you need anything?"

"No, I don't think so."

"I just wanted to touch base. As you know, we're having dinner tomorrow at Troy's parents' house, but we'll be at your mom's for dessert later in the day."

"Great. When's your mom getting here?"

"She said she'll be at your mother's house by later this afternoon. I just hung up with her. Okay. I have to run. See you tomorrow."

I hung up and put a fingertip to the mini-cakes cooling on the wire rack, a smile crossing my face. Since Orli was a toddler we'd had a Thanksgiving morning tradition of having these for breakfast before a big dinner at my parents' house. They were my own recipe and similar to pumpkin muffins, but instead of baking them in muffin tins I always used a Bundt pan that produced six individual huge muffins in a distinctive ring shape. Orli loved them, and by the time she was four, she called them clunkerdunkers and the name had stuck.

I had just placed them into my Tupperware holder and secured the lid when the phone rang again.

"Are you busy cooking for tomorrow?" I heard Simon ask, and I smiled.

It had been four weeks since our pizza together, and although he'd called a few times for office-related questions, we hadn't seen each other again.

"I'm baking but was just going to sit down to enjoy my second cup of coffee. How've you been?"

"Busy. I'll really be glad to get over there and get settled in. That's why I'm calling. All the furniture for both the office and my apartment is being delivered next week. So I'll be tied up getting everything arranged and in order. Gloria's going to come over and help me get my apartment together, and I should be an official resident of Cedar Key by the second week in December."

"That's terrific," I told him. "Things are moving along fast now."

"Right and I . . . was wondering . . . well, I'd like to give you the tour of the office first. You know . . . as the nurse there, maybe you'll have something to add that's slipped my mind."

"That would be great. Sure." No, it wasn't a bona fide date, but hey, I wasn't turning down a chance to be with Simon again.

"Wonderful. After I give you the tour of the office, I'd like to show you my apartment upstairs, so I'm inviting you to dinner."

Oh, this was sounding a bit more like a date. "Yeah, that would be great, but you don't have to cook. I can just see your apartment without dinner."

Simon laughed. "Yes, I know that but as my colleague, I'd enjoy cooking dinner for you."

Colleague? Maybe not a date after all. "That would be nice. Thanks," I said, wanting to kick myself for feeling a bit disappointed.

"Would Tuesday evening the ninth work for you? At seven?"

I glanced at the calendar hanging on the wall. "Yes, fine. I look forward to it."

"Wonderful," I heard him say again with a definite tone of excitement. "What are your plans for tomorrow?"

"Dinner at my parents' house, and you?"

"Yes, the same. We'll have quite a gang over there. Well, happy Thanksgiving, Josie. I look forward to seeing you in a couple weeks."

I hung up the phone with mixed feelings. I was definitely attracted to this guy. I think he liked me, too, but I wasn't sure he liked me as a romantic interest. Using the word *colleague,* he probably didn't. He was just being nice, inviting me to dinner. And anyway, wouldn't that be a bit sticky, working so closely with somebody that you were actually dating? And then I recalled all of the doctor/nurse stories I'd heard at the hospital during my training. In public they had remained quite professional, so I was usually surprised to hear about this or that doctor and nurse being a couple. So, yes, of course it was possible to have a romantic relationship and to maintain the professionalism at work. *But whoa, Josie,* I thought. *This is simply a dinner at his apartment. Don't go assuming things that may never happen.*

I opened the shop at ten and didn't think we'd be too busy the day before Thanksgiving. Most women were more focused on cooking and baking rather than knitting the day before a holiday.

About an hour later Chloe walked in just as I was unpacking some scrumptious cashmere yarn.

"Uh-oh," she said, walking over to finger it. "I see another dent in my checking account."

I looked up and laughed. "I know the feeling, but I've appreciated the discount since I've been working here. I bet you're happy to be back knitting full time with that cast gone."

"I am," she said, holding her arm out. "I was lucky that it healed so well. We'll probably be slow today, and I think we can close by two."

"Yeah, I was thinking the same thing. What're your plans for to-morrow?"

"Dinner at Aunt Maude's with Grace, Lucas, and Solange. Are you going to your parents?"

I nodded. "Yeah, and Jane is driving over today to spend a few days at their house. Mallory and her family will be over later in the day for dessert."

"And what's our new doc in town doing? Has he moved in yet?"

"He's moving in next week when all of his furniture is delivered. He did call me this morning and said he'll be spending the holiday at his parents' house in Gainesville."

"Do you have a class tonight?"

"Yeah, I asked the guys if they wanted one. Saxton said that Berkley's doing the cooking and they invited Doyle, but he's free this evening and the others agreed. So they said it was up to me and I have no prep to do tonight. You know my mother—won't let me do a thing. I baked some pumpkin bread this morning for the guys. What about Gabe? What's he doing tomorrow? He's alone here on the island."

"Yeah, I know," was all she said.

Gabe had taken Chloe to have her cast removed and out for lunch. According to her, they seemed to enjoy each other's company, but that was four weeks ago and since then he hadn't made any overtures toward getting together again.

She went to pour herself a cup of coffee and then plunked down on the sofa. "I'm not sure he likes me. Christ, I sound like a silly teenager, don't I?"

I filled my mug and joined her. "No, not at all. You said you both seemed to have a great time spending the day together."

"We did. Well, at least I *thought* we did."

"Maybe he's waiting for you to make the next move."

"Me?"

"Yeah, you," I said, then laughed. "You're right—you're not teenagers, so all those rules like never call the boy, wait till he asks you out, they don't apply anymore."

A smile crossed her face. "Says who?"

"Chloe, those days are gone. Women are more assertive and independent now."

"So you're suggesting that I ask him on a *date?*"

"Well, not necessarily a date, but you could invite him for Thanksgiving dinner. I seriously doubt that Maude would mind one more at the table."

She took another sip of coffee as a thoughtful expression crossed her face. "Hmm, maybe you're right. Maybe he's waiting to see if I'm interested or if I was just being nice by accepting his ride to Gainesville. Maybe I should stop by the class this evening and ask him to dinner tomorrow."

I reached over and patted her hand. "Now you're talkin'. If he's truly not interested, he'll make up some excuse for tomorrow and at least you'll know how he feels."

She nodded emphatically. "Right. I'd rather know upfront and not be blindsided like I was with Parker. God, this dating scene, it's a slippery slope, isn't it? You don't want to appear too interested, but then if you don't show enough interest, that's not good either. I thought these days were behind me."

I laughed. "Afraid not. Like I said, there's no expiration date on attraction or romance."

"Thanks for your advice, Josie."

"Anytime," I said.

Now if only I could figure out my exact relationship with Dr. Simon Mancini, my advice might be worth something.

20

My dad was the one who answered the intercom when Orli and I pulled up to their gate, and he was the one who opened the front door to greet us.

"Happy Thanksgiving," he said with a huge smile on his face before scooping both of us into a hug.

"Same to you, Dad. Where's Mom?"

"Oh, she and Jane are sitting outside on the patio having a cup of tea. Come on in."

Sitting on the patio? Having tea? On Thanksgiving morning? Why wasn't she in her usual mode of rushing around the kitchen, wearing an apron, finishing up all of her last-minute details?

But as Orli and I headed to the back of the house I did inhale the wonderful aroma of the turkey cooking away in the oven.

"Happy Thanksgiving," I said, walking over to place a kiss on my mother's cheek and then Jane's.

"Happy Turkey Day, Nana," Orli said.

"And to both of you," my mother said.

She was curled up on the lounge, her legs tucked under her with a mug between both hands. I took a really good look at her and realized that she looked a bit pale. When did those shadows suddenly appear beneath her eyes?

"Are you okay?" I asked.

"Of course, why?"

"Well, because you're normally in the kitchen bustling around on Thanksgiving morning—not reclined out here like a diva."

Jane laughed. "Your mother had Delilah help her yesterday with all the baking, stuffing the turkey, peeling the veggies, so all of the work is done. By the time I got here at three, they'd already finished."

Okay. Something definitely was not right. Never in all the years that I'd lived in this house had my mother allowed Delilah to help her do the prep for a holiday meal. My mother prided herself on doing it all. Alone.

"How's your stomach feeling?" I asked.

"Fine. Fine."

"Mom, don't tell me fine. Something not's right."

"Are you not feeling well, Nana?" I saw the concern on Orli's face.

My mother waved a hand in the air. "Don't be silly. Just a little tired. I've been quite busy working to finish up my manuscript before the holidays. You know how hectic it gets this time of year. And now it's completed and in the hands of my editor. So that's it for me till after the first of the year."

I still wasn't convinced, but I dropped the subject.

"I just love coming here for Thanksgiving," Jane said, as if she also was trying to skirt the issue. "I spoke to Mallory this morning, and they'll be over around four. Gosh, I can't believe how Carter is growing. Ten years old already, and look at you, Orli. About to turn sixteen."

Orli shot her a smile and nodded. "I know. I'm going to be taking driving lessons in January."

"Here we go, girls." My father came outside holding a tray of glasses, which he placed on the table. "Mimosas for everyone. Well, a virgin one for Orli," he said, causing her to giggle.

We held the champagne flutes up as my mother said, "Happy Thanksgiving to the four people who I love most in life."

"And we love you back," all of us said, which was our traditional response each year.

I took a sip. "Is there anything left that I can do?" I glanced inside the French doors and saw that the dining room table had already been elaborately set.

"I don't think so," Jane replied. "I got the table set this morning."

Jane had set the table? Another odd occurrence. Setting the table for a holiday dinner was something else my mother had claimed as her domain many years ago.

"No, no. Everything is all ready. We'll be eating at noon. So did that new doctor open his practice yet? I haven't been downtown in a couple weeks, so I've been out of the loop."

I took another sip of my champagne and orange juice. "Not till after the first of the year. He hasn't told me a definite date yet that he'll be opening the office, but he's moving into his apartment next week."

"Imagine," Jane said. "We're going to have a doctor on the island again after all these years. There hasn't been a doctor here since the 1950s."

"Yeah, maybe if there had been one in 1966, Wendy would still be alive." My mother took a deep gulp of her drink.

My head shot up and I saw the look that passed between my mother and Jane. Wendy was my mother's younger sister, who had passed away at the age of eight from pneumonia. Despite my repeated questions as a child, my mother always refused to talk very much about my aunt Wendy, so I was surprised that she should mention her now.

"I heard that he's hired Brandy as your receptionist," Jane said, completely ignoring my mother's statement. "I bet she's thrilled to have that job."

I felt as if something was going on that I wasn't privy to. My mom and Jane were more like sisters than girlfriends. Although they were both close to the other three women in their Sisters group, there had always been a unique and extraspecial closeness between these two. I understood this because Mallory and I shared the same kind of bond. Many times we could just read each other's mind and know what the other was thinking or was going to say. It was both comforting and eerie. And for the first time that I could remember I felt a twinge of jealousy that my mother shared this kind of closeness with Jane and not with me.

"Yes, Brandy's pretty excited," I said. "I think she'll be good for the office." I felt a surge of sulkiness come over me and remained silent while my parents and Jane continued to talk about the weather, news on the island, and other mundane subjects.

"Joe," I heard my mother say, "it's time for the turkey to come out of the oven. It's always best to let it sit for a while before you carve it. Orli, did you select the Christmas CDs to play after dinner?"

Orli jumped up and headed inside. "I'll do it now."

The uneasy feeling that I'd had since I arrived slowly began to dissipate. My mother's instructions to my father on the turkey removal and to Orli were the same things I'd been hearing since I was a little girl—the selection of music used to be my job as a child. It was my mom's tradition that after Thanksgiving dinner Christmas songs would be played for the first time that season. Everything seemed to be back in sync, making me think that perhaps I'd been overreacting about my mother.

By the time Mallory arrived with Troy and Carter, I was feeling more relaxed. Of course three glasses of wine might have also accounted for that.

"Hey," she said, pulling me into a bear hug with one arm while trying to juggle a covered pie plate with the other. "Happy Thanksgiving."

"Same to you, but how come you get to bring some dessert and I'm not allowed to?"

Mallory laughed as we headed to the dining room. "Your mother didn't *allow* me—I just baked a pecan pie and here it is."

"I stand up to her all the time. Never seems to do me much good. Hey, Carter, how're you doing?" I ruffled the top of his head and gave him a hug before hugging Troy. "You look great, as usual," I told him.

"Must be all of Mallory's devoted attention," he said with a smile.

After all the holiday greetings and hugs were exchanged, Mallory and I headed into the kitchen to begin preparing the coffeemaker, uncover pies, and place items on two trays. That was one chore that my mother had always allowed Mallory and me to do from the time we were around twelve.

"Hey," I whispered to her. "After dessert, take a walk with me down near the water."

"Sure. What's up?"

"Just wanna discuss something with you."

She nodded, and we each carried a tray into the dining room.

About an hour after dessert the cleanup began—a chore in which everybody took part. By the time the dishwasher was loaded, food covered and put away, my father and Troy were ready to chill out in front of the TV with one of the many football games being televised. My mother, Jane, and Orli headed to the patio with coffee.

I caught Mallory's glance and nodded.

"Josie and I are going to walk down by the water," she said.

My mother smiled. "Ah, Christmas secrets beginning already?"

"Something like that," I said as we quickly exited the patio, walked around the side of the house, and headed to the far end of the yard.

The sun was just about ready to call it quits for another day. The sky was streaked with pinks and blues, and I knew that no matter how many sunsets I witnessed, I'd never tire of them. We both remained silent for a few minutes until we reached the bench near the fence and sat down.

"So what's up?" she asked.

I shook my head. "I'm not sure. Has your mother mentioned anything about my mother?"

"Like what?"

"Like my mother not feeling well?"

Mallory shifted on the bench to face me. "No. Not at all. Is something wrong?"

I shrugged. "I don't know. Things just don't seem right. She's been having what she calls *tummy twinges* for a couple months now." I went on to tell her about Delilah assisting Mom yesterday with the baking and preparation.

"Hmm, that *is* unusual. The day before a holiday that kitchen is normally off limits to everybody except your mother."

"Exactly." And then I told her the strange thing she'd said about my aunt.

"Yeah, she never mentions her. Actually, she's gone out of her way over the years to avoid talking about her sister. Geez, Josie, I don't know what to think."

"Neither do I."

We were both silent for a few moments, and then she patted my arm. "Well, don't worry about it. It might be nothing at all, but I'll see if I can get my mom to talk. She's going to be here till Saturday. If there *is* anything going on, we both know that my mother already knows about it."

I nodded and put my arm around her shoulder for a hug. "Thanks, Mallory. I knew I could depend on you."

❧ 21 ❧

During the week following Thanksgiving I made a point of stopping by my parents' house more often than usual. If my mother was suspicious, she didn't say anything. Mallory had called me after the holiday weekend, and although she had questioned her mother, there was nothing to report. Jane had assured her daughter that Shelby was fine, just tired. And I had to admit that my mother did look a bit better than she had on Thanksgiving.

I awoke on Tuesday morning with a sense of anticipation. I was having dinner at Simon's apartment that evening. I turned over and hugged the pillow to me while I let my mind wander. Thinking about Simon made me realize that in many ways he reminded me of Grant—good looks, an abundance of sex appeal, and easy to be with. Not for the first time I wondered if maybe I'd been wrong not to give Grant a chance years ago. Although he had never come right out and asked me to marry him, there had been an instance when Orli was about three years old and he was visiting us. He hadn't said it in so many words but had definitely hinted that perhaps I'd changed my mind about our relationship. I was quick to brush him off because I was pretty sure he definitely had marriage on his mind. I tried to analyze what it was, exactly, about the thought of marriage that I was so against, and once again couldn't come up with a solid reason. *Ah, well, too late for hindsight now,* I thought as I headed to the shower.

Later that evening I was putting the finishing touches to my makeup when Orli walked into my room and plunked down in the middle of my bed.

"Hey, what's up?" I asked, reaching for my silver hoop earrings.

"I was just wondering . . . did you love Dad?"

I spun around to face her. "What brought this up?"

She pulled her legs up to her chest, grasping them with her arms. "I was just wondering."

I went to sit beside her and patted her knee. "Yes. I did love him. Very much. I *still* love him, Orli. How could I not? He gave me the greatest gift ever. You."

This brought a smile from her. "How did you know? How did you know that you loved him?"

My inner mom radar went off. This really wasn't about Grant and me. It was about our daughter.

"It's difficult to explain exactly how one knows, and of course everybody is different. Why? Somebody special in your life?"

I saw a faint crimson tinge her cheeks, and she nodded. "Yeah. Jared Stevens."

I racked my brain, trying to remember which fellow he was in her class. "Oh, the one who works at the Market part-time?"

She nodded.

"Nice-looking guy. You have good taste," I said, causing her smile to grow wider. "So what's the problem?"

"I'm not sure he likes me. How'd you know that Dad was interested in you?"

"Geez, that was so long ago, Orli," I said, forcing myself to think back to my freshman year of college. Those exciting, exhilarating, sometimes over-the-top days. "Well, he flirted with me, for one thing. I was at a local coffee shop with some of my friends, and he was sitting at a table across from us with a group of guys. I could feel him staring over at me, but I thought it was my imagination. He was drop-dead gorgeous."

Orli laughed. "He still is."

She had a point. "I remember it was pouring out—I mean raining cats and dogs—and when I gathered up my books to leave, between trying to balance my textbooks and open my umbrella, my books landed everywhere, and before I knew it—your dad was there, ready to help me. When I saw him up close and looked into his eyes . . . I don't know . . . I just knew there was something extraspecial going on."

"Oh, I remember the story now. Didn't he get your phone number from your girlfriend and call you for a date?"

I nodded. "Yup. He did, and the rest is history."

Orli laughed again. "Well, that's just it. I *think* Jared is interested, and Laura's boyfriend, Mark, is good friends with him and said that he is. But he hasn't even called me yet."

I pulled her into a hug. "Stop stressing. Give it some time," I told my daughter. "Sometimes the wheels of romance turn very slowly."

I walked up the back steps to Simon's apartment while trying to balance a wrapped gift and a bottle of wine.

"Hey," he said, opening the door wide and gesturing with his arm. "Come on in, and welcome to my new place."

I stepped into the kitchen and smiled. "This is gorgeous," I told him, and it was. Not in an overstated way, but the stainless steel appliances, granite counters, painted yellow walls and oak table and chairs would lure any chef. From the exquisite aroma filling the kitchen, it already had. "And something smells yummy."

"My signature spaghetti sauce is simmering with meatballs and sausage. But I can't lie; most of it is my mom's recipe."

"I think I'm in for a treat. Here," I said, passing him the bottle of wine and gift. "Just a little something as a housewarming gift."

"Thanks, Josie. That's really nice of you." He read the wine label. "Perfect. The Chianti will go great with the meal. Should I open this now?"

"Definitely," I said as I watched him remove the paper and bow from the package.

"Oh, Josie, this is beautiful." He held the framed and matted print out in front of him. "What a gorgeous shot of the Gulf with the pelicans. Was this taken near the Seabreeze?"

I nodded. "Yes. Taken by a local photographer. I found it at the Arts Center."

"Thank you so much. I have the perfect spot for it." He then brought the print closer and read, *Always flow like the water,* which was written at the bottom. "A good saying for everybody to keep in mind. Thank you again. Come on, I'll show you the rest of the place."

The living room was cozy and comfortable, done in tones of green and blue.

"I love your sofa and armchairs," I told him. Wide stripes of celery green and a deeper green covered the fabric. I glanced around and saw a large flat-screen television, CD player, and pine tables, all of which coordinated with the hunter green walls. "Very nice."

"I have to give all the credit to Gloria. Bedrooms and baths are this way."

I followed him down a short hallway. Both bedrooms and their attached bathrooms were also tastefully decorated, but it was easy to see which one would be Lily's space. Lavender and pale pink dominated the room. A twin maple sleigh bed was filled with stuffed animals and a gorgeous rolltop oak desk took up half a wall, in addition to an armoire and a smaller flat-screen TV perched on a maple table.

"Your daughter is going to love this," I said, and then felt a catch in my throat. But she wouldn't be able to *see* any of it.

"I hope so. Let's crack open that bottle of wine."

I settled myself on the stool at the counter that acted as a divider between the kitchen and the living room and noticed that the table had been set with brightly colored yellow and blue placemats, nice dishes, and glassware. Simon Mancini seemed to have a bit of experience in being a dinner host.

He passed me a wineglass, and this time I made the toast first. "Here's to your new home. I hope you'll have years of happiness here."

"Thanks, Josie. Dinner will be ready in about a half hour. Let's go downstairs so I can show you the office."

I followed him down the stairs, around the side of the house, and to the porch. He slipped a key into the lock, and we stepped inside to a waiting room that was both professional and comfortable. A chocolate brown leather sofa, love seat, and three matching armchairs lined the wall, which was painted a pale blue with a border print of small blue and yellow flowers. In an alcove to my right were a large oak desk, leather office chair, and two cherrywood file cabinets. Behind the desk was a printer and fax machine.

"Oh, Simon, this is a beautiful office. It looks wonderful."

"You think it's okay?" he asked.

"Okay? God, patients are going to love coming here, and Brandy will think she's in heaven working at that desk."

He laughed. "Good. I guess Gloria got it right again. And over here is your office," he said, leading me down the long hallway.

"My office?" I'd had no idea that I'd actually have an office.

He opened the door to reveal a medium-size room with another oak desk, two armchairs in a buttery yellow leather and a file cabinet, all of it overlooking the bay window that looked out to Second Street.

"Sure. You have to have an office too. You can bring patients in here to talk with them, go over their meds, that sort of thing."

I felt excitement bubble up. "God, I love it, Simon. I've never had an office before. I really love it."

"Good. I'm glad." I saw a huge smile cross his face. "Here's my office down here."

I followed him to the end of the hallway to a larger version of my office, and then he showed me the three exam rooms along the inner part of the hallway.

We walked back out to the reception area, and he said, "So. What do you think? Will you be happy working here?"

"Happy? That's putting it mildly," I said, then laughed. "Gosh, yes. This is so perfect. All of it. I'm going to love working here." And I knew that I would.

We went back upstairs, and Simon refilled our wineglasses before draining the pasta that had been on a slow boil and sliding garlic bread into the oven.

"Can I do something?" I asked.

He shook his head. "Nope, I'm all set."

I watched him scoop sauce, meatballs, and sausage over the spaghetti. This man looked quite at home in his kitchen. I recalled the discussion that I'd had at the yarn shop about stereotypes and smiled. Simon Mancini oozed masculinity—even cooking. No doubt about it.

"Oh, Josie, could you get the salad plates out of the fridge, please?"

I jumped up and found the glass plates covered with plastic wrap, which I removed before putting them on the table.

"I think we're all set," he said.

Following his delicious dinner, we both opted for wine rather than coffee, and Simon opened a bottle of cabernet before we settled on the sofa and resumed our conversation.

"So Lily is arriving here on Friday. I'll go to Gainesville and pick her up," he told me.

"That's great. I have no doubt that she'll love this place."

"I hope so," he said, and then got quiet for a few moments. "There's something that I want you to know, Josie." He paused again. "My daughter is blind."

"Oh," was all I said. I felt like a phony, having already known this fact. "I'm sorry."

He smiled. "Oh, don't be. Lily reminds me a bit of you. She's extremely independent, despite her lack of sight. She has a guide dog, Leo, and they're quite the team. There's very little that Lily isn't able to do."

I took a sip of wine. "That's wonderful. She sounds like quite a young woman. You must be so proud of her."

He nodded, but I noticed sadness in his eyes. "Lily wasn't born blind. She lost her sight at age eight."

"Was it an illness?" I wasn't sure which was better—to be born without sight or to lose it after knowing what it was like to see.

Simon shook his head. "No, it was an accident. A car accident. I was driving her to her ballet lesson, and we were hit by a reckless teen driver who thought it was more important to text than keep his eyes on the road."

"God, I'm so sorry," I said, and instinctively reached over to touch his hand.

I felt him grasp mine and gave his hand a squeeze before he took a gulp of wine and nodded. "Yeah, it was a pretty rough time for a while for all of us."

I wondered if, even though Simon wasn't at fault, he felt a certain amount of guilt.

"But . . . we got through it," he said, placing his empty wineglass on the coffee table. "And as I said, Lily does exceptionally well. After she recuperated from the accident and we realized her vision was permanently gone, we got her enrolled at the Florida School for the Deaf and Blind in St. Augustine. I credit them with making Lily as independent as she is."

"That's wonderful. And to think she's such an accomplished knitter. She really does sound like one very special young woman."

A smile covered Simon's face. "She is, and I think you'll enjoy meeting her."

"I look forward to it," I said, and glanced at my watch. I brought it closer to my face. Surely it was wrong. Eleven-fifteen?

"Oh, my God. I can't believe it's so late!" I exclaimed, and heard Simon laugh as he glanced at his own watch.

"We do have a way of getting carried away talking, don't we?"

I took the last sip of my wine and nodded. "Yeah, I really have to get going."

"I'll walk you home," he said, standing up.

"No, it's just down . . ."

But he cut me off. "I know it's just down the street and I'm walking you there."

When we got to my front door, I smiled. "Thank you so much, Simon, for such a lovely evening. Gosh, I had a great time and the food was delicious."

"I enjoyed it just as much," he said, and then moved a bit closer, grazing my lips with his. "I'll see you soon, I hope."

✑ 22 ✑

The following Wednesday morning I'd had the shop open about an hour when I heard the chimes tinkle and looked up to see Simon accompanied by a young woman and a huge golden retriever. I knew this was his daughter, and quite simply, she was stunning. Tall, slim, with thick, dark hair that fell to her shoulders in waves. Her hair color and olive skin made it obvious that she'd gotten most of her genes from Simon's Italian side of the family. She walked into the shop with an air of confidence, the leash clasped in her hand, the dog leading the way, and designer sunglasses covering her eyes. Had I not known, I never would have guessed that this striking young woman was blind.

"Good morning," I said.

The sound of my voice seemed to direct both Lily and the dog toward me.

"Josie, I'd like you to meet my daughter, Lily, and this is Leo."

Lily extended her hand, which I grasped in both of mine.

"It's so nice to meet you," I told her.

"Same here," she said. "My dad's told me a lot about you, and I couldn't wait to visit your shop."

I let out a chuckle. "Oh, I'm afraid I'm only working here part time till I start working for your dad. Is it okay to pat the dog?"

"Oh, yes, it's fine. Leo's very friendly."

"He's gorgeous," I said, running my hand along his thick coat. "Have you ever thought about getting his fur spun into fiber for knitting? That fur would make a nice scarf."

Lily laughed. "I have heard about that, and I should do it."

"The original owner of this shop, Sydney Webster, started her business by doing just that. She spun dog and cat fur into yarn. People seem to like the idea of always having a keepsake from their beloved pets. Would you like to look around the shop?" I asked, and then felt stupid. It was obvious that she couldn't *look* around the shop.

But she surprised me by saying, "Yes, I'd love to. If you could just verbally cue me as to where the yarn is located, I think Leo and I can manage."

I proceeded to explain that there were four display tables in the center of the room and the rest of the yarn was in cubbyholes along the two walls.

"Thanks," she said, and moved toward the first table with Leo beside her.

I watched her hand reach out and begin stroking a skein of Elsbeth Lavold ViSilk.

"Oh, this is nice," she said.

"It is. It has the touch of silk with matte tufts that provide a contrast to the smooth viscose. Perfect for comfortable warm-weather garments, and it's made in Italy."

"Does it come in any shades of green?" she asked.

"It does. I have it available in a celery green, grass green, and a deep emerald."

She nodded. "Thanks. I'll keep browsing."

I glanced at Simon and saw the look of pride on his face. He had been right—he had one very independent daughter.

"She's lovely," I said. "Such a pretty girl."

"Thanks. Lily arrived Friday, and I spent the weekend letting her get used to the apartment and taking her around the island. But she couldn't wait until you opened the shop this morning." He laughed. "You know. That knitter thing."

I nodded. "Oh, yeah," I said as I watched Lily making her way around the shop like any other sighted customer. "I'm leaving on Monday for Boston, but I'd love to have you and Lily to dinner before I go. Any chance you're free Saturday evening? Orli said she's anxious to meet both you and your daughter. But . . . I'm not sure I can guarantee such a delicious dinner as you prepared."

Simon laughed. "I tend to doubt that, and yes, I think so. Lily." He called over to his daughter. "Josie would like to have us for dinner Saturday evening, and you can meet her daughter, Orli."

Lily turned around and a smile crossed her face. "Oh, thanks. Yes, that sounds great. I'd love to go. She's not allergic to dogs, though, is she? Leo goes everywhere I do."

"No, she's not, and we both love dogs. Of course Leo is also invited."

"Great," she said before resuming her yarn browse.

"So are you all packed and ready for your trip?" Simon asked.

I let out a chuckle. "Not quite. I'm usually pretty organized, but I've been busy Christmas shopping, wrapping gifts, that sort of thing. After tonight's yarn class I'll be officially finished working here. Today's my last day in the shop, so that'll give me a few days to focus on packing."

"Will tonight be the end of your knitting classes too?"

"Well, it's the final night for the sweater class, but Dora said if the men want to do another class after the first of the year, its fine with her. So we'll see what they say. It won't interfere with my day job, because it's in the evening."

"You seem to really enjoy the class, so I hope it'll continue for you."

I noticed that Lily had found the wicker basket for purchases on her own and had quite a few skeins of various yarn filling it.

"Well, I think this will keep me busy for a while," she said, walking back toward the counter.

I peeked inside and saw that she had good taste in yarn. "Nice choices," I said. "Will that be all?"

"I think so." She reached into the bag that hung from her shoulder and removed her wallet.

Simon's hand shot out to stop her. "My treat," he said.

"Dad," she groaned. "I have money. You don't need to be buying my yarn for me."

Yup, she did remind me of myself in that respect, and I smiled. I hated it when my mother did the same thing when we were out shopping together.

But Simon was adamant. "I know you do, but this is my little 'welcome to the island' present for you."

She let out an exasperated sigh, leading me to believe this happened a lot, but she smiled, gave her father's arm a squeeze, and said, "Thank you."

I began ringing up the purchases, and a thought hit me. "Oh, Lily, we have a knitting group that meets here every Thursday evening. We're off till after the holidays, but I'd love for you to join us after the first of the year. We meet from seven till nine and then have coffee and tea and some goodies after. I'm afraid everybody is older than you, but you might like to join us."

The smile on her face increased. "Thank you so much. And absolutely, I'd love to come. I've found that when it comes to knitting, age is totally irrelevant."

"Great," I said. I liked this girl. She might not have her sight, but she didn't lack in other truly important qualities.

"I seem to be the one lagging behind here," Saxton said that evening at our class. "I have the front of my sweater finished, but I'm just starting the back."

"Not to worry," I assured him. "Knitting isn't a race. We all knit at different speeds, plus we all have different schedules for our knitting time."

I glanced over at Gabe, who was finishing up his final sleeve. For a new knitter, he had developed amazing speed, not to mention the fact that knitting for him seemed to come quite naturally. He seldom asked me a question or was stumped by any of the techniques.

"I have to say, Gabe, you've really caught on fast. If I didn't know better, I'd think maybe you're not a beginner at all," I joked with him.

I saw a flush creep up his neck.

"Oh . . . well." He cleared his throat.

The other three men stopped knitting and looked at Gabe, waiting for an explanation.

"Yeah, I noticed that too," Doyle said. "You really caught on fast, and you're sure much further along on the sweater than the rest of us."

Gabe placed his sweater in his lap and looked across the table at me. "Well . . . maybe I wasn't as honest as I should have been with you, Josie."

"What do you mean?"

"Yeah, I've been knitting for a while. Quite a while."

My father laughed and shook his head. "So you've been holding back on us. For how long?"

There was a pause before Gabe said, "Ah . . . since I was four years old."

"What?" all of us exclaimed at the same time.

"Are you serious?" I asked.

Gabe nodded. "Yeah, I'm afraid so. I'm a fraud."

Doyle laughed. "Well, I wouldn't say that, but why the hell would you lie to us?"

"Because the sign said *beginners'* knitting class. I very much wanted to join the group. You know, get to know some guys, be part of the crowd. So I figured I'd join and just keep a low profile."

The room erupted in laughter.

"Well, you dirty dog, you," Saxton said, clapping Gabe on the back.

A grin covered my father's face. "And did you think you'd never get caught?"

Gabe laughed. "Yeah, something like that."

I shook my head. "But, geez, Gabe, you still could have attended the class. I wouldn't have booted you out." But then another thought occurred to me. "Ah, you didn't want to intimidate the new knitters, did you? *Or* the instructor, for that matter. Just how proficient are you in knitting?"

A sheepish grin crossed his face. "Well . . . my mother owned a yarn shop up in Philly. I was teaching kids to knit by the time I was six or so. Mothers would come to the shop with their kids, who would see me sitting there knitting, and before you knew it, both boys and girls were asking how to do it. So before long my mother got the idea of having me teach a kids' class while the mothers shopped and then joined the women in another room for their own classes."

My father shook his head. "Well, I'll be darned. That's really great. So you've been knitting all your life."

Gabe nodded. "Pretty much."

"And I'd bet anything you're certified, aren't you?" I asked.

He pursed his lips, raised his eyebrows, and nodded. "Yeah . . . I'm a master knitter with TKGA—The Knitting Guild Association."

Again the room filled with laughter.

"Well, good for you," my dad said. "So see, once again this proves that knitting is *definitely* for men."

All of us looked up as Chloe walked into the room.

"Hey, guess what?" Doyle said to her. "Gabe's come out of the closet."

I saw her face blanch as she said, "What? You mean he's *gay?*"

❧ 23 ❧

I was staring into my bedroom closet Friday morning when the phone rang.

"Are you busy?" Grant asked.

"I'm trying to decide what to pack. How's the weather up there?"

"Actually, so far, we're having a very mild winter. Here it is December nineteenth and we'll have a high of fifty-two today. We're down in the thirties and forties overnight though, so definitely a winter coat and some warm sweaters."

I nodded. "Oh, good. Both Orli and I will be able to wear some of the knitted items I've made this past year. So what's up?"

"My brother and his family arrive at my mom's this weekend, so I'll be tied up over there and just wanted to double-check on everything for Monday."

"Oh, Jeff and Melissa are coming? Will we get to see them?"

"Yes. They both managed to get a week off from work and they'll be at my mom's for Christmas. They'll be with us for a week and of course, Dirk is on semester break."

I adored Grant's older brother and his wife. They lived in a suburb outside of Manhattan, where they were both attorneys. And Dirk was in his junior year at NYU. Orli would be thrilled to spend some time with her cousin.

"Great. I'm looking forward to it."

"So listen, just in case I don't get a chance to get back to you before Monday, I wanted to let you know that I'll meet you and Orli downstairs at the baggage area. Your flight is due in at three."

"Yup, I have the app on my cell phone, just in case there are any changes. I can't wait to see you, Grant, thanks for calling. Now I'd better get back to this packing or I won't have any luggage arriving at that baggage carrousel."

He laughed across the line. "Same here, Josie. I'm looking forward to spending the week with you."

I hung up and realized that he hadn't said with you *and Orli,* but of course I knew he was thrilled to be spending time with our daughter. I reached for my calf-length, black leather winter coat and placed it on the bed, wondering what, after sixteen years, Grant's feelings were toward me. Sure, I was the mother of his child and we were very good friends, but I recalled my mother's hints over the years about my being much more than just a friend to Grant.

Don't be silly, I thought, and continued packing.

Orli and I had just finished lunch when my mother called.

"Just wanted to remind you that Maggie arrives tomorrow and our Christmas get-together is Sunday at three."

"Yup, I haven't forgotten. Is Jane going to be able to make it?"

"Yes. She arrives at Mallory's house tomorrow, and she said she'll drop by for a drink early in the evening."

"Great. Anything I can bring for Sunday?"

"Not a thing. Delilah helped me get everything prepared yesterday and this morning. So it'll be a matter of popping things into the oven. Nice and easy."

Delilah had helped her cook again? "How are you feeling, Mom?"

"Well . . . I'm sure it's nothing. Nothing at all. But that tummy twinge hasn't gone away. So . . . I decided to make an appointment with my gynecologist in Gainesville. It's probably some minor female thing. I have an appointment for Tuesday."

"Tuesday? Damn. I won't be here and I would have gone with you."

"Don't be silly. Besides, Jane and Mags said they'll both take me, and then we're going shopping and out for lunch."

I couldn't help wondering if she had purposely made the appointment for when she knew I'd be gone.

"Okay, but I'll call you from the Boston area after your appointment. And I'll see you on Sunday."

"Everything all right?" Orli questioned when I hung up.

"Hmm, I'm not sure. Nana has had some stomach discomfort and she's seeing the doctor on Tuesday. We'll know more then."

"Gee, maybe it's just a flu or something. Hope she isn't sick for the holidays."

"Hmm, maybe," I said, but my nursing instinct notched up a level.

"It's me," I heard Mallory holler as she came through the front door.

"In the kitchen," I hollered back.

"Hey, guys," she said, walking directly to the coffeemaker, reaching for a mug, and filling it. "All packed, Orli? You must be so excited about your trip."

"I just have a few last minute items to toss in my carry-on, but other than that, yeah, I'm finished. Unlike Mom."

"Hey, hey. I'm *almost* finished. I've had some interruptions this morning."

"Well, since I'm good to go, I'm meeting Laura at the library. Our books are due back. I'll be home by five."

She placed a kiss on my cheek and then Mallory's.

Mallory shook her head as Orli walked out the door. "She's one special kid, you know."

I smiled. "I *do* know. Every single day. So what brings you over here?"

"Oh, any chance I can borrow your punch bowl? Mine broke a couple months ago and I still haven't replaced it. I offered to bring the punch for the Garden Club Christmas party on Monday, and you'll be gone."

"Sure," I said, reaching up into the cabinet and removing the crystal set. Twelve small cups with handles rested inside the bowl.

"I'm glad it's getting used. My mother gave me this years ago, with the hope that I'd entertain as much as she does."

Mallory laughed. "Thanks. Oh, before I forget . . . my mother told me on the phone this morning that your mom has an appointment in Gainesville next Tuesday with her doctor."

I nodded. "Yeah, my mom called this morning to tell me the same thing. No hint of what might be going on?"

Mallory shook her head. "Nope, none. And I know you'll be gone next week, but if I hear anything beyond what she tells you, I'll keep you in the loop."

"Thanks."

"So you're finished at the yarn shop, huh? Chloe's all set to resume work?"

"Yeah, she's doing great. I think she's happy to be back there full time. I also think things might be heating up between her and Gabe."

"Really? She invited him to Maude's for Thanksgiving dinner, didn't she?"

"Yeah, and he accepted and it went really well, and since then he's taken her out to dinner a few times."

"That's great. I've met him only a couple times, but he seems like a nice guy."

"He really is. I think Chloe likes him a lot, but she's keeping a little quiet on the subject."

"Hmm, just like you."

"What do you mean?"

"You and Simon."

"Mallory, there is no *me and Simon*. We've just had a few friendly dinners together. Actually I'm having Simon and his daughter here tomorrow evening for dinner. Orli has been anxious to meet both of them."

"Oh, that's great. I passed them walking along Second Street the other day when I drove past. I love her dog. I assume he's her guide dog?"

"Yeah, that's Leo, and he's really great. He's also invited to dinner. I'm just amazed at how independent she is. Oh, Simon did give

me some more info on how she lost her sight." I proceeded to fill
Mallory in on the details.

"Gosh, that's so sad, isn't it? So she wasn't born without sight.
But from what you've said, she certainly seems to do very well. Did
you find out yet how she's able to knit? Do they make patterns in
Braille?"

"I have no clue. But she's going to join our knitting group, so
maybe we'll find out then."

Mallory nodded. "God, life sure is strange, isn't it? I mean, really,
we just never know from one day to the next what might happen and
how our lives can so easily be turned upside down."

"Isn't that the truth."

"One decision can alter the entire path of our life. You know, if
Lily hadn't had the ballet class that day . . . well, who knows. Do
you ever think about how different your own life would have been
if you'd married Grant?"

I was surprised by her question. "Sometimes, yeah, I do. But
I've always felt strongly that it just wasn't meant to be. We were
young, he was just starting a career, and I really don't think we
would have lasted."

"Yet look at the two of you all these years later. Still very close.
You support each other, you've raised your daughter together as
much as possible, and you get along better than many married couples."

"My point exactly."

Mallory laughed. "Oh, come on. You're not still against marriage, are you?"

"I've never been *against* it. I'm just not sure it's right for me."

"And you're too damn independent to give it a chance, aren't you?"

I remained silent for a few moments. "Hey, I thought you always
supported my decision about Grant."

"I did support it and I support you, Josie, but it doesn't mean
that I have to agree with you. It's pretty obvious that you've always
been the one great love in Grant's life."

My head shot up and I stared at her. I waited for her to add
something to what she'd just said, but she didn't.

"Well, if you've finished philosophizing for today, I really have to finish packing."

She got up and came to give me a hug. "Kicking me out, are you? Glad I asked for the punch bowl before our conversation."

I laughed and nudged her in the ribs. "Get outta here. I'll see you on Sunday at my mom's."

❧ 24 ❧

By the time Saturday evening arrived, I was fully packed except for last-minute carry-on items.

I had spent most of Friday trying to decide what to make for dinner for Simon and Lily. It was times like that when I wished I'd paid more attention to my mother's offer of cooking instructions. I didn't dare do any of my Italian dishes since Simon had already proved his own skill in that area, so I eventually decided on a casserole with stew beef, cheese, potatoes, and herbs. I figured salad and my homemade biscuits would complete a nice meal, in addition to my cheesecake with blueberries.

"I have the dining room table all set," Orli said, walking into the kitchen. "Anything else I can do?"

"I don't think so. I have brie in the fridge to go with crackers before we eat, and white wine is chilling. Thanks for your help."

"I'm looking forward to meeting Lily," she said. "Well, Simon too." She let out a chuckle. "But I think it's so great that despite lack of sight, Lily seems to manage pretty well."

"I agree. I know Simon is quite proud of her," I said as the doorbell chimed. "There they are."

I opened the door to see Simon holding a bottle of wine and a bouquet of flowers. Lily stood there with Leo beside her on a leash.

"Welcome. Come on in."

I made the introductions and noticed that Lily wasn't wearing the sunglasses; her eyes were closed.

"I thought this red zinfandel might go with dinner, and the flowers are for you," Simon said, passing me a beautiful arrangement of orange roses and pale yellow lilies, accented with burgundy mums and lush greens.

"Oh, Simon, thank you so much. They're gorgeous," I said, bending my head to inhale the heady fragrance. "Have a seat in the family room." I gestured with my arm. "I'll just get these into a vase."

Orli followed me into the kitchen as I reached into the cabinet and then filled my best crystal vase with water.

"Cute," she whispered into my ear. "He's really cute."

"Shh!" I whispered back and tried to suppress a giggle. "Bring out the brie and crackers while I get these arranged."

"They really are so pretty, Simon. Thanks again," I said, placing the vase in the middle of the dining room table. "Okay. We have some brie and crackers, and what can I get you to drink? I have some pinot grigio that's cold, and Lily, I have diet soda, sweet tea, lemonade?"

"Pinot for me," Simon said.

"Sweet tea sounds great." Lily had Leo already curled up beside her feet.

"Does Leo need a bowl of water or anything?" I asked. I was a novice at being a hostess to a dog.

Lily laughed. "No, no. He's fine. Thanks."

"He's just beautiful," I heard Orli say as I headed to the kitchen. "It's okay to pat him?"

"Oh, sure. He loves people."

I turned around to see Simon behind me as I removed the wine bottle from the fridge.

"Here, let me open that for you."

"Thanks. Corkscrew is there on the counter."

"Your daughter resembles you closely. Very pretty girl."

"Thank you. Actually, she did manage to get Grant's lovely green eyes."

I proceeded to pour the sweet tea and got out two wineglasses, which I placed on a tray.

"It's so nice of you to invite us to dinner, Josie. Lily was looking forward to meeting Orli."

"Good, I'm glad. I know Orli felt the same."

Simon filled the glasses and said, "I'll take these for you."

We returned to the family room to hear both girls involved in a conversation about some current singer or band that they both seemed to love.

I lifted my wineglass. "Here's to both of you, and welcome to Cedar Key. I hope you'll be happy here and your practice will be successful, Simon."

"Thanks," they both said.

"My dad said you're leaving on Monday for the Boston area. You must be so excited, Orli. Christmas in New England and celebrating a special birthday."

"I am. I love being up there. Oh, I love it here too." I saw her shoot me a quick glance. "But there's just something about the Boston area. So much to see and do. Have you ever visited there?"

Lily nodded. "We have. My dad took me to Boston a few years ago. The history of the city is amazing. Are you considering Boston for college?"

Orli surprised me by saying, "Actually, yes, I am. I've been doing some research on various colleges there."

She was? I knew she'd mentioned in passing that she'd like to go out of state and might have even hinted at Boston, but somehow this sounded a bit more definite, and I noticed how she avoided looking at me.

"Well, we're happy to announce that Lily has made her college decision," Simon said.

"Oh, how exciting. Where're you going?" Orli leaned forward on the sofa.

A smile crossed Lily's face. "I finally decided last week to attend the University of North Florida in Jacksonville."

"Congratulations," I said, and from the look on Simon's face, I knew he was happy with her choice.

"Actually, it was Lily's first choice when she got accepted but she wanted to be sure, so we also visited a few other campuses."

"What made you decide on UNF?" Orli asked.

"Well," she said, leaning forward to stroke Leo's ears. "It's a nice campus. Not too big, and I think it'll be easy for Leo and me to get around. But they have an excellent Disability Resource Center and that was important to me. I had an interview with the DRC team and I was impressed with the services and accommodations that they provide."

"That's wonderful," I said. "You must be so excited."

"Are all of the course materials accessible?" Orli asked.

Lily nodded. "Yeah, they are. They have digital conversions of the textbooks for electronic book readers and accessible text-to-speech functions. It's still a foggy area with many of the colleges and the Disabilities Act, but the U.S. Justice Department has been very good about addressing any violations. There was a recent lawsuit filed against Louisiana Tech University, and they agreed to stop using learning materials that limit access for students with visual disabilities."

"That's wonderful," I said. "And it sounds like you're very well informed on the subject."

Simon laughed. "Oh, yeah. Sometimes she's like a dog with a bone on this issue, but I do applaud her involvement."

"What are you majoring in at college?" Orli asked.

"Communication, with a focus on public relations and the media. Have you decided on a major yet?"

Orli shook her head. "Ah . . . no . . . not quite. I'm considering maybe something in business."

"Well," I said, glancing at my watch. "Dinner is almost ready. Just give me a few minutes to get out the casserole and pop my biscuits into the oven, and we can eat."

"Everything was delicious, Miss Josie," Lily said, wiping her lips with a napkin.

"It certainly was," Simon agreed, shooting me a smile across the table.

"Thank you. As soon as I get the table cleared we can have some of my blueberry cheesecake."

Orli jumped up to help me remove the dinnerware.

"Coffee or tea?" I asked.

"Coffee would be great," Simon said. "But let me help you."

"No, no. We're fine." I raised my hand in the air.

"I'll have tea, please," Lily said.

I followed Orli to the kitchen and stacked the dishes on the counter. "Just leave those and I'll rinse them after and get the dishwasher loaded," I said, removing my cheesecake from the fridge. "You can take out the dessert plates and forks and I'll get the rest."

"They're so nice, aren't they? I really like them both a lot."

I smiled at my social butterfly. Orli always did feel comfortable meeting new people. "They are," I agreed.

Following dessert, Orli took Lily into her room to listen to some of her CDs and Simon insisted on helping me clean up in the kitchen.

"Thank you again," he said. "I know that Lily has enjoyed this evening as much as I have."

I looked up from loading the dishwasher and smiled. "Good. Then we'll definitely have to do it again after I get back."

"It's a date," he said, making me wonder if we'd ever have a bona fide *date*.

⤜ 25 ⤚

Sunday flew by with the Christmas gathering at my parents' house. It was great to see Maggie again, and the entire day was filled with laughter. By the time Orli and I boarded our flight in Atlanta, I was feeling less concern about my mother.

She'd seemed her perky self the day before, and even seemed resigned and accepting of the fact that both Orli and I would be absent from her house on Christmas day.

I settled back in my seat as we got airborne and patted Orli's hand.

"A girl could get used to first class pretty fast, couldn't she?"

Orli giggled. "I know. So much more room, and that pre-flight drink was nice, wasn't it?"

I nodded. "Yes, having a glass of wine at the gate makes me feel special."

"You *are*," Orli assured me.

I let out a sigh and once again wondered how Grant and I had gotten so lucky to produce such an outstanding daughter.

I reached into my carry-on and removed the scarf that I was working on for Grant's mother. A few more rows and it would be finished. Not a knitter herself, Molly always showed great appreciation of the knitted items I'd made for her over the years.

I had liked Molly from the first time Grant had introduced me to her. His dad had passed away the year before we met, but I remembered thinking how self-assured and independent Molly was despite being a new widow. And how vastly different she was from my own mother. I'm not sure she ever agreed with my decision not to marry her son, but she never voiced her thoughts and had always assured me that whatever Grant and I chose to do was up to us.

I nodded off following lunch and woke to see Orli dozing beside me with her iPod earbuds in place. Glancing out the window, I saw the Boston skyline in the distance and felt the air pressure inside the cabin begin to change.

Orli yawned and stretched. "Are we almost there?"

"Almost," I said, pointing out the window.

She leaned across me and smiled. "I can't wait to see Dad."

It had been nine months since I'd seen him, and I realized I was also looking forward to it.

As we descended on the escalator to baggage, I saw Grant immediately and my stomach gave a lurch. Leaning against a wall, hands in his jean pockets, he looked every bit as handsome as the day I met him. His cranberry turtleneck and black cashmere sport jacket boosted his good looks, and his dark hair streaked with gray added to his appeal.

As if feeling my stare, he glanced up, smiled, and waved.

"There he is," Orli exclaimed, waving back before leaving the escalator to run into his open arms.

I laughed as I walked toward them. He kissed Orli on the cheek and released her to envelop me with his hug. I loved the ease and familiarity that Grant always managed to make me feel in his arms. He surprised me by brushing my lips with his rather than the usual peck on the cheek.

Swinging his arms around our shoulders, he said, "How great! I have both of my girls together again. Good flight?"

"Oh, it was," Orli bubbled. "First class was great, Dad. Thanks."

"Yes, thank you, Grant. We both enjoyed it."

"Good. Ah, here we go," he said. "Baggage is coming out."

We walked closer to the carousel, his arms still around us.

Within a few minutes, we had our bags and headed to the parking lot.

The Boston sun was shining and the air was crisp, making it feel more like autumn than December.

"You really are having a mild winter," I said as Grant placed our luggage in the trunk.

He nodded. "Yeah, there's a cold front coming in this evening though. We could end up having a white Christmas after all."

"Oh, good," Orli said as she got into the backseat, leaving me to sit up front next to Grant.

Grant drove along 1A, heading north. There were other routes he could have taken, and I wondered if he recalled my fondness for driving along Lynn Shore Drive with the mighty Atlantic to my right.

"I always forget how pretty it is up here," I said, and all of a sudden had a flashback to that spring of sixteen years before when Grant and I had sat huddled on a blanket at this very beach, making out and declaring eternal love for each other. I smiled at the memory.

"It is," was all he said, and I wondered if he was having the same recall.

Orli carried most of the conversation as we made our way to Danvers and Route 62.

"Oh, wow, there it is," I heard her say, and glanced up from the road to see the familiar imposing structure. Although I could tell that it had received a facelift, the buildings still looked down on the town of Danvers from high atop the hill.

Grant turned onto the long, winding road that led up to Kirkbride Village and slowed down halfway at a guard hut, where he waved to the man inside, and the security gate lifted for us to enter. As we curved to the entrance I saw that four brick buildings stood in the late afternoon sun, which lent a softness and coziness to what many local residents remembered as a frightening and eerie place. The developer had preserved the outside shell of the original Kirkbride Building, where Grant now resided, once home to so many lost souls. Now gone were the confining black bars, replaced with white shutters on each side of the stylish, large windows, creating a sense of warmth. Large trees that still had not shed all of their autumn leaves gave an atmosphere of peace rather than horror to the place. I had to admit that the uncomfortable feeling I'd had years ago on seeing the former mental facility was gone.

"Oh, this really *is* pretty," I said as Grant pulled into a spot in front of the first building.

"I told you," he said, and I saw the smile on his face.

"Wow, it doesn't look anything like the scary place it used to be." Orli jumped out of the car and looked around her.

I got out and followed Grant to the trunk. I had to agree. The malevolent aura the place had always exuded had disappeared and in its place was a very pretty condo complex.

"I hope you'll like it here," he said as we followed him to a triple-size glass front door that allowed the beauty of the inside atrium to be seen from outside.

Grant swiped a card in the security pad, and I stepped inside to see five condo units in the shape of a U. The developer had strategically placed a huge crystal chandelier in the center of the glass-peaked roof, allowing the prisms to catch rays of sunlight, which distributed splashes of color throughout the atrium. Beneath the chandelier I saw an intricate freshwater fishpond. Varying tiers held aquatic plants and flowers, with ceramic statues of mermaids, fairies, and angels adding serenity. The waterfalls flowed into the pond from various directions, creating a soft, trickling sound while colorful fish swam among the lily pads. Throughout the atrium, metal benches added welcome and respite from the outside world.

"This is *so* upscale, Grant. Really gorgeous!" I looked around and saw there were two condos on either side of the entrance and a larger one at the rear, which completed the U shape.

"Oh, Dad, I just love it," Orli said as she went to give her father a squeeze. "It's hard to believe this was a mental hospital years ago."

He nodded, and the three of us looked over as the door on our right opened and an elderly woman emerged, holding a watering can.

"Hello, hello," she said, walking toward us with her hand outstretched.

I saw a smile cover Grant's face. "This is Estelle Fletcher, my neighbor. And, Estelle, this is my daughter, Orli, and her mother, Josie."

"Well, well," she said, nodding. I wondered if the woman always spoke with double words.

Grant's description of her had been understated. I took in the white frizzy hair that was pulled tightly back from her forehead and had managed to escape the purple silk scarf at the nape of her neck. Dramatically arched dark brown eyebrows caused a questioning expression, and blood-red lipstick had been applied beyond the natural contours of her lips. She wore a bright orange and red caftan, which added to her unusual appearance.

"So nice to meet you," I said while accepting her outstretched hand. I noticed she held on to it longer than necessary as she stared into my eyes.

"Yes, yes. Same here." She gave my hand a squeeze before letting go, and said, "You have good energy."

Orli chuckled and shook the old woman's hand. "Do I have it too?" she questioned.

"You? You, my dear, have a very special gift. The gift of love."

Orli looked at me and shrugged.

"Okay," Grant said, directing us to the unit straight ahead. "Let's get you settled in. Take care, Estelle."

"Oh, I will, I will."

Yup, she definitely spoke in double words.

"Oh, and Josie, do stop by my place while you're here. We'll have some tea and muffins."

"Thanks." I followed Grant and Orli. "Thanks. Maybe I will," I told her, and wondered if speaking with double words was catching.

I stepped inside the condo and gasped. "Oh, Grant. This is positively stunning."

My eyes took in the spacious and open great room with a large kitchen behind it and French doors leading outside to a brick patio and greenery. Jutting out above the great room with a staircase to the right was a loft with skylights, creating a warm glow from the sun streaming in.

"Oh, it is, Dad," Orli gushed. "I just love it."

I saw the look of pride that covered Grant's face. "Good. I'm glad you both like it. And over here," he said, walking to the left, "is your room. I'm in the loft."

We deposited our wheeled luggage as I took in the large rectangular room, complete with twin beds, a desk, and two bureaus. The plum and cream color scheme was very chic.

"Beautiful," I said, walking to inspect the attached bathroom.

"It is," Orli agreed. "But I bet Gram did the decorating."

Grant laughed. "Yeah, she did, and she also came over this morning and brought a casserole for our dinner this evening. So after you both get unpacked, we can relax a little before we eat. A glass of wine, Josie? And I bet you'd like a hot chocolate, Orli?"

"Thanks, yes," I said.

"That would be great." Orli ran over to give Grant another hug, making me question if I'd been wrong not to allow our daughter to grow up in a household with both parents.

26

Following dinner, the three of us sat in the great room, laughing and talking. Orli was curled up on the sofa beside Grant, and I was stretched out in the armchair, my legs propped on the hassock. I let out a sigh of contentment. This was nice. Very nice. I was surprised to realize that this was the first time we'd been together as a family in Grant's home. When he visited Cedar Key, he came to dinner at our house, but this was different. Orli and I were both going to be living and sleeping under the same roof as Grant for an entire week.

"And so you think you might consider Boston?" I heard Grant say, and tuned back in to their conversation.

I saw Orli shoot a glance over to me. "I . . . don't know. Maybe."

I sat up straighter in my chair. "What's this about? I'm afraid I zoned out."

"Orli's been telling me that she might consider college in Boston."

I recalled that she'd recently said the same thing to Simon's daughter.

"Yeah, I heard you say that the other evening," I said. "So what's up with that?"

"Well . . . I've been giving it a lot of thought. And I did some research. I don't think I want to major in business after all."

I leaned forward in my chair. "Oh?" I wasn't sure which surprised me most—the fact that she seemed serious about Boston and had discarded business as a major or the fact that she hadn't discussed any of it with me.

Grant patted her knee. "Ah, are you considering a nursing degree like your mom?"

Orli shook her head. "No. A degree in journalism, like Nana."

This news was beyond surprising and the first that I was hearing about it.

"Really?" Where on earth had this come from? "I had no idea you were interested in writing."

She nodded as she fingered the tassels on the afghan beside her. "I've always enjoyed writing, but I'm thinking more along the lines of journalism in relation to the media."

Grant laughed. "Oh, like an anchor person on our nightly news?"

Orli gave him a playful jab. "Well, more like somebody who travels and does interviews with important people for the news."

I blew out a breath. "Wow. I had no idea, Orli, but I think it's great if you think you'd enjoy that as a career. There's certainly lots of opportunity." I tried to banish the images in my mind of my daughter in some war-torn country doing interviews.

"Really? Then you'd be okay with it?"

I laughed. "Orli, this is *your* choice and *your* life. Not mine. You know how I feel about a woman making her own choices."

She nodded. "Well . . . that's why I'm considering Emerson College. Where you went."

Emerson—what was to have been my alma mater; now my daughter might make it hers. "It's a great college," I said.

"It certainly is," Grant added. "And I won't lie; I'd love having you so close and living up here during the school year."

I felt my heart skip a beat. Sure, I knew that day would come when Orli would leave home for college just as I had. But now I felt a twinge of jealousy. For some reason, I felt left out, left behind—

because the place that I had always occupied in Orli's life would now be filled by Grant.

By nine o'clock Orli said she was going to take a shower and get to bed.

She stood up and stifled a yawn. "I'm tired. What are the plans for tomorrow, Dad?"

"That's up to both of you. Gram would like us to stop by, though, for a quick hello. So maybe we could do lunch in Marblehead."

"Sounds great," I said.

"Could we take a drive up the coast to Gloucester and Rockport?" Orli asked.

"Sure. We'll go to my mother's in the morning, then get lunch and go for a drive."

"Sounds like fun," she said, kissing both of us good night and heading to the bedroom.

Grant watched her leave the room and smiled. "We have one special daughter, don't we?"

I nodded. "We do."

"How about a nightcap? A glass of wine?"

"Yes, that would be nice."

I followed him into the kitchen and perched on a stool as he uncorked a bottle of cabernet and filled two glasses.

"Here you go," he said, passing one to me. "And here's to our amazing daughter and her future."

I nodded. "Yes, to Orli's future."

"Would you be okay with Orli going to college up here?" he asked.

"I'd miss her, but no matter where she goes, I'll miss her, so yes, of course."

"You seemed surprised about the journalism major."

"Yeah, I was, in a way. But at this age most young women still aren't exactly sure what they want."

"Ah, unlike you, huh?"

I looked across the counter and saw a smile cover Grant's face.

"I thought I was sure about journalism, but as we know now, it really wasn't what I wanted."

He took a sip of wine before saying, "Actually, I was referring to you and me. I recall a young woman of nineteen who was very adamant that she shouldn't marry and should raise her daughter pretty much on her own."

Over the years I couldn't recall Grant ever bringing this topic up in a conversation, so I was surprised that he did now.

I blew out a breath. "It wasn't so much the not getting married, Grant. I just think the *timing* was wrong. There you were about to graduate college, heading toward a career in law. It wouldn't have been easy for you."

He nodded. "Hmm, you're right. I know that." He took a gulp of wine and shook his head. "Odd, though, how life is, isn't it? Do you ever think how your life might have been different had we married before Orli was born?"

"I have thought about that. I don't think I would have become a nurse for one thing. I would have been a stay-at-home mom, I'm sure."

"Probably. Would you have minded that?"

I thought about his question for a few moments. "Not at all when Orli was small. Actually, I would have welcomed it. It was tough trying to juggle low-paying jobs and spending quality time with Orli."

Grant nodded, and I went on, "But I think once she got into high school I would have wanted to find myself outside of the home. Do you know what I mean?"

"I do. Yes, of course, and I think that's natural. So maybe that's when you would have gone to college and become a nurse."

"You could be right. But we were young when I got pregnant with Orli, so who knows if our marriage would have lasted. And look at what we have now . . . a wonderful and close friendship. We might have jeopardized this by getting married at that time."

I saw a thoughtful expression cross Grant's face, and he let out a deep sigh. "Hmm, you could be right. So when do you begin your new job?"

"The week after New Year's, January seventh."

"Are you excited?" he asked.

"I am. It'll be nice working so close to home, and I think Simon will be a dream to work with."

"Simon?"

I laughed. "Well, Dr. Mancini, but he told me to call him by his first name outside of office hours."

"I see," was all he said, and if I didn't know better, I'd think there was a tad of jealousy there.

As if to confirm this, he asked, "So are you and Simon . . . seeing each other outside of the office?"

"Well, we haven't begun working together yet, but . . . yeah, we've had a couple dinners together. But they really can't qualify as dates. Just friendly, informal dinners."

I took the last sip of my wine and glanced up to the clock on the wall. "Gosh, it's ten-fifteen already. No wonder I'm tired. I'm sure Orli is fast asleep, so I'm going to take a quick shower and jump in bed myself."

I got up to place my wineglass in the sink and felt Grant's hands on my shoulders. I spun around to find his face inches from mine.

"I'm glad you're here," he said. "I've always loved being with you."

"Same here," I told him before his lips touched my cheek. "I'll see you in the morning."

"Sleep well," I heard him say as I walked toward the bedroom. For the first time in sixteen years I felt unsure of myself with him.

❧ 27 ❧

The following morning I woke to the sound of laughter. Turning over in bed, I realized it was Grant and Orli. The bedside clock read 8:30. God, I'd slept like a rock and couldn't believe it was that time already. I got up, hit the bathroom, and put on my robe before I walked into the kitchen to find father and daughter engrossed in a crossword puzzle as they stood near each other at the counter.

"Good morning, sleepyhead," Grant said with a huge grin on his face. "Coffee?"

He walked to the Bunn coffeemaker on the counter, filled a stoneware mug, and passed it to me.

"Thanks, and gosh, I didn't mean to sleep so late. What time did you get up, Orli?"

She waved her hand in the air. "Oh, hours ago. Dad and I have been waiting for you so we could get going."

I glanced at her and saw she was still in her pajamas. "You little fibber, you," I said, going over to give her hug.

She let out a laugh. "Nah, I only got up about a half hour ago, about the same time Dad did."

"Yeah, there's no rush," he said. "How about some French toast for breakfast?"

"Cool," Orli said before bending her head back over the puzzle.

Grant began removing items from the fridge and cabinets. "So you slept well?"

"Very well, thanks, but can I help?"

"Nope. I've got this under control. Just relax."

I walked toward the French doors and looked out to the patio. Another sunny day. I cracked the door and then shivered. "Oh, you were right. Definitely cooler out there this morning."

"Yeah, I caught the weather when I got up, and you might get your wish, Orli. There's a possibility of snow flurries tomorrow evening."

"Sweet. On Christmas Eve."

"Oh, did my box arrive with all the Christmas presents?" I'd decided it was much easier to ship the gifts rather than lug them on the plane.

Grant nodded as he poured batter onto a large skillet. "Yes, I put the box into the hall closet."

"Thanks." I perched on a stool next to Orli as I watched Grant display an ease in the kitchen that I remembered from our college days at his apartment.

Orli continued to study the crossword as I sat and watched Grant cook bacon to go with the French toast. Such a normal everyday scene in most households, but the three of us were experiencing it for the first time—and I discovered I liked it.

"Here we go," I heard Grant say as he placed plates on the table. "Chef Cooper bids you *bon appétit*."

Orli and I both laughed as we joined him.

"Gosh, your cooking skills put mine to shame," I said after taking a bite. "Delicious."

"That's not true, Mom. I think you're a good cook."

My daughter, ever the diplomat.

After a few minutes, she said, "You know . . . I was kinda wondering . . . maybe Friday or Saturday we could take a drive to Boston. To see the Emerson campus."

Grant stared at me from across the table, leaving the ball in my court.

I took a sip of juice and nodded. "Well . . . yeah. I think we could probably do that. They're closed for Christmas break though, so you wouldn't be able to go inside."

"Right, I know, but I think I'd just like to see the area."

"You're sounding pretty interested in Emerson," I said.

"I think I might be."

"If it's okay with your mom, sure, we could make a day of it and then have dinner in the North End after."

"Yeah, that sounds great," I said. Then why did I have a nagging ache inside of me?

A few hours later we pulled up in front of Grant's childhood home, located on a narrow side street in Old Town. I'd always loved this house. The white clapboard building sat back from the sidewalk surrounded by a small garden that was now in its winter slumber. With gabled roof, brick chimneys and bay windows, the two-story structure was the quintessential historical home in Marblehead.

Walking down the brick path, I looked up to see that Molly had already flung open the front door and was standing on the porch to greet us.

Orli rushed into her arms. "Merry Christmas, Gram. You look great."

Molly did look great. At sixty-six she had maintained her youthful figure and the cut of her short, stylish silver hair very much resembled mine.

She opened her other arm to me. "Josie, how wonderful you're here. You and Orli both get prettier each time I see you."

I laughed and placed a kiss on her cheek.

"Come on inside. It's getting nippy out here. I think they're predicting flurries for tomorrow night."

We followed her into the large hallway and the spacious sitting room on the right.

"That's what Dad said. I'm hoping we do get a bit of snow. Makes it more festive, don't you think?"

Molly laughed. "It's festive until you have to shovel it. How about some tea, coffee? Hot chocolate for you, Orli?"

I nodded. "Coffee would be great, thanks. Can I help with anything?"

"Oh, I'll help her," Orli said before Molly could respond.

"Sit down and make yourself comfortable," Grant told me.

I looked around the room and smiled. There was a lot to be said for things not changing. The room looked much as it had years before on my first visit to this house. Same cushy furniture, antique tables and lamps, and Persian carpet covering the center of the hardwood floor. Late-morning sunlight streamed through the bay windows, adding to the coziness, and in front of the windows a huge Christmas tree dominated the room. I could smell the scent of pine and walked over to admire the many ornaments and decorations.

"This is such a great house, Grant. I've always loved it, and your mom did an outstanding job with the tree." I sank into one of the armchairs.

He nodded. "Yeah, I agree, and the house has been in our family for generations, so that makes it extraspecial."

I thought of my grandmother's house where Orli and I lived and knew what he meant. Glancing around I saw that one lacquered table held framed photographs and got up to take a look.

Grant's parents' wedding photo stood beside one of Jeff and Melissa. There were images of both Orli and Dirk at various stages of growth and one photo that I hadn't seen in years: Grant and I taken during the first year we met. We'd gone on a picnic to Devereux Beach in Marblehead with a group of friends from college. It was an exceptionally mild day in November. Grant and I sat atop the stone wall with the ocean behind us. My long hair was blowing in the wind, and we were snuggled into each other's arms. I lifted the photo to look closer and saw the emotion of pure joy and love on our faces.

"You had that photo blown up and gave it to me for Christmas that year, remember?"

I spun around to see Grant standing behind me, a somber expression on his face.

"I do," was all I said as I vividly recalled that magical day. Later that evening at his apartment we'd made love for the first time.

"Here we go," Molly said, coming into the room with Orli behind her carrying a tray. "Hot drinks and some gingerbread cookies I baked this morning."

My memory evaporated, and I returned to the armchair.

"So are your plans all made for the birthday celebration Sunday evening?" Molly asked.

Grant hadn't said a word to me about what he had planned, so I was as curious as his mother.

He nodded. "Yes, and now that they're here I can tell them. I made reservations at Marliave in Boston."

"Marliave? Did you, Dad? That's my favorite place. You took me there for a birthday lunch when I turned ten."

"That's right. I did and knew it was your favorite, so I thought it would be the perfect place to celebrate your Sweet Sixteen."

My hand trembled as I reached for my coffee cup. *Marliave.* The place where I'd told Grant over dinner that I was pregnant with Orli. In the last twenty-four hours my past seemed to be on a collision course with my present.

I yawned as Grant pulled into the space in front of his building.

He reached over and patted my knee. "Tired? I promise we'll have an easier day tomorrow."

"No, no. I'm fine." I got out of the car and followed Orli and Grant into the building.

It *had* been a full day, but a very enjoyable one. After visiting with Molly, we had lunch at the Barnacle overlooking the harbor in Marblehead, followed by the coastal drive that Orli had requested. On the way home we stopped for pizza at a little place in Danvers Square.

"I'm going to go call Laura," Orli said, heading to our room. "She won't believe the amazing day that we had."

I glanced at my watch and saw it was already seven. "My mother still hasn't called about her doctor's appointment today. I'm going to give her a call," I told Grant as I settled myself at the kitchen counter.

"Would you like some wine?"

I nodded as I tapped my parents' number on my cell. "Yes, please."

I was surprised to hear my father answer. "Dad? How's Mom doing? How'd her appointment go today?"

"Josie, hi. Well . . . ah . . . we're still not sure what's going on. The doctor arranged for a scan on Friday."

A scan the day after Christmas? This didn't sound good.

"What exactly do they think it is?"

"Well . . . it's too soon to get concerned. We'll know more on Friday, I think. Your mother's resting."

I felt a shiver of fear crawl up my back. "Is Maggie there? Let me speak to Mags."

"Okay, and Josie, I hope you and Orli are having a good time."

"We are, Dad. Let me talk to Mags."

"Josie, sweetie." Maggie's voice came across the line.

"Mags, what's up with my mom?" I knew Maggie would be honest.

I heard her let out a deep sigh. "Josie, honey, the doctor suspects that your mother could have uterine cancer."

~ 28 ~

I disconnected my call with Mags and stood in Grant's kitchen as if I were slowly waking from a dream. This couldn't be possible. *My mother hadn't appeared sick,* I thought and then my mind quickly shifted from that of daughter to that of nurse. I knew that sometimes with gynecological cancers there were very few symptoms.

"Everything okay?" I heard Grant say before he saw the look on my face. After placing the wineglasses on the counter, he came over to scoop me into his arms. "Are *you* okay, Josie?"

I fought to hold back the tears ready to spill out of my eyes and whispered, "They think my mom could have cancer of the uterus."

"Oh, Josie. Oh, God, I'm so sorry."

I felt his hand on the back of my head and I pushed away from his chest as I swiped at the tears still threatening.

Taking a deep breath, I said, "Don't say a word. I don't want Orli to know right now. She doesn't need this special time ruined."

Grant nodded and squeezed my hand. "We'll talk later. Here, have some wine."

A few minutes later Orli came out of the bedroom full of excitement from talking with Laura. "She said Clovelly is doing fine. She went over to feed him and visit twice today. Is it okay if I have some ice cream, Dad?"

"Of course, help yourself."

I took another gulp of wine and felt Grant's eyes on mine.

Orli spun around as she removed a carton of Rocky Road from the freezer. "Oh, did you call Nana? What happened at the doctor?"

"Yeah, I did. Well, they're not sure what's going on. She's having more tests on Friday."

"Oh, that's good. I bet it's not serious," she said as she began spooning ice cream into a bowl.

I attempted to hold on to my daughter's optimism as the three of us passed the evening playing gin rummy. If Orli thought I was unusually quiet, she didn't say anything.

She got up from the kitchen table and stretched when we finished the second game. "I'm going to shower and then read in bed before I go to sleep. What's up for tomorrow, Dad?"

"Well, it's Christmas Eve so how about if we go out for brunch late morning and then spend the day decorating the tree? I'm going to make my famous shrimp scampi for dinner, so it'll be a nice quiet day with just the three of us."

"Cool," Orli said, bending to kiss Grant's cheek. "Gram's tree was gorgeous, but I was hoping we'd decorate one here too."

Orli kissed me good night and headed to the bedroom.

"How about another glass of wine?" Grant asked.

"Sounds good," I said, and curled up at one end of the sofa.

Thoughts of my mother kept swirling in my head. I wanted to think positive. I really did, but this was one of those times when a little bit of knowledge could be dangerous. From my nursing experience I knew that people didn't always get the happy solutions they longed for.

"Here ya go."

Grant passed me the wineglass before settling beside me.

"To your mother," he said, touching my glass with his. "To her good health."

"Thanks." I took a sip and then rested my head against the sofa. "I'm worried, Grant."

He reached for my hand and gave it a squeeze. "Of course you are. That's only natural."

I took another sip of wine. "God, I'd be the first one to say my mother can be such a pain in the ass. But . . ." The tears that I'd struggled to hold back earlier now escaped, and I felt myself being wrapped in Grant's arms.

"Shh. It's okay. It'll be all right."

I felt his hand stroking my back as I attempted to get control of my emotions.

"It's so damn scary," I said against his chest.

I felt his head nod. "I know, but as a nurse you should also know that many times the problem is something simple. Something benign that has an easy fix."

I sat up and took a deep breath. "Right. I know you're right. Thanks, Grant."

I took another sip of wine. "Oh, your mom took me aside and told me about the surprise birthday party she planned for Orli on Christmas day."

He smiled and nodded. "Yeah, she knew I wanted to have the special dinner Sunday evening for the three of us, but she wanted to celebrate Orli's birthday too."

"She said she's baking Orli's favorite raspberry velvet cake and they have birthday gifts for her to open. That's really nice. And Jeff, Melissa, and Dirk will be there to help her celebrate." I paused for a second before saying, "Just like a real family."

By the time I headed to bed an hour later, I realized two things—I was very grateful that I'd been with Grant when I got the news about my mother, and there was a distinct possibility I was falling in love with him all over again.

I woke the following morning to find the weather predictions had been accurate. Pulling aside the bedroom curtain, I saw white, fluffy snow falling from the sky. There was very little accumulation, and the cars in the parking lot had just a dusting of what looked like sugar.

Orli was still asleep and the clock read 6:45. I put on my robe and crept quietly out of the room. I was surprised to see Grant already sitting at the kitchen table, bent over the newspaper with a coffee mug in front of him.

He looked up and smiled. "Good morning. Sleep okay?"

"Surprisingly, yes. I think the wine helped." I filled my own mug with coffee and joined him. "How about you? Are you sleeping okay with us in the house?"

"Better than I have in years. This being alone isn't all that it's cracked up to be."

Grant was probably right. I had Orli at home, but his house was completely empty.

"Hey, the weatherman was right. There's a bit of snow out there."

"Yeah, although I don't think it's going to amount to much, I think Orli will be happy." He took a sip of coffee, and I instinctively knew there was something he wanted to tell me. From the very beginning we'd had this magic gift of almost knowing each other's thoughts.

Sure enough, a few moments later, he said, "You know, Josie, there's something I wanted to discuss with you. I know you have a lot on your mind with your mother, but while Orli's still asleep, I thought I should tell you."

I leaned forward, my eyes glued to his face. "What is it?"

He cleared his throat before saying, "Orli has told me something and she's quite nervous that it might cause you to be upset."

What the hell? "Just tell me, Grant." I felt my annoyance notching up.

"Well . . . she was wondering . . . if maybe she could finish her senior year of high school up here."

"What?" What the hell was he talking about? Orli told me everything. We'd never had secrets and yet . . . she was considering something like this and had never told me?

"She hasn't mentioned anything to you because it's just something she's thinking about. So she wanted to tell me first, and I think she wanted me to pave the way with you."

I knew I'd probably lose Orli when she set off for college, but that was over a year away. I'd had no idea that I could be losing my daughter as soon as the coming spring.

I shook my head. "I don't know what to say. No, she's not said a word about this to me." I blew out a breath. "Why the hell would she want to do this? I don't understand. I thought she liked living in Cedar Key. She has loads of friends there. Why on earth would she want to leave and complete her senior year at a strange high school? I don't get it." My initial surprise was now beginning to turn to anger.

"I'm not sure either," Grant said. "She didn't give me a reason why. She only said it's something she's giving some thought. I'll let you handle it, Josie. It's up to you whether you want to mention this to her."

Once again, Grant deferred to me. Something he had done from the moment I'd told him that I was pregnant. I felt a sliver of selfishness creep through me. Despite the visits, the holidays, the phone calls, Grant had never really been allowed to spend long periods of time with his daughter. Had I been too selfish with Orli, wanting to keep her all to myself? I thought of my mother and questioned the fine line between being a control freak and being independent.

"So . . . how would you feel about that, Grant? How would you feel about taking on a teenage daughter full time? Would you want her living here with you? Having a kid around can certainly cramp somebody's single lifestyle." I knew I sounded bitchy, but I couldn't help it.

He waited a few moments before answering. "First of all, despite what you might think, I don't have a single lifestyle, Josie. Sure, like you, I've dated a bit here and there, but there's only been . . ." He cleared his throat. "I have a very boring life." A smile crossed his face. "If Orli made the decision to live here with me, and you agreed, then yes, of course, I'd love to have her. But I wouldn't go against you. She means the world to you. I know that. But Josie, just don't forget . . . she means the world to me too."

I nodded and remained silent.

29

Somehow I'd managed to put aside my concerns about Orli and had enjoyed the spirit of Christmas Eve.

On the drive to Grant's mother's house the next morning, my cell phone rang and I answered to hear my mother say, "Merry Christmas, Josie. I hope I'm not interrupting the festivities."

"No, no, not at all. We're driving to Molly's house. Merry Christmas, Mom. How're you feeling?"

"Actually, quite well. Give me a head's up . . . have you said anything to Orli?"

"Not really."

"Okay. Good. No sense ruining her time up there over something that might turn out to be nothing."

I had a million questions for my mother, but Orli's presence in the backseat prevented me from asking. "So you and Dad are having a good Christmas morning? And Mags is there?"

"Yes, yes. She's here. I made eggs benedict for breakfast. We're enjoying some coffee on the patio."

"Who's going with you for the testing tomorrow?"

"Your father is. Mags is going to spend some time visiting with Jane."

"Promise to call me as soon as the tests are over and you leave Gainesville?"

"Yes, I will. But Josie, it's probably going to take a while before we have any results."

If they were rushing the scan, I had a feeling they'd also rush the results.

"Listen, honey, I'll let you go. Wish Grant and Orli a Merry Christmas from all of us here and give them our love. I'll call you tomorrow. Promise."

I disconnected the call and let out a sigh.

Grant reached across the seat and squeezed my hand. "Everything okay?"

I nodded and turned around to face Orli, who had been listening to music on her iPod. "That was Nana. She wished you a Merry Christmas and sent her love. To you too, Grant."

"Oh, good. Is she feeling okay?" Orli removed the earbuds.

"Yeah, fine. She'll have those tests tomorrow and then we'll know more."

I took a sip of coffee and looked around Molly's dining room table. It had been such a great morning and afternoon. When we'd arrived, Jeff, Melissa, and Dirk were already there. I was astonished at how much my nephew had grown in the few years since I'd last seen him. He was a tall, good-looking young man, and it was obvious that he and Orli enjoyed each other's company. They'd been talking nonstop since we got there. It was good for her to have a relationship with her only cousin.

I glanced across the table, where Grant and his brother were discussing something political and Melissa and Molly were talking about a segment they'd seen on the *Today* show the week before, and I smiled. This was nice. The entire day had been nice—exchanging gifts by the tree, enjoying a turkey dinner, and now lingering over dessert and coffee. It made me realize all the holidays that I'd missed with Grant's family. All the closeness and various events. All because of a choice that I had made sixteen years before.

"Any more coffee? Pie?" I heard Molly say, and I shook my head.

"None for me. Thanks. I'm stuffed." I took the last sip of my coffee.

Melissa followed Molly into the kitchen, and a few minutes later they returned with Molly carrying a candlelit cake and both singing "Happy Birthday." All of us joined in, and I saw the look of surprise and delight on Orli's face.

Molly placed the cake in front of her granddaughter, and Orli quickly blew out sixteen candles.

"Oh, wow! Thank you. I had no idea you were doing this . . . but I'm glad you did," she said, causing all of us to laugh.

"Did you make your wish?" Grant asked.

Her glance went from her father to me, and she nodded. "Yes, I did."

She then opened gifts of bath products, books, and a lovely gold necklace from Molly.

"Your mom and I are giving you your gift on Sunday," Grant said.

"Oh, good. I like spreading out my birthday over a few days."

Dirk laughed. "Doesn't look like you missed out celebrating your day right after Christmas, cuz."

"Not in the least," Orli assured him.

Following birthday cake and more conversation around the table, I glanced at my watch and was surprised to see that it was already seven.

Molly got up to begin removing plates and glasses, and Melissa and I did the same. We followed her to the kitchen, and I had to smile because the three of us seemed so in sync. Molly began filling the dishwasher, Melissa was covering leftovers with plastic wrap, and I continued cleaning off the table.

When I walked back in, Molly said, "Oh, Josie, I wanted to ask you. Do you think it would be okay if Orli spent the night with me Saturday evening? I know Grant has lots of plans, but I'd love to spend some time alone with her."

"Of course it's okay. I know Orli would love that. We're driving her to see the campus at Emerson on Saturday, and we could drop her off here on the way back."

Melissa looked up from covering the cake. "Emerson? That's great. So she's going to be going to your alma mater?"

I leaned against the counter and shrugged. "Still not sure. This really just came up over the past few days, but yeah, I think she's strongly considering it."

"Even though it's still over a year away, I know I'd love having my granddaughter so close," Molly said.

Little do you know, I thought, *there's a possibility you could have her very close by the time this school year ends.*

Following the cleanup we found the guys watching a football game in the den and Orli and Dirk playing a game of Monopoly at the dining room table. It was refreshing to see two young people playing an old-fashioned board game rather than glued to some tech device.

"Tea, coffee, or a drink in front of the tree?" Molly asked.

"Tea would be great," Melissa said.

"Same here," I said. "Let me help."

She shooed us into the sitting room. "No, no. You gals sit and gab. I won't be very long."

I chose my usual armchair, and Melissa took a spot on the sofa.

"Molly sure does an exceptional job with the tree, doesn't she?" I said.

"She does. We come here pretty much every Christmas, so I never bother to put one up at our house. Not that I'm complaining."

I let out a chuckle and nodded. "Yeah, it's a lot of work, but with both my mom and Molly, it's a labor of love."

Melissa reached over and patted my knee. "I'm so glad you're here with us this year, Josie. I'm really happy you came."

"Thanks. I'm having such a good time."

"I know Grant's thrilled that you're here."

"Yeah, he loves having Orli for the holidays."

"True, he does." Melissa shifted on the sofa and leaned forward. "But I meant *you.*"

I wasn't sure what to say and could feel a flush creeping up my neck.

"God, Josie, you have to know . . . he still loves you so much. He always has, and no matter what . . . I don't think that's ever going to change."

"Well . . . I love him too. I mean, geez . . . we did have a daughter together."

Melissa raised her eyebrows and took a deep breath. "Look, I've known you since the first time Grant brought you to this house. I've always liked you, so I've never wanted to offend you and say anything. Besides, it's really none of my business, but . . . there's so much more going on between the two of you than simply parenting a child together. I respect the decision you made when you found out you were pregnant with Orli, but . . . you have to know . . . Grant's always been crazy in love with you. That'll never change. I just want to make sure that you *do* realize this."

Did I realize it? I wasn't sure. Actually, I'd never given it much thought. He was always so good to Orli and me. He always agreed with me, no matter what the issue, about how our daughter should be raised. But hadn't it always been about Orli? Surely, it wasn't about *me*.

Melissa reached over and gave my arm a squeeze. "I'm sorry. I probably shouldn't have said anything. It's just that . . . I see the way Grant looks at you, the way he talks about you, and it always makes me feel so bad. I adore my brother-in-law and I'd love for him to have what Jeff and I have shared all these years. And of course . . . life is so short."

I nodded and recalled what Mallory had recently said to me: You've always been that one great love in Grant's life.

"Thanks, Melissa. Thanks for being so honest. I do appreciate it."

No doubt about it—my past was definitely on a collision course with my present. And the worst part was, I didn't have a clue what to do about it.

∽ 30 ∽

Saturday was turning out to be another perfect day. The snowflakes had disappeared along with the overcast sky. Although it was cooler than when I'd arrived, the sun was shining, and it felt good to wear a winter coat along with one of my knitted hats and scarves.

It had been sixteen years since I'd returned to Boylston Street and Emerson College. It was located across the street from Boston Common, and Grant, Orli, and I walked around so that she could see the various buildings. I could tell by the look on her face that she was captivated.

"Which one was your dorm, Mom?" she asked.

Before I had a chance to respond, Grant said, "She was in the Colonial Building. Just down here."

The residence hall and suite-style accommodations were on the floors above the historic Colonial Theater, which was the oldest continuously operating theater in New England.

Orli nodded. "I bet it was so much fun being in the heart of Boston, so close to everything. You never stayed in touch with your roommate or any of your classmates, did you?"

I shook my head. "No, unfortunately, I didn't." Although I didn't say it, I knew the main reason was because of my circumstances. Leaving college, pregnant, at the end of my freshman year put me into a whole different world from the girls who stayed on at Emerson. Had I chosen to stay and had I married Grant, there was no reason why I couldn't have also continued on with my education. But sixteen years ago that wasn't the choice I'd made.

Since Orli wanted to spend the night with Molly, Grant suggested we have lunch in the North End rather than dinner. By the time we dropped her off in Marblehead, it was close to four.

"Anything special you'd like to do?" he asked as we drove away from his mother's house.

"No. I'd be happy just to go back to your place and relax."

He laughed. "You're going to need a vacation by the time you get home. I think I'm wearing you out."

I looked over at his handsome face and smiled. "Not in the least."

We entered the atrium to find Estelle Fletcher watering various plants.

"Hello, hello," she greeted us as she pointed a finger in my direction. "You still haven't come over to visit me."

I smiled, but she made me feel like a recalcitrant teen. "I know and I'm sorry. We've just been so busy since I got here."

She waved a hand in the air. "Not to worry, but maybe you could stop by in the morning for coffee."

"Yes, that would be great. Around ten?"

"Perfect," she said before bending over to water a large ficus tree in a terra cotta tub.

Grant let out a chuckle when we entered his condo. "I'm really sorry about that. Estelle can be a bit overpowering."

I laughed as I headed to the kitchen. "Nah, not a problem. I'll pop by in the morning to have a chat with her."

"How about some of my mom's turkey pie for supper? I can warm it in the oven now."

"Sounds great," I said as my cell phone went off. I saw that it was my mother.

"Josie," I heard her say. "Am I interrupting anything?"

"No, we dropped Orli to spend the night at Molly's and just got back to the condo. What's up?"

There was a pause before she said, "Well . . . I have some news for you. I had my CAT scan yesterday and we'll have those results on Monday, but . . . the doctor did a biopsy when I was there this past week, and he called this morning to tell me they got the lab report back."

"So what did it show?"

"Josie . . . I'm afraid it indicates uterine cancer."

I found my way to the stool at the counter and plunked down. "Oh," was all I could manage to say for a moment before I mustered up my nursing voice. "Well, okay. At least now we know what's going on. Did he indicate what stage it is?"

"Stage? No, he didn't mention that and I didn't think to ask. He wants to see me in his office next Tuesday. What with the bleeding, I think he wants to move on this fast."

"Bleeding? What bleeding?" This was the first I was hearing about bleeding.

"Oh . . . uh . . . I had some breakthrough bleeding the week before last. That's why I thought I should see the doctor, as I'm finished with menopause."

I ran a hand through my hair. "God, Mom! Why didn't you tell me? Yes, that's pretty significant."

"Okay. Yes, I know that. That's why I made the appointment, and now's not the time to be reprimanding me."

She was right. "I'm sorry. What can I do, Mom? What can I do to help?"

"Well, I know you're flying home on Tuesday and you arrive in Gainesville at twelve-thirty. So I made the appointment for two." There was a pause before she said, "I was wondering . . . well, I'd really like . . . for you to go with me to the appointment."

A warm feeling went through me to hear my mother request that I be the person by her side. "Yes, yes. Of course I'll go with you."

"Your father and I will pick you up at the airport, and he'll take Orli for lunch while you and I go for the appointment. Will that work for you?"

"Yes, that'll work out fine. How're you feeling, Mom? Any pain?"

"No, no. I'm okay. Still a little tired."

I had no doubt she was minimizing what was going on.

"Okay, I'll definitely go with you and I'll call you tomorrow. I love you, Mom."

"Love you too, Josie," she said before hanging up.

I turned around to see Grant holding a bottle of wine, a concerned expression on his face. "It's not good, is it?"

I swallowed the lump in my throat and shook my head, and before I knew it, tears were streaming down my face and I found myself in Grant's arms as he patted my back and attempted to soothe me.

"Come on," he said, leading me to the sofa. "I'll pour the wine, and you can tell me what's going on."

My mom has uterine cancer, I thought. *She could die. That's what's going on.* Bad news always has a way of allowing our rational thoughts to be replaced with the worst-case scenario.

"Here you go," Grant said, passing me a glass and sitting beside me.

I took a deep gulp and nodded. "Thank you," I said before blowing out a breath. "She had a biopsy and the results show uterine cancer. I don't know much more than that except she's seeing the doctor on Tuesday afternoon and she asked me to go with her."

Grant grasped my hand in his. "I admit, it doesn't sound good, but Josie, you know that there are some remarkable treatments for cancer."

I nodded. He was right. Then why did I feel so scared?

"I know it's easier said than done, but you have to think positive." He waited a few moments before saying, "Do you want to fly home sooner? I could arrange a flight for tomorrow."

I realized that once again Grant was putting me and my situation above his own. He relished the fact that Orli and I had two more full days with him, and yet . . .

Before I knew it, tears were running down my face again. I didn't deserve such a caring and thoughtful man.

I felt his arms around me as he whispered, "It's okay, Josie. Whatever you want. Whatever you think is best."

After a few moments I got my tears under control, sat back, and swiped at my face. I let out a deep breath along with a hiccup and smiled. "Thank you, but no. No. We're not ruining this trip or Orlie's birthday tomorrow. We'll fly back on Tuesday, as planned."

His smile matched mine. "Okay. We'll enjoy our wine and then have dinner."

I pushed my food around on the plate, consuming very little of it. My appetite had vanished with my mother's news.

"More wine or coffee?" Grant asked after we filled the dishwasher and cleaned up.

I knew I'd already had a few glasses but said, "Wine, please."

I settled myself on one end of the sofa while Grant poured the wine. He placed the glasses on the coffee table and then went to the CD player and inserted some discs.

By the time he sat down beside me and picked up his glass Roberta Flack's voice was filling the room with "The First Time Ever I Saw Your Face."

I looked at Grant and smiled. That was our song. It had played on the car radio the night Grant picked me up for our first date, and we had both agreed the words were written for us. I thought back to that coffee shop in Boston and the first time ever I'd seen his face. I did think that the sun rose in his eyes. And the first time we made love, I knew our joy would last forever.

"We were wrong, weren't we?" I asked.

He shifted on the sofa to look at me. "What do you mean?"

"We always thought our joy would go on forever, didn't we?"

He took a sip of wine and smiled. "It has. We have Orli. She's our joy."

I nodded, and we both remained silent for a few moments.

"You asked me a question a few nights ago, remember? Whether I ever think how different my life would be had I married you."

Grant nodded.

"I have a question for you." I took a gulp of wine. "Something I've wondered about and always wanted to ask you."

"What is it?"

I paused a moment before saying, "Why did you never ask me

to marry you, Grant? Not once did you ask, even after I told you that I was pregnant."

He fingered the stem of his wineglass and remained silent, making me think perhaps he wasn't going to answer.

And then he said very softly, "Because you never let me."

I took another sip of wine and waited.

"You never gave me the chance, Josie. You told me right up front which way it was going to go. You were leaving college, leaving Boston, and going back to Cedar Key. You told me you wanted to raise our child alone. You gave me no options." He took my hand in his. "And I couldn't pressure you. You said you'd allow me to be part of our child's life and that was the most I could hope for."

"So that was enough for you?"

He let out an exaggerated chuckle. "Enough? God, no. It was never enough. I wanted it all to be so different, but I knew you didn't. And . . . I loved you enough . . . enough to let you go. I couldn't risk losing you completely, and I didn't want the tension of my disappointment coming between us."

The words from *The Prophet* by Kahlil Gibran flashed into my mind—something about loving somebody and letting them go.

I leaned toward Grant, putting my arms around his neck and pulling his face to mine. Without even thinking, I placed my lips on his. And with no hesitation I felt his mouth responding in a long, deep, passionate kiss. Gone was the benign kiss on the cheek, and in its place I felt a surge of desire I had never felt with any other man. The kiss continued as he slid me down on the sofa and awakened a part of me that only at that moment I realized had been dormant for sixteen years.

With both of us breathing heavily, we broke apart and Grant stretched alongside me, holding me in his arms as he stroked my face.

"I've always loved you, Josie. I've never stopped loving you. I want you to know that. I want you understand why I didn't ask you to marry me, and it had nothing to do with love."

I felt my head nod as I began to realize this. Grant hadn't asked because he knew back then what my answer would be.

I lifted my face to his as his lips met mine again, and again I was consumed with desire. I felt his hands on my body before he pulled away and stared into my eyes.

"God knows I want you, Josie. But if this is going to happen, I want it to be right. I want it to be right with you, and after the news you got this evening . . . I don't think it's the right time."

I heard the huskiness in his voice, and although my body rebelled, my mind knew that once again it had to do with timing and he was right. I was confused and upset, and I felt like my life was being turned upside down.

"Okay," I whispered. "Okay. But don't leave me. Stay here with me."

He kissed my forehead as I snuggled deeper into his arms. "I'll always be with you, Josie."

⫷ 31 ⫸

Sun streaming through the living room windows woke me the next morning. Grant was still curled beside me. I pulled back a bit to stare at his face. That face I'd fallen in love with sixteen years ago. We'd come very close to making love the night before, and in all honesty, I was pretty sure that if Grant hadn't stopped, it would have happened.

I let out a soft sigh. What the hell was I doing? What was I thinking? And Simon? What about Simon Mancini? A week ago it seemed that relationship might be headed somewhere. But was that what I really wanted? I had no idea.

Grant stirred, opened his eyes, and smiled. He kissed my cheek before running his fingertip slowly across my lip. "Good morning. Did you sleep okay?"

"I did. Actually, very well."

He stood up and stretched. "Me too. *Very* well. I'm going to hit the shower if you want to start the coffee."

"Deal," I said as I stood up and fluffed the pillows on the sofa.

I spooned the coffee into the filter, filled the carafe with water, and poured the water into the coffeemaker. "Now what?" I said out loud. "Where do we go from here?"

I headed to my bathroom to take a shower and get dressed.

When I walked back into the kitchen, Grant was standing by the French doors, coffee mug in hand, looking out to the yard.

"It's our daughter's birthday today," he said.

I smiled and filled my own mug before sitting at the counter. "I know. Hard to believe it's been sixteen years."

"About last night . . ." he started to say.

I put up my hand. "No, no. It's okay. Really."

He sat across from me at the counter. "No, it's not okay. I have no idea where we might be headed, Josie."

Well, at least he was as confused as I was.

He reached for my hand. "But I want you to know you mean the world to me. I know you have a lot on your plate right now. With your mother, a new job . . . even this doctor, who seems pretty interested in you."

"Oh, no, really. He's only . . ."

"Stop. You have no idea where that might go. It might just be a colleague relationship, true. But . . . I have to face the fact that you could fall in love with him. You need to choose for yourself, Josie. I can wait until you're sure. So . . . you're going to go home on Tuesday and focus on your mother. That's your priority right now. You'll be there for her and help her through this. And I want you to know . . . I'll only be a phone call away if you need me."

I nodded. "And what about us?"

He paused for a second before saying, "Well, we'll always have a connection because of our daughter, but I'm hoping when the time is right, you and I will have something more."

I stepped into Estelle Fletcher's condo and smiled. It was like stepping back in time to a Victorian sitting room. Heavy mahogany furniture dominated the room, but instead of brocade drapes at the windows, sheer lace curtains let in the morning sunshine, giving the room a cozy rather than sinister feel.

"Come in, come in," she said, indicating that I should sit on the sofa. "I'll get the coffee and muffins."

"Can I help?"

"No, no. I'm fine."

I looked around and noticed a large painting above the credenza, realizing it was an image of the original brick structure of Danvers State Hospital.

"Here we go," she said, placing a tray on the coffee table.

I saw the oversized blueberry muffins and smiled. "Those are Jordan Marsh muffins, aren't they?"

"They are. Do you have the recipe too?"

"No, but Grant's mother does, and I used to love these."

"Ah, yes. They were quite popular around this area in the sixties. I think every housewife had the recipe."

"Did they ever discover how it got out to the public?" Jordan Marsh department store in Boston had been famous for the muffins sold only in their bakery, until somehow the secret got out.

Estelle laughed. "No, but the rumor was always that it came from some disgruntled bakery employee."

She filled my china cup with coffee as I took a bite of muffin. "Oh, they're as delicious as I always remember." I reached for a napkin and wiped crumbs from my mouth. "Isn't that the original mental facility?" I asked, pointing to the painting.

"It is. I wanted a painting of the structure and hired a local artist to compose it for me." She took a dainty sip of coffee. "My mother resided here, you know."

"Oh, she lived with you here at the condo?"

"No, unfortunately, she did not. She was a patient at the facility."

"Oh, I see," was all I said.

"She wasn't mentally ill though. No, far from it. She had the misfortune to go through menopause with the emotional symptoms that many women have."

I nodded. "I remember Grant's mother telling me that. How tragic that those women had no recourse back then."

Estelle broke off a piece of muffin, popped it into her mouth, and nodded. "No, back then women had precious few rights. My father had a mistress, you understand, and the easiest way to deal with both my mother and the mistress was to have my mother committed here."

"God, that's so sad. How old were you at the time?"

"Twelve. I went to live with my mother's sister in Lynnfield. My mother passed away about a year later. They said it was pneumonia. And a year or so after that, my father was killed in an automobile accident." She took another sip of coffee. "It was karma, you see."

I remained silent and took another bite of my muffin.

"Yes, karma. He never was able to go on and enjoy his life with his mistress. Although many people don't believe in it, it's the entire cycle of cause and effect. Like you being here at this particular time. Do you believe everything happens for a reason?"

"I'm not quite sure," I replied.

"Oh, it does, my dear. It certainly does. You might think it strange that I'd want to come and live in a structure that caused my mother so much heartache, but you see, being here allows me to fill my home with joy and love. Jerome and I had a few good years here before he passed on. We brought light to our home, and with light comes understanding and love. Much like with you."

My head snapped up. "What do you mean?"

Estelle smiled and reached over to pat my hand. "Ah, my dear. Your life is in a state of flux right now, is it not?"

How the hell did she know that?

"But you have good energy and with time, everything will balance out."

"I'm not sure I understand. I mean, gosh, you just met me for the first time the other day. You don't know me at all."

"Are you familiar with *The Wizard of Oz*?"

I was beginning to think perhaps Grant's neighbor was suffering from a mild case of dementia. "Yes, of course. I've watched the movie many times with my daughter."

She nodded. "Right. Well, always remember one of its most profound lessons—what you're looking for has been inside you all along."

Was she talking about Grant? About me?

She leaned across the table and gave my hand a squeeze. "I'm sorry if I've disturbed you." She waved a hand in the air. "But thank you for indulging me. I'm just an old woman with silly thoughts. So tell me about the birthday celebration this evening."

The sense of unease that I'd begun to feel slipped away. "We're going to a restaurant in Boston," I said, and went on to explain it was Orli's favorite.

Estelle asked me questions about Cedar Key and then launched into a tale about the history of Danvers State.

"But you see, although it has a tragic past, I firmly believe that those of us who choose to live here now have put the troubled souls to rest."

I nodded and glanced at my watch. "Gosh, it's already eleven. I really need to get going. We're picking Orli up at her grandmother's this afternoon for the birthday dinner." I stood up to leave and felt myself being embraced by Estelle.

"Thank you so much for coming to visit, Josie. I very much enjoyed it. And when you come back up here, please be sure to drop by."

She walked me to the door and gave me another hug.

"Thank you for the coffee and muffin," I told her.

"My pleasure. Oh, and Josie . . . just remember . . . every behavior has a reason and a deeper layer to it."

I walked across the atrium back to Grant's condo, convinced the poor woman talked in riddles, because I had understood very little of what she said.

I sat across the table from Grant and Orli and smiled. He had booked a corner table for us with a view of the cityscape. Candlelight danced across their faces, creating a glow, but I knew that the real reason for Orli's happiness was having her parents together for her special birthday.

We had just finished dessert and Grant and I were sipping coffee when he reached into his jacket pocket and produced a small, beautifully wrapped present.

"Happy birthday, Orli. Happy Sweet Sixteen."

He got up to kiss her cheek and placed the gift in front of her.

She shot me a huge smile and as she removed the paper, I could see the signature blue Tiffany box and white satin ribbon.

"Oh, Dad, thank you," she exclaimed as she held up a gorgeous gold chain with a gold disc dangling from it. "I love it. Look, Mom."

I took the necklace in my hand and smiled. On the front was engraved *Orli* with her birthstones forming the small numbers of 1 and 6. I turned it over to read *Love, Mom and Dad*.

How like Grant to also include me in the gift. "It's gorgeous," I said. "And I bet it was custom designed."

Grant smiled and nodded.

I reached into my handbag and passed my present to my daughter. She removed the paper and opened the box to reveal a gold bracelet that held charms that were meaningful to her.

"Oh, Mom, it's beautiful. I love it." She held it up to catch the light and then noticed a heart-shaped charm with three birthstones. "Look, Dad, it's for the three of us."

Grant took the bracelet, looked at the charm, and sent me a smile. "Thank you for including me," he said, and I was positive I saw his eyes glisten.

❧ 32 ❧

I had dreaded telling Orli about her grandmother, and coward that I was, I put it off until Tuesday morning before we left for the airport.

The day before had been spent visiting with Molly, and I didn't have the heart to ruin my daughter's last day in the Boston area.

We'd set the alarm for six, gotten up, showered, dressed, and were finishing up French toast prepared by Grant.

"Orli," I said, before taking a sip of coffee. "There's something I need to tell you. I found out three days ago . . . but I didn't want to ruin the rest of your time here."

"Is it Nana?" she asked, amazing me again with her insight.

I shot a glance to Grant, who nodded with a weak smile, attempting to give me a boost of courage.

"Yes, it is, sweetie." I reached for her hand and felt the clamminess on mine. "I'm afraid the news wasn't as good as we'd hoped. They did a biopsy last week . . . and it shows that Nana has cancer of the uterus."

Her eyes never left my face, but she remained silent.

"And so . . . they're picking us up at the airport today and Grandpa will take you to lunch while I go with Nana to meet with her doctor."

This was when Orli burst into tears, and both Grant and I jumped up to put our arms around our daughter. "Will she . . . will she . . . will she die?"

It's so true that parents would gladly endure the pain and heart-break brought to their child, because in that moment I wanted to extinguish the pain from my daughter's heart and I knew by the look on Grant's face that he felt the same.

"No, no, Orli," I heard him say. "We're thinking positive. They're making great strides today with treatment. We're going to hope for the best until the doctor explains everything later today."

She reached for her napkin and rubbed her eyes.

"Will she have to have surgery and then chemo and radiation?" she asked.

"That's what we'll find out today, Orli," I told her. "We'll know much more after we see the doctor."

"Okay," she said, and then left the table, walked into our room, and closed the door.

I let out a deep sigh. "Shit, this isn't going to be easy," I said.

Grant pulled me into his arms and put his chin on top of my head. "I know," he said. "I know."

Standing at security with Orli and Grant, I almost wished he'd just dropped us off outside. But he insisted on parking the car and coming in with us. I hated good-byes. I was never good at them, and watching while Orli and Grant hugged, I felt a sense of empti-ness.

He turned to pull me into an embrace and kissed my cheek. "You call me, okay? Call me this evening and let me know how everything went."

I nodded, too choked up to say anything.

"Okay," he said, giving Orli a last hug. "Now I want my girls to have a good flight. Orli, call me when you land."

"I will, Dad, I promise, and thank you for everything. It was the best Christmas and birthday I've ever had."

"Yes, thank you, Grant." I swallowed to prevent any tears from leaving my eyes. "Thank you so much, and I'll call you this evening."

He turned and walked away, heading to the exit without looking back.

Both Orli and I were quiet on the flight to Atlanta. I was glad that we only had enough time to use the restroom and grab coffee before boarding the Gainesville flight.

Orli dozed and listened to her music during the hour before we landed, and I held a book in front of me, reading the same paragraph over and over. My mother, Grant, and Simon consumed my thoughts, and I was grateful when we finally landed on the tarmac.

My parents were waiting for us on the other side of the glass as we walked into the gate area. I had sunglasses on, so my mother couldn't see that I was staring at her, and I was relieved to see she looked exactly as she had the week before. Dressed in an ankle-length skirt, fashion boots, and a beautiful emerald green pullover, she actually looked like the epitome of good health.

"Hey," she said, scooping both Orli and me into her arms. "We ordered up this seventy-degree weather especially for you."

Orli laughed and then went to hug my father. "You look great, Nana. Are you feeling okay?"

"Yes, yes. Fine." She waved her hand in the air, and I was certain she was putting on a good show for Orli's sake. "Now, your grandfather will drop us at the medical center. Oh, we can get coffee there, Josie, and you two are going out for lunch. Gee, maybe you're hungry too, Josie?"

"No, not at all, but coffee will be great."

At precisely two o'clock my mother and I were ushered into the doctor's office. I was certain some strings had been pulled by my mother's gynecologist to secure an appointment with the oncologist so fast on the day before New Year's Eve.

He stood up from his desk to greet us, extending his hand. Tall, in his midfifties and distinguished looking, he had a warm smile and welcoming demeanor.

"I'm Dr. Girone, Mrs. Sullivan. And is this your daughter?"

My mother and I sat in the chairs across from him, and she nodded. "Yes, this is Josie."

He sat down and folded his hands into a tent. "Okay, I have

your biopsy and CAT scan here," he said, and began shuffling through papers. "The good news is that you have a stage 1 cancer. At this point, there doesn't appear to be any lymph node involvement."

My mother sat silent while I digested his information. He was right. This was pretty good news, and I let out a sigh of relief.

"I'm told that you're an RN, Josie?"

"Yes, I am."

"Good, because from experience I'm pretty sure your mother will take in only about half of what I say, so you can be her advocate and explain more later."

I nodded.

"So what does this mean?" my mother asked. "What do we do now?"

Dr. Girone leaned back in his chair and shot her a smile. "Well, in my professional opinion and based on your health history, I'd say you're a very good candidate for robotic surgery."

"For *what?*" she asked and leaned forward.

"Robotic surgery. We're getting very good results with this. I'll send you home with information so you can read more about it, but it's less invasive, with less chance of infection, and the recovery is much faster than conventional surgery. The plan would be to remove the uterus, thereby removing the cancer. We'd also do another biopsy . . . and then, we'll see where we're at."

My mother was quiet for a few moments and then said, "And what if I choose to do nothing?"

"Nothing?" the doctor and I said at the same time.

"Yes. What if I choose to just . . . wait . . . and see where we're at."

Dr. Girone leaned across the desk and folded his hands. "I would strongly advise against that. We're dealing with a stage 1. If you wait, it could possibly increase, which would make the prognosis less favorable."

"What about chemo and radiation? Would I have to have that?"

"It's too soon to determine that right now. We'll know more after the surgery."

My mother sat back and let out a sigh. "Well . . . I think for right now . . . I'm going to choose to wait."

I'd remained silent up to this point. I glanced at the doctor and saw his pursed lips and raised eyebrows, but he said nothing.

Shifting in my chair, I looked at my mother and felt my concern, anger, and fear erupting. "What the hell! Are you serious, Mom? You're going to *wait* and do nothing? That's not an option, and this is not one of your novels where you can manipulate everything and everyone to give you that satisfying, happy ending. This is *real*. What the hell are you thinking?" I heard my voice getting louder and couldn't help it. "Don't you want to get better? How about Dad? Are you even thinking of him? My God, you're being so selfish."

Dr. Girone stretched his palm toward us as my mother remained silent. "Okay, I understand where you're both coming from. Believe me, I do. Josie, as a professional I think you know we can never force anyone when it comes to medical decisions. Mrs. Sullivan, although I don't agree with you, it is *your* decision to make. However, I want you to take the information in this packet, go home, relax, take a few days, and think about it. Will you at least do that?"

My mother reached for the packet and held it against her chest. "Yes."

I caught the wink in my direction from the doctor as he stood up.

"Good. I'll be out of the office the rest of the week. So I'd like you to call me next Monday. That gives you some time to make a decision."

My mother and I both stood up and shook his extended hand.

"If I were to have this surgery, how long would I be in the hospital, and when would it be done?"

"You'd only be there overnight. We'd have you admitted early on the morning of surgery, and you should be able to go home the next evening. As to when it could be done . . . when you let me know the route we're going, I could have you scheduled within a couple weeks."

My mother let out a sigh and nodded. "Okay. Thank you." Then she turned around, opened the door, and headed to the elevators.

❧ 33 ❧

The one-hour drive back to Cedar Key was grueling. My mother had sugarcoated the information to my father and Orli. I wasn't sure if that was for Orli's sake or if she planned to withhold all the details from my father even after they got home. She made it sound like there wasn't too much to be concerned about and surgery was something that could be considered months from now. It was difficult, but I kept my mouth shut and refrained from giving them the truth.

When they dropped us off at home, my good-bye to my mother was strained.

I kissed her cheek and said, "Call me," before taking my luggage and pulling it up the walkway.

Clovelly came running to greet us, and Orli scooped him into her arms. "Oh, I missed you," she said. "But Laura said you were a good boy."

I wheeled my luggage into my bedroom and left it there. Tomorrow was another day, and I was exhausted. We had stopped for dinner in Gainesville, and even though my poor father and Orli did most of the talking, I was grateful I didn't have to tackle supper now.

I was filling the kettle with water when the phone rang. My gaze went to the clock on the kitchen wall. I saw it was just after seven, and I had no doubt that it was Grant.

"Orli called when you landed," he said. "But I was getting a little concerned not hearing from you. How'd it go at the doctor's?"

I turned on the stove and then perched on the stool as I ran a hand through my hair. "Good and bad," I told him, and then brought him up to date.

"Yeah, your mother is trying to keep control of the situation," he said.

"Right, but this is no time for her to be the control freak she's been all her life."

"Josie, look, you know yourself that bottom line . . . whatever she decides, it's her choice. You've always prided yourself on your own independent choices."

I let out a sigh. *Yeah,* I thought, *and now I'm beginning to question if perhaps I've been wrong.*

"I know that, Grant, but it's so frustrating. Knowing, medically, what would be best for her."

"I understand that, but give her a little time. She just might come to see that waiting and doing nothing is not the way to go. I just hate seeing you so upset. Promise me you'll have an early night and get a good night's sleep. Any plans for New Year's Eve?"

I let out a chuckle. "No and since it's tomorrow night, I seriously doubt I'll have any. Orli is spending the night at Laura's, so I think I'll chill out with a few chick flicks, some wine, and popcorn."

"Sounds good. Take care of yourself, and call if you need me." There was a pause before he said, "Oh, and Josie, thanks again for coming up here with Orli. It was a great week."

"It was," I said before hanging up.

I had just settled myself on the sofa with my cup of tea when the phone rang again. *It has to be Mallory,* I thought. So I was surprised to hear Simon's voice.

"Josie, welcome back. I hope you had a good visit to the Boston area."

"Thanks, and yes, both Orli and I enjoyed it very much. How've you been?"

"Good. I had a busy week doing last-minute things in the office before we open next Wednesday." There was a slight pause, and then he said, "Listen, I was wondering . . . well, a friend of mine in Gainesville is having an informal gathering tomorrow evening at his place, and I was . . . thinking that maybe you'd like to join me."

"Oh. For New Year's Eve?"

"Right. Actually, it's more of a late afternoon dinner with drinks. He's from France and now a surgeon at Shands. His significant other is from Morocco, and she's preparing tajine. Are you familiar with it?"

"Isn't that some sort of stew?"

"Right. It's quite good, and I think you might enjoy it. Plus, the group that will be there is a lot of fun."

My first thought was Grant, but then I recalled what he'd told me, about giving Simon a chance, seeing where it might lead.

"Okay," I said. "Yes, I'd love to go, and thanks for inviting me."

"Great. Lily is with her mother for a few days. Does Orli have plans for tomorrow evening?"

"Yes, she does. A slumber party at a friend's house."

"Very good. Okay, how about if I pick you up about three? Will that work for you?"

"Perfect," I said before hanging up the phone.

I returned to the sofa and took a sip of tea. *So,* I thought, *I do believe that this qualifies as a bona fide date.* There was only one problem—I wasn't certain a date still ranked high on my wish list.

I rolled over in bed and was surprised to see the bedside clock read 8:30. Today was the last day of the old year, and what a year it had been. I'd lost a job and managed to get a new one. My daughter had turned sixteen. I'd met Simon Mancini. I had developed more of an understanding about Grant Cooper and the man that he was. And my mother had been diagnosed with cancer. I let out a yawn and stretched my arms above my head. Yes, it had been an interesting year. I headed to the bathroom as I wondered what the coming year had in store.

Walking into the kitchen, I smelled the aroma of fresh brewed coffee and smiled. My gaze caught Orli's note on the counter telling me she'd prepared my coffee and was at Laura's house.

I had no sooner sat down with my mug than I heard Mallory's voice coming through the front door.

"Are you up?" she hollered.

"Kitchen," I hollered back.

"Oh, gosh, you're still in your jammies. Did you just get up?"

"Yup. I think I needed to sleep in."

Mallory gave me a tight hug, walked to the cabinet, got a mug, filled it with coffee, and joined me at the counter. "Well, welcome home. I'm not surprised. You were constantly on the go up there, but you had a great time, didn't you?"

"I did. I'm glad I went."

"I'm so sorry about your mom, Josie. She called my mom and I found out the other day. How'd the visit go yesterday?"

I shook my head. "Not as well as I'd hoped. Oh, the prognosis actually seems fairly good, but..." I went on to give Mallory the details.

"God, she really can be such a control freak, can't she? Doesn't she realize that she has no control over this situation and by doing nothing, she'll possibly make it worse?"

"I told her all that. Grant told me last night on the phone to let go of it for right now. Let my mother have a few days to think about all of it. I mean, God, I know how devastating and scary news like this can be. I saw it with patients all the time. So...all I can do is hope my mom will do the right thing and what's best for her."

"Hmm, you're right. And so...how'd it go spending an entire week under the same roof as Grant?"

My mind flashed back to Saturday evening, wrapped in his arms all night on the sofa, and I felt a flush creeping up my neck. "Good. Very good."

Mallory leaned across the counter. "Good? Very good? That's all you have to say? Okay, what's going on?"

I let out a chuckle. "Damn you, Mallory. You're as bad as that Estelle Fletcher, practically reading my mind."

"Oh, right, what was she like? You met her?"

"Oh, yeah. I had coffee with her Sunday morning. I'm not sure what to make of her. Eccentric is putting it mildly. She told me all kinds of things. And she was full of teasing hints about things she wanted me to consider."

"Sounds interesting. Like what?"

"Some silliness about *The Wizard of Oz*. She said what I'm look-ing for has been inside of me all along. I have no idea what she means."

Mallory remained silent, causing me to stare at her. "What?" I said. "Don't tell me you know what she's talking about."

"Well . . . I'm wondering if it was in relation to Grant."

"Hmm, I did consider that, but what would it have to do with him?"

"You've avoided telling me very much about being with Grant, which leads me to think something is brewing there. I've always known how Grant feels about *you*. Maybe your feelings for him, and I don't mean friendship, have been inside of *you* all along. Things changed this past week, didn't they? I can tell."

I ran a hand through my hair and jumped up to refill my mug. "I don't know. Maybe. Yes. Actually, they did." I blew out a breath and sat back down. "It was all so . . . subtle. I mean it's not like we planned it or anything, but yeah . . . something seems to have shifted." I took a sip of coffee and fingered the spoon on the counter. "I don't know. It's almost like . . . well, like I'm falling in love with him all over again."

Mallory reached across the counter and gave my hand a squeeze. "And maybe you are. So where does that leave Simon?"

"I have no idea . . . but we have a date for tonight."

"What?"

"Yeah, he called last evening. Oh, it's a group thing. Dinner at a friend's house in Gainesville, but . . . he is actually picking me up. I'm not meeting him there."

Mallory laughed. "Well, this only gets more interesting. And how do you think Grant would feel about that?"

"He's fine with it. Actually, he told me to see Simon, to see where it might lead. He said he's willing to take a chance."

Mallory rolled her eyes. "Hmm, very gallant of him, but don't be too sure he's fine with it. Once again, he doesn't want to pres-sure you. He's giving you the freedom to make your own choice."

I nodded. "Yeah, that's exactly what I was thinking."

34

"Mom, you look great," I heard Orli say, and turned around to find her in the doorway of my bedroom.

"Thanks." I took a final look in the mirror. I'd chosen black slacks, a red pullover sweater I'd made a few years before, and black flats. "Yeah, I thought the sweater would be festive. Are you all set to go to Laura's?"

"Yup. On my way over there now. Thanks for putting together my goodie bag. We're all bringing snack food, so we'll have plenty."

"And you have your sleeping bag?"

She came to give me a kiss and hug. "Yeah, I've got everything. And you have a good time with Simon. Tell him hi for me. I'll be home by noon tomorrow."

"Okay, and you have a fun night too."

After Orli left, I walked into the family room to wait for Simon and smiled at the thought that she wished me a good time with somebody who wasn't her father. I had a strong feeling that no matter what happened, Orli would always be in my corner with her support.

Simon arrived a few minutes later, looking very nice with an open collar shirt, navy sport jacket, and gray slacks. And to my surprise, I found myself comparing him to Grant. Although they were fairly equal in the good looks department, I was pretty sure Grant scored a tad higher.

"Hey," he said, stepping into the foyer and placing a kiss on my cheek. "It's so good to see you again, Josie. You look great."

"Thanks," I told him, and realized I was also happy to see him.

"All set?"

"I am. Just let me get my handbag."

He opened the passenger door of his Lexus, and I slid in. He walked around the car and got behind the wheel, and as he settled himself in the seat, I noticed he grimaced.

"Are you okay?" I asked.

"Yeah, yeah. Fine. Just my back acting up a bit."

I recalled how it had bothered him that afternoon we'd had lunch at the Pelican and realized now that it was probably a residual injury from the car accident with Lily.

"Have you taken anything? An anti-inflammatory or pain med?"

"No, it'll be fine. Really. So tell me about your Boston visit. From the weather reports, I saw you had pretty mild weather for December."

"We did, but Orli got her wish, because we had a light dusting of snow Christmas Eve, so she was happy."

"And everything went okay staying with Grant? You liked his new place? I take it he had plenty of room for two guests."

I got the feeling he was quizzing me on the sleeping arrangements. "Yes, it's a beautiful condo. The developer did an amazing job with the restoration, and yes, Orli and I had our own guest room."

"Good. Were you able to get into Boston at all or did you stay on the North Shore?"

"We did. I was surprised to find out that Orli is considering my alma mater for college, so we took her to see the Emerson campus, and then Sunday evening we went back into Boston for her birthday celebration."

"That's great. Yeah, Boston has some superb restaurants. So your daughter might be heading to the northeast, huh? Are you okay with that?"

I glanced out the car window and let out a sigh. "I'm not really sure. Well, I mean, of course it's up to Orli where she wants to go for college, but . . . yeah, it'll take a bit of getting used to, having her so far away."

"I'm very pleased that Lily will be in Jacksonville, so I understand how you feel. Have you ever considered going back there yourself?"

I shifted in my seat to see his face better. "You mean like live there? Permanently?"

He nodded.

"No. Not ever," I said, and wondered why he'd ask that question. I also wondered why I'd neglected to tell him that Orli was also considering doing her senior year up there. "So tell me about Lily. You said she's with her mother for a few days?"

"Yeah, she'll be back with me on Saturday."

I noticed he wasn't quite as talkative as he normally was and thought perhaps his back was bothering him more than he'd admitted.

"There is some other news," I said. "I don't think my mother has shared it around town yet, so consider it doctor confidentiality."

"Of course. Is she okay?"

"She's been diagnosed with uterine cancer."

He reached over and squeezed my arm. "God, Josie, I'm so sorry to hear this. Is she seeing somebody in Gainesville?"

"Yes, an oncologist, Dr. Girone. I went with her yesterday for her appointment. She's a stage 1, and he's recommending robotic surgery. He feels she's a good candidate for that type of procedure."

"Well, if it makes you feel better, I know Dr. Girone, and he's brilliant. He's a good doctor to have. Knows his stuff, and as you probably know, they're getting very good results with this type of treatment."

"Yes, I know."

"Has she been scheduled for surgery yet?"

I shook my head. "Not yet, but hopefully within the next few weeks."

"Well, Josie, if you need any time off work, it's yours. I'm hoping the practice will be steady, but I don't want you worrying that you can't take time off to be with your mother, okay?"

"Thanks, Simon. I appreciate that," I said, and wondered if the surgery would actually come to pass.

We pulled up in front of a brick cottage in the historic district of town. I didn't wait for Simon to open my door and noticed when he turned to get out, his face scrunched up again in discomfort. He reached into the backseat and removed two bottles of wine.

The front door was opened by a dark-haired man of medium height, and even before he uttered a word, I knew this was the French surgeon. He had a cosmopolitan air about him and hugged Simon before kissing both of my cheeks.

"Welcome and Happy New Year," he said, gesturing with his arm for us to come in. "Amelle, Simon and his guest are here," he called over his shoulder.

A petite, black-haired woman in her late thirties came from the back of the house. With dark, olive skin and long glossy hair, she bordered on exotic.

"I am Jean-Paul, and this is Amelle," Simon's friend said, as they both extended their hands.

"And this is Josie," Simon told them.

"It's so nice to meet you," I said.

"And Happy New Year to both of you." Simon passed them the wine.

"Thank you. Come on in. The others are out on the patio. A mild day we're having, so we will enjoy the good weather, no?"

As we walked along the hallway and through the kitchen, a delectable aroma filled the air. I saw two other couples on the patio, standing around, holding glasses of wine.

Jean-Paul made the introductions and then went to the bar that had been set up outside. "White or red wine?" he asked.

"Red for me, please," I said.

"So Josie, we're told you're going to be Simon's new nurse," one of the women said.

"Yes, actually, he's opening the practice next week."

Her partner laughed. "Well, he can be a slave driver, so you make sure he doesn't overwork you."

Amelle jabbed his arm playfully. "Oh, Jim, stop picking on poor Simon. I'm sure he'll be a lovely boss."

Simon came to stand beside me, passing me a wineglass.

"Right, look who's talking," he said. "How many nurses have you gone through over the years?"

Jim chuckled and raised a hand. "No, no. That had nothing to do with what kind of boss I am. They left either to get married or to start a family."

They were a nice group, and I realized it was fun to socialize with medical colleagues. After about an hour, Amelle clapped her hands and said, "Okay, dinner is ready. Everybody, please go inside to wash your hands and then choose a seat at the table out here."

I looked at Simon and saw a grin on his face. I knew we were taught as children to wash our hands before meals, but this seemed like an odd request for a group of adults.

Simon and I waited outside the bathroom to use the sink. He leaned over my shoulder and whispered, "It's tradition. You'll see."

After the requested hand washing, we sat down while Jean-Paul went around refilling wineglasses. Then Amelle emerged from the kitchen carrying a unique piece of orange clay cookware that I'd never seen before. The bottom was a wide, circular, shallow dish, and the top was distinctively shaped into a rounded cone. She placed it in the center of the table.

"Have you had tajine before?" Amelle asked me.

"No, never, but it certainly smells wonderful."

"Ah," Jean-Paul said. "Then you are in for a treat."

Amelle had gone back inside and returned with loaves of French bread, which she placed around the clay pot.

"Okay," she said, taking a seat beside Jean-Paul. "In Morocco, we do not eat this meal with silverware. However, you may use a fork and knife, if you like."

"I've had tajine before, and I wouldn't ruin the experience with utensils," one of the women said, causing us to laugh.

"It is a slow-cooked stew," Amelle explained. "With chicken, vegetables, some onions, and spices. The meal is cooked in this piece of clay cookware very slowly. The lid traps the steam and returns the condensed liquid to the pot, causing the meat and vegetables to be very tender."

"Not to mention delicious," Jim said.

Amelle nodded and went on to explain. "The traditional way to eat tajine is to break off a piece of bread, dip it into the stew, and with your thumb push the food onto the bread before eating it. *Bon appétit,*" she said, breaking off a piece of the crusty bread and demonstrating.

Ah, the hand washing certainly makes perfect sense now, I thought.

Simon smiled at me. "Go ahead, give it a try."

I did and found it was quite easy to scoop a bit of chicken and vegetables onto my piece of bread. I brought it to my mouth, took a bite, and instantly knew that the flavor hitting my palete was exquisite.

"Oh, my, gosh," I exclaimed. "This is so good."

A round of laughter filled the air as the others joined in. I was immediately struck by the fact that we were taking the experience of *breaking bread* to a new level. I watched as the others broke off bread, scooped, and ate, and I was enveloped by a strong sense of communal camaraderie. Here I was with strangers I'd only met an hour before, and yet this simple cultural tradition gave me a feeling of belonging. Conversation and laughter filtered around the table, and it made me happy to be a part of it.

I happened to glance at Simon sitting beside me, and from the expression on his face, I was positive he was experiencing more back discomfort.

"Are you okay?" I whispered.

He nodded, but I could tell that he wasn't.

The eight of us had managed to finish off the entire meal. "That was delicious," I said, wiping my lips with a napkin. "Thank you so much for sharing your culture with me, Amelle."

She smiled at me from across the table. "Ah, but we're not finished. After we clear this away, we will have some Moroccan tea, and Jean-Paul wants to share one of his customs with all of you."

I joined the other three women in helping to clear the table, and again I could see that Simon appeared to be in pain. I leaned over his shoulder and whispered, "We can leave, you know. If you're in pain, we don't have to stay."

He reached up and gave my hand a squeeze. "No, I'm okay. We'll have tea and dessert."

Amelle came onto the patio carrying a beautifully ornate tea pot with a long, thin spout and proceeded to fill our cups. "Mint tea," she informed us.

"And this," Jean-Paul said, following her out, "is *La Galette des Rois,* the French cake for New Year's." He placed a round cake with flaky puff pastry in the center of the table. Sitting atop the cake was a gold paper crown. "Normally, we have this on January 6, the feast of the Epiphany, to celebrate the arrival of the Three Kings or Magi. But we will have it this evening with our friends."

"Oh, is this the cake with the prize in it?" Jim asked.

Jean-Paul smiled. "*Oui.* One slice will have a porcelain trinket inside, and that person will be the king, wear the crown, and have a good year ahead."

I had read about this French tradition and smiled as Jean-Paul sliced the cake into eight pieces, passing plates around the table.

I took a bite, and it was delicious. I detected the taste of frangipane, and on my second bite my tooth hit something hard. Careful not to swallow it, I laughed and then held up a beautiful, tiny baby Jesus. "I have it," I said, holding the prize up in the air.

A round of applause went around the table as Jean-Paul jumped up, placed the crown on my head, and proclaimed, "Bravo! You shall have a wonderful year ahead."

"Congratulations," Simon said, leaning over to kiss my cheek.

I glanced down at the porcelain trinket, thinking that since my daughter was born so close to the date of the Epiphany, it was both special and appropriate.

Following dessert, Jean-Paul built a fire in the stone pit at the end of the patio, and everyone drifted to chairs surrounding it.

I was quite surprised to glance at my watch and see that it was going on ten. It had been a wonderful evening, but I could tell that Simon's discomfort hadn't lessened.

I reached for his arm as we went to follow the others. "We can leave, Simon. Really. I can tell you're uncomfortable."

He let out a deep sigh. "I don't want to ruin your evening. I can stay."

"No, no," I insisted. "I think we should go. It's already ten, and it's an hour drive back to the island."

"You're sure?"

"Absolutely," I assured him.

We made our round of good-byes, and then I thanked Jean-Paul and Amelle for such a memorable evening.

"Thank you so much for inviting me and sharing your culture and traditions with me," I told them.

"It was our pleasure," Amelle said, and I noticed that Jean-Paul was whispering something in Simon's ear as he clasped his arm around his shoulder.

Simon nodded and caught me looking at them. "Okay, and yes, thank you both for a wonderful evening."

"I can drive back," I said as we headed to the car. "I had very little wine. You might be more comfortable in the passenger seat."

"No, I'm fine. Really."

As we headed along SR 24, Simon was quiet. He'd tuned the radio to a soft jazz station.

"That was nice," I said. "I enjoyed it so much. Thank you for inviting me."

He nodded but remained silent.

When we were entering Bronson, he said, "Josie, there's something that I need to tell you. Something that you need to know, especially if we're going to be working together."

Red flags flew up as I shifted in my seat to look at him. "What is it?"

"You've probably wondered why I don't take any pain meds for my back discomfort." He paused for a moment before saying, "It's because I can't. I'm a recovering drug addict."

I knew that the medical profession had its share of addicts. A nurse I'd trained with had a problem with alcohol, so his confession wasn't a total shock to me. Alcohol and substance abuse affected people from all walks of life—from corporate leaders to street people.

"Okay," I said, waiting for him to go on.

"It all goes back to the car accident with Lily almost ten years ago. I wasn't the cause of the accident, but I carried a lot of the blame. Stephanie was the one who was supposed to originally drive Lily to that ballet class, but at the last minute it interfered with one of her social events, so I drove. For months after the accident it bothered me that if Stephanie had driven her, if anything had been different, the accident wouldn't have happened. In addition to the guilt, I was having extreme back pain from the injuries I'd sustained. Of course my doctor prescribed pain meds."

He paused for a moment, gauging my reaction. "And you got hooked," I said softly.

I saw him nod. "Yup, as simple as that, except it was far from simple. Within a few months I discovered that it was becoming increasingly difficult to get through my workday without oxycodone. Instead of cutting back on it as the doctor suggested, I was increasing my dosage. Long story short, I basically overdosed, went into respiratory depression, and passed out. Stephanie found me on the living room floor. She called 911, and I was rushed to the ER."

My hand flew to my mouth. "Oh, my God."

He nodded. "Yeah, it was pretty damn scary, I won't lie. I woke in ICU, and I knew that was the beginning of the end. I was fortunate that I didn't lose my license to practice or my job. But with the help of a counselor at the hospital, I began attending a twelve-step program at the hospital. I was also fortunate that my partner took over my patients at the office, and when I was discharged, I went from the hospital directly to a rehab facility in Jacksonville, where I spent three months in recovery."

"My God, I had no idea. So it was pretty bad, but you wanted to get better. You're the one who did the footwork."

"Exactly. I'd seen enough in my own practice of medicine to know the addict must *want* to get better, and I did. But I admit it's not easy, because unfortunately the back pain is chronic. Something I've learned to live with. When it gets really bad, I go for acupuncture, and that does help."

"So it's still a day at a time, huh? And I know you drink wine. That doesn't bother you?"

"No, I've never had a problem with a few glasses of wine. Never had a desire to keep drinking. It's the pills that are my problem, and, yes, it's still one day at a time. But I'm doing okay. I still attend meetings in Gainesville, but I wanted you to know what was going on. As a nurse, I knew you'd think it silly that I don't even take an acetaminophen. My closest colleagues, like Jean-Paul, know my history, but I don't advertise it."

I reached over and patted his hand. "I understand and, Simon, thank you for telling me. For being so honest."

He squeezed my hand in return and said, "Thank you for understanding, Josie. I had a feeling that you would."

35

I awoke the following morning about eight and was sitting at the kitchen counter enjoying my first cup of coffee when the phone rang.

"Happy New Year," I heard Grant say.

His voice brought a smile to my face as I felt a twinge of loneliness. "And Happy New Year to you. You're up early. Weren't you out painting the town red last night?"

His laughter came across the line. "I could say the same of you, and no, I'm afraid I had a pretty boring evening. I took my mother out for an early dinner, came back here, and fell asleep by ten. Didn't even see that ball drop. How about you?"

"Actually, I did end up going out." I paused for a second, feeling a bit awkward. "Simon invited me to a friend's home in Gainesville. There were two other couples, and I had a Moroccan dish called tajine for the first time. Simon wasn't feeling well, so we were back here by 11 and I was fast asleep by midnight too."

"Oh, I see," he said, and I wondered if that was relief I heard in his tone. "Ah, tajine. It's a great dish, isn't it? I had it years ago when I visited some Moroccan friends in France."

"It was delicious, and I'm glad I had a chance to try it."

"Any word from your mother?"

I let out a sigh. "None. I don't want to badger her, but I still don't know what she's decided. If she's decided anything."

"Hang in there, Josie. I have a feeling that Shelby will end up doing the right thing. Is Orli around?"

"No. She had a sleepover last night at Laura's house. She's due home about noon."

"Okay, well, give her my love. I just wanted to call and wish you a Happy New Year."

"Thanks, Grant. I'll be in touch soon."

I hung up the phone and poured myself another cup of coffee. Taking my mug, I curled up on the sofa, deep in thought.

I thought about Simon and what he'd told me the night before. It certainly didn't affect the way I felt about him. I knew he was a competent and well-regarded physician, and I gave him credit for the struggle he lived with every single day. But I knew something had changed between us. At least on my part. I enjoyed being with him, but it now hit me that my enjoyment was more that of a friend—not a lover. I had been attracted to him in the beginning, but I now wondered if that attraction had any depth to it. Much like with Ben. Before Simon left me at the door the previous evening, he had kissed me, and that was when I realized that it was *me* who had changed. Gone were the initial sparks, and I found my mind straying to Grant and recalling the evening we'd spent on his sofa.

When the phone rang again, I was more confused than ever.

"Josie, are you busy?" I heard my mother say.

"No, not at all. Still in my jammies having coffee. How are you?"

"I'm okay. Is Orli home?"

"No, she's at Laura's till around noon. Why? What's going on?"

"I was wondering if I could come over to talk to you."

"Of course you can. Now?"

"I'll be there in about fifteen minutes," she said, and then hung up.

By the time my mother arrived, I'd thrown on a pair of sweatpants and a T-shirt. I was sitting on the sofa when she walked through the front door. My first impression was that she still looked good, dressed in tan slacks, a pale yellow blouse, and a matching cardigan that I knew she had knitted.

"You look good," I said, getting up to give her a hug. "Coffee?"

"No, I've had my fill this morning." She went to sit on the edge of the sofa.

"Did Mags get home okay?"

"Yes, she called me last night, and Jane went home yesterday."

"I'm glad they came to visit, but you're going to miss them," I said, wondering what was so important that she needed to see me at nine in the morning.

As if reading my mind she said, "I didn't come to talk about Mags and Jane. There's something I wanted to discuss with you."

I leaned forward on the chair. "About your diagnosis?"

She brushed some hair behind her ear. "Yes and no."

I took a sip of coffee and waited for her to go on.

"I was twelve when my sister, Wendy, passed away, and she was only eight." My mother fingered the strap on her handbag.

I saw no connection at all to my mother's health issue, but I nodded. "Right. It must have been difficult for you to lose a sister so young," I said, and then wondered if death was the subject my mother wanted to discuss.

She let out a sigh. "It was devastating, and I always felt it was my fault."

"Your fault? You know that you couldn't have prevented the pneumonia that took her life."

A look of anguish crossed my mother's face. "It wasn't pneumonia, Josie. It wasn't pneumonia that killed her. . . . She drowned."

"What?" I got up to sit beside her. "What do you mean she drowned? This is the first that I'm hearing of this."

She nodded, and I saw tears glistening in her eyes as she let out another deep sigh. "That's because I never wanted you to know. The locals know the real story, but being my loyal friends, they never said a word when I refused to discuss the drowning and explained that her cause of death was pneumonia."

I felt my own eyes filling with moisture. "But it wasn't?" I asked, softly reaching for her hand.

My mother shook her head and reached in her bag for a tissue. "No, it wasn't. She drowned at the beach we used to have on First

Street. Something else that you've never known, Josie, is that my
mother was a drinker."

This news astonished me. "What? Grandma Helen? I never saw
her take a drop of alcohol."

"That's because she never did again after Wendy died, but . . .
by then, it was too late. The damage had been done." She dabbed
her eyes with the tissue. "Because my mother drank, much of
Wendy's care fell to me. I really didn't mind. I adored my younger
sister. Jane and I took her everywhere with us. But that afternoon
Wendy begged me to take her to the beach, and I had already made
plans with Jane. There was some type of event going on at the library for my age group. Wendy wasn't able to follow us as usual. I
told her I'd take her the following day, but I knew she wasn't
happy. So I left her with my mother and went with Jane. Somehow,
Wendy snuck out of the house and went to the beach alone. She
couldn't swim, and that was why I was always so strict about her
not going without me."

"Oh, my God," I said as I gripped my mother's hand.

"The next thing I knew somebody was racing into the library
looking for me. They said Wendy had been in an accident at the
beach. Jane and I flew out of there, but when we got to the beach . . .
there was my little sister laid out on the sand . . . with people hovering over her. We didn't have a doctor on the island back then, but it
probably wouldn't have saved her anyway. She was already gone."

I pulled my mother into my arms and felt the tears wetting both
of our faces. "I'm so sorry, Mom," I whispered. "I'm so terribly
sorry for your loss."

After a few moments my mother pushed away from me, wiped
her eyes, and let out a deep breath as she emphatically nodded. "I
wanted you to know the truth, Josie, because I'm hoping it will
help to explain why I've been so controlling all my life. I'm not ex-
cusing my behavior . . . but I just need you to understand why."

I instantly recalled what Estelle Fletcher had said to me: *Every
behavior has a reason and a deeper layer to it.*

"And you felt responsible, didn't you? You felt guilty because
you weren't with your sister. You lost control of the situation."

My mother nodded. "I see that now, but it's taken me until very recently to understand. I did feel responsible. I felt guilty for doing what twelve-year-olds do—simply being a kid. And so I think I lived all the years since then thinking that if I controlled every situation, if I stayed on top of things, if I made sure no harm came to you or your father . . . then nothing bad would ever happen."

"And now?" I asked.

My mother reached for my hand. "And now . . . now I see that life doesn't work that way, Josie. I got slammed with my diagnosis, and that was my wake-up call. You were correct at the doctor's office when you said that I have no control over this situation. I don't. I have no control over the outcome, but I realize now that I *do* have control over what I do about it."

I let out a sigh of relief and felt my vision blurring. "And so, what are you planning to do?"

"I'm calling Dr. Girone on Monday. Your father and I have discussed it over the past few days. I'm going to have the surgery, and then . . . well, we'll hope for the best."

I scooped my mother into my arms. "I love you, Mom. You're doing the right thing, and I'll be with you every step of the way."

When my mother left, my immediate thought was to share the news with Grant.

"Oh, Josie, I'm so happy for you. I told you she'd do the right thing. What made her finally change her mind?"

I proceeded to share the story of my aunt, Wendy.

"Wow," I heard Grant say. "I guess it's true that everybody has a story, isn't it? I know you're relieved, and I'm sure Orli will be too. When is the surgery, do you know?"

"No, but we should find out next week. I know I'll be a wreck, but at least she's decided to try to get better."

"Exactly. Call me next week and keep me posted."

I disconnected with Grant for the second time that day and thought about both Simon and my mother—how each of them had encountered a life-changing experience and yet they both had the strength needed to go forward with their lives.

And that was when it hit me. Despite what I liked to think, my own life was in a state of limbo.

❧ 36 ❧

I walked into the office of Dr. Simon Mancini at nine-thirty the following Wednesday and was shocked to see the waiting room filled with people. Actually, overflowing with people, because every seat was taken and some were standing.

My gaze flew to Brandy, who smiled and shrugged. "Guess we have a huge run on sick people," she said.

"We don't even open till ten," I told her.

She shrugged again. "What can I say? They were all out there on the sidewalk and porch when I got here a little while ago."

This was crazy. I raised my hand in the air. "Okay, people. What's going on? Are *all* of you sick and in need of a doctor?"

Raylene was the first to respond. "Well, yes. I have a bunion that I think he should look at, but"—I saw a smirk cross her lips—"I also want to meet our new doctor face-to-face."

Ah, so *that* was what this was all about. "Okay," I said again. "Those of you who are really sick, of course you'll be seen. If you think it can wait a day or so"—I directed my stare toward Raylene—"then make an appointment with Brandy. As for the rest of you . . . well . . . you'll just have to wait until Dr. Mancini has his open house."

"Open house?" Brandy said. "What open house?"

I shushed her with my glare and whispered, "Beats the hell outta me," before heading to my office. I sat down in my chair and laughed. What had I been thinking? Of course the locals would come and want to meet the new doctor. Shame on me for not considering that.

I looked up as Simon appeared in the doorway. "I just peeked into the waiting room. My God, is there a flu outbreak or something?"

I let out a chuckle. "Not quite. I'm afraid I neglected to tell you we have a fair number of nosey and inquisitive residents on the island."

"So they're not all sick?"

"Right. That's the good news. The bad news is . . . you're going to have to throw an open house."

"Are you serious?" he asked, but I saw the smile that crossed his face.

"Yup. 'Fraid so."

He stepped into my office and closed the door behind him. "Well, I think that can be arranged. With your help, of course. Gosh, I guess I should have thought of that."

"You and me both, and yes, I'd be happy to help."

"Josie, I heard the news about your mom. I'm so glad to hear she's agreed to have the surgery. Do you know when it's scheduled?"

"Yes, a week from Friday, the sixteenth."

"Okay, well, I'm officially giving you Friday off and the following Monday."

I began to protest, but he held up his hand. "Doctor's orders," he said, and left my office.

When I returned to the waiting room, I saw that things were more in control, with only about six people sitting there, including Grace with Solange.

I walked over to her and bent down to take the baby's hand. "Are you sick?"

"No," Grace said. "I'm afraid it's Solange. I think she might have an ear infection. She's been up all night crying, pulling at her ear, and she has a fever."

I nodded. "Yeah, that's what it sounds like. It shouldn't be too long till you're seen."

"Thanks, Josie." She grabbed my wrist. "And Josie, I'm so sorry. I saw your mom at the coffee café earlier. She's having surgery next week?"

"Yeah, but we're all thinking positive," I told her.

The day went pretty smoothly for a first day. We had a steady flow of patients with cold symptoms, concerns about blood pressure, and even two who required sutures from a fishhook laceration and a fall on oyster shells. We closed the office at four. I raced home, popped a meatloaf into the oven for supper, and had just poured myself a cup of coffee when there was a knock at the back door.

"Hey, Chloe. Come on in. I just brewed a fresh pot of coffee. Would you like some?"

"That would be great," she said, settling herself at the counter. "With you not working at the yarn shop anymore, I haven't seen much of you since you got back from Boston. I wanted to tell you how sorry I am to hear about your mom."

I filled another mug and joined her. "Yeah, thanks. It's been a bit nerve-racking, but we're all thinking positive. The surgery is a week from Friday."

"Right. Well, I had an idea but wanted to discuss it with you first. I thought it might be nice if I designed a cowl for your mother, to wish her well in her recovery and to let her know how much she means to all of us at the yarn shop."

"Oh, Chloe. What a great idea. She'd love that. I know she would."

"Okay, great. I did a little research and I found out that the color for uterine cancer is peach. I haven't decided yet what type of yarn I'll use, but I'll start working on a design. I'm sure all the women in the knit group will want to make these cowls to sell at the Arts Festival in April, the way they did with the Compassion Shawl that Dora designed. So we can also raise some money for a good cause."

"That's a terrific idea. I know my mom will be so pleased, and you're right, as soon as the women see your design, I'm sure they'll want to use it for a fund-raiser."

"So you and Orli had a nice time in Boston?"

"We did. It was great to be back up there again, and it was a special time for Orli."

"Have you ever considered relocating up there? After all, Orli's dad lives in the Boston area, and I know you liked it years ago when you were there for college."

"Actually, I haven't said anything, but Orli is thinking she might like to attend Emerson. So... who knows what might happen. I do love that area, but I've never given any thought to leaving Cedar Key."

"No, I didn't either when I first came here after my marriage with Parker broke up. And I love being so close to Grace and her family and Aunt Maude, but... sometimes things change in life. Sometimes we're given an opportunity to move on and begin a new chapter."

I leaned across the counter. "What are you saying? Are you thinking of moving?"

Chloe laughed and waved a hand in the air. "No. Not at the moment anyway, but... well, Gabe has asked me to go away with him for a weekend."

"That sounds promising. I take it the two of you are getting serious?"

"He's a really nice guy, Josie. We've spent a lot of time together the past few months, and I love being with him. That doesn't happen all the time. Hey, everybody has flaws, but it's so nice to meet somebody and truly enjoy their company and discover you have a lot of things in common."

Hmm, I knew what she was saying.

"That's great, Chloe, and I'm happy for you. Is he still leaving Cedar Key in April? Does he want you to go to Philly with him?"

"I think he will return to Philly, at least for a while. He'd like me to visit Ormond Beach with him for a weekend."

"Oh, on the east coast. I was there a few years ago. Orli and I went over for a few days. It's a nice, small town. Well, not as small as Cedar Key," I said, then smiled. "But it's also a coastal town, though on the Atlantic rather than the Gulf. Why Ormond Beach?"

"Gabe has been there a number of times, and he's fallen in love with it. He wanted to spend the winter here to give himself some time to consider his long-term plans."

I raised my eyebrows and waited for her to go on.

"I've discussed it with Grace but not Aunt Maude yet, although knowing her, I have no doubt that she'd encourage me. Ormond Beach doesn't have a yarn shop, so . . ."

"Oh, wow, Gabe is such an expert knitter. Is he considering opening a yarn shop over there?"

Chloe laughed. "Well, that's one of the plans, yeah. But the bigger one is that he'd like to purchase a farm along with a few alpacas and spin the fiber to sell at the shop."

"Oh, my gosh, that's quite a venture. But are there farms over there? I thought it was pretty much city."

"Just off SR 40, before you get to the downtown area, there's still a country setting with some farms, yet it's only a ten-minute drive to where the yarn shop would be located."

"That really sounds ideal," I said, and then it hit me. "Oh! And he'd like you to live there, too, and help him run the shop?"

Chloe nodded. "Nothing is definite. I mean, he hasn't even found property with a house or business space. It's just something that we've been discussing, so that's why he'd like me to spend a weekend there with him."

"Well, I think it's a great idea and you should at least go for the weekend. Have you ever been to Ormond Beach?"

She shook her head. "No, never been over there. Grace said the same thing, that I should at least go and check it out."

"I agree, and I think you're right about Aunt Maude. I have no doubt that she'd encourage you. Remember when Grace went to Paris for those months with Lucas? Both you and Maude supported her, and I know they'll do the same for you now."

"You're probably right, and Ormond Beach is certainly a lot closer than Paris. It's not quite a three-hour drive from here, so we'd be able to visit frequently."

"Of course you would. I'm excited for you, and like you said, it could be a whole new chapter opening up."

After Chloe left, I began peeling potatoes to go with the meat-loaf and gave some thought to her news. I was genuinely happy for Chloe, but her situation only intensified my realization that my own life was definitely in a state of limbo.

In the week since I'd returned home, I'd seen Simon twice: the New Year's Eve dinner and today at work. On his part, nothing seemed to have changed. Even at the office earlier, he'd seemed attentive to me, friendly. We'd joked back and forth a bit. So what was nagging at me?

I had to be honest. I liked Simon. I liked him a lot, as a friend and as my employer, but that was as far as it would go. I knew that now—because it was Grant whom I couldn't seem to get out of my mind. And it was Grant I missed.

❧ 37 ❧

The following evening at the yarn shop, we had a full house for our knitting group. I was very happy that both my mother and Lily had decided to attend.

I glanced over and saw that Leo was curled up beside Lily's feet as she knitted away and answered questions from the group.

"So what you're saying," I heard Dora comment, "is that all of your patterns have been converted to Braille? And you read a portion and then knit a portion?"

"Exactly," Lily said. "I can download books through the National Library System, but I can also access many free patterns, just like all of you, from Ravelry and other sites. I then convert text documents into Braille for my personal use."

"Do any of the patterns already come in Braille form?" Chloe asked.

Lily nodded. "Yes, there's a wonderful lady in Arizona, Marjorie Arnott, who has a small Braille embossing business, and she produces knitting and crochet pattern books and I can read them in hard-copy Braille."

"Well, I think that's just wonderful," Dora said.

I agreed, but what impressed me the most was the fact that despite Lily's independent attitude, she also understood the need to depend on others when it was required.

The conversation shifted to my mother, and I heard Sydney say, "So the surgery is a week from tomorrow?"

My mother nodded and let out a deep sigh. "Yeah. The doctor wanted to move on it as soon as possible."

"Oh, I agree. And you'll be back home the next evening?"

"That's the plan," my mother said. "Josie wants to go with us, so we've decided the three of us will drive to Gainesville on Thursday, book a hotel, and be there for my early check-in on Friday morning."

"That's a very good idea," Dora said. "And how nice to have a nurse in the family."

"Oh, I almost forgot," Chloe said, looking up from her knitting. "As soon as you have any information, Josie, please call me. We have a telephone tree in place. Then I'll call Dora, and she'll call the next person on the list. This way, you won't get all the calls to find out how Shelby is doing, but we'll all know what's going on."

I felt a smile cross my face. "Sounds like a plan to me."

"What's this I heard about an open house at the doctor's office?" Raylene questioned.

"Yes, Dr. Mancini has decided an open house might be a good way for him to meet his patients. We're working on the details, but I think it'll be held the end of the month."

"Oh, that *is* a good idea," Sydney said. "I heard you were overflowing on opening day, and many were curiosity seekers."

I shot a glance at Raylene and laughed. "Yeah, you could say that."

"Well, I'm very happy to have him here on the island," Grace said. "He saved me a trip to Gainesville for Solange and her ear infection. She's already feeling much better."

Just before nine Sydney helped Dora prepare the coffee and carrot cake for the evening's snack, and Chloe appeared from the back room carrying a basket, which she presented to my mother.

"This is for you, Shelby. All of us baked something, and we added some chocolate, jams, and other goodies to help you recuperate from your surgery." She leaned over to place a kiss on my mom's cheek.

I saw the moisture in my mother's eyes as she hugged the basket to her chest. "Thank you so much. You guys are just the best."

They were. The knitting group embodied the kind of female friendship and community that became even more important during times of difficulty.

The following week at work brought a steady stream of patients, and Simon continued to be friendly. We had just closed the office for the day on Wednesday afternoon and I was going over some patient charts in my office when I looked up to see him standing in the doorway.

"Have you got a minute?" he asked.

"Sure," I said, waving to a chair. "What's up?"

"I hoped maybe we could discuss the open house. I was thinking late afternoon on the thirtieth?"

I glanced at the calendar on my desk. "Yeah, that sounds good. My mother's surgery will be out of the way, and a Friday is good."

He nodded. "We should have some food. What do you suggest?"

"Well, probably pastry would be best with coffee and tea. I know if I put the word out, the women will all want to donate something." I looked at the appointment book. "We have patients only till noon, so that'll give us some time to set up and get organized."

"So should we say three till five?"

"Yeah, that would be good. Oh, how about if I do up a flyer and we have it posted around town at the Market and other shops?"

"Good idea."

I recalled the telephone tree that Chloe had mentioned. "What I'll do is call Chloe about the women donating baked items and I'll get a list put together, so we don't end up with too many of the same things."

Simon chuckled. "Not only did I not think to even have an open house, but I would have no idea how to get it together. So thanks, Josie. I really appreciate your input."

I smiled. "It'll be fun. Hey," I said as an idea struck me. "Why don't you and Lily come for dinner Monday evening, and then you and I can go over the list of things we need to get done."

"Oh, that's great, but Lily is leaving on Saturday for a few days with her mother. I can come solo though, if that's okay."

"Of course it is." I glanced at my watch and saw it was almost five. "Well, if you don't have anything else for me to do, I think I'll head home."

"I'm all set," he said, walking around my desk to lean down and give me a quick hug. "And Josie, I'm wishing your mother all the best with the surgery. You're leaving tomorrow afternoon for Gainesville, right?"

I nodded. "Yeah, and I won't lie, I'll be damn glad when this is all over with."

He squeezed my arm. "It's pretty nerve-racking but keep thinking positive, and do me a favor . . . could you call me after the surgery to let me know how it went?"

"Absolutely. Thanks, Simon."

I walked in the back door at home to find Orli on the telephone, and I heard her say, "Oh, here she is now."

"It's Dad," she said, passing me the phone.

"Hey, Grant. What's up?"

"I just wanted to make sure everything was on track with your mother. You're going to the hotel tomorrow afternoon, right?"

"Yeah, that made more sense than leaving so early Friday morning. Orli is going to be spending the night at Laura's house, so that's all been arranged."

"Good. And yes, it's better to do that rather than rushing. Maybe you can chill out tomorrow evening at the hotel. Okay, well, I'll be in touch. And Josie . . . stay strong."

I hung up the phone and smiled. Grant always did have the utmost trust in me. Although I've never considered myself a strong person, I knew that right now I had to be for my mother's sake.

❧ 38 ❧

The alarm clock woke me at five Friday morning. Before I hit the shower, I brewed myself a cup of coffee and stood gazing out the hotel window at the dark parking lot. I was scared. Damn scared. Not just about my mother's diagnosis, but because none of us had any control over the outcome. There I was trying to explain this to my mother when in truth I hated the fact as much as she did. I let out a deep breath. This was one of those times when I realized that no matter what, it was out of our hands.

I met my parents downstairs in the lobby at six-thirty as we'd planned.

I saw my mother and had to smile. She looked more like she was heading to one of her book signings than to a hospital for surgery. Her hair looked great, makeup perfect, and she was wearing black slacks with a gorgeous, pale blue cashmere pullover. I had opted for jeans and a sweatshirt.

I walked up to give her a hug and heard her say, "Oh, Josie. Really? Didn't you pack more appropriate . . ."

She didn't finish her sentence but waved a hand in the air, a sheepish expression covering her face, and kissed my cheek. "Okay," she said. "Let's get this show on the road."

* * *

My dad dropped my mother and me off at the front door of the hospital while he went to park the car.

When he returned, the three of us headed to the elevator that the receptionist indicated and ascended to the designated floor. I found a seat in the waiting room while my parents tended to the admitting paperwork. They returned a short time later with a woman leading the way.

She explained that she'd escort my mother to the surgical floor and show my father and me where we could wait. Another elevator took us to that area, and she indicated a large room already crowded with waiting loved ones.

"Now, one of you may come with us to the holding area before Mrs. Sullivan is taken into surgery."

"I'll wait here," I said.

The woman nodded. "Very good, and your father will return here. This is where Dr. Girone will come to find you when he finishes."

I leaned over to hug my mother and kissed her cheek. "Be a good patient. I love you," I told her, and was glad she returned my hug quickly and allowed my father to take her arm, because I could feel my eyes filling with tears.

I walked into the waiting area and found a seat isolated from the groups of people. I had brought some knitting in a tote bag, but I knew I wouldn't be able to focus on my sock pattern.

I glanced across to an elderly woman, who gave me a smile. "There's a coffee machine over there," she said, pointing to a counter along one of the walls.

"Oh, thank you," I told her, standing up. "Can I get you a cup?"

"No, dear. I've had my quota for this morning."

I returned with my coffee and shot her a smile. "Is your husband in surgery?" I asked.

She nodded. "Yes, I'm afraid so, dear. Yours too?"

I shook my head. "No, my mother."

"It doesn't matter who it is, it's always difficult. This may sound silly," she said, and brought a tissue to her eyes, "But tonight . . . it will be the first time in sixty-eight years that I won't be sleeping with my husband."

I jumped up to sit beside her and patted her hand. "It's not silly at all. I don't imagine that you'll sleep very well," I told her.

"No, I don't think that I will."

Both of us remained silent, lost in our own thoughts.

After a few minutes she stood and patted my hand. "I think I need some fresh air. If I don't see you again, I wish you the best."

"Same to you."

I watched her leave and did a double take as I saw a man enter the waiting area, scan the room, and catch my eye.

I jumped up. "Grant?" I ran toward him as his arms opened to envelop me. "What on earth are you doing here?"

He laughed and kissed my cheek. "Surprise! You didn't think I'd let you go through this alone, did you?"

"When . . . how . . ." My thoughts were an incoherent mess, and he laughed again, leading me to a quiet area of the room.

"I flew down late last night."

I shook my head in disbelief. "I can't believe you're here. Wait until Orli finds out."

A grin covered his face. "Our daughter already knows. She and your parents were in on the surprise."

I reached for his hand and then gave it a squeeze. "Thank you. Thank you for coming." Until that moment I hadn't realized how alone I had felt.

"Your mom's gone to surgery?"

"Yeah, my dad is with her in the holding area. He'll be back here shortly."

"She's going to be okay, Josie."

Hearing him say the words made me feel better.

My father found us a little while later. "Ah, you made it," he told Grant, giving him a hug. "Got in all right last night?"

"Yes, it was a good flight. I got the rental car and made it to the hotel by eleven."

"Is Mom okay?"

"A little nervous, but she'll be fine. She was already pretty drowsy when I left her. Let's find the cafeteria and get some breakfast. It's going to be at least three hours till we hear anything."

* * *

It was just past noon when I looked up and saw Dr. Girone walking toward us. The three of us jumped up as if we were one person.

He extended his hand to my father. "Shelby is in recovery. The surgery went well, and she should be back in her room in about an hour. I'll meet you there at that time."

"Thank you," my father told him, and I heard the sigh escape his lips.

I gave my father a hug and patted his back. "Okay, let's go get some coffee and then we'll head to Mom's room."

We arrived just as they had transferred her into her bed. She was awake but groggy. My father went to her side, taking her hand and kissing her cheek.

"Dr. Girone said the surgery went well and he'll be in here shortly to talk with us."

She nodded and forced a smile. "Is Josie here? Where's Josie?"

"Right here, Mom," I said, going to the other side of the bed and reaching for her hand. "You did great."

She smiled again, and I could tell she was fighting to keep her eyes open. "Is Grant here?"

"Right here," he said, coming to stand behind me as he put a hand on my shoulder.

Her smile increased and she nodded. "Good."

A few minutes later, Dr. Girone entered the room with a nurse.

"You did very well, Shelby. I don't like to speak too soon, but from what I can tell right now, I don't think you'll need radiation or chemo. I'll know more in ten days when I get the path report back."

"Oh, thank God," I whispered, and the flood of tears that I'd held back all morning was released as I felt Grant's arms go around me.

"That sounds like good news," my mother said.

A huge smile covered my father's face. "It certainly does."

"Okay, then." Dr. Girone patted my mother's arm. "The nurses will be coming in to check on you, and Mr. Sullivan, you indicated you'd like to spend the night here with your wife, so later this evening they'll bring in a cot for you. And if you do as well as I think you will, you'll probably be released to go home tomorrow evening. I'll see you before you're discharged."

"Thank you," my parents said at the same time.

I went back to my mother's bedside. "Are you in pain? Do you need anything for discomfort?"

"No, I'm fine at the moment. Josie, I'm going to be dozing most of the day. Why don't you and Grant go home? You can call your father later to check on me."

I looked at Grant and saw him nod. Leaning over, I kissed my mother's cheek. "Okay. I have to call Chloe and give her the good news so she can let everybody know." I went to kiss my dad and noticed that the worried expression from that morning had disappeared. "I'll call you later, and make sure you eat."

"Will do," he said.

We arrived back on the island by late afternoon, and that was when I wondered where Grant planned to stay during his visit.

He was just pulling up to my house when I asked, "Did you book a room somewhere?"

"Oh . . . ah . . . no. Actually, I need to do that."

He turned off the ignition, and I looked over to see an uncomfortable expression on his face.

"Well . . . no. You really don't have to. I mean, that would be silly. You've come all the way down here . . . and we do have a guest room."

"Are you sure?"

I paused for one brief second. "I'm sure," I said, and headed to the front door.

"Coffee?" I asked, going to the kitchen just as my cell phone rang.

"Sounds good," Grant said, taking a stool at the counter.

It was Orli on the phone. I had called her from the hospital with the good news. She was grateful and happy about her grandmother but also found it humorous that Grant had managed to surprise me.

"I was wondering if it would be okay if I stayed at Laura's again tonight, but I was going to come home to see Dad and get a few things."

"Sure, that's fine," I told her as I filled the coffee carafe with water. My devious mind now wondered if perhaps Grant's staying here alone with me was part of the plan as well.

⧉ 39 ⧉

Orli had just left to return to Laura's with fresh clothes, and Grant and I were finishing up our coffee when I heard Mallory coming through the front door.

"It's me," she called, and came into the kitchen to pull me into her arms. "I'm so happy about the good news."

I noticed that her hug was extratight, and when she pulled away I saw the tears in her eyes. "We're all so happy! My mother is planning to visit next week. She was so worried. We were *all* worried. My mom called the rest of the Sisters to let them know what's going on. God, listen to me, I'm rambling." She let out a laugh. "Hey, Grant. Good to see you."

Grant and I both laughed. "How about some coffee? Looks like you could use more of a jolt."

Mallory wiped at her eyes and chuckled. "God, I was such a wreck, but I didn't want to say that to you."

That's what a good friend does, I thought. *Hides her own fears.*

I passed Mallory a coffee mug. "I think she's going to be okay, but we'll know more when she sees the doctor in ten days."

She sat down to join Grant and me at the counter and took a gulp of coffee. "You were so strong, Josie. I don't know how you did it. I would have fallen apart completely if it had been my mother."

I smiled and shook my head. "No, Mallory, you wouldn't have. I know you as well as you know me."

She waved a hand in the air. "Well, I'm just so glad this is behind us. Oh, hey, my mother said that Mags wants to plan a get-together for the five of them."

"Really? Like a trip somewhere?"

"No, a gathering here. On the island. Mags called it a celebration of life and said she'll organize all of it. And you and I are invited."

I let out a chuckle. "Oh, Lord. They're going to allow us into their inner sanctum?"

"Guess so. They must think we're big girls now." She placed her mug in the sink. "So how long are you staying, Grant?"

"I'm booked to fly back next Wednesday."

I didn't realize this. I'd assumed he'd probably return to Boston in a day or so.

"Well, great. You and Josie will have to come for dinner one evening. Where're you staying?"

He remained silent for a moment, shot a glance at me, and said, "Ah . . . right here. Josie offered her guest room."

Mallory's gaze went from me to Grant. "Oh . . . I see. Well, listen, I need to get going. You guys take care, have fun, and Josie, call me and we'll confirm for dinner."

Her wink and smile as she left didn't escape me, or the fact that she'd shown no surprise at Grant being in town.

"So," I said, suddenly feeling awkward. "We need to think about dinner. I did defrost some steak before I left yesterday."

"Sounds great. I'll fire up the grill."

I watched Grant head out to the patio and felt my heart turn over. An insignificant task—a man about to cook steak. But it wasn't that—it was everything. It was the fact that he'd always allowed me to grow and become the person I was meant to be. It was his loyalty and continued caring. It was that he'd left everything in Boston to fly down here and be with me when he knew I most needed him. It was his eternal and everlasting love for me. And in that moment I knew without a doubt that Grant was everything to me and that Mallory had been right. I had loved Grant from the moment that I'd met him. The only difference now was the fact that I was mature enough to realize it.

I smiled as I began preparing a salad. Grant had gotten the grill going and was staring through the French doors at me. Our eyes met and locked, and my smile grew wider before I pulled my gaze back to the salad. A minute later he walked into the kitchen.

"How about some wine?" he said.

"Perfect. I have a nice Beaujolais in the wine rack. Is rice pilaf okay with you?"

"Sounds good. I have the grill on low, so just let me know when you want me to put the steaks on."

"You can start them in about twenty minutes." I watched him uncork the wine and took the glass he offered me.

"Here's to life," he said, lifting his glass and touching mine. "And to your mother's recovery."

I nodded. "And . . . here's to you and me."

He stared at me, paused for a second, and said, "I'll drink to that."

I joined him at the counter, and staring at his face I realized that Grant had aged well over the years. Except for a bit of gray at his temples, he didn't look much different from the man I'd met at the coffee shop years before—the man I'd fallen in love with.

I took a sip of wine and then asked, "Has Orli said any more about wanting to finish her senior year with you?"

He shook his head. "No. Not a word." He reached across the counter and took my hand. "You know, Josie, I won't go against you. If you'd rather she stay here, I'll back you on that."

I nodded. I knew he would. "It's up to Orli. It's not fair of me to deny her this experience if that's what she wants, but thank you for your support."

Grant cleared his throat before asking, "So how's it going with you and Simon? Are you still dating?"

I let out a chuckle. "Oh, I'm not sure dating is the right term.

He's a good friend. A nice person and pleasant to work for. But . . . beyond that . . ." I shook my head. "No. There's no romantic interest on my part. Oh, shit," I said as a thought occurred to me.

"What is it?"

"Damn. I just remembered . . . I invited Simon for dinner on Monday."

"Oh. Why would you do that if you're not interested in him?"

"We're having an open house at the office. So people in town can come and meet him without faking a sickness to do so."

Grant laughed. "Did they really?"

"They really did, so I suggested we have an open house, which will be at the end of the month. We're working on the list for food and trying to get it organized. I asked Simon to dinner so we could discuss it. But now . . . well . . ."

"Ah, now I understand. I'm staying here and you think that might create a problem?"

I nodded.

"Nah, not a problem at all. I look forward to meeting Simon."

I was afraid he'd say that.

"Can I refill your glass?" Grant asked as I curled up at one end of the sofa.

"Yes, thanks. That steak was cooked to perfection."

"It was a good dinner. I enjoyed it too," he said, passing me my glass.

I took a sip and let out a deep sigh. "This is nice," I told him.

I had called my father earlier, and he said my mother was doing well and resting comfortably. If she was doing as well in the morning, she'd be able to come home the next evening. A sense of contentment came over me; all was right in my world.

Grant reached for my ankle and began massaging it. "It is, and you look the most relaxed I've seen you in a while."

I put the wineglass on the coffee table and scooted next to him. His arm went around my shoulder.

"I am," I said softly, and raised my face to his. "I also feel like I've turned a corner."

He reached for my hand and brought it to his lips. "In which way?"

The surge of desire that I'd felt at Grant's condo was returning. "Remember when you mentioned timing at your place? You said you didn't think the timing was right?"

He nodded before placing his lips on mine. What began as a flicker quickly turned to a deep and passionate kiss. As I felt his hands on my body, I knew in my soul that I loved Grant. I had always loved Grant. And I always would.

"That timing," I whispered as I pulled my lips away from his. "That timing is *finally . . .* perfect."

I stood and reached out my hand. "I want you, Grant. I want you to make love to me."

As he clasped my hand and followed me to the bedroom, I also knew in my soul that Estelle Fletcher had been spot on—the love I felt for Grant Cooper had really been inside of me all along.

≈ 40 ≈

I woke the following morning the way I'd fallen asleep—curled in Grant's arms, my head on his chest. I felt the smile that covered my face as I recalled the previous evening of lovemaking. Sex had never been a problem with us, and after sixteen years it had proved to be even better. Grant was a passionate and giving lover. A man who not only received pleasure but easily returned it.

I felt him stir and pulled away to stare at his handsome face.

He brushed a strand of hair behind my ear. "Good morning, beautiful," he whispered.

"Good morning to you. Sleep well?"

"The best," he said as I felt his hand slide down my thigh.

"Oh, hey, our daughter could be coming in the door any minute."

"And your point is?" he asked as he pulled me closer.

Whatever my point had been quickly vanished in the heat of the moment.

An hour later I was still curled up in Grant's arms, relishing the emotion of what we had just shared again, when I heard the front door slam and Orli's voice calling, "Mom, I'm home."

I leaped out of bed, searching for my nightgown, and caught the grin on Grant's face.

"What? You think this is humorous?"

He let out a chuckle but did get up and begin putting on his jeans. "Josie, really? I think Orli has a complete understanding of how she came to be."

"Yeah ... well ..." I flung my nightgown over my head and reached for my robe. "Whatever. Maybe you should stay in here until she goes into her room."

"Right, and you think she won't notice that the guest room bed wasn't slept in?"

"Damn," I said, and heard the knock on my door.

"Mom? Are you awake?"

"I'll be right out," I called, and heard my voice crack.

"Okay, just wanted to let you know I'm back."

I let out a deep breath, ran a hand through my hair, and shot Grant a withering glance before leaving the room.

Walking into the kitchen, I saw Orli preparing the coffeemaker.

"Oh, thanks," I said as I placed a kiss on her cheek.

"I thought Dad was staying here last night," she said, and then I saw her gaze shift behind me.

I turned to see Grant emerging from my bedroom.

"Oh." She let out a giggle. "I guess he *did* stay here. Good morning, Dad."

Grant walked over to Orli, placed a kiss on her cheek, and said, "Good morning, sunshine. Ah, coffee brewing. Well done."

"How's Nana?" she asked as if we were the typical American family enjoying morning conversation while I stood in my kitchen feeling like a naughty teenager.

I cleared my throat and nodded. "Fine. She's fine. I spoke to Grandpa last evening, and it looks like she'll be able to come home later today."

Orli smiled and reached for two mugs from the cabinet. "Oh, good! I just knew she'd do well. Can we go visit her when she gets home?"

"Well, we'll have to check with Grandpa. But yes, I'm sure we can stop by for a brief visit."

She placed the filled mugs in front of us. "Okay. Let me know what time we can go. Enjoy your coffee. I'm going to take a shower."

I swear that was a smirk I saw cross my daughter's face.

As soon as she left the kitchen, Grant burst out laughing. "Josie, you need to chill out. I have a feeling our daughter knows precisely what went on here last night . . . and from what I can see, she's entirely fine with it."

Maybe he was right. I felt a grin cross my lips. I pulled up a stool and joined him at the counter. Placing my chin in my hands and leaning toward him, I said, "Okay, Mr. Know-It-All . . . and where do we go from here?"

"I thought you'd never ask," he replied, reaching out to squeeze my hand. "When we have some private time, we'll discuss it."

The phone rang and I answered. "And so . . . did you behave yourself with your housemate?" Mallory teased.

"That depends what your definition of *behave* is," I told her.

There was a pause before she said, "No! You slept with Grant, didn't you?"

I shot him a grin and winked before saying, "Hey, we're not in high school anymore. A woman never kisses and tells."

I heard her laughter come across the line. "Oh. My. God. You did! Well, all I can say is, it's about damn time. Good for you. Hey, the reason I'm calling is to invite you to dinner tomorrow evening. Are you free?"

"Yeah, we are."

"Great. How's six?"

"Perfect. Thanks, Mallory. We'll see you then."

It had been Orli's idea that the three of us spend the afternoon walking around the downtown area. Strolling Dock Street, licking my ice-cream cone, I recalled doing the same exact thing as a child with my parents. Both of my parents. We headed to the City Park and found a bench overlooking the water.

"Come on, Dad," Orli coaxed as she removed her socks and shoes. "Let's walk along the shore."

He looked at me with raised eyebrows. "Sure, why not? Are you coming, Josie?"

I laughed and waved a hand. "I'll pass, but you two go ahead."

I watched as Orli ran toward the water with Grant following and heard their squeals as the incoming tide lapped at their feet.

It felt good to watch the two of them, and although I knew that I'd done a good job raising our daughter and that I'd never deprived either one of them of time together, I also knew that perhaps the time had arrived to let Orli decide where she wanted to be. I would miss her. A lot. I had always encouraged her to experience what gave her happiness, and lately I could see that at this time in her life, that happiness might be with Grant in the Boston area.

They returned to the bench a few minutes later, laughing and joking with each other. Orli leaned over to brush the sand from her feet.

"Dad said we could go to the book café for hot chocolate and coffee."

"Right," he said, laughing. "My old bones need to warm up."

Orli nudged him playfully on the arm. "Oh, Dad. You're not old. You're just . . . seasoned."

Grant and I burst out laughing.

"That's one way of putting it, I guess, but you make me sound like a roast beef."

"Come on," she called, running ahead of us.

"I'm just going to pop next door and see if Lucas has the latest Ken Follett novel. Grab us a table," Grant said as he walked through the archway to the book shop.

"Hey," Suellen greeted me. "I heard your mom was doing pretty well."

"She is, and she'll be home in a few hours. We're all really grateful."

"That's wonderful news."

I gave her our order, and then Orli and I sat down.

"Oh, I'm glad I found you."

I looked up to see Chloe walk in. She reached into a tote bag and removed a gorgeous piece of knitting.

"I wanted to show you the cowl I designed for your mother. It's not finished yet, but I think it's turning out well."

I picked up the peach-colored piece of work and nodded. "It's beautiful, Chloe. She's going to love it."

"Oh, it is," Orli said, reaching to touch it. "That's for Nana?"

Chloe nodded. "Yeah, I'm calling it the Healing Cowl, and I hope it'll help with her recovery."

"Can you join us?" I asked.

"No, I'm afraid not. I'm on my way home, but I peeked in the window and saw you. Gabe is coming for dinner, so I have to get cooking."

"Give him my best," I said.

"Oh, I will. . . . By the way, we're definitely going to Ormond Beach next weekend."

"Well, good for you. I'll be anxious to hear about it."

I watched her leave the shop and had no doubt that she was about to embark on a whole new adventure—which caused me to wonder where, exactly, I might be headed myself.

Spending the previous afternoon with Grant and Orli had given me a sense of family, but walking up to Mallory's front door with Grant at my side made me feel complete—the other half of a whole.

"Hey," she said, swinging open the door and hugging both of us. "Troy," she hollered. "They're here."

Troy came to greet us, pulling me into a hug and extending his hand to Grant. "Good to see you again. It's been a while," he told him. "Come join me in the family room. I'm catching the end of the Bucs game."

"Right," Mallory said. "And we'll be in the kitchen." She shot me a grin. "Men and their sports."

"Where's Carter?" I asked.

"Oh, he's at a friend's house for supper tonight. They're working on a school project. Glass of wine?"

"Great," I said, sitting at the table. "Oh, I see we're going fancy tonight. Eating in the dining room, huh?"

She popped the cork on a bottle of Pinot and laughed. "Well, sure. It seems this might be a special occasion."

"Really? For you?"

She slapped my arm. "No. For you, silly."

I took a sip of wine and shook my head. "Well, I hate to disappoint you, but nothing's going on."

"Oh, come on, Jos. It sounded pretty promising yesterday."

"Shh! Geez, you don't have to let Grant hear us talking about him. I really don't know what's going on. Things do seem to be on a good track. Probably more so than in sixteen years, but . . . well, he said we'd talk when we had some private time. I thought he'd bring the subject up last night after Orli went to bed, but . . ." I could feel a flush creeping up my face.

Mallory turned from the stove and laughed. "Oh, I get it. You had other things on your mind."

"Something like that," I mumbled.

"Well, I hate to sound like an old record, but . . ."

"I do love him, Mallory. I guess I never really stopped. I just needed time to grow up and find *me*."

"Exactly," she said, coming over to give my shoulders a squeeze. "And you have done a remarkable job of doing just that, but now . . . well, it might be time to take inventory and see where you're headed."

Mallory was right. I knew that. But I also knew that in life there are never any easy solutions.

"I think you're forgetting one thing," I told her.

She spun around to look at me. "What's that?"

"Grant's livelihood is in the Boston area. You don't seriously think he'd consider uprooting, giving up his law practice, and moving to Cedar Key, do you?"

I saw the frown on her face. "Oh, shit. I never thought of that. That you might leave Cedar Key?"

"Exactly. This could turn out to be a case of be careful what you wish for."

✌ 41 ✌

As soon as the doorbell rang Monday evening, I realized that I should have called Simon to let him know that Grant was also going to join us for dinner. *Too late now,* I thought as I glanced out to the patio where Grant was reading the newspaper. I ran a hand through my hair and headed to the front door.

"Simon, come on in," I said, and found myself in an embrace as he handed me a gorgeous bouquet of flowers.

"They're beautiful. Thank you."

"They certainly are," I heard Grant say behind me and I spun around. "Oh . . . ah . . . Simon, this is Grant . . . Orli's father."

I saw the surprised expression on Simon's face as he extended his hand. "Nice to meet you. I didn't realize you were in town."

"Yeah, I flew down last week to help Josie through the ordeal with her mother."

I noticed that he hadn't included Orli's name in that sentence.

"Right," I said, gesturing toward the family room. "Simon, come in and sit down. Dinner will be ready shortly. How about a glass of wine?"

"Sounds good," he said, settling himself on the sofa.

"Coming right up," Grant replied, heading to the kitchen as if he were the man of the house.

I went to the rolltop desk and removed a notebook. "So . . . I have a list of the women and what each one will be bringing for the open house. We'll also have to get some paper plates and cups, that sort of thing."

He nodded and looked up as Grant came into the room expertly carrying three wineglasses. After passing one to Simon and to me, he held his in the air and said, "Dr. Mancini, here's to your new practice. I wish you much success."

"Thank you," he said before taking a sip.

"Josie tells me you're having an open house at the end of the month. I'm sure your patients will appreciate that." He settled himself on the arm of my chair, displaying a relaxed attitude as if he'd lived in the house forever before he reached over and patted my hand. "You're fortunate to have such an excellent nurse working for you."

Oh, Lord! What had I been thinking? Maybe this dinner wasn't such a good idea after all.

Simon cleared his throat. "Yes, I was very fortunate that a colleague of mine suggested that I interview Josie. . . . I knew immediately she'd be perfect for my office."

Grant sent me a smile and, of all things, a wink. "Yeah, Josie can be quite perfect."

I jumped up, sloshing a bit of wine over the rim of the glass. "I need to check on the casserole. I'll be right back."

Yanking open the oven door, I shook my head. What the hell was Grant doing? I'd never seen him act like this before. I removed the casserole to allow it to cool a bit before serving. I popped a tray of biscuits into the oven and took a gulp of wine before heading back to the family room.

"Right, the winters can be pretty brutal, but I guess when you're born and raised in New England you get used to it," I heard Grant say.

I was pleased that I was no longer the topic of conversation.

"Biscuits are in the oven," I said. "Just a few more minutes."

"Josie, how's your mother doing?" Simon asked.

"Better than I would have expected. She came home Saturday evening and she looks great. Still a bit tired, but I know she's relieved. She sees the doctor a week from today."

"Right. I'm sure he'll have the path report by then, but it's great that his initial assessment sounds good. Is Orli joining us?"

"No, she's at Laura's. But she said to be sure to tell you hello."

Simon smiled. "And Lily said the same to you."

"It's been nice being able to spend a few days with my daughter," Grant said. "Josie told me that your daughter is living with you for a while."

If I didn't know better, I'd think Grant wanted to make sure that Simon knew I shared all information with him.

"Yes, father-daughter time is very special. And I think when they hit a certain age, even more so. Lily will be off to college this summer."

I heard the timer on the oven buzz. "Okay," I said. "Dinner is ready."

Both men jumped up to follow me into the kitchen.

"Simon, you can take that seat," Grant took it upon himself to say, as if he had his designated spot beside me.

I managed to place the casserole and biscuits on the table without dropping anything, but I could feel the tension surrounding me.

We made small talk throughout the meal, and I thought I'd choke when both men reached for the wine bottle at the same time, saying, "More wine, Josie?"

I could feel my annoyance building as Simon appeared ready to challenge Grant. There was no doubt that testosterone levels were rising and a test of the alpha male was in play here. Had I not been so nervous and irritated, it would have been humorous.

"No, thanks," I mumbled.

Somehow we managed to get through dinner and the cleanup. When we finished, I put my hands on my hips, faced both of them, and said, "Okay. Grant, do me a favor and let Simon and me sit here and finish discussing the open house. Didn't you mention earlier that you wanted to watch something on PBS this evening?"

The bewildered expression on his face caused me to suppress a grin, but the glare I sent him was well understood.

"Oh . . . right. I'll leave you to it," he said, turning around and heading to the family room.

I heard the volume from the television and brought the notebook to the table. "Okay. Flowers. Maybe we should get a few bouquets for the waiting room."

"Very good idea," Simon said. "I can pick those up Thursday evening. I'm sure they'll stay fresh for the next day. And you did the flyers to place around town, right?"

"Oh, yes. I did." I reached to the back of the notebook and removed a folded sheet of paper. "What do you think?"

"Excellent. Maybe I should put one on the outside door of the office too."

"Good idea. I'll make copies tomorrow when I come into the office."

"Well, I think we're in pretty good shape. The food is accounted for, flowers, the flyers. Can you think of anything else?"

"Oh . . . do you have business cards?"

"Gosh, I meant to get some printed and never got around to it."

"Don't worry. There's still time. Jot down what you'd like to have on them, and I'll run into the printer in Chiefland. It would be nice to pass those out, with your phone number on them."

"Great. I'll have that for you tomorrow." Simon took the last sip of wine in his glass and stood up. "Thank you so much, Josie. For the wonderful dinner and for all your help getting this open house together."

"I'm glad I could help," I said, following him to the front door.

He ducked his head into the family room. "Good night, Grant. Have a good trip back to Boston."

I couldn't resist a smile. Was that his parting dig?

Grant raised his hand in a salute. "Thanks, and all the best with your open house. With Josie's assistance, I know it'll be a success."

Yup, definitely snarky.

I closed the front door and walked into the family room. Grant's eyes were glued to the TV screen and he avoided looking at me. I positioned myself between him and the television, hands on hips, and said, "Well? What the hell was that?"

He raised his eyebrows as if he had no idea what I was talking about. "What do you mean?" he asked, but I saw the sheepish expression that crossed his face.

"What do I mean? I mean you acting like some silly, lovestruck, jealous teenager. That's what I mean. You embarrassed the hell outta me."

He jumped up and pulled me into his arms. "Aw, Josie, come on. I didn't mean to embarrass you. But it's pretty obvious that guy is interested in you."

I pushed him away and plunked on the sofa. "Oh, and I guess it doesn't matter what I think?"

"What *do* you think?" he asked, sitting down beside me.

"I think we still haven't discussed where we're going from here. You and I."

He reached for my hand and this time I didn't pull away. He let out a deep sigh and nodded. "Okay. Where I want to be is with you. I've always wanted that, and while I understood your reasoning years ago . . . things are different now, and I think you know this. From what you've told me and shown me over the past month, I've come to believe that you love me as much as I love you."

I remained silent for a few moments. "I do love you, Grant," I whispered. "Very much, and I always will."

"And do you want to be with me and spend the rest of your life with me?"

"I do," I said again.

He squeezed my hand. "And that's what I want, but we have to be realistic. My job, my career, is in the Boston area. We know that Orli wants to come there when school finishes in May, and she seems pretty certain about attending college in Boston. And so . . . I want you to come too. I want you to marry me, but at the very least I want you to live with me, be in my life, every single day. It took sixteen years, but I'm asking you to marry me."

I wasn't surprised at his request. And I knew I wanted to marry him. I just wasn't sure if I wanted to give up everything that had formed my life till now—my family, my friends—and live permanently in the Boston area.

I leaned forward and brushed his lips with mine. "I do love you, Grant, with all my heart and soul. And I *do* want to marry you, but . . ."

I saw the intense expression on his face.

"Could I think about it? Could I have a little time to get everything straight in my head? I know how I feel about you, I'm absolutely sure of that. I just need to consider everything else that's involved."

I saw a huge smile cover his face as he pulled me into his arms. "I've waited sixteen years, Josie. What's a little longer?" he whispered in my ear.

42

Grant flew back to Boston on Wednesday as planned, and by Friday, I knew I had to have a talk with Simon. Although he hadn't mentioned a word about Grant and the dinner, I felt like there was an elephant in the room and I hated the uncomfortable feeling it was causing.

At the close of office hours on Friday, Brandy popped her head into my office. "Anything you need done before I go?"

"No, I'm all set. Thanks, and have a great weekend."

"Will do. You too," she called as she left.

I got up and stood in the doorway of Simon's office. His head was bent over as he read papers on his desk. I quietly observed him for a moment. No doubt about it, he was a really handsome guy. Not to mention also a caring and nice person. He just wasn't the one for me.

I cleared my throat and he looked up.

"Have you got a second?" I asked.

"Sure," he said, sliding the papers aside. "Have a seat."

"I wanted to apologize for Grant's behavior the other night."

A quizzical expression crossed his face. "His behavior?"

"Yeah, I'm afraid he was ... well, actually, I'm not quite sure what he was doing, but I'm sorry if he made you feel uncomfortable."

Simon let out a chuckle and shook his head. "No apology needed, and what he was doing was . . . staking out his territory." His chuckle turned to a laugh. "I understood his tactics."

"You did?"

He nodded. "Yeah, I'm afraid it's a guy thing. In an old-fashioned world I think it was called one-upmanship." He leaned across the desk. "He seems to love you very much, Josie. And it's easy to see that you feel the same way about him."

When I remained silent, he went on. "I've known that ever since I met you and the first time you mentioned Grant's name. The way you spoke about him, I could see it in your face. But, hey, you can't blame a guy for trying."

I felt a grin cross my face.

"Seriously," he said. "I'm very happy for both of you. So . . . where do you go from here? With him in the Boston area and you down here?"

I let out a sigh. "Good question. At the very least Grant would like me to relocate up there with him."

"I'm not surprised. I thought that might be coming. Are you going?"

"I'm not sure yet. I asked him to give me some time to think about it. But I'd give you plenty of notice if I was planning to leave," I hastened to add.

"Don't worry about that, Josie. You have to do what's best for you."

I stood up to leave. "Thanks, Simon. Thanks for being so understanding."

A smile covered his face as he nodded. "That's what friends are for, and Josie, I wish you all the best no matter what you decide."

I spent a lot of time over the next few days thinking about Grant's request. I knew I loved him, but did I actually want to leave my hometown and begin a whole new life elsewhere? More and more, I was beginning to realize that yes, I did. That old saying was true: home is where the heart is, and my heart was with Grant.

He had been gone for a week now, and it seemed each day I missed him more. I missed being with him, his laughter and his love. We had talked on the phone a lot over the past week, and he had refrained from asking if I'd made a choice yet. But that was Grant, again giving me the space I needed without pressure.

Orli and I had just finished cleaning up after supper.

"Your knitting class is at seven, right?" she asked, cutting into my thoughts.

"Yeah, it is, why?"

"Lily called earlier and asked if I could stop by and visit with her for a while. Would that be okay?"

"Sure. Be home by nine."

"Okay," she said, placing a kiss on my cheek before leaving. "I will."

Orli still hadn't brought up the subject of her senior year in the Boston area. I also hadn't told her about Grant asking to marry me or his request that I move in with him. I felt that before I discussed this with her, I wanted to be sure of my decision.

Just as I was about to walk out the door for the yarn shop, the phone rang.

"Josie, do you have a second?" my mom asked.

"Sure. What's up?"

"Well, Mags called earlier today. Needless to say, she's thrilled that my path report showed good news on Monday. So she wants to have a gathering for a long weekend here on the island."

"Yeah, Mallory had mentioned something about that."

"Well, the plans are in the works, and it's going to be held mid-April, just after my three-month checkup with the doctor."

"That's great. I know that'll be a fun time."

"I think it will be. Mags is renting a house for the five of us to stay in, and you'll never believe what she managed to do."

I let out a chuckle. "I give up."

I heard my mother's laugher across the line and had to admit it was a good sound. "Well, it seems she's coerced Sydney and Noah into letting us stay at their place for four nights."

"What? The Lighthouse? She's kicking Sydney out of her own home?"

My mother laughed again. "That's just it. Sydney and Noah have had plans to spend the month of April back in Paris. She said it would be empty anyway, so why not."

"Oh, wow! The Lighthouse is the perfect place for your gathering. That's great."

"I know. I'm really excited about this, and all of us want you and Mallory to come by on the first night to join us. I think it'll be fun."

I laughed again. "Oh, no doubt it will be, especially with Mags there. Absolutely I'll come, and I know Mallory will too."

"Great. Okay, then if I don't see you before, I'll see you on Friday at the open house."

I hung up the phone and smiled. It was good to hear my mother excited and positive, and I was grateful for the friendship she had with her four friends. I didn't have a wide circle of close friends, which made me even more appreciative to have Mallory. Being a busy, young, single mom had forced me to work long hours and then attending college had cut into my free time, so I'd never formed numerous friendships. But having Mallory always in my life had more than made up for that.

That's when it hit me. If I left Cedar Key, I'd be leaving both Mallory and my mother. My mother. Oh, God, I could only imagine what her feelings on this would be. She got upset if I canceled out a dinner at her house. I doubted that she'd be accepting of her one and only daughter moving to the Boston area. Getting her to finally accept the fact that I'd be attending college there had been tough enough.

"You guys are doing so great, I'm not sure you'll continue to need an instructor," I said, looking across the table. "Well, that excludes you, Gabe. You never needed me."

All four men laughed, and Gabe held up his hand while shaking his head. "That's not true, Josie. I've enjoyed these classes very much."

"Hey, what's this I hear about you heading to Ormond Beach this weekend?" Saxton asked.

I saw a faint crimson creep up Gabe's neck. "Yeah, Chloe and I are going over there to check out some property. I'm giving some serious thought to relocating there by the end of the year."

"That's great," Doyle said. "Not so far a drive that you couldn't come back here for a visit. Did I hear you're considering opening a yarn shop over there?"

Gabe nodded. "I'm giving it some serious consideration, yeah. That's always been a dream of mine. To open my own place like my mother did. But I'd like to take it a step further and have enough land with my house to keep a few alpacas. I haven't done any spinning in a few years, but I'd enjoy getting back to that."

"It sounds like a great plan to me," my father said. "And I have no doubt that Shelby and I would drive over to visit your place."

"That *is* exciting," I said, recalling Chloe's words about beginning a new chapter in her life.

Maybe I'd reached a point in my own life where it was time to do the exact same thing.

∽ 43 ∽

Orli had just left for school and I was savoring my morning coffee while I watered the plants on the patio when I heard the phone ring.

"Do you know what next week is?" I heard Grant ask when I answered.

I headed to the calendar on the wall. "And good morning to you too," I said as a smile covered my face. "Ah, yeah. The second week of February."

I heard Grant's laughter. "Right, and that means Valentine's Day is next Saturday."

"Okay."

"Well, I hope you don't mind, but I just booked myself a flight to Gainesville next Thursday. I didn't think it would be right for us to be apart on such a special day. We've spent too many Valentine's Days without each other."

I felt excitement bubble up. "Really? You did that? That's wonderful, and God, no, I don't mind. It's been three weeks since we've seen each other, and it feels like a year."

"Exactly. I'll arrive on the twelve-thirty flight, get the rental car, and should be on the island by two."

"I can't wait. I've missed you, Grant."

"You have no idea how much I've missed *you*. I love you, Josie."

"I love you more," I said, and I meant it.

I heard him chuckle. "I doubt that's possible. I have to be in court in a half hour, but I'll call you this evening."

I hung up the phone and smiled. Not only was I happy that I'd get to see Grant in one week, I was thrilled that I'd finally be able to give him my answer in person. Now I had to call my mother to see if she was home so that I could stop by and prepare to do battle with her.

Delilah opened the door with a huge smile when I arrived at my parents' house. "Miss Josie, come on in. I don't see nearly enough of you."

And soon, you'll be seeing much less of me, I thought.

"Your mother will be right down. Would you like some coffee or tea?"

"Coffee would be great. Thanks. Is my father home?" I asked as I headed to the family room.

"He just ran down to the library. Should be back shortly."

I walked to the large window that looked out to the ocean. I would miss this. I knew I would. My childhood home, the Gulf, my parents. But I also knew that the time was right for me to embrace the love of my life and all that went with it.

"Josie, I'm so glad you stopped by," my mother said as she joined me. "Your father's at the library, but he'll be right back. Is Delilah getting you something to drink?"

I turned to give my mother a hug and felt bad that within a few minutes I'd probably be robbing her of this happy mood.

"Yeah, she's getting coffee," I said, sitting down.

"Good. Well, you look happy this morning. Everything's going well?"

I nodded. "Yeah, it is. Actually, that's what I wanted to talk to you about."

Delilah walked in holding a tray with two coffee mugs. "Would you like cookies or anything to go with this?"

"None for me," my mother said.

"No, I'm fine. Thanks."

"Okay, then. I'll be cleaning upstairs if you need me."

"So what's going on?" my mother asked.

"Well . . . as you know, Grant was here last month."

My mother nodded. "Right. That was so nice of him to fly down here for you and Orli."

"It was. And of course you know I spent a week up there over Christmas."

"Yes."

"Well . . . ah . . . it seems . . ."

"Oh, for heaven's sake, Josie, just spit it out. What's going on?"

I felt perspiration wetting my forehead as I fingered the coffee mug. "Things have changed."

My mother leaned forward. "Changed? In what way?"

"I've fallen in love with Grant all over again."

I expected anger. I expected a snarky retort. I did not expect my mother to throw her head back laughing and reach for my hand.

"All over again? My darling daughter, you've never stopped loving Grant. I knew that. Your father knew that, and Grant knew it. You were the only one who was so stubborn that you refused to admit it."

It didn't happen often, but I was at a loss for words.

"You silly girl," she said. "Well, actually, if you finally realize this, you're no longer a *girl*. You've finally matured into a woman."

"So you're not surprised?" I managed to find my voice again.

"Not in the least. I've been hoping that you'd discover this before it was too late. I honestly give Grant the utmost credit. Waiting around for sixteen years for you to wake up and smell the coffee, so to speak."

I shook my head and started laughing. "Why have you never said anything?"

She waved a hand in the air. "Oh, Josie, really? You felt I interfered in your life too much as it was. I wasn't about to point out the obvious to you."

She was right. How many times had I accused her of being a control freak?

"And so . . ." she said. "Do I dare ask where all of this goes from here?"

Here it comes, I thought.

"Well." I cleared my throat. "I'm not sure if you're aware, but Orli has been hinting that she'd like to finish her senior year in the Boston area and live with Grant and . . . it seems that she'd also like to attend Emerson. As a . . . journalism major."

I saw a look of surprise and joy cover my mother's face.

"No. I had no idea. Journalism? She's never said a word to me."

"She's only recently shared this with Grant and me."

"So she wants to leave Cedar Key at the end of this school year? Won't that be difficult for her, making new friends and trying to fit in for her senior year in a new school?"

"That's what I thought too, but she seems excited about the idea."

"Well, that makes sense."

"It does?"

"Perfect sense. First of all, Orli is at an age now where it's understandable that she'd want to spend more time with her father. No matter what you think, Josie, she did miss out on special times with her dad. You, of all people, should know this. Look at the close relationship you have with your father. And it was never formed with phone calls and occasional visits."

She was right, and I felt a twinge of guilt.

"But knowing my granddaughter as I do, I think there was a method to her madness."

"What do you mean?"

My mother laughed. "Oh, Josie, Orli has always been a fixer. The one who ran interference between you and me, the one who organized those kids to fix up Mr. Al's house years ago. My granddaughter is the peacemaker. I have no doubt that if she indicated she wanted to live up there with Grant . . . it might have been the nudge you needed to wake up and see that you belong there as well."

"You think? You're saying this was all planned on Orli's part?"

"Well, I'm not saying that was her *only* reason for wanting to be up there. No, I think she truly wants to spend more time with Grant. And Molly too, for that matter. She does have another grandmother, Josie. Molly has missed out too. But . . . yes, I do think that girl of ours has enough insight to realize that her decision just might affect you too."

I shook my head and smiled. "You could be right. I've always taken pride in the way that Orli takes charge and handles situations." And then what my mother was really saying hit me. "So . . . are you okay with me also moving up there? Leaving Cedar Key?"

"Of course I am, Josie. Maybe I was a bit overbearing at times, but as you'll find with Orli someday, children are only a loan. We love them, we raise them, we do the best we can, but eventually they have to fly off on their own and become who they're meant to be. Sometimes it's only around the corner or in the same town. Sometimes it's across the country or the world. But nothing ever . . . and you can trust me on this . . . nothing *ever* breaks the bond of a parent and child."

I had no control of the tears streaming down my face. All of the stress of the past month seemed to be pouring out of my eyes in a huge flood of welcome relief. I leaned over as my mother opened her arms to me. I felt her patting my back, and I knew in that moment that she was right. It didn't matter where we were geographically, because love is love and family is family, despite any distance.

"And so," I heard her say, "is Grant expecting you to live in sin, or is there a wedding on the horizon?"

I pulled away laughing as I wiped my eyes. "Actually, he did ask me to marry him when he was here last month. He said, at the very least, he wants me to move in with him, but I asked for some time to think about it. He called this morning, and he's flying down here next week for Valentine's Day."

My mother reached up to brush a tear from my cheek and nodded. "And I know that this time, my brilliant and beautiful daughter will make the right choice."

44

When Orli arrived home that afternoon, she entered the house to hear the CD player going full blast, and she heard me singing away as I prepared her favorite meal of baked macaroni and cheese. I looked up and saw the smile on her face along with raised eyebrows.

I slid the casserole into the oven, ran over, grabbed Orli's hands, and began dancing around the kitchen with her to an ABBA song. When it ended, we both collapsed in laughter as I caught my breath.

"What's all this about?" she said, still laughing as her eyes caught the chocolate cake on the counter that I'd baked that morning.

"This is about celebrating."

"What are we celebrating?"

"Life. Love. The month of February. You. Me. Us. Everything," I exclaimed, throwing my arms in the air.

Orli narrowed her eyes. "Seriously, Mom. What's going on?"

I shot her a smile. "Seriously . . . I will tell you later after we finish your favorite supper."

She ran over to peek inside the oven. "Mac and cheese?"

"Yup."

"This must be pretty serious," she said before heading to her room.

* * *

"Thanks, Mom. That was delicious," Orli told me after her second helping of her favorite meal.

"My pleasure and now . . . let's have a talk."

She took a sip of water, folded her arms, and leaned across the table. "I'm ready."

"Okay. Now, I want you to be perfectly honest with me. Do you want to go live with your dad and finish your senior year up there?" She started to say something, but I held up my hand. "Wait. I'm not finished. Because if you do, I want you to know I approve one hundred percent. If this is what you truly want."

She nodded. "I do. I really want to do this, but . . . I feel bad about leaving you here."

"Orli, first of all . . . that's not for you to be concerned about. You're sixteen. You're not a little girl anymore, and you have to begin doing what you feel is best for you. And besides . . . I don't want you to think that I'm following you, but . . . I've also been invited to live with your dad."

I saw a confused expression cross her face, but bright girl that she is, it took only a moment for her to realize what I was saying.

"Oh, my God! Dad asked you to marry him, didn't he?"

"He did," was all I could say before she jumped up and wrapped her arms around me.

"When? When's the wedding?"

"Whoa. Hold on. I haven't exactly said yes yet."

"What do you mean?"

"Well, he gave me some time to think about it, which I have, and between you and me, my answer is yes. But he doesn't know that yet."

Orli let out a giggle. "So when are you telling him?"

"Your dad called this morning and he's flying down next Thursday . . . to spend Valentine's Day with me. With us."

"Oh, wow! That's great. And you'll tell him then?"

I nodded. "Right. What better time than Valentine's Day?"

"Pure romance," Orli gushed. "Wait till Laura hears this."

I put up my hand. "Do me a favor—don't tell anybody until I've told your dad."

"Oh, right. No problem. Does Mallory know?"

"Nope. Not yet. Only you and Nana."

"Oh, God! Nana? She's probably not going to be very happy about *both* of us leaving here."

I tapped her on the nose with my finger. "Don't be too sure of that, sweet pea. Nana is full of surprises lately. Come on, help me clean up so I can get to the yarn shop. I want to pick up a piece of needlepoint before the knitting group starts."

"Do you have anything specific in mind?" Marin asked.

"Yeah," I said, browsing through the multitude of canvases that hung from the racks. "You don't have anything that's a map, do you?"

"I do. I have state maps. Is that what you want?"

"Yeah."

She pointed to a rack at the back of the shop. "Right back there. I have quite a selection. Which state?"

"Massachusetts," I said.

Marin reached into the rack, withdrew a hand-painted canvas, and held it up. "Is this what you want?"

"Yes. Perfect. I'll take it." I looked at the outline and saw the hook of Cape Cod and in small letters BOSTON and other large cities throughout the state. "Would it be possible to put my own mark on it?"

"I'm not sure I know what you mean."

I pointed to an empty spot just north of Boston. "Like right here, would it be possible to stitch maybe a heart?"

Marin held the canvas closer. "Sure. I don't see why not. That's a white empty space, so you could do that."

"Great. I'll pick out my threads now."

By the time I finished choosing and she rang up my sale, I could hear the women arriving in the yarn shop. I walked through the archway to see Dora, Chloe, Sydney, and my mother talking.

"Hey, Josie," Chloe said. "Shopping for needlepoint?"

"Yeah, I enjoy switching between that and knitting."

Sydney laughed. "Don't we all."

Within twenty minutes, the shop was filled with ladies chattering, knitting, and laughing.

"Sydney, I heard you're getting booted out of your house," I said.

She laughed as she knitted away on a gorgeous blue cable pullover that I knew was for one of Monica's triplets. "Not exactly. As all of you know, Noah and I have decided to spend the month of April in Paris. And it seems the Sisters of '68 were looking for a place to stay for a long weekend."

"So you're giving them your house?" Raylene said.

"I'm offering it to them for the long weekend. It's the perfect spot for a gathering."

My mother nodded. "It's ideal. We're all just thrilled. And we promise not to behave so badly that Officer Steve has to come out and quiet us down."

Everybody laughed as Berkley said, "Geez, now, that's no fun. Behaving badly is a girl's claim to fame."

Raylene sniffed as her needles increased their speed. "Well, in my day . . ."

"Yes, Raylene," Dora said, cutting her off. "In your day girls and women were perfect angels. But we still managed to have some fun. At least some of us did." She looked up from her knitting and winked at the group.

This brought forth another round of laughter.

I heard Chloe clear her voice. "Well, I have some news," she said. "The only ones that know about it are Dora, Maude, and Grace, but I may as well share it here."

I saw some raised eyebrows, and Grace shot her sister a smile.

"As you know, I've been seeing Gabe Brunell, and as some of you know, a couple of weeks ago we took a weekend trip to Ormond Beach. Gabe is an expert knitter and it's been his dream to open his own yarn shop someday. Well, it looks like that's going to happen. He's found the perfect spot over there and . . . he's also found the perfect house with some farmland, so he plans to keep a few alpacas and use the fiber for spinning."

"Oh, that sounds wonderful," Berkley said. "If he needs any suggestions or info on alpacas, I'd be more than happy to help him or have my friend Jill talk to him."

"Thanks so much. I'll be sure to let Gabe know."

"This is really exciting news," Sydney said. "How great to be setting off on a new venture."

"It certainly is," my mother told her. "Sometimes we reach a point in life when it's time to take a leap and head in a whole new direction."

I saw the smile she gave me and nodded.

"Wait a minute," Raylene said, placing her knitting in her lap. "I don't understand. What does any of this have to do with you, Chloe?"

"Geez, Raylene, connect the dots," Berkley said, laughing. "Chloe is going with Gabe. She'll help him run the yarn shop over there."

"What? You're leaving Cedar Key? You mean you're going to be living with him there? In *his* house?"

"Yeah, I am," Chloe said. "That's exactly what I'll be doing."

"Well, what about Maude? And your sister? You're just leaving them?"

Raylene's indignant tone left no doubt that she found the idea preposterous.

"She's not *leaving* us, Raylene." Grace put her knitting in her lap. "Chloe is a grown woman. She knows what she's doing, and even better, she knows what she wants. Aunt Maude and I support her decision completely. We're very happy for her, and besides, it's not even a three-hour drive to visit each other."

Raylene shrugged. "Well, I still don't get it. Why on earth would you want to do something like that?"

Without missing a beat, Chloe leaned toward Raylene and said, "Because I *can* . . . and because life is too short *not* to."

A round of applause went up in the shop before we moved on to other subjects.

About an hour later, Dora announced it was time for tea, coffee, and our pastry. "Berkley brought a beautiful red velvet cake, but before we get to that, I think Chloe has another announcement."

"Now what?" Raylene said with a frown on her face.

Chloe jumped up, ran into the back room, and returned with a gift bag, which she passed to my mother.

"Shelby, this is for you. I designed it and knitted it, and I hope you'll like it."

My mother reached into the bag and removed the gorgeous peach-colored cowl.

"I've called it the Healing Cowl. I hope it will help in your continued recovery and bring you good health."

My mother placed it around her neck, and I saw the moisture in her eyes as she got up to give Chloe a hug. "Thank you so much. This means the world to me."

My thought at that moment was the hope that once I got settled into my new home, it wouldn't take me long to find a yarn shop with a new group of women who would make me feel part of that very unique alliance—female friendship.

❧ 45 ❧

Thursday morning I was busy polishing furniture, running the vacuum through the house, and thinking that for the first time in a long time my life seemed to be on track and I was in my element. I also realized that everything that had happened over the past sixteen years had brought me here. Meeting Ben and meeting Simon were things I needed to do. I couldn't help but feel that I'd come full circle.

After I finished cleaning, I was about to prepare myself a sandwich for lunch when I heard Mallory come in the front door.

"Hey," she said. "Oh, good, just in time for lunch. Can you make me one of those?" She pointed to the rye bread, turkey breast, and cheese.

"Sure. Sweet tea with it?"

"Sounds great," she said, positioning herself on the stool. "So Grant's due here about two?"

I nodded.

"Has he mentioned yet what you're doing for Valentine's Day?"

"He booked a reservation at the Island Room for us."

"Hmm, nice. What're you wearing?"

I laughed. "Haven't given it a thought."

"Josie, Josie, Josie, what would you do without me? We'll go through your closet after lunch."

"I can't guarantee we'll find anything worthy in there."

"Well, if all else fails, we can raid my closet." She took a sip of the tea that I placed in front of her. "You're telling him yes, aren't you?"

I laughed. "You've always been such a nosy friend."

"Well?" she said before taking a bite of her sandwich.

"Maybe."

"You have to promise me that, except for Orli and your mom, you tell me first. I expect a phone call from you at seven Sunday morning . . . with all the details."

"Eat your sandwich," I ordered.

After we finished, we headed to my bedroom, where I began removing dresses from my closet. Each one I held up brought an emphatic shake of Mallory's head.

"None of those will do, Josie. You want to look glamorous. Sexy. Seductive."

I laughed. "You seem to forget, this is Cedar Key. Nobody gets quite that dressed up."

"Too bad. You mean to tell me you have nothing else?"

As soon as she said this, I remembered the garment bag hanging in the guest room closet. Cocktail dresses from my college days that I was never able to part with.

"Follow me," I said.

I removed a blood-red dress, sleeveless, V-neck, with a scalloped hemline, and I recalled wearing it the night that Grant took me to Marliave to celebrate our first Valentine's Day together.

"Bingo," Mallory said. "Oh, Josie, it's stunning. Try it on."

I slipped it over my head and was grateful that, even sixteen years later, it fit to perfection. I walked to the full-length mirror and twirled around. I felt like I was nineteen again, but the image in the mirror showed me that the college freshman had been replaced by an attractive woman—a woman who had grown and evolved, and a woman I was proud to be.

"You think?" I said.

She gave me a thumbs-up. "Perfect. Grant will love it."

I wondered if he'd remember it. "Oh, no," I wailed. "I know I don't have any heels to go with this."

"Not to worry. We're the same size, and I have a pair of black strappy ones that will be perfect. With your black cashmere shawl, you'll be a vision."

I removed the dress, hung it carefully on the hanger, and slipped back into my jeans and sweatshirt.

"Okay," Mallory said. "Mission accomplished. Thanks for the lunch, but I have to scoot. You take a nice scented bubble bath, put something pretty on, and be ready when Grant gets here."

I followed her to the front door and gave her a hug. "Thanks for your help."

"Just don't forget," she said as she jogged down the walkway, "Sunday morning. Seven o'clock. Phone call."

I laughed and closed the door just as the phone rang.

"Hey," I heard Grant say. "Landed right on time. I need to stop to pick up a few things, so it might be closer to three before I get there."

I thought of the bubble bath that Mallory had mentioned. "That's fine," I said. "I'll be here, and I love you."

"I love you too. See you soon."

I walked into my bathroom and wondered when I'd last used my garden tub. *Too long ago,* I thought.

After turning on the faucets, I poured some lavender bubble bath into the water and realized that Sydney had brought me the bottle from Paris the year before and it was almost full. I grabbed the igniter from the drawer and proceeded to light the candles surrounding the tub.

After I slid down into the warm water, I let out a sigh. I really should do this more often. It was pure luxury. I thought about Grant arriving in a few hours, and my excitement at seeing him again grew. I did feel like I was about to embark on a whole new life, and that made me wonder about my house. Technically, it belonged to my mother, but I was pretty sure that she wouldn't part with it and would rather keep it for when Grant, Orli, and I came to visit. That gave me a sense of comfort, to know that I wasn't cutting all my ties to Cedar Key.

When the water began to cool, I got out and decided that jeans and my black cotton pullover were perfect for a casual evening. After I dressed, I sprayed on a bit of Shalimar and headed to the kitchen. Orli was home from school and nibbling on an oatmeal cookie.

"What time will Dad be here?" she asked.

I glanced at the clock. "In about an hour or so. He called from the airport and said he had a few things to pick up and he'd be on his way."

"I'm glad he's coming for a few days."

I turned on the oven and began stuffing the chicken that I planned to roast for dinner. "Me too," I said.

"I'm going to go get my homework done before he gets here." She poured herself a glass of milk, grabbed two more cookies, and headed to her room.

By the time Grant arrived, the aroma of roasting chicken was filling the kitchen, the dining room table was set, and I had just uncorked a bottle of wine.

I ran to the front door to greet him, and laughed. I couldn't see his face because two huge bouquets of flowers were covering it.

He peeked from behind one of them and grinned. "For my two best girls for Valentine's Day."

I reached out for the bouquet he passed me and placed a kiss on his lips. "Oh, Grant. They're gorgeous."

Orli came running from her bedroom. "Hey, Dad," she said, sliding into his free arm.

"Happy Valentine's Day," he told her.

"Wow, they're so pretty. Thank you."

I headed to the kitchen. "Let's find some vases for these."

Grant and I had a glass of wine before supper as we relaxed on the patio.

"How's your mother doing?" he asked.

"Still doing well. She's changed."

He shifted in the lounge. "In which way?"

"More mellow. Relaxed."

He nodded. "Yeah, sometimes we're slammed with a life-changing event and we see that things that seemed important before aren't important at all."

"I'm glad. Well, I'm not glad she was diagnosed with cancer . . . but I'm glad she's . . . different."

Grant reached for my hand. "So are you," he said.

"What do you mean?"

"I mean this in a good way, but you're less defensive. I think you always felt you had to prove yourself. As the good single mom. The responsible breadwinner. I think you know now that you've accomplished both of these things."

I nodded. "You're right. Maybe no matter what I said or tried to project, I think deep down I felt some guilt that I didn't cave to tradition."

He brought my hand to his lips. "And now?"

"Now I'm not sorry that I did it my way . . . but I love being exactly where I am in my life. With you."

"I was hoping you'd say that."

I enjoyed watching Orli and Grant converse and joke with each other throughout dinner. It reminded me of my teen years at my parents' table. Mothers and daughters can have a complex and sometimes adversarial relationship, and I was grateful that so far Orli and I had never had that. But there was something very special about the father-daughter relationship. A father is the first man a girl loves, the one she depends on and looks up to, the role model for the man she chooses to spend the rest of her life with. Grant was that person to me.

The three of us pitched in together to clean up the kitchen after we ate, and even this mundane task took on new meaning with Grant to help us.

"I'm going to go watch TV in my room," Orli said when we finished, and I couldn't help but think she was purposely giving Grant and me some private time. She kissed us and said good night before heading to her room.

"Another glass of wine?" I asked.

"Sounds good," Grant said as he sat on the sofa.

I passed him a glass and curled up beside him. "Oh, no," I said. "I just realized, I'm working till noon tomorrow. Simon's been so nice giving me time off because of my mom, I didn't want to ask for another day."

"That's not a problem." Grant took a sip of wine as he slid his arm around my shoulders. "I'm sure I can manage to stay busy. I think I'll go over and visit with your parents for a while, and then I can pick you up at the office and take you to lunch."

I recalled the last encounter between Grant and Simon and pulled away to stare at him. "Are you coming inside?"

"Sure. Why not? I haven't seen the office yet."

I shook a finger at him. "Because you were very naughty the last time you two were together. That's why."

He threw his head back, laughing. "Oh. That. Well, I promise to be on my best behavior. You can trust me."

I did trust him. In all ways.

"Come on," he said, standing up and taking my hand. "I guess you're going to allow me to share your bed again? It's been a long day. Let's take our wine and go relax in your room for a while before we fall asleep."

I gave him a smile and had a feeling that sleep was the last thing on either of our minds.

❧ 46 ❧

The alarm went off at six, and I reached across Grant to turn it off. He opened his eyes, smiled, and said, "Good morning, beautiful."

"Good morning," I told him as I snuggled into the crook of his arm. "Sleep well?"

"With you? Always."

We lay there for a few minutes slowly waking up and relishing the closeness of each other. Then I leaned over to kiss his cheek and said, "I need to hit the shower. I have to be at the office to open at eight."

Grant's embrace tightened around me. "Hmm, can't you prolong this a little?"

"No, Mr. Cooper, I cannot," I said, laughing, and jumped out of bed.

"Well, if you insist. I'll get the coffee going . . . or . . . I could join you in the shower first."

I laughed again. "Not this morning, but hold that thought," I said, and headed to the bathroom.

I walked into the kitchen dressed in my light blue scrubs to find Grant sitting at the counter reading the morning paper. I walked over to place a kiss on his cheek. His arm went out to encircle my waist and pull me to him.

"You look pretty damn sexy in those scrubs," he whispered in my ear, his voice husky.

I gave him a smile and pulled away. "Oh, no, you don't. Seducing me again."

Orli walked into the kitchen, a grin on her face, and put an end to Grant's attempt. "Good morning," she said as she pulled a box of cereal from the cabinet and then milk from the fridge.

"Would you rather have eggs or something?" I asked her.

"Nah, this is fine, but tomorrow morning it'd be nice if Dad could make his famous French toast."

"Done deal," he told her.

"Grant, would you like some eggs?"

He shook his head. "No, but those blueberry muffins look good."

I'd baked a batch the day before and removed the plastic wrap, placing them on the table.

"So what's up for today, Dad? I'm sorry you'll be alone while I'm at school and Mom's at work."

"Not a problem. I'm going to go visit your grandparents for a while later this morning and then I'm picking your mom up at the office to go to lunch."

"Sounds good," she said, spooning cereal into her mouth. "Are we eating here tonight?"

"Oh, I almost forgot. Nana called and invited us over for dinner. Supposed to be there at six. I told her I'd check with you, Grant."

"Yes, I'd like to go, and I'll let her know when I drop by later."

Within an hour, Orli had grabbed her backpack, kissed us both good-bye, and headed off to school.

"Are you sure you don't want me to drive you?" Grant said.

Orli laughed. "No, Dad. Thanks, but I'm a big girl."

We watched her walk out the door, and he let out a sigh. "She *is* a big girl, isn't she? All grown up. The years went too fast."

I nodded. "Yeah, but I think the best are yet to come."

He pulled me into his arms and brushed his lips over mine. "I think you're right. I'm going in the shower and then I'll drop you at work."

I walked into the office to find Brandy already seated behind her desk going over the appointment book. She had turned out to be a very valuable employee. She was dependable, great with the patients, and seemed to enjoy her job.

Her head popped up, and I saw the excitement covering her face. "Look," she said, pointing to a vase of very pretty pink lilies, daisies, and assorted greenery.

I leaned over to inhale the heady fragrance. "Oh, gorgeous. From a secret admirer?"

"No, from Dr. Mancini for Valentine's Day. You have one too on . . ." she started to say, and then clamped her hand over her mouth. "Sorry. I didn't mean to ruin the surprise."

I laughed and headed to my office as I called, "That's okay," over my shoulder.

An identical bouquet sat on my desk in a glass vase, and I turned as I heard Simon say, "Just a little something for Valentine's Day."

"Thank you. That was very thoughtful, and I think you made Brandy's week."

"Did Grant get in okay yesterday?"

"He did, yeah, and he'll be picking me up at noon to go to lunch."

"Great. Well, I think we have a busy morning."

We did. There seemed to be a respiratory infection going around the island, and everybody was hoping for instant relief. I was shocked to look at my watch and see it was already noon when I headed to the waiting room to escort our final patient into Simon's office. I returned to see Grant coming in the door and heard Brandy say, "Can I help you?"

"I'm here to . . ." he said before I interrupted him.

"He's here to pick me up," I told Brandy. "This is Grant Cooper, Orli's father."

I saw her eyes light up as she stared at him and a huge smile cross her face as she gave him a quick body scan.

"Oh," she said. "Oh. Right." She jumped up to shake his hand. "I'm Brandy, Dr. Mancini's receptionist."

"Very nice to meet you," Grant said, returning her handshake. "Josie has told me what a great employee you are."

Her eyes never left his face. "She has?" She then seemed to regain her equilibrium and said, "Oh, I just love working with Josie. She's the best."

Grant laughed. "She is, isn't she?"

"We're on our last patient," I told him. "You can wait in my office. I shouldn't be too much longer."

"And you can put the phones on service now," I told Brandy.

When Grant turned to follow me, she gave me a thumbs-up and mouthed the words *He's smokin'*.

I felt a grin cross my face as I showed Grant into my office.

"Very nice," he said, sitting down. I saw his gaze go to the flowers, but he never said a word.

A few minutes later Simon walked in, and if he was surprised to see Grant sitting in front of my desk, he didn't show it.

"Hey, Grant," he said, extending his hand. "Good to see you again."

Grant stood up and returned the handshake. "Same here. You've got quite a nice place. Josie told me how much work went into the remodeling."

"Yeah, it did, but I think it was worth it. Josie, there are no more appointments, so we're finished for the day. I just sent Mr. Fred on his way with an antibiotic."

"Oh, okay, great." I reached for my handbag and sweater. "Well, then we'll scoot along. Tell Lily I said hi."

"Will do," he said as I followed Grant to the door.

"Have a good weekend, Brandy. Any plans for Valentine's Day tomorrow?"

She let out a chuckle. "Nah, no romance in my life. I'll spend it watching a chick flick with a bowl of popcorn. But you enjoy yours."

The look on her face told me that she knew I would.

* * *

Grant and I headed to the Pickled Pelican for lunch, and the weather was too gorgeous not to sit outside on the deck overlooking the water.

After we gave our order for wine, I smiled and said, "I must commend you. You were very well behaved at the office just now."

Grant laughed. "Told ya I would be. But . . . were the flowers on your desk from Simon?"

It was hard to suppress my giggle, and I nodded. "Yes, they were."

He held his hand in the air. "Oh, that's fine. Very nice of him. Especially since I saw the same bouquet on Brandy's desk."

I shook my head as I muttered, "Men!"

Our wine was brought to the table and we put in our order for sandwiches.

"There's something that I wanted to discuss with you," he said.

I took a sip of wine and looked up at him. "What is it?"

"Well . . . if you do decide to come to the Boston area . . . you'll have to give up your job here."

"Right," I said, unsure where he was going with this.

"So I just wanted you to know that whatever you choose to do about working up there is fine with me."

"Okay," I said, and then smiled.

"If you'd like to take a nursing position around Danvers or if you'd like to work in one of the large hospitals in Boston, that wouldn't be a problem, because you could drive in with me if the hours worked out."

I thought of Beth Israel, Massachusetts General, and all of the top-notch hospitals I'd be able to choose from, and I had to admit that it was mighty enticing.

"Or," he said, reaching for my hand, "you don't have to work at all, Josie. There would be no need to do so unless you *wanted* to. I just want you to know that. Whatever would make you happy."

It had been like that from the beginning—always. Whatever made *me* happy had always been Grant's primary concern.

❧ 47 ❧

I woke the following morning to find the space beside me empty. I sat up and looked around the room. No Grant. I headed to the bathroom before walking into the kitchen to find him at the counter whipping up a batch of French toast. And my eyes went to the two red boxes on the counter.

"Happy Valentine's Day," he said, coming to kiss me and pass me one of them. "For you, the love of my life."

I took the box and smiled. "Thank you. I love you," I said as I removed the paper to find two pounds of French dark chocolate. "You had these sent from France, didn't you?"

He nodded. "I did, and I hope Berkley will forgive me."

I laughed. "Hey, as good as her chocolate might be, nothing compares to authentic French chocolate."

"Good. I hope you'll enjoy it."

"Oh, I have no doubt I'll enjoy it, but I think my hips might regret it."

He slid a hand down the side of my body as he whispered, "Nothing wrong with those hips at all.

"I had an idea," he said as he poured me a mug of coffee. "I thought maybe the three of us could take a drive to Gainesville and take Orli for lunch to that restaurant that she loves."

"Oh, the Red Onion? Yeah, she loves their salads."

"Good, that's what we'll do and we'll still be back in plenty of time for our dinner reservation at seven."

I sat across the table at the restaurant, watching Grant and Orli discussing a legal case that she'd recently seen on television, and I smiled. Seeing the two of them together felt so natural. I recalled a few instances when I'd experienced jealousy about Orli flying to the Boston area, but now, not only did I feel secure in my daughter's love, but I also knew she felt secure with her father. And that made me happy.

"I wanted to ask you both something," she said.

I looked at Grant, but he didn't seem to know what it was. "What is it?" he asked.

Orli shifted in the booth and began fingering the spoon on the table. "Well . . . I was just kind of wondering . . . would it be possible to change my name?"

My heart fell. I had always loved Orli's name and had chosen it specifically because it meant *You are my light,* which she certainly was. "Oh, I didn't realize you didn't like it," I said.

"Oh, no, I mean . . . Sullivan is fine, but . . ."

I began laughing and interrupted her. "You mean your *last* name?"

She nodded and then caught on and also laughed. "Oh, no, not my first name. But . . . I just thought . . . since Dad's name is on my birth certificate, that you know . . . maybe when I register for high school up there, I could go by Orli Cooper."

I saw the surprise on Grant's face. He cleared his throat before saying, "Well, yes, of course you could do that, Orli. But . . . why would you want to do this?"

I had a pretty good idea why. When I married Grant, I would become Josie Cooper, and I had a feeling that Orli wanted the three of us to have the same name.

"Well . . . I just thought . . ."

"I think it's a wonderful idea," I said.

"You do?" Grant shot me a smile, and I knew he liked the idea a lot.

"Yes, I really do. You are her father, so why not? And I'm sure you know how to make it legal. You're a lawyer. Don't you do those sorts of things?"

Grant laughed and nodded. "It wouldn't be much of a problem at all. If that's what you think you want, Orli, then yes, after you move up to Boston, we can get it done."

I saw her let out a sigh and realized that as much as she might have wanted this, she also didn't want to hurt my feelings. She leaned over to hug her father. "Oh, good," she said, but I was the one she was looking at. "Thanks, Mom."

We got back to the island just before four. Orli reminded me that Laura was coming to spend the night.

"Oh, that's right," I said. "How about if I whip up a batch of brownies for you guys? And we have plenty of chips and dip. Anything else you'd like?"

"No, brownies will be great. Thanks."

After I got them into the oven, I asked Orli what she'd like for supper.

"I'm still full from lunch, and we'll be snacking all evening. You need to go get ready," she informed me.

Grant said I could have the master bathroom and he'd shower and dress in the guest room. I took extra time applying my makeup, and by the time I slid the red dress over my head, I realized that I was nervous. I thought back to that first Valentine's Day in Boston. So excited, so in love. Little did I know that the following month I'd get pregnant with Orli and my entire life would change. Just as it was about to again—but this time, it would change with Grant beside me. I slipped into Mallory's black heels, sprayed a bit of Shalimar on my neck, and gave a smile of approval to myself in the mirror.

I walked out into the family room and heard Grant whistle. "You look stunning," he said, coming to encircle me in his arms. He paused for a second, and then pointed as recognition crossed his face. "That dress. Isn't it the one you wore to Marliave our first Valentine's Day together?"

He *did* remember. "It is," I said, as I took in his tan sport jacket, white shirt, and chocolate brown slacks. He could easily have passed for a *GQ* model. "You look *so* handsome."

We both turned around to see Orli and Laura standing in the doorway and heard Orli say, "Wow! You guys clean up really nice."

Grant bowed as I took a curtsy, and we both laughed.

Laura nodded. "Gosh, you both look like you belong in a fashion magazine."

I reached for my shawl and small bag on the sofa. "Thank you both. If you need me, we'll be at the Island Room. You guys enjoy your evening."

"We will," Orli hollered as we headed down the walk to Grant's car. "You too."

It was a mild evening so we chose to sit outside on the deck to eat rather than in the restaurant. The sky was crystal clear with stars and the moon hovering over the water. I smiled and thought the setting could be straight out of a romantic film.

"I think the special occasion calls for a bottle of champagne this evening," Grant told the waiter when we were seated. He looked at the wine list before indicating his choice.

"Valentine's Day *is* pretty special," he replied as he passed us menus. "I'll be right back with that."

A few minutes later he returned with the bottle and an ice bucket on a stand, popped the cork, and filled a flute for Grant to sample.

Grant nodded. "Very good."

He then filled my flute and said he'd be back shortly to take our order.

Grant leaned across the table, holding his glass toward me. "Here's to the love of my life and the rest of our life together."

I touched the rim of his glass. "To us," I said.

We each took a sip and then he reached for my hand. "I want tonight to be very special. I've waited sixteen years for this moment. I said that I'd give you some time, and I think the time has arrived."

He let go of my hand to reach into his coat pocket, removing a small black velvet box, which he flipped open. "Will you marry me, Josie? Will you spend the rest of your life with me?"

My gaze went to the incredible sparkle of the diamond nestled in the box. He reached for my left hand, then slid the ring onto my finger.

I hadn't given much thought to a ring. Despite the fact that I'd been pretty sure he'd ask me to marry him, I hadn't expected a ring right away.

I felt moisture wetting my eyes and dabbed at the corners as I nodded. "Yes, God, yes, I'll marry you. The ring is absolutely stunning!"

And it was—a beautiful solitaire in an antique platinum setting.

He brought my right hand to his lips and placed a kiss there as he smiled. "It took a while, but you were worth the wait, Josie. I love you."

"And I love you, Grant. I'll love you forever."

He let out a deep sigh, which made me wonder if he'd been nervous. Surely, he hadn't thought that I might refuse, had he?

"I couldn't be any happier," I told him.

"You really like the ring?"

"I love it. It's just gorgeous. You have excellent taste."

A grin crossed his face. "Yes, I do," he said. "I chose you." He took a sip of champagne. "It was my grandmother's ring. My mother gave it to me sixteen years ago, the day I told her you were pregnant."

"What? You've held on to it all this time?"

He nodded. "Yeah, I guess she assumed back then that we'd be getting married, but when that didn't happen, she told me to keep it. She said she had a feeling that someday the time would be right and I'd be giving it to you."

I shook my head. "Oh, my God, really? She never gave up on us, did she?"

"Nope. Never. Just like I didn't."

It was difficult to take my eyes away from the ring. I held out my left hand and smiled. It made my hand look different. But I *was* different. I wasn't the young woman who had been unsure of herself, unsure of her life path or where she was headed. Now I knew. I knew that I was meant to be with Grant and meant to share the rest of my life with him.

I pulled my gaze from the ring and looked into Grant's eyes. In that moment I saw love staring back at me. And in that moment I knew I had never been happier.

Grant told me later that he'd tipped the waiter to hold off on coming to take our dinner order, giving us the private time he wanted. Just another example of his thoughtfulness.

When we had finally finished with dinner and dessert and were lingering over coffee, he said, "So, do we have a date?"

"A date?"

He laughed and nodded toward my ring. "Yes, I've asked you to marry me. You accepted. The next step would be to choose a date for the wedding."

"Oh, gosh. I have no idea. And not only a date . . . but where? Here? Boston?"

"I'm going to leave the location to you. Whatever you decide will be fine with me."

"If I don't get married here, on the island, I don't think my mother will ever forgive me." I took a sip of coffee and then it hit me. "Oh, I know. I'd love to get married in my parents' backyard. You know, down by the water. Wouldn't that be a beautiful setting?"

Grant nodded and smiled. "It would be, and I know your parents would like that."

"Okay, then, that's settled. Mom will want to do the reception there too. God, she'll be in her element planning this wedding."

"I think you're right."

"And will your mother, Jeff, Melissa, and Dirk fly down to attend?"

Grant laughed. "Are you kidding? Of *course* they will. They've been waiting for this day too."

I recalled what Melissa had said to me on Christmas, and I knew he was right. It also hit me that I'd never had a sister, but I'd be getting a sister-in-law.

"Okay," he said, taking the last sip of his coffee. "We have the where worked out, but that still leaves the when."

I nodded. "Right. Well, how about if I move up to Boston when Orli finishes school here in May and we plan the wedding for October. The weather is cooler down here late October, and it would be a perfect time for an outdoor wedding."

I saw a frown cover Grant's face. "We have to wait *that* long?"

"It's only eight months, and weddings take time to organize and plan. Besides, knowing my mother, she'll need all that time to make sure it's the perfect wedding. Unless . . ."

He looked up with a hopeful expression. "Unless what?"

"Unless you'd rather we just run away and elope."

"Absolutely not," he said, a grin covering his face. "I've waited this long, and I want us to have a proper wedding. October it is."

I had a feeling he'd say that. "Good," I said. "Because it'll probably take me that long to choose the perfect gown."

Grant laughed as he stood up and reached for my hand. "Let's go. This is the first night of the rest of our lives," he said before placing a kiss on my lips.

48

The next few days were a frenzy of visits and phone calls. First stop was my parents' house the following morning.

My mother opened the door and scooped both Grant and me into a tight embrace. Her eyes immediately went to my left hand.

"Oh, your ring is gorgeous. Congratulations to both of you," she said as she directed us to the patio. "Your father and I are having coffee. Come and join us."

My father pulled me into a hug, lifted my hand, and smiled. "Best wishes to both of you." He clapped Grant on the back. "And welcome to the family. Officially."

"So," my mother said as she filled two china cups with coffee. "Have you set a date yet?"

"Not a definite date, but late October."

"Oh, good. That'll give you plenty of time to get it all planned." I shot a glance to Grant and smiled.

"Have you decided on a location yet?" my father asked.

"Actually, yes, we have." I took a sip of coffee. "We were wondering if we could have the wedding and reception here."

My mother clapped her hands together in excitement. "Really? Here? Oh, Josie, yes. That would be wonderful. Of course you can."

"Good. We were thinking we'd have the ceremony down by the water. It's such a pretty spot."

My mother nodded. "Oh, it is. Definitely. We'll have a trellis with flowers, and I'll arrange to have seating for the guests. Oh, and tents. I'll rent some tents for the reception. We certainly have plenty of room to do all that. It'll be so much fun."

I laughed. I knew my mother would enjoy every second of the planning.

"How did Orli take the news?" she asked.

Grant smiled. "I'd say she's over the moon. We told her this morning, and she's really happy for us."

"I'm not surprised," my father said. "I think she's always hoped this would happen."

"Have you decided who will be in the wedding?" my mother asked.

"I want Orli to be my maid of honor, and Grant will have Jeff as his best man."

"Perfect," my mother said. "And colors? Have you chosen colors yet for them to wear?"

I laughed. "Not yet, Mom. I need to think about that."

"And your gown? And your plans to leave Cedar Key? Will you be staying here till October?"

I shook my head. "No, Grant and I have discussed it, and after Orli gets out of school in May, we're going to fly to Boston and settle in there. Get Orli registered at school for her senior year in the fall and let her get used to living in Danvers. We'll all fly back here the week before the wedding, so we'll have plenty of time to do last-minute things. And my gown . . . I think I'd like to shop in Boston for that, and I was wondering . . . maybe you could come up this summer and go shopping with Orli, Molly, and me."

"Oh, I'd love to. Yes, absolutely, your father and I will fly up for a few days." She shot a glance to my dad and said, "But we have some news too."

I saw the grin on my father's face. "What's going on?"

"Well, your mother and I have decided we're going to take the month of June and spend it in Paris."

"Oh, wow! Really? That's great. I know you loved it when you went before."

"We did," my mother said. "We were only there a week, so this time, we thought . . . well, life is too short. Why not rent an apartment and spend the whole month of June there."

"Good for you," Grant said and reached for my hand. "Which reminds me, we have to decide on a honeymoon destination."

"We do," I said. "There's a lot to planning a wedding, so I'm glad we have eight months to get everything done." I looked at my watch. "Well, we need to get going. I promised Mallory we'd stop by."

Before I even had a chance to open the car door, Mallory was running out of the house. She pulled me into a hug and grabbed my hand.

"Oh, Josie! I'm so happy for you. Your ring is stunning. Well done, Grant," she said, running over to give him a hug too. "Come on in. You have to stay and have lunch with us. I made crab salad sandwiches."

I gave Mallory all the wedding details over lunch. We were enjoying coffee when we finished, and Grant was watching football with Troy.

"Will Orli be your maid of honor?" she asked.

I avoided eye contact and nodded. "You don't mind, do you?"

A huge smile crossed her face. "Mind? Don't be silly. Of course, I don't mind. It's only appropriate that Orli be part of the wedding party. Besides, I'm a tad too old for one of those fussy gowns."

I let out a chuckle. "Knowing Orli, she won't allow it to be fussy. I think she'll choose something elegant but chic."

"Have you decided on colors yet?"

"Not yet, but since its late October I was thinking of maybe autumn colors for Orli's gown, the flowers, and place settings. And I'd love it if you could fly up to Boston for a few days so we could shop together. My mother's coming up, and you could also help me choose my gown."

"Oh, Josie, I'd love to. You know that."

"Great. Grant has a guest room, and we'd love for you to stay with us."

"It's a deal," she said, jumping up to place a kiss on my cheek.

Our next stop was the book café. We walked in to find it pretty full for a Sunday afternoon. Some tourists, but I spied Grace and Chloe at a back table and waved as Grant and I grabbed a spot up front.

Suellen came to take our order and immediately saw my ring. Her hand flew to her mouth as she gasped and yelled, "Oh. My. God," yanking my hand toward her. "You're engaged!" Which caused heads to turn and Grace and Chloe to come running over, laughing.

"I am," I said as Suellen relinquished my hand to let them have a look.

"When? When did this happen?" Chloe said. "And congratulations to both of you."

"Last night," I told them. "Grant took me for dinner to the Island Room."

"How romantic," Grace said. "And your ring is just beautiful. So when's the big day?"

"Late October," both Grant and I said together.

Chloe pulled up a chair. "Okay, we want all the details."

Grace stood there laughing. "Maybe they'd rather be alone."

I waved to the empty chair. "No, no. Join us."

Grace sat down and I launched into another description of our plans.

"Wow," Chloe said when I finished. "So you're leaving the island too. Well, I'm glad your wedding will be here in Cedar Key. It won't be a problem at all for Gabe and me to come and stay a few days. That is . . . if we're invited." She let out a chuckle.

"Of course you're invited," I told her.

"I'm so happy for you." Grace reached over to pat my arm. "For both of you. Are you planning a large wedding?"

I smiled. "Hmm, knowing my mother, yes, I'd say pretty large."

"Oh, that's great. And what a perfect spot for a wedding—your parents' property. Well, it looks like we'll be having a dual going-away party at the yarn shop."

I looked at Chloe, who nodded. "Yup, Gabe made an offer on the house and farm in Ormond Beach, and it was accepted. We're waiting now to hear about the business space downtown for the yarn shop, but it looks like we'll be moving over there by late summer."

"Oh, Chloe. That's wonderful news and congratulations to *you*."

"Thanks, and yeah, I'm pretty excited about all the changes ahead for me. But . . . I don't think I see a wedding on the horizon for us. At our age, I think we might just opt to live in sin."

All of us laughed as I replied, "Hey, whatever floats your boat, I always say," and I saw the wink that Grant gave me.

49

Like many other newly engaged women, I'd suddenly become very left-handed. Wherever I went during the next couple of weeks, my ring and upcoming marriage were the topics of conversation as soon as anybody glanced at my hand.

Simon had been sincerely happy for me when I broke the news to him and quite understanding about the fact that I was giving my notice to leave my position in early May. Although I felt bad about leaving him without a nurse, he assured me the office would be fine and I was to focus on getting ready for my move.

Keeping so busy made the days go even faster. Within eight weeks Orli and I would be on our way to Boston to begin a whole new life.

I walked into the office on a beautiful spring morning to find Brandy gabbing excitedly on the phone. "Oh, have to go," she said, before jumping up to grab me in a bear hug. "You'll never guess. You'll never guess what happened yesterday."

I let out a chuckle and shook my head. "No, I have no clue. What's going on?"

She backed away and took a curtsy. "Well . . . I've been accepted into the medical assistant program at Santa Fe Community College."

"What?" This was the first I'd heard about any such plan. "What do you mean? You're leaving the office too?"

She waved a hand in the air. "No, no. I'm staying here. I'll be taking evening classes, after work. Well, I started thinking about you leaving and, you know, about poor Dr. Mancini not having a nurse. So I decided that maybe if I became a medical assistant, I could help him out in addition to handling the front desk."

"Wow, I didn't even know you were considering this, Brandy."

She nodded her head emphatically. "Right. Nobody knew except Dr. Mancini and me. He thought it was a great idea and told me to apply, so I did . . . and I got accepted for the fall classes. I called him last night to tell him, and he's really happy for me."

I pulled her into another hug. "So am I. Good for you. I think that's great news. You're such an asset to this office."

"Well, I have *you* to thank for that. For giving me a chance. That day you told me about the job and then helped me with the interview. None of this would have happened if you hadn't given me an opportunity."

"I did give you a chance, but *you* made it work out. You're an excellent employee, and I have no doubt you'll be a great medical assistant. Hey, who knows, maybe your next step will be nursing school."

A look of surprise crossed her face. "No! You think?"

I laughed. "I think you can be and do whatever you want."

By the first week in April, my house was looking more like a storage unit than a place where two people resided. Boxes filled the family room; photographs and paintings on the wall had been removed; and brochures for florists, photographers, and caterers filled the desk.

I had just finished packing up a box of yarn in the guest room when I heard Mallory come through the front door.

"Guest room," I called to her.

She walked in and shook her head. "Geez, what a mess. Are you moving *everything* up there with you?"

I laughed as I brushed a strand of hair out of my eyes with the back of my wrist and stood up. "No. Not quite. But we're taking important things like books and yarn, and certain photographs and paintings that are special to us. A lot of it will stay here, but Grant said to box up what we want to take and have it shipped."

I turned around to hear Clovelly let out a meow and scooped him up in my arms. "Yes, fella, you are definitely coming with us too. Not to worry."

Mallory reached out to pat him. "How do you think he'll do on the flight?"

"Probably fine. Grant bought a ticket for him to fly in his carrier in first class with us. Remember when Marin flew all the way back from Paris with Toulouse? He did great."

"Yeah, he's such a great cat, so I'm sure Clovelly'll do okay too."

"Time for a lunch break," I said, putting Clovelly back on the bed to curl up. "Can you stay?"

"Definitely," she said, following me into the kitchen. "So your mom sees the doctor in a couple weeks, doesn't she?"

I nodded as I pulled items from the cabinet and fridge to prepare a tuna sandwich for us. "Yeah, she does. I think she's a little nervous, but she's doing so well, and I'm so grateful for that. Since her diagnosis, she's really mellowed out."

"I've noticed it too. Sometimes a life-changing event will do that—cause a transformation. Well, I'm happy for you, Josie. I know it wasn't always easy getting along with your mom."

I diced some onions into the tuna fish and added some mayonnaise. "Yeah, it's much more pleasant now. She's so excited about planning the wedding. Oh, Grant and I have chosen the date—Saturday, October 24."

"Sounds great. I can't wait. It'll be the gala event of Cedar Key."

I laughed and placed the sandwich plate in front of her. "Sweet tea?"

She nodded. "Yeah, thanks. I bet Orli is getting pretty excited too. In a subtle way, I think that little instigator has been planning this event for years."

I let out a chuckle. "Could be. But I think whatever I decided, she would have supported me. But yeah, I know she's thrilled that Grant and I are getting married."

"Oh, did you hear that Gabe is holding off going back to Philly till early June?"

"No, I didn't. Why's that?"

"Well, he and Chloe are going to do a road trip up there. They have plans to spend a few days outside of Atlanta so she can meet his daughter and family, and then Chloe will stay with him in Philly while he puts his condo up for sale and arranges for a mover."

"That's great. I'm so happy for her. I remember when she first came to the island after her marriage broke up, she was so miserable and angry."

"Yeah, she really turned her life around, didn't she? And the best part was reconnecting with Grace."

"Well, you know what they say about all behavior having a reason. Once Grace found out why her sister had always been so difficult, I think it made it easier for her to understand Chloe's behavior all those years." I chewed a bite of my sandwich, thinking about my mother and her sister.

Mallory hit the side of her head with her palm. "Geez, I forgot to tell you the big news. Did you hear about CC? My mom said she called her last night, and it seems she's broken it off with her boy toy."

"No! Really? What happened? I wonder if my mother knows."

"Yeah, I think she does, because CC planned to call all the girls. Well, I guess that it *was* just a fling for her and it had run its course. And . . . apparently she's put in her paperwork to take an early retirement."

"Oh, wow. She's leaving the advertising agency? Gosh, I wonder what brought all of that about? I did think she really liked that Matthew and her job."

"Well, according to my mother, she did. But I guess she felt it was time for a life change. She has plans to return to Italy next year after she retires—alone. She wants to rent a villa there and focus on her other love—painting."

"Gosh, so many changes going on. I do remember that CC was a great artist, but for some reason she never pursued it. Well, good for her. I'm happy that she's following her passion."

I noticed Mallory had become quiet. "What's wrong?"

She let out a deep sigh. "I'm just feeling like a failure, I think. So many women are not only discovering what they really want in life, they're actually taking a risk and doing it. I mean, look at you. How far you've come. From the beginning you did things on your terms. Then you wanted to become a nurse and you *did* it. Now you're marrying Grant and moving away. Me? I've only ever been a wife and mother."

I saw the tears rolling down her face and jumped up to hug her as I wondered how much this actually had to do with her self-identity and how much with her best friend leaving for good.

"Oh, Mallory, don't be silly," I told her and patted her back. "That's what you always wanted—to be Troy's wife and to be a mother. There's nothing wrong with that. Nothing at all."

She swiped at her eyes and sniffed. "Yeah, I know, but now . . . maybe I want more."

I pulled away to stare at her. "You do? Like what?" This was the first time I'd heard Mallory talk this way.

She reached for a tissue and blew her nose. "That's just it . . . I don't know what I'd like to do. I only know I'd like to do *something*."

"Okay, then," I said, sitting back down on the stool. "Let's figure out what that something might be. Do you think you'd like to go to college and take some courses? Train for a career maybe?"

She shook her head. "No, I don't think so."

"Hmm. Knitting. You love knitting and you're very good. With Chloe leaving, maybe you'd like to work with Dora in the yarn shop?"

"I did consider that, but no . . . what I've been thinking about is my photography."

"Oh, my gosh, I'd forgotten all about that." I thought back to our teen years when I never saw Mallory without her Canon AE-1 swinging from around her neck. "That's right, you loved photography. And you were good. Damn good! So why don't you pursue that? Get back to taking photos and maybe even enter something in the Arts Festival."

She nodded. "Yeah," she said doubtfully. "But I just don't know if I'm good anymore, and everything is done now with digital cameras. Call me old-fashioned, but I still prefer using film. Remember when I thought about turning our extra room into a darkroom?"

I did. "Well, I think it's a great idea, Mallory. I think you should do it. Get back to taking photos, have a darkroom, and hey, you could open a photography studio right here on the island."

I saw her face brighten. "You think? But I'd need to build up some customers."

"Yes, I *do* think you can do this. And you know what? I'm hiring you for my wedding. I want you to be my photographer. There isn't anybody who knows me better than you. Anybody who could capture the real *me* better than you could. It would give a boost to your new career, doing a big wedding." *Not to mention a boost to her confidence,* I thought.

Her brightness turned to pure joy with the smile that covered her face. "Oh, my God! Really, Josie? You'd let me shoot your wedding? That really would be a major boost."

She jumped up to pull me into a hug.

"Yes, I really want you to be my wedding photographer," I told her as I tried to push out my mother's reaction to this news; she had recently informed me she planned to hire some posh photo studio in Gainesville.

❧ 50 ❧

Four days before the Sisters weekend, my mother saw the doctor and got another good medical report. My parents were ecstatic, and everybody was feeling grateful. Dr. Girone told her he'd see her again in July for another three-month checkup.

She phoned me at seven the morning of the gathering, still on a high from her good news. "So you and Mallory will come by this evening, right? Jane is already here. She arrived yesterday and stayed at Mallory's last night. Mags and CC landed in Gainesville last evening, and Elly is driving from Atlanta and should be here by early afternoon. I just wanted to let you know that I'm leaving shortly with Mags and CC to go pick up some things in Gainesville."

"Well, aren't you the early bird," I said, laughing. "And yes, Mallory and I will come by tonight about seven or so. Anything I can bring?"

"Nope, not a thing. We're picking up wine and food this morning. Mags is going to make some seafood concoction for an early dinner for us. Okay, then, I'll see you at the Lighthouse later this evening. Love you."

I hung up the phone and smiled. My mother was definitely in her element, surrounded by her dearest and closest friends. I was glad that Mags had thought to organize something like this to get them all together for a celebration.

I phoned Mallory later in the morning. "All set for the big event tonight?"

Her laugh came across the line. "Yeah, I am. I swear my mom's been acting like a college student since she got here yesterday. Jumping around the house dancing, cracking jokes, and so excited. There's some good energy when you put those five women together. They gave my mom the key to the Lighthouse, so she just left to go open it up and get it ready. I think the rest of them have gone to Gainesville shopping."

"Yeah, they have, and Elly is due here in a couple hours. You want to drive over around seven together?"

"Sounds good. I'll pick you up. Be ready to party."

As soon as Mallory pulled the car onto the crushed oyster shell area in front of the Lighthouse, I could hear the music blaring. We got out and began walking up the stairs when I heard my mother's voice belting out "Dancing Queen" by ABBA.

I looked at Mallory. "What the hell?"

She shrugged and laughed. "Have no clue."

I opened the door, stepped into the kitchen, and saw my mother holding a karaoke microphone with the lyrics of the song flashing on a monitor screen. But what really made my jaw drop was my mother's appearance. Gone was her tailored dress code. She was wearing skinny jeans and a hot pink tank top with the sparkly silver words *Bite Me* splashed across the front. On her head was a floral wreath of fresh flowers, and beneath that wreath was no sign of her traditional chic hairstyle. It had been replaced with a pixie cut, which very much resembled my own style. Her auburn color also looked a shade brighter.

While my mother sang into the mic, Mags shook a tambourine as Jane, CC, and Elly danced around the family room, joining in the singing, all five contradicting the fact that they were older than sixty.

I looked at Mallory, and both of us burst out laughing as my mother noticed us standing there and motioned us to join the dancing.

I heard my mother singing the words, and I knew without a doubt that she *was* having the time of her life. When the song ended, there was an eruption of laugher and my mother rushed over to pull me into a tight hug.

"What the hell is this?" I asked, touching her cropped hair.

"You don't like it?"

Actually, I liked it a lot. The cut was very becoming and made her look ten years younger, but I couldn't help recall how she'd always indicated she never cared for my choice of hairstyle.

"I love it, but . . ."

She laughed and said, "I know. Mags talked me into it today at the salon. So I figured, what the hell! Life is too short not to try new things, right?"

"Absolutely right." It was then that I noticed the aroma floating around the room. "Mom! Are you guys smoking pot?"

She waved a hand in the air. "Oh, I think Mags may have snuck some in. Come on," she said, grabbing my hand. "Come say hello to everybody."

Mags was wearing a tie-dyed T-shirt with psychedelic colors of turquoise, orange, yellow, and blue splashed across the front. The colors matched the bandana tied around her forehead, and I felt like I'd stepped back in time to a 1960s sorority party.

She pulled me into a tight embrace. "Isn't this great, Jos? It's like time has stood still."

Yup, she was definitely taking some hits of marijuana and was more bubbly than usual.

Elly and CC came over to hug me. Both of them were wearing long, gauzy dresses that fell to their ankles, and I noticed they were both barefoot. Floral wreaths also sat atop their heads.

"This is going to be a great four days," Elly said. "I'd forgotten how much fun we used to have in college."

"And I think we're proving we're never too old to celebrate and have fun," CC added.

"Look at my mom," I heard Mallory say, and turned around to see Jane wearing a floral print minidress with a pair of white boots that came just below her knees. Perched on her head was a red floppy hat with a wide brim.

I shook my head, laughing. "This is too funny. I think they hung on to all those clothes from the sixties."

Mags clapped her hands to get our attention as she waved a peace sign flag in the air. "Okay, everybody, get yourself a glass of wine. There's plenty of food, so dig in, and let's keep singing and dancing. CC, your turn. Choose a song, grab the mic, and let it rip."

I'd been to other gatherings over the years with the Sisters of '68, but they were pretty demure compared to this one—laughter and fun, but not the inspiring energy that seemed to fill the room this evening. Was this what happened as one got older? You began to appreciate the moments more? You began to understand that more time was behind you rather than ahead of you? You celebrated more and truly embraced the essence of life? If these five women were any example, I'd have to say yes, that was exactly what could happen.

I poured myself a glass of white wine as I listened to CC singing "If Not For You," a popular 1970s Bob Dylan song, which made me think of the bond these five women had forged over fifty years ago as freshmen in college. They had been together through all of life's ups and downs, good times and bad, and most important, all five had contributed something special to their relationships that made them continue to grow and flourish. I glanced over to see the joy on my mother's face as she moved her body to the rhythm of the music, and I knew I owed Mags a lot for coming up with the idea of this get-together.

"They're quite a group, aren't they?" I heard Mallory say as she came to stand beside me. "I can't ever remember a time that they weren't in my life."

I nodded. "I know. They're very fortunate to have one another, but we're pretty lucky, too, to be a part of it. I haven't seen my mother this happy in ages."

"What do you think of her hair? I just love it."

"I do too." I felt the smile cross my face. "She sure surprised the hell outta me with that. It's like she's transforming into a whole new person. For the better," I added.

"Hmm, seems to be running in the family lately," Mallory said with a grin on her face.

I was nibbling on a delicious cream cheese hors d'oeuvre when my mother ran over and put her arm around my shoulder.

"Fill up your wineglass and come with me," she said.

I topped off my wine and followed her outside to the wrap-around deck. It was pitch dark with no light pollution, and looking up, I saw the starlit sky and a silver full moon.

"Isn't this gorgeous?" she said as we both leaned our elbows on the railing and looked out at the water.

I nodded as I savored the moment. "It is," I whispered.

She turned to me and took my hand. "Josie, I just want you to know how much I love you and how happy I am about your up-coming marriage to Grant. I also want you to know how much it means to me that you're here with us tonight."

I gave her hand a squeeze. "I love you too, Mom, and I wouldn't have missed this for anything. I hope you know how much I appreciate you doing all the planning for the wedding."

She let out a chuckle. "Are you kidding? I love having carte blanche organizing my daughter's special day."

"Ah, wait a sec," I told her. "Not *quite* carte blanche. No frocks and definitely *no* parasols. Promise?"

Her laughter matched mine. "Yeah, I promise. I've chosen the florist. So you'll have to choose your wedding bouquet. I have loads of photos at the house for you to look at, or you can design your own. We still have to decide on the photographer, but I've found a few spectacular ones in Gainesville."

I took a sip of my wine. "About the photographer . . . I've al-ready found one."

Her head shot up. "Oh, really? I wasn't aware of that."

"Right. Well . . . ah . . . I've decided to hire Mallory."

Surprise covered her face. "Mallory? Mallory Wilson?"

"Yes. My best friend since forever."

"I don't understand. I mean, Mallory's not a photographer. Josie, what on earth are you thinking? This is the most special day of your life. You can't take a chance and not have perfect pictures to capture that day. Does Mallory even own a camera?"

Traces of the old mom quickly returned in her attitude and tone of voice.

"Mallory happens to own a very good camera. Photography has always been her passion, and she recently shared with me that she plans to return to it, take some courses over the summer and maybe even open a shop on the island. She needs to build her confidence, and I want to help her with that. So yes, I want Mallory to be my photographer on my wedding day. Nobody could capture Grant and me better than she can."

My mother remained silent for a few moments, and then she leaned over and kissed my cheek. "If you want Mallory . . . then Mallory it is. The photographer is settled. Come on," she said, grabbing my hand and pulling me inside. "It's your turn to choose a song to sing."

After looking through the various selections, I knew I wanted to sing another ABBA song, "I Have A Dream," because those words were appropriate to where I'd come from, where I was at, and where I was headed in my life. Like the song said, when I know the time is right for me, I'll cross the stream. And I had—with both my mother and Grant.

51

The five weeks following the Sisters of '68 gathering literally flew by as I knew they would. Between planning for a major move and my autumn wedding, there was constant activity. Orli had finished school a few weeks earlier and had spent the night at my parents' house.

I was enjoying my second cup of coffee on the patio, soaking in the warm May morning, when the phone rang, and I answered to hear Grant's voice.

"All set for your going-away party tonight?" he asked.

"Yeah, I am. It was so nice of Dora and Marin to organize a get-together at the yarn shop."

"I think it'll be a good time, and one week from today you and Orli will be on your way to Boston. I can't wait to have both my girls here with me."

"We're pretty excited about that. I'm headed to the post office this morning to ship up the final boxes."

"Great. Have a good time tonight and call me when you get home. I love you, Josie."

"I love you too, Grant. I can't wait to be up there with you."

I hung up the phone, finished my coffee, hit the shower, and then headed downtown.

Coming out of the post office, I saw Simon walking toward me.

"Hey, Josie. Still sending boxes up to Boston?"

I laughed and nodded. "Yeah, that was the last of them. Poor Grant will be sorry he told me to ship things up there."

"Oh, I doubt that. So everything's on track for you to leave next week?"

"Yup. Orli and I fly out a week from today."

"Well, you know I wish you all the best. You have a whole new adventure ahead, and you'd better not forget to invite me to the wedding."

I laughed again. "Absolutely. You and Lily are on the guest list—with a plus one."

"A plus one?"

"Sure. Never know who you might meet between now and then, and you might want to escort her to the wedding."

A smile crossed Simon's face. "You could be right. And don't forget to stop into the office this summer when you're back here visiting."

"Will do," I told him as he leaned toward me for a hug.

I arrived at the yarn shop that evening to find it overflowing with women. Chloe spied me and came to grab my arm.

"Can you believe it? All this for us," she said, laughing. "Get a load of that chocolate fountain Berkley put together."

I saw a long table filled with various foods and in the center a beautiful two-foot-tall cone of chocolate with stacked tiers over a silver basin at the bottom. From the top crown, chocolate flowed over the tiers, creating a waterfall. Bowls of fresh strawberries sat in front of it.

"Oh, wow," I said. "That's magnificent."

"I know. Berkley really outdid herself on this. Go grab a strawberry and dig in."

"Hey, everybody," I heard Marin call out. "Both of our guests of honor are now here. So help yourself to wine and food, and have a great time."

I headed to the chocolate fountain first and savored the flavor.

"You're going to miss my chocolate when you move," I heard Berkley say.

I turned around and laughed. "You're right. I am. Maybe we can arrange for me to have some shipped to Boston."

"Of course you can. I do mail order."

"Here you go." My mother passed me a glass of wine. "What a nice gathering this is."

"Thanks, and yeah, it is." I took a sip of wine and looked at the crowded room. It suddenly hit me that I'd be leaving all of this. The yarn shop, friends and family. Although I felt a twinge of nostalgia, I also felt excitement about the doors that were opening to me.

I walked around the room mingling with everyone.

Sydney came to give me a hug. "I'm so happy for you, Josie. Your leaving has gotten me thinking about my own venture, when I first came to Cedar Key to stay with Ali."

"Yeah, that opened a whole new chapter for you, didn't it?"

She nodded and took a sip of wine. "It certainly did. I had no idea where that trip would lead me. At first, I thought I was only coming here to do some healing. But then I discovered Sybile and Saren and a family I never knew I had. Plus, coming here allowed me to find Noah. We just never know what's around that next corner."

"No, we don't," I said as Grace came to give me a hug.

"You must be so excited, Josie. I know Chloe is really looking forward to Ormond Beach. So much ahead for both of you. I remember when I first came here. I never could have guessed Cedar Key would lead me to Lucas and having a daughter."

"That's true," I heard Monica say. "I had never intended to stay here permanently, but I met Adam and well . . . the rest is history. So like my mother said, we just never know what's ahead, but we have to be willing to take a risk to find out."

I let out a deep sigh and nodded. Once I had decided to pay attention and listen to my heart, everything had fallen into place.

We looked over as Dora clapped her hands to get our notice.

"Ladies, thank you to everybody for coming this evening as we bid farewell to Josie and Chloe. We're going to miss both of you, but we share your excitement. Josie has a wedding to look forward to, and Chloe is on the brink of a new relationship and a new business venture. So we wish you both well, and we'll never forgive you if you don't come back to visit often."

Laughter and applause filled the room.

"We have a little something for both of you, so if you'll come up here. . . ."

Chloe and I went to stand beside Dora as she passed us each a large wrapped present.

I took off the paper to reveal a gorgeous matted and framed photograph taken from the Number Four bridge, looking out to the saw grass and water beyond.

"Oh," I gasped. "This is just beautiful. Thank you so much."

Chloe had unwrapped hers and held up another matted and framed photograph taken from the Big Dock looking out to Atsena Otie. It was then that I caught Mallory's eye in the crowd and smiled.

"You shot these, didn't you?" I said.

"She did," Dora explained. "And all of us commissioned her to take the photos, so Mallory's new business is now official and she's made her first two sales."

I rushed over to give Mallory a hug.

"Thank you so much. And thank you, all of you, for this gift and the party."

"Well, we didn't want you to forget Cedar Key," Mallory whispered in my ear.

As if that could ever happen.

I took one last look around the house and then followed my daughter out to my parents' waiting car. Clovelly sat in his cat carrier on the backseat, and I scooted in on the other side.

"All set for the airport?" my dad asked.

"We are," I told him.

"One last thing." My mother turned around from the front seat and passed me a small piece of paper and pen. "Here, Josie. I want you to write one word on this paper and don't ask questions."

"One word?" I looked at Orli, who shrugged and smiled.

"Yes. Just one word that means something to you."

I thought about it for a second and wrote the word *love,* passed it back to her and heard her tell my father, "Okay. We're ready."

When we got to the Number Four bridge, my dad pulled off the road.

"Something wrong?" I asked.

"Nope. Here," my mother said, and passed me a small glass bottle with a cork on top. "Fold up your piece of paper, put it in the bottle, and throw it over the railing into the water. You want to leave a part of yourself here on the island."

I folded up the paper very small and squished it into the bottle, placed the cork on top, and walked to the railing. The sun was shining on the water, causing reflections from the boats and saw grass. I took in a deep breath and felt the moisture in my eyes. This place would always be my home. I had drifted for a while just like the boats bobbing on the water. But I had finally come to realize that Grant was my anchor. Many people fall in love with the wrong person, but all along—I had fallen in love with the *right* one. I was leaving Cedar Key, but all endings lead to a new beginning, and before the day was over I'd be with Grant taking the first steps on a new journey.

I lifted my arm up in the air, felt the smile on my face broaden, and flung the bottle into the water before I blew it all a kiss good-bye.

AUTHOR'S NOTE

Ellen Johnson is the owner of Serendipity Needleworks in Tuscaloosa, Alabama, where I've done many book signings. She has designed the Healing Cowl for my readers, and we do hope that you'll enjoy making one.

If you have any questions about the cowl, please contact Ellen at emj@bellsouth.net.

Happy knitting!

Healing Cowl

BY ELLEN JOHNSON

Note: This pattern is knitted with the wrong side facing you.

Supplies

1 skein of Lorna's Laces Shepherd's Worsted (or 225 yards of worsted weight yarn)

Size (U.S.) 9 needles

Directions

Cast on 96 stitches.

Place marker and join for working in the round, taking care not to twist.

Round 1—P

Round 2—K

Begin Trinity Stitch Pattern.

Round 1—(right side K)

   2—*(K1, P1, K1) all in the same stitch, P3tog. Repeat from *around.

   3—P

   4—*P3tog, (K1, P1, K1) all in the same stitch. Repeat from *around.

Work in Trinity Stitch Pattern for 6 inches. Work Transition Round.

Transition Round—*YO, K2tog. Repeat from * around.

Begin Ripple Pattern.

Round 1—*[(K2tog) 4 times, (K1, YO) 4 times], repeat from * around.

Round 2—P

Round 3—K

Round 4—K

Repeat the four rounds of Ripple Pattern four times around, for a total of 16 rounds.

Bottom Edge

Round 1—P

Round 2—K

Bind off, purl wise. Weave in tails, block lightly, if desired, and enjoy!

Eager to revisit Cedar Key? Go back to where it all started with this preview of *Spinning Forward,* available in bookstores and online.

1

Whining drew my attention to the fawn-colored Boxer curled up beside the bed. Lilly had been my constant companion for four years and now she was my salvation. With my home, my assets, my life as I knew it taken from me, Lilly was my one factor of stability.

Living on an island off the west coast of Florida wasn't something that I planned to be doing at age fifty-two. Twenty-eight years of marriage to a successful physician provided a lifestyle that I not only enjoyed, but took for granted. Okay, so maybe Stephen wasn't the most passionate and romantic man on the planet, but he created a sense of security in my life. That is, until his Mercedes crashed into a cement barrier on I-495 in Lowell, leaving me a widow with no sense of direction and no knowledge of a secret he harbored.

Two weeks following his funeral, I had been working my way through the grieving process when I was zapped with another shock. I opened the door of my Lexington, Massachusetts home to find a sheriff standing on my front porch, knowing full well this wasn't going to be good news. My first thought was concern for Monica, my twenty-six-year-old daughter.

"Are you Sydney Webster?" he'd questioned.

"Yes. Yes, I am. What's wrong?" Despite the chill of the October day, beads of perspiration formed on my upper lip.

He'd cleared his throat and with downcast eyes passed me a large envelope.

"Ma'am, I'm sorry to have to deliver this to you, but it's a certified notice for your eviction."

"My *what?*" I felt lightheaded and gripped the door frame.

"Eviction of premises. You have thirty days to pack up your belongings and vacate the house."

I'd thought it was a joke. Somebody had seen Stephen's funeral announcement in the paper and was playing a prank on me. The house had been paid for years ago. Nobody could just show up and kick me out of my own house. This didn't happen to law-abiding citizens.

Clutching the envelope with sweaty palms, I'd torn it open and removed an official-looking piece of paper. All I saw was a blur of words, making no sense out of what was happening.

"I'm sorry, Mrs. Webster," he'd told me. "I really am. I'll return in thirty days at nine A.M. to make sure your belongings are removed and obtain the house keys from you."

"This is a mistake," I babbled. "A major mistake." Closing the door, I slid down the length of the wall, my sobs shattering the quiet of the house.

And here I was five weeks later on an island off the west coast of Florida. In a quaint but small room at the Cedar Key B&B, and I knew for certain none of it had been a mistake. Stephen's secret vice of gambling and the events that followed were what had brought me to this small town of nine hundred permanent residents, relying on the hospitality of my best friend Alison.

"Come on, girl," I said, swinging my legs to the side of the bed. "Time for you to go out and for me to get some coffee."

The bedside clock read 6:15. At home I never woke before 9:00 and was amazed that in the week I'd been staying at Alison's B&B, I didn't sleep beyond 6:30. Slipping into sweat pants and a T-shirt, I grabbed my pack of cigarettes and with Lilly close at my heels we descended the stairs to the porch.

Opening the door to the small L-shaped dining room, I saw a

middle-aged couple quietly conversing over coffee and made my way to the kitchen.

"Mornin'," Twila Faye said as she removed freshly baked blueberry muffins from the oven.

Twila Faye was Alison's right hand running the B&B and I liked her. She'd raised her only son alone after her philandering husband had left town twenty years before with a tourist visiting from Macon, Georgia. Raised in the Boston area, I didn't know much about Southern women, but I knew Twila Faye represented what they called *true grit*.

Pouring myself a cup of dark, strong coffee, I asked if Alison was around.

"Lord, child, she's already out for her walk with Winston."

I should have known. I felt slothful when I had discovered that Ali woke seven days a week at 5:00 A.M. She never varied from her routine. Up at five, she prepared muffins, brewed the coffee, squeezed oranges for fresh juice, and by 6:00, her guests had breakfast waiting for them. Then she rounded up her Scottish terrier for a walk downtown to the beach.

I looked at the clock over the table and saw it would be another twenty minutes before she returned.

"I'm going to sit in the garden with my coffee," I told Twila Faye.

"Take one of these muffins with you."

Patting my tummy, I shook my head. "I'm trying to lose the twenty pounds I packed on this past year. I'll have some cereal later."

Settling myself on the swing in the far corner of the garden, I lit up a cigarette. Blowing out the smoke, it crossed my mind once again that perhaps smoking was another bad habit I should consider discarding.

I watched Lilly sniffing around the artfully arranged flower beds. Bright, vivid azalea bushes in shades of red. Yellow hibiscus gave forth cheer even on a dreary day. And dominating all of it was the huge, four-hundred-year-old cypress tree. I looked up at the leaves creating shade over the garden and wondered about something being on this earth that length of time. Having withstood tropical storms and hurricanes, drought and floods, it stood proud and secure. Right now secure was the last thing I was feeling. I had an overpowering urge to climb the tree. All the way to the top. And maybe absorb some of the positive energy that it seemed to contain. But with arthritis recently affecting my knees, I decided to stay put on the swing.

Physically, I was in pretty good shape for my age. If we discount the extra twenty pounds and smoking, that is. But emotionally, my life was a train wreck.

"Good morning," Ali called, walking through the gate along the brick walkway. "Let me put these shells inside and I'll join you with coffee."

I nodded and smiled. Ali always had a way of cheering me up. Ever since our college days as roommates, she'd always been there for me as a good friend. A no-nonsense-type person, she stepped in when I called her about my eviction. She demanded I drive down with Lilly, a few belongings, and stay with her at the B&B. She apologized that the second-floor apartment in the Tree House was rented till January, but I could stay in one of the rooms in the main part of the house. The Tree House was detached and located on the side of the garden. Ali had her apartment on the first floor and sometimes rented the one above. Feeling like a homeless person— actually, I was—I was grateful to have any space where Lilly and I could stay. But I won't lie . . . going from a 4,500-square-foot luxury home to a 12 x 12 bedroom with adjoining bath was like giving up a BMW 700 for a military jeep.

"I see you still haven't given up those disgusting things," Ali said, settling in the lounge beside me.

I snubbed out my cigarette in the ashtray and remained silent. I could have said plenty. Like she was the one that turned me on to cigarettes in the first place, during our freshman year in college. Everyone smoked back then, until it became a health issue long after our college days. I also could have said, unlike her, I hadn't dabbled in smoking pot. But I let it slide and took a sip of my coffee. The only rule that Ali had imposed when I moved in was no smoking inside the B&B.

Ali flung the long salt-and-pepper braid hanging over her shoulder to her back. She hadn't changed much since our college graduation. Tall and still very slim. Only faint lines beside her eyes attested to the passing years. She was wearing shorts that showed off her long legs, and a crisp white blouse. Her bronze tan reminded me of the days we used to spend (without sunscreen) on the beaches of Cape Cod.

"So what are your plans today?" she asked.

Plans? I was beginning to feel like an inert creature since arriving in Cedar Key. I had ventured downtown a couple of times. Taken a few walks with Lilly. Read a couple books. But other than that, I felt lost. It had even crossed my mind a few times that maybe I should return to the Boston area. Which always led me to question, *to what?* My life, as I knew it, had been snatched away from me.

As if reading my mind, Ali said, "Look, Syd, I know you've been through a hell of a lot these past couple months. Losing Stephen and then the eviction, but you've got to pull yourself together and decide what you'll be doing for the rest of your life. You can't just turn off."

Anger simmered inside of me. "What the hell would you suggest I do? I have no job. I haven't worked as a nurse in twenty-six years. I'm not sure I'd even remember which end of a syringe to use. I have no training in anything else. My bank account is on low. I have no clue what I'm going to do." I swiped at the tears now falling down my cheeks.

Ali reached over and patted my hand. "I don't mean to be hard on you, but it's very easy for a woman in your situation to regress. You're in a funk and you need to do something to get yourself moving forward. What happened to that girl I knew in college? The take-charge, independent woman, who knew where she was going and how she was going to get there?"

"She married Stephen," I said and realized that was true. "He wasn't supposed to die at fifty-five. And he sure as hell wasn't supposed to leave me financially insecure. It's damn difficult not to be angry with the rotten hand life suddenly dealt me."

As soon as I said the words, I felt embarrassed. Alison had gone through similar circumstances twenty years before. Gary had died suddenly after a three-month battle with cancer. Leaving her alone, with no children and no future. Within a year of his death, she had shocked me with the news that she was uprooting. Relocating to an island off the west coast of Florida where she had vacationed as a child. She explained the place was calling to her and she felt certain she could heal there. She had been right. Purchasing the B&B had turned her into a savvy businesswoman, and given her an increased confidence. Something I definitely lacked.

"That's total bullshit and you know it. Life isn't fair, so you move along and make the best of it."